# THE GHOUL ON THE HILL

THE HIPPOSYNC ARCHIVES
BOOK 2

DC FARMER

WYRMWOOD
BOOKS

# COPYRIGHT

Copyright © Wyrmwood Media Ltd 2024. All rights reserved.

The right of DC Farmer to be identified as the author of this work has been asserted in accordance with the Copyright, Design and Patents Act 1988. Names, characters, businesses, places, events and incidents are either the products of the author's imagination or used in a purely fictitious manner. Any resemblance to actual persons, living or dead, or actual events is purely coincidental. No part of this book may be reproduced in any form or by any electronic or mechanical means, including information storage and retrieval systems, without written permission from the author, except for the use of brief quotations in a book review.

First published 2017 as Frivolous Pursuits by Spencer Hill Press

This edition published by Wyrmwood Books 2024

A CIP catalogue record for this book is available from the British Library

eBook ISBN- 978-1-915185-28-0
Print ISBN - 978-1-915185-29-7

Published by Wyrmwood Books.
An imprint of Wyrmwood Media.

# EXCLUSIVE OFFER

**WOULD YOU LIKE A FREE NOVELLA**

Please look out for the link near the end of the book for your chance to sign up to the no-spam guaranteed Readers' Club and receive a FREE DC Farmer novella as well as news of upcoming releases. HERE ARE THE BOOKS!

FIENDS IN HIGH PLACES*
THE GHOUL ON THE HILL
BLAME IT ON THE BOGEY (MAN)
CAN'T BUY ME BLOOD
**COMING SOON**
TROLL LOTTA LOVE
SOMEWHERE OGRE THE RAINBOW

# PROLOGUE

**SOME PEOPLE HAVE** great difficulty remembering what it's like to be nine.

They forget that the world, at that age, is full of unending wonder. They forget how amazing frogspawn smells and how brilliant mud is as a dam-building material. They forget how, after an hour's lunchtime football, water from the brass tap in the corner of the schoolyard will never taste as deliciously, brain-freezingly, cool. Everything is bigger, brighter, and gut-tinglingly new. Best of all, the grey filter of teendom is yet to cloak the imagination with hormone-dunked cynicism.

In a nine-year-old's head, it's only a matter of time before a Hogwarts owl arrives with a letter tied to its talon, or a wardrobe door opens on to a snow-covered wood. Yet for all the same reasons, when the improbable jumps out of a box and bites you on the ankle, the vivid scars it leaves behind are much deeper and slower to heal.

Darren Trott was nine when the improbable sank its long and poisonous fangs into him.

———

APRIL SUN SPARKLED off the rain speckling the window. The kitchen smelled of burnt toast, and a radio played middle-of-the-road hum-alongs while Darren's mother made ham and lettuce sandwiches for his lunch. His father had long since departed for work and Darren had six minutes before leaving to catch the school bus. Time enough to open and examine the little figure he'd found at the bottom of the box of Snappy Pops.

The cellophane wrapping around the figure crackled between his fingers. Through the crinkled surface he saw a man in a torn suit carrying a briefcase splashed with red. He frowned in mild confusion. The advert on the box had promised a woad-daubed warrior; part of a promotion for a film called Legends of the Cave set to burst across cinema screens everywhere over Easter. Yet there was nothing remotely blue about the corporate drone staring back at him through the cellophane.

Disappointed, Darren ripped off the paper and examined the figure as he strode upstairs. He set the model down on his bedroom desk and went to the bathroom. Toothbrush lodged behind his rear molars, he grabbed a washcloth from the sink and went back to the desk to wipe the red smudges off the figure's briefcase. Carefully, he applied the damp cloth and rubbed. Instantly, the hard plastic under his fingers changed, softening to rubbery putty. It was as if he'd picked up a moribund bird from under a window, only to find that his touch instigated the faint and disconcerting fluttering of a wing.

A thrill of horror danced up Darren's young arm. A grunt of disgust burst from his throat. He flung the figure down on the desk, threw his hands up, and danced back reflexively. But his eyes could not give up the now wriggling figure.

He tasted half-chewed Snappy Pops in the back of his throat as an ort of breakfast made an unwelcome return visit. He swallowed it back with a grimacing cough, as the tiny figure stopped writhing and propped itself up on one elbow.

Darren went rigid. The air in the room froze solid and his lungs seized. He couldn't breathe, but neither could he turn away. His organ-stop focus was locked on a four-inch man clutching a briefcase, looking right back at him from a terror-filled face and speaking in a tinny, pleading voice.

'You have to warn them. Please…they're taking innocent

people. You have to warn the others. Tell the Porter…Hippos in Oxford. You have to warn the others.'

Darren made a noise that would have passed for a scream had it not been for the obstructing toothbrush still clamped between his teeth. Instead, the noise emerged as a passable imitation of a baby elephant finally winning its two-day battle against constipation.

He could do nothing but stare while his nine-year-old brain suffered an earthquake. Toothpaste dribbled down his chin and dropped onto the carpet. A voice in his head was screaming at him to run, but the quivering lumps of flesh that were his legs had lost the power of locomotion in their fight to keep him upright. His teeth spasmed on the toothbrush, he heard plastic crack and felt a searing pain in his jaw. His mind, well on its way to visiting a nice dark room to lie down in, finally got the message.

In the ten seconds it took for his legs to respond to the orders his brain had issued, the slumped figure on the desk went rigid, its tiny face distorting in agony, its voice emerging through cracked lips.

'Please…The porter…' were the last words Darren heard before he turned and fled, discovering at last his non-baby elephant voice to howl with lung-top volume, leaving a trail of warm urine on the bedroom floor in his wake. He flew along the landing, hurtling headlong toward a tumultuous wave of doctors, child psychiatrists, a blighted education, and peer-driven ridicule.

It would be ten years before he could find the strength to use a washcloth again.

Some nice, caring doctors in cardigans and thick-rimmed glasses would want to know what had happened so that they could help him heal. Some nice, caring teachers—experts in damage limitation like always having a spare pair of pants in the stationery cupboard for those damp patch, or even brown stain, moments—would want to know what had happened so that they could help him learn. Some not so nice kids adept at disinhibited and inventive vocabulary would find out what had happened and pour scorn, unmercifully, from a very great height.

From that day onwards he was saddled with a name that

followed him through another nine years of miserable education and taught him what it was like to be one of the afflicted.

Dolly Darren.

A daily reminder of thirty seconds of arcane madness in his bedroom that he never asked for and wished, with all his young, bewildered heart, had never happened.

Unlike most people, being nine years old was something Darren Trott was not likely to forget.

Not ever.

# CHAPTER ONE

**Dusty daylight illuminated** the room in which the spy stood, filtering in through slatted blinds to lend the scene just the right measure of seedy mystery. It suggested somewhere tenebrous and gloomy, a place you would not want to linger, and yet the spy looked uncannily at home. The wooden floor suggested austerity, but the walls were what lent the place a very Third Man atmosphere that set the shot apart. Grainy, sepia photographs stretched as canvases from floor to ceiling on three sides. On one was the image of a pointed bone, pale as a bleached skull, nestling amongst stone stalagmites. On another, a phantom snake coiled on the same dank subterranean floor, its headless state the only clue that it was nothing more than a shed serpent skin. On a third wall, half in shadow, glistened a large facetted boulder shot through with gleaming metal. At first glance these images appeared unrelated, yet it was clear that they had been taken in the same, harsh, sunless setting.

But the spy's features were what drew the eye. He had a dark, cropped beard, a full-lipped, cruel mouth, a flattened nose that spoke of violent past encounters, and sharp, intelligent, calculating eyes. The way the light reflected off the spy's ice-cold corneas added a delicious frisson of menace. In terms of image, all he was really missing was a shark tank and an eyepatch.

'Almost there,' Darren whispered, shifting his head from

behind the lens for a bird's eye view of the set. 'Maybe a little more head tilt to the left might help.'

The spy, being of inanimate resin, said nothing and Darren expected no answer.

That's not strictly true though, is it Dolly Darren?

Darren squeezed his eyes shut to suppress the trite challenge his subconscious threw up and did a distractive sweep of his brain's hard drive. The mental equivalent of putting fingers in your ears and la-la-ing the chorus of 'Yellow Submarine' so as to not have to listen to some idiot spoiling the end of a must-see film. His method of steering his thoughts away from the little 'That's not strictly true though, is it?' qualifier always wanting to poke its ugly head above the parapet of his sanity. He was quite good at the technique by now. He'd had years and years of practice.

Darren dragged his mind back into focus. He couldn't quite decide how best to describe the spy's expression. Treacherous, perhaps? Calculating, possibly? Imperious, definitely. Whatever the term, he knew he was very close to capturing it in the shot he'd set up.

He stepped away from the tripod supporting his camera and walked around to a point where he could lean over to adjust the spy's angle of gaze without disturbing the lights he'd spent such a long time arranging. Gingerly, a millimetre at a time, he rotated the spy to the left and went back to view the change through his camera lens.

'Better,' he muttered. 'Much better.'

He squeezed the button on the remote shutter cable (he always used one so as to eliminate any camera shake). The shutter clicked and he studied the result in the LED screen: black and white, his preferred format. Still Darren wasn't happy. He'd been planning this shot for weeks, months even, letting the idea grow and ferment in his head, sketching the layout and background on a storyboard. The spy was one of his favourite figures, but because of its striking physical features, Darren had struggled with the portrayal for fear of it coming across as too overt. To modify the trope, to give it his stamp, he sought subtlety and mystery in his work.

As he studied the recent photograph, he let the vivid memory of where he'd bought the model bubble to the surface of his consciousness. It took no effort because Darren could recall every detail of every model purchased.

Some might say he was obsessed.

One or two frequently did.

As for the spy, the manner of its acquisition was memorable for the simple reason that Amanda had, by chance, colluded in its purchase. And since Amanda generally liked his little plastic models about as much as iced porridge, the rarity of this event deserved its own special plaque on the crowded walls of Darren's memory bank.

## CHAPTER TWO

They'd stumbled across the strange little shop as they'd wandered back to the train station from the bed and breakfast. Norwich was the third city Darren had visited with Amanda on Trey Lushton's 'Fabulush' concert tour, having been with her to Birmingham and Leeds too. The fact that luscious Lushton had to name his tour 'Fabulush'—to ensure those attending were left in no doubt as to how they were expected to react—confirmed Darren's conviction the bloke was a wannabe, band-waggoning, runner-up-in-a-national-talent-contest drain on the oxygen supply of the first water, with about as much charisma as rancid chum.

By the time Norwich came around, Darren was almost catatonically bored with the prospect of another 'Fabulush' evening and knew that if he had to clap along once more to 'My Dingaling'—Lushton's innuendo-laden encore—he would scream. And scream he did, along with almost forty-thousand other, mostly female, fans. Only his scream reverberated with pent-up disgust and ennui, not the vacuous adulation so hysterically evident in those around him.

Amanda had a Pavlovian response to anything Lushton-related. Having suffered through two hours of ludicrous, choreographed, auto-tuned drivel the night before, Darren hoped he might avoid seeing the berk for another year or so at least. So when, the following morning, Amanda stopped outside the shop and pointed to the poster of a permatanned man in his late twenties with dimpled cheeks and laser-etched teeth grinning back at them, Darren felt a groan begin to emanate from his toes and ooze up through his whole body like some awful reverse peristalsis. It was only when he glanced at the rest of the shop that Darren managed to halt the protest an inch before it broke through the barrier of his front teeth.

The Lushton poster took up one half of the double-fronted windows. The other half was full of glass shelves crammed with scale models and figures. Second World War military uniformed battalions jostled for position with Egyptian pharaohs and Agincourt bowmen. This was exactly the sort of place Darren could lose himself in for hours and that Amanda avoided like Yersinia pestis. But the juxtaposition would not compute in Darren's head until he realised just how far the Lushton merch-machine tentacles could stretch. To the left of the Lushton poster, in black ink on a fluorescent orange background, a banner announced;

**TREY LUSHTON MERCHANDISE ON SALE HERE: T-SHIRTS
SIGNED PROGRAMMES
POSTERS
ACTION FIGURES**

Amanda gazed in rapture, cheeks pink, lips parted as she yielded to her obsession to purchase yet another reminder of her idol.

'Let's go in,' she breathed.

It took a moment for Darren to respond: A moment during which he resisted the sardonic urge to tap at his ear with an open palm, pretending to dislodge some clogging water or wax with great difficulty.

'Okay, if you want to,' he replied, with a dollop of nonchalance that would have easily won him a second interview at RADA. He had to turn away to prevent her seeing him grin like a loon, knowing she would never have any idea how much pleasure he'd got from saying those words. The monumental irony of it was lost on her, or at least deliberately ignored by her since it usually took a team of wild mustangs for Amanda to even consider allowing him to enter a shop like this. And then only if some convenient, distracting, shopping opportunities were within fifteen yards. Darren would grade these according to the time they bought him. An Yves Saint Laurent, Zara or Top Shop rated fifteen minutes; a coffee shop, ten; any bookshop, three— and even then, only for the time it took to choose and pay for two magazines.

But that post 'Fabulush' concert day was different. They'd gone in together, and while Amanda thumbed through glossy concert photos and squealed over the Trey Lushton dolls—variously attired in spangly suits or jeans and a bomber jacket, or bronzed and bare-chested in surfer shorts, holding a body board —Darren browsed the rest of the shop.

The spy stood in the middle of a collection of German animal models from a recently discontinued line, but Darren's collector's eye had zeroed in on the quality of the craftsmanship and detail like a pro. In short, it was a must-have item, and when he'd gone to the desk and paid for it, as well as a signed Fabulush program, two posters, a Surfer Trey and a Concert Trey ('Complete with microphone!'), for once, Amanda said nothing.

Surfer Trey now sat next to Amanda's jewellery box, watching her dress and undress every day. Concert Trey and the spy had gone to Darren's garage. He'd tried photographing Concert Trey, but the imagery it inspired involved monstrous clowns holding the bastard down and trying to ram the microphone somewhere it wouldn't quite fit, at least not without a lot of lubrication and a drill. Or the twit cowering in a forest, about to be attacked by a bear with very long claws. Darren couldn't help that. It was what the idiot inspired in him. But he knew that Amanda would not be amused, and so the photographs remained unprinted on Darren's hard drive while Concert Trey languished at the bottom of a box. Amanda, meanwhile, had never asked.

But the spy proved to be something else altogether; genuine

rocket fuel for Darren's imagination and the shots said imagination inspired. And if Darren began wondering how much of an aide de fantasy having a miniature Trey Lushton on your dresser was, he told himself not to. He was in no position to criticise. How could he when he spent most of his own spare time fantasising with the aid of plastic models?

## CHAPTER THREE

JUXTAPOSING AND PERSONIFYING toy characters through forced perspective was what melted his butter. Harmless, technically demanding, and highly absorbing, it had become Darren's 'thing'. That he featured as part of the 'urban vinyl art-toy' movement made him feel a tad uncomfortable, though that was how the critics who judged his photography in the many competitions he entered often labelled him. Pseuds' phrases like, 'His utilisation of the simulacra of actual setting allows an exploration of the narrative reality and exploits the potential of toys as objects of artistic expression,' did not sit happily in Darren's head. Art, with a capital 'A', was a foreign concept to a boy from his sort of background, or so he believed. So, yeah, okay, it sounded a bit pretentious written down, but the truth was Darren liked to see the expression on people's faces when they realised that the figures weren't human. The 'narrative reality' hogwash had come from someone else's overblown prose. What he strove for was hyperreality. And, more than anything, the pleasure it gave him in trying.

Darren dragged his mind back to the shoot. All he had to do was capture the right moment. Yet angst over the perfect shot was not the only anxiety hanging over him cumulonimbus-like this evening. He looked up from the camera at the 'studio' he'd created in the garage. Trestle tables set in a U-shape bore the sets he'd crafted from wood and papier mâché. Underneath, on palettes, nestled a dozen others. Jungles, mountains, deserts, industrial sites; all modelled by his own hand. Surrounding them were half-packed boxes of the sets he'd already dismantled.

Something leaden shifted in his guts. The triggered sigh emerged heavy with self-recrimination and doubt. Could this be the last time he was ever going to be able to do this?

And as if that thought evoked a mental incantation that summoned the lurking demon of his dread, the garage door opened and in strode the reason that Darren's world was about to be turned upside down, looking good enough to eat.

Amanda Cray was five four, had a boyish figure with slim hips, and wore her hair cut pixie-short above an unseasonably bronzed face, thanks to something called Summer Kiss Vita Dermatone that cost a week's wage for a bottle the size of a sparrow's egg. Darren was struck by how Amanda's facial tan was always at odds with the paleness of her hands. Of course, he said nothing, though in his opinion she didn't need the warpaint, or the row of gel-whitened teeth, since he thought that she was more than pretty enough without. His voice, however, was a whistle into the wind compared to a billion-dollar cosmetic industry that excelled at convincing people to paint themselves ochre. And at some point, someone was going to have to ask if the entire cosmetic industry was actually an ancient curse laid on a modern world by some mad Druid, who'd been spinning with laughter in her sacred grove ever since someone invented the word 'serum'.

'Dar-ren,' Amanda broke his name up into two long syllables laden with familiar accusation, 'I can't believe you're still out here when the bins need putting out and the dishwasher needs emptying.'

'Thought it was your turn for dishwasher emptying?' He played it cool, parrying her thrust, hoping to infer that one of them might have made a teensy, easily made, mistake.

'I've just touched up my nails, Darren.' Amanda shook her head in a way that beggared the need for further explanation.

'Thank God you didn't have a full manicure then or we'd be

having this conversation in Intensive Care.' Darren grinned and watched his humour-torpedo swerve yards wide of the mark.

Amanda pierced him with an annoyed expression. 'They got horribly chipped when I put petrol in the car yesterday.'

'Ah, right,' Darren said. By far his favourite word, 'right' covered a multitude of nuanced subtext responses such as 'serves you right', 'too bloody right' and 'I reserve the right to remain silent'. Amanda might have heard an anodyne, but in his mind, he was screaming, 'But it was you who left the car empty from the last time, and you who wanted to pop along to the shops again yesterday, unless I am very much mistaken. Only "right" that you put some petrol in it, is it not?'

When she didn't reply, Darren guessed that his silent sarcasm scattergun had probably penetrated her armour by no more than a tenth of millimetre. Not enough to cause annoyance, but enough to possibly prick the surface of her conscience. A guess confirmed by her immediately going on the offence.

'God, I'll be glad when you get rid of all this… junk,' Amanda waved her hands and zipped up her lips, a sure-fire signal that she was about to enter Lecture Mode, which was one of the less endearing traits she'd inherited from her father. From the set of her jaw, Darren guessed it was going to be a variation on the ambition theme. The 'I-don't-know-about-you-Darren-Trott-but-I-have-no-intention-of-spending-the-next-twenty-years-as-a-clerk-in-the-back-office-of-Dobson-and-Crank's-because-I've-got-dreams-and-I-thought-you wanted-to-be-a-part-of-them,' talk.

'Yeah, I've been thinking about that,' Darren said.

She rounded on him, her eyebrows set in a challenging frown.

'It's just that you're asking me to give up the one thing I really enjoy doing on my own,' Darren explained, wondering why it sounded so much like an apology. Her glare could have started a forest fire. As it was, Darren thought he could smell singed hair. '…Okay, the second thing I really enjoy doing on my own.'

'I'm not asking you to give it up, Darren,' Amanda said, ignoring his limp stab at humour. 'I only want what's best for you. I mean it's not even like it's a proper hobby, like fishing, or football, or golf.' She sighed a little long-suffering sigh to indicate that her search for understanding, when it came to Darren's artistic endeavours, had long ago crashed and burned with no survivors. 'Taking photos of plastic dolls is bordering on the sad... distic.'

Darren couldn't let that one go. 'Sadistic?'

Amanda picked up a plastic dinosaur with a cannon glued to its back, grimaced and put on her best understanding-a-four-year-old expression. 'Let's face it Darren, you're a grown man, and like my dad says this is...well it's a bit of a frivolous pursuit, isn't it?'

Darren inclined his head. A gesture that was the nearest Darren came to being angry. 'Frivolous pursuit' had Harry Cray's reactionary stamp all over it, under it and running right through it like end stage cholera. But before Darren could even think of marshalling a response, Amanda had thrown down the dinosaur and taken three steps forward into the garage, morphing seamlessly into Planning Mode.

'And this place is ideal for a studio. We can have the nail bar here,' she pointed towards a stack of photographic paper. 'And Dad knows someone who can get us a proper dentist's chair for pedicures and stuff. I've even been thinking about training for Botox.' She turned her animated, fake-tanned, face towards him. 'You can, you know. There's this clinic in London. And it's not expensive. Only five thousand.'

Darren's eyebrows went up and he saw the light dim in her eyes, even though she retained a tight-lipped smile. She turned towards him and walked forward, perfume heady, mascara thick, lips moist from a recent coat of gloss. Putting forward a manicured nail, she walked her fingers up his chest. When she spoke, her voice had dropped an octave. 'All I'm asking is that you move some of this stuff so I can share the garage with you. I don't need it all, half...two thirds, tops. You know how much I've wanted this.'

She smiled and Darren felt something stir inside him that he was powerless to prevent and unable to easily hide. Amanda's smile was what had first attracted him to her. It was a smile capable of lighting up half of England, even if a little stone-in-the-shoe awareness nagged at him. Of late Darren seemed to be seeing less and less of those dazzling pearly whites when there were just the two of them in the equation.

'And,' Amanda went on, giving it her best pout, 'when it's done, I was thinking maybe we'd make Saturday nights "our night". Proper you-sleeping-with-me-in-the-bed night.'

'I thought you said you didn't want to do all that until we'd set a date?' Darren asked, adjusting his groin area uncomfortably.

'You know I promised my dad we wouldn't live together until we were married.'

'We do live together.'

'I mean live together. Biblely.'

'You mean biblically.'

'Whatever. A promise is a promise, Darren,' Amanda said.

'How could your dad possibly know we were sharing a bedroom?' Darren asked, the question dripping with feigned innocence.

'Alright, there's no need to be sarky. You know I made him take all those hidden cameras out of the bedroom… as well as the microphones from the toilet downstairs…and the CCTV from the living room. It's not the point. I'd know.'

Darren shook his head.

She pouted again. It was one of her top three expressions. 'Don't you want us to be a proper couple?'

Being male and in his late twenties and…male and in his late twenties, Darren did very much want him and Amanda to be a proper couple, if by couple she meant the verb and not the noun. And yet Amanda's propensity for using the bedroom as currency to ensure his hobby-abandoning compliance sat uneasily in Darren's core. Of course, perhaps this was the way relationship politics were conducted in the big wide minefield world between two consenting adults. After all, he was on the upslope of the learning curve still, his only other physical dalliances having been drunken fumblings after nightclub encounters and once, a memorable couple of hours in the back of an estate car covered with flower stencils with a thirty-year-old hippy when he'd worked as a steward at a local music festival. Still, Amanda's controlled physicality was a blueprint for the future he didn't much relish. Being male and in his late twenties, and possessing an active imagination, Darren hankered after spontaneity of the kitchen work surface, or halfway up the stairs, or hanging from the chandeliers twice a day variety. Unfortunately, none of those scenarios were in Amanda's playbook. In fact, lately the pages had been totally blank thanks to a prolonged spot of bladder infection, so he was not going to sneeze at this offer of a regular slot.

With admirable restraint, he refrained from mumbling 'regular slot', and instead, gave her a meek nod.

'Good,' Amanda stepped away, suddenly all businesslike, leaving Darren fresh air against which to press his…argument. 'Do you want me to ask Dad to get my cousin Pete to come round with the van on the weekend? Get all of this lot to the dump in one go?' Amanda asked.

'No thanks. I told you, it's going into storage. No need for the van or the dump.' He regretted it as soon as he'd said it because he had no idea where it was all going to go.

Amanda tilted her head but didn't press the point. 'Okay,' she said brightly and turned to leave. 'I'll probably be late so don't wait up. It's Julianna's birthday, so some of us are going out for a drink afterwards. I've left some packet ham in the fridge if you get hungry. Bye.'

Darren watched her go, deflated in more ways than he could readily explain, only just resisting the urge to cry out after her, 'Just as well that inspector from the Michelin Guide cried off supper tonight, then,' with great difficulty. Instead, he suppressed a sigh and told himself not to be such an arse. Just because Amanda lived with him didn't make her his domestic lackey, as she was never slow to point out.

Nothing stopping him from preparing his own delicious meal based on the leftover packet ham and some spaghetti hoops if he wanted to, right?

Stop it, he told himself. After all, in the current economic climate there were lots of people who would give one, if not two, limbs as well as their signatures in blood to have what he had: a house bequeathed to him by his mother, a tidy little nest egg which his mother had carefully nurtured courtesy of an insurance payout when his dad had died, a pretty (in an elfin sort of way) younger girlfriend, and a job—of sorts. And someone with his lack of qualifications was lucky to be in employment. You only needed to pick up a newspaper any day of the week to know that. When he took a step back like this, he knew he was a lucky bloke. Perhaps not exactly living the dream, but living, certainly, and dreaming definitely.

And the one dream locked in the chambers of his heart, the one he didn't let out other than to graze on the grasslands of his own fertile imagination, involved photography and writing as the tools of his trade. Perhaps in a studio on a smallholding, somewhere way out in the country. Somewhere where a handful of kids could play and raise those silkie chickens with fluffy feet, and where he'd keep horses and goats and a clutch of dogs. He'd always wanted dogs.

This dream he'd never dared share with Amanda. Whenever tempted, a klaxon sounded in his head accompanied by a weird German voice, screeching, 'Verboten!' He had no idea where the voice came from: years of black and white films on TV on wet Saturday afternoons in all probability. Yet, it was one he could not disregard.

The voice, like Darren, couldn't quite see Amanda in muck-coated wellies, bottle-feeding a lamb at 3.00am on a freezing February morning.

Darren stamped on his wool-gathering. He had a lot to be thankful for. Granted, his had not been an easy transition to adulthood, blighted as it was by watching his mother waste away from an appalling and aggressive form of multiple sclerosis that went by the laughingly innocuous eponym of Marburg Disease.

He'd needed support and Amanda had been there for him.

Okay, so she'd started picking out curtains for her (their) bedroom while his mum had still been in the hospice, and emptied his mother's wardrobe and stored the contents in the attic before they'd decided on the hymns for the funeral. Yet Darren realised that those things had needed doing and he was grateful for her being there at a time when he'd needed strong support.

But the fact was, it would have been better if that support had been upholstered in a little padding called subtlety and not constructed as rigidly as a piece of tempered steel. He'd tentatively pointed that out after he caught Amanda thumbing through a sampler book for the curtains one night after visiting his mother on her deathbed. Amanda simply shrugged and said, 'Let's face it, Darren. Your mum isn't coming home and the place looks like a Dickensian dosshouse and smells of stale cabbage.'

Amanda liked to speak her mind, no matter what. And in most cases the what had already taken a look at the opposition and crawled away to lie under a bush. Darren found it difficult arguing with her because he sensed that her way of looking at things reflected the way that most pragmatic people would. And Amanda's pragmatism came fired from the hip and loaded with ten-bore ammo.

Taking photographs of collectable figures was, indeed, a pretty frivolous pursuit. But then, so was golf when you came to think about it. Harry Cray played golf every weekend. A game he, Darren, was thus constantly encouraged to take up. The thought always left him cold. What was so profound about hitting a small white ball around three miles of damp fields, other than a good walk and learning that a tee was exactly the right tool for removing dog dirt from under your shoe?

Darren's stomach rumbled. Thoughts of packet ham and congealing spaghetti hoops did nothing to assuage his appetite. Amanda would be gone for three hours at least. He reached for his mobile and tapped out a text message.

ANY FOOD GOING SPARE?

Ten seconds later, his phone chirped with the reply.

LAMB KOFTA WITH DAL AND CHAPATTIS IN TEN. WANT SOME?

Darren grinned and sent back, ON MY WAY.

He looked again at the spy through the viewfinder, adjusted the angle of the slats so that a single horizontal beam illuminated the eyes and threw the rest of the face into shadow, and took four quick shots, adjusting the spy's stance between each one. The first and second were good, the third outstanding.

Darren's skin tingled. He made a fist and uttered, 'Result.'

The words were understated, but inside he was singing because he knew he'd captured the nuance he'd been searching for in that single snap. He allowed himself a wry smile. It was so often like this with photography. Hours of contemplation and planning and it all came down to a single shot taken in a throwaway moment. He'd given up asking the gods for answers. It was obviously beneath them.

Darren locked the door behind him and fetched his coat from the house before heading out for his supper, wondering, and not for the first time, why he felt not one jot of guilt.

# CHAPTER FOUR

Sanjay Bobal lived with his dad in an end of terrace house that backed onto a railway embankment on Shunter Street. A 1930s brick railway worker's house, it, along with the rest of the terrace, had been earmarked by the local council for demolition at least three times as part of one regeneration project or another. A change of administration, lack of money, and a light bulb moment from the local planners—who one day realised that the houses were all still structurally sound—resulted in renovation grants for insulation and double glazing instead of bulldozers and a wrecking ball. Shunter Street was a quiet cul-de-sac, not overly troubled by the trundling noise of trains, thanks to the streamlined service introduced by the Spanish-owned company running the local railways. A glance in the local newspaper property section revealed that Shunter Street was now a 'convenient for transport links' spot well on the way to being 'up and coming', although to call the area 'much sought after' quite yet would have been stretching things a bit.

On either side of the cracked path leading up the rectangular, postage-stamp front garden stood a pile of carefully stacked breeze blocks and a stone flower tub. The tub had never contained any flowers in all the years that Darren passed it on his way to the front door. Ever since, in fact, he'd met Sanjay on his first day at Millbrook Nursery School. They'd been classmates through primary and secondary too and throughout those years, Sanjay had been the one, and sometimes the only, friend on whom Darren could rely.

He rang the doorbell and waited. Twenty yards away, a man walked his dog along a path adjacent to the railway line. In the street behind some kids were laughing uproariously at someone's attempt at using a hula hoop. For one frozen moment, Darren wondered if he'd wandered on to the set of a Fifties Ealing comedy, so timeless was the scene. A woman dressed in a sari emerged from the door of Number Fifteen and wandered out to the gate to supervise half a dozen boisterous children. In her arms she held a child of no more than two, wearing the contented, wide-eyed look of a spaced-out junkie that came with having a dummy in its mouth.

Darren hailed her. 'Hi, Mrs. Roopal. You've been to a sale at the orphanage again, I see,'.

Mrs. Roopal nodded and tutted, showing Darren a row of gleaming teeth. 'Rita's gone to the bloody pictures and dumped the grandkids on me.'

'Come off it, Mrs. R. You're in your element.'

Mrs. Roopal shook her head in denial. 'You wait, Darren. One day you will have the grandkids.'

Though the words suggested that Mrs. Roopal harboured misgivings of the long-suffering kind, the way the giggling children gathered about her, and her reciprocal smiles, all suggested a huge dollop of grandmotherly disingenuousness. It was obvious that she loved it really. Yet she looked up at Darren beseechingly as the two-year-old mewled to be let down to play with the older ones.

'They are like pimples, Darren. Get rid of one and two grow in its place.'

Darren had two seconds to consider this little gem of tortuous dermatological wisdom before the door in front of him opened to reveal a skinny, round-shouldered man of Darren's approximate age with unruly hair and a lopsided grin.

'Hi Dar, you coming in or what?'

Darren waved to Mrs. Roopal and stepped across the threshold. He followed Sanjay along the passage that had a new coir mat on the floor and marigold walls sporting gloriously colourful stylised prints of elephants and the goddess, Kali. Sanjay paused halfway along and stuck his head through a doorway.

'Darren's here, Dad,' he sang. 'We'll be out the back.'

The first room of the ground floor had been remodelled from what had once been a parlour into a studio apartment for Sanjay's dad. He was sitting on a leather sofa watching television, a pair of nasal oxygen tubes snaking from his nostrils to a cylinder on a trolley at his feet, head bobbing in response to the documentary narrator's spiel. The lardy grocer flesh that had once sheathed Mr. Bobal had melted away to leave a wiry-framed man whose head now looked much too big for the stick-limbed body beneath. Thick, heavy-framed glasses magnified his eyes and showed up the veins on the jaundiced sclera in stark detail. There seemed to be too many teeth in his head, and his lips were pale and dry. Sickness was rescaling Mr. Bobal, turning him from Mr. Chubby The Shopkeeper into a cachectic marionette.

'Darren,' Mr. Bobal said, his liverish eyes crinkling, two ropy hands reaching up to clasp Darren's. 'Good to see you. Sanjay, get Darren something to eat.'

A huge thirty-six-inch screen showed a wild-eyed wildebeest coming to a sticky end courtesy of a pride of lions. 'I'm fine, Mr. B,' Darren said, noting the close-up of a lioness, jaws dripping with gore. 'Still glued to the comedy channel then, I see?'

'National Geographic, you see. Bloody fantastic. Last night, I watched a hippo eat a wildebeest. Nothing like nature to put us in our place, Darren. Sure you don't want a sandwich?'

'Sanjay is sorting me out, Mr. B,' Darren said, grimacing at the bloodbath on TV. He followed Sanjay through to the kitchen, where delicious aromas wafted up from bubbling pans on the stove. Two places were set at the table. Saliva flooded Darren's mouth and he helped himself to the food. Hot, spicy flavours exploded on his tongue, eliciting little grunts of spontaneous approval he was helpless to prevent. 'Mmm, this is really good.'

'Mrs. Roopal's,' Sanjay said, between mouthfuls of dal-laden chapatti. 'She brings stuff around every Thursday. Mrs. Gupta does Monday and my auntie Anitha does weekends. I never cook at all now. My dad eats hardly anything so there's always way too much. One meal normally lasts me three days.'

*Brilliant*, thought Darren. *That's the way to do it.* Mr. B had, over the years, offered a service to the community and stayed open all hours long before twenty-four-hour shopping was the vogue, just in case people *needed* something. And now his *need* was greater than theirs and they'd responded in kind with food and herbal remedies. All very old fashioned, but bloody fantastic when you came to think about what a community was all about. Though he corrected himself on the herbal remedy bit since calling Dealer Dave's cakes simply 'herbal' was like calling Godzilla a lizard.

Darren and Sanjay ate in appreciative silence for several minutes, wrapped in a fuzzy cloud of Mrs. Roopal's delicious cuisine.

'Your dad seems good, you know…considering,' Darren said eventually, letting 'considering' droop under its own weight.

'Yeah. He's lost another half a stone though,' Sanjay said with a slight shrug.

Darren pondered this and came up blank. He glanced up, but Sanjay did not return it. What was there to say? A heavy smoker for as long as Darren could remember, the chronic bronchitis that wracked Mr. Bobal every winter had started producing red flecks every time he coughed. One visit to Outpatients, an X-ray and a CT scan had delivered a jackpot diagnosis of carcinoma of the lung, with the disturbingly wholesome typology of 'oat cell'.

'He's amazingly cheerful,' Darren said, looking down into his food and successfully suppressing the urge to sympathise. Such unnecessary and maudlin sentiments had long ago been banished from the Sanjay/Darren agenda. They both had 'Lost Parent' T-shirts folded away in their psychological drawers. Years before his mother's death, Darren's dad had succumbed to a heart attack when Darren was twelve and Mrs. Bobal to TB when Sanjay was seventeen.

'I know. Always been pretty chilled, my dad,' Sanjay said.

'Is that to do with him being Hindu?' Darren asked.

'Nah. It's them cannabis cakes Dave the Dealer from Number Six keeps bringing him for pain relief.'

'Right,' Darren said, with a glance at Sanjay to see if he was smiling.

He was. 'We can split one for afters if you like.'

'No, better not,' Darren said, his own smile laden with Dealer Dave reminiscences. 'Last time we did that, I didn't get home 'til five in the morning because we watched the fainting goats clip on YouTube at least a hundred times.'

When Darren couldn't force another morsel of naan past his lips, Sanjay cleared the table and, gaze averted, muttered a throwaway, 'Got a new pump for the rivers.'

'What?' Darren asked, grinning.

Sanjay nodded, unable to stop a smile from bursting through.

'This I've got to see,' Darren said, grinning in reciprocal anticipation.

## CHAPTER FIVE

**He followed Sanjay** out and along the narrow back garden to a wooden door in a wall in the far corner. The wall, a bricked-up arch under the railway bridge, was resplendent with ivy. The storage space it provided had been one of the prime reasons for Mr. Bobal buying Number One Shunter Street. He'd used it to store the goods he sold in Bobal's Stores. But the shop soon became shops, all now supplied by shiny vans that arrived in the early hours of the morning to fill up the shelves. As the business no longer needed a dark cavern under a railway bridge to store goods, the lock-up became Sanjay's Den. One thousand square feet of floor space with curving whitewashed walls and a concrete floor; power for light; heaters for the cold winter months; and, more importantly, ample room for Sanjay's hobby.

Unlike Darren, whose photographic obsession with plastic figurines required set pieces—simulations of the real world on three square foot foundations of hardboard—Sanjay's hobby was on an altogether grander canvas. He had designed, and made, his own scale model of the Babylonian Empire, complete with cities, tall ziggurats, rugged mountains and a vast plain between two rivers. The burgeoning project covered at least half the floor space in the cavernous room.

That it was a thing of breathtaking beauty, worthy of an admission fee any day of the week, interested Sanjay not one bit.

It was in the making that Sanjay found his escape, together with the buying of the military models, construction of the rivers and the growing of miniature plants in the rich flood plains: a work of passion and total preoccupation.

Sanjay created this miniature Mesopotamia such that every hill and well was accessible. Beginning with the desert and climbing to the mountainous regions, it was best perceived at eye level. And to the mountains Darren went. Out of view, he heard Sanjay flick a switch. The low hum of an electric pump filled in the room, and water trickled out from a pass and cascaded down the hills to fill the arid riverbeds, flowing through Sanjay's Euphrates and Tigris towards the Gulf—a buried baby bath—in the South. Sanjay wore a triumphant smile, but something caught Darren's eye. To the north of where he stood, on higher ground, a vanguard of horsemen crested a rise. They were static models; nevertheless, the last time Darren had been in this room, they had not been present.

'What's happening over there, Sanj?' Darren pointed to the troops breaking free of their lines.

'Ah, the Egyptian incursion,' Sanjay nodded. 'Neb'll sort them out, no trouble.' 'Neb' referred to Nebuchadnezzar, the ruler of Sanjay's Babylon, the great empire of ancient history to which this masterpiece paid homage.

'When's the battle?' Darren asked.

'Next Friday, I reckon. Fancy coming round? Wadi-you say?'

Darren groaned but came back with, 'Just asp and Nile be there.'

'Oughtn't you clear it with Amanda first? Fez to fez?'

'Shut your cheops. What sort of Giza do you take me for?'

Sanjay groaned with cringing admiration. Darren shrugged but kept a triumphant grin on his face. Being present at one of Sanjay's staged battles was always an experience—mainly because he ran them with the utmost accuracy and detail, using authentic weaponry and strategy.

'Sure?' Sanjay asked, the question genuine and pun-free this time.

'Yeah, no probs,' Darren replied, trying not to sound too

crestfallen. 'I'll not be doing anything. I expect the garage will be a spa by that time.'

'Oh great. Bring me some washing up powder and a *Hello!* back the next time you're there.'

'Very funny.'

Sanjay grinned, looking highly pleased with himself. 'She's determined to see this through then?'

'You know Amanda,' Darren said. If he did see the resigned look that came over Sanjay's face, he decided not to comment. 'She's even offered some of her cousins to help me move out.'

Sanjay gave him a sharp look to check if he was joking. 'Where are you going to put all your stuff?'

'Don't know. I'll keep some of it, of course. Quite a lot of it will end up in the skip.'

'Oh, man.' Sanjay's pained expression reflected his heartfelt tone. 'That would be like, such a crime.'

Darren's shrug came with a downturned mouth. 'She won't have it in the house. She's right, I suppose, there's far too much of it. I've never been able to throw anything away, that's my problem.'

'But those are your sets. I mean, some of those are genius, man.'

Darren shook his head. 'I've promised Amanda. By the time she gets all her stuff in there I'll be lucky to end up with a broom cupboard. All I'd need is an owl and a giant on a motorbike and I'd be under the sorting hat before you can say French tips. No, she might as well have the whole garage.'

'Yeah but, I mean, what about what *you* want, Dar?'

A moment's very uncomfortable silence followed, broken by Darren turning away. 'I'll survive,' he said and flinched inwardly at how hollow the sentence sounded.

Sanjay stared at his feet while Darren turned back to study the mountains. Another silence followed, this one with both barrels wadded down and primed. Suddenly Sanjay looked up, his face unexpectedly animated.

'Bring your stuff here.'

Darren's pulse did the quick step. He stared at Sanjay and then around at the lock-up. Despite its size, Sanjay's project and the accompanying flotsam filled the space. Towards the rear stood a workstation where Sanjay made landscapes and painted his models. The space around the edge was cluttered with boxes and rags, leaving visitors in no doubt that this Mesopotamia was a work in progress. Darren knew for certain that trying to crowbar his sets in here would only cramp Sanjay's style, and he couldn't do that.

'Thanks mate, but no thanks. There's no room in here for my rubbish.'

'Who said anything about in here?' Sanjay said, grinning. 'Come with me, oh-soon-to-be-gobsmacked one.' He turned and hurried back up the garden to the house. Darren followed up the stairs to the first floor. 'It's so obvious. Should have thought of it before. Be perfect for you…' Sanjay threw out the words over his shoulder. A moment later, Darren entered a large room overlooking the tiny front garden. Light from the street outside flooded in through a large bay window.

'Mum and Dad's old bedroom,' Sanjay announced, flicking on the light, sounding pleased with himself.

'Wow,' Darren commented, looking around. 'Didn't know your mum and dad were Time Lords.'

A bright pendant light in a paper shade illuminated a huge room. Bare floorboards and moulded plastic furniture hailed straight from a seventies sitcom. The two landscapes depicting jungle and mountains on the walls were lost against the eye-catching—if not mind-bending—brown wallpaper spattered with circles of yellow, orange and red. All that was missing was a disco ball and some idiot in flares and platforms, wiggling his hips and miming trying to pick some low-hanging fruit and place it in a holster on the opposite hip.

But as a space it was ideal.

'What about your dad?' Darren levelled his eyes on Sanjay, trying not to look too beseeching.

'He's downstairs permanently, man,' Sanjay shrugged. 'Walking up and down these stairs would give him a stroke. Look at this place. There's loads of natural light. It's perfect.'

'Well, it's big enough alright. They could launch the Space Shuttle from that corner alone. You sure your dad won't mind?'

Sanjay shook his head and frowned. 'My dad loves you, man, you know that.'

'Still, bringing all my stuff here…'

Sanjay tutted, went back to the landing and called out in a slightly bored voice, 'Dad? Okay if Darren brings his photography stuff and sets it up in your bedroom?'

A cheerful disembodied voice yelled back, 'Tell him to bugger off.'

Sanjay grinned and turned back to Darren. 'See, told you.'

Darren found himself grinning, too. It was the obvious answer. Plus, it would get Amanda totally off his case.

'That would be brilliant, mate. Amanda'll be over the moon.'

Sanjay frowned. 'Let's get one thing straight. I'm not doing this for *Amanda*; I'm doing it for *you*. I know she's got a plan and stuff, but I hope she appreciates your sacrifice. That's all I'm saying.'

Darren recognised the invitation for what it was: a chance for him to talk to Sanjay about…*things*. Talking about Amanda to other people, though, even Sanjay, made him very uncomfortable. Especially as Amanda's opinion of Sanjay never deviated from cast-iron, no-way-back, loser geek.

*Failure is so unattractive in a man, Darren.* He could hear her voicing it loud in his mental memory bank. You could always rely on her to come out with that little dagger thrust of thoughtless rudeness masquerading as blunt honesty wrapped up in a bit of petty malice. Sanjay's opinion of Amanda, on the other hand, was one of polite distrust, though he would never say so. Darren had long ago accepted the fact that they were not going to befriend one another, and he'd fallen into the role of uncomfortable piggy in the middle. At least Sanjay did not take every opportunity to discuss Amanda, though the same could not be said when the tables were turned.

'Thanks, mate,' Darren held out a hand and Sanjay shook it. 'You're a brick.'

'Like you'd use to smash someone's head in with?'

'You've been reading those Swedish thrillers again, haven't you?'

'*Super Mario Kart on the Wii?*'

'Lead on, Nebmeister.'

Much later, after an hour of pleasurable virtual karting to the tune of *Pretzel Logic* blasting out through the sound system, Darren said his goodbyes to Sanjay and Mr. Bobal.

At the door, Darren had a thought. 'About shifting my stuff…'

'I'll borrow my uncle's van this weekend. Get it shifted in no time,' Sanjay volunteered. 'Oh, and say hello to Amanda for us.'

# CHAPTER SIX

DARREN WOULD, of course, do just that. Since he would be redolent of Mrs. Roopal's curry, there'd be no hiding the fact of his visit from Amanda. He knew, too, that the Bobals' vicarious greeting, though delivered, would go unanswered. Amanda had a thing about Sanjay and his dad. She had visited them when she and Darren had first started going out, but after a couple of times, she said she didn't like the way the house smelt. After Mr Bobal's diagnosis, she added that she was uneasy in the presence of someone who knew he was dying. Which spoke volumes for her discomfort around Darren's mum. An irony of admission that was, of course, totally lost on Amanda whose monochrome view of the world did not stretch to any, let alone much, self-analysis.

So, Darren was well aware that Amanda didn't like Sanjay—though if you asked the audience to list the things not to like about him, it would be sugar cube-sized. In fact, other than a propensity for awful puns and a need to quote two-minute sections of *Python* movies to anyone who would listen, Sanjay was completely harmless. One could do a lot worse than use, 'Always Look on the Bright Side of Life' as your creed, even if humming it incessantly while sculpting Mesopotamian landscapes could get a teeny bit wearisome.

Darren had other theories for Amanda's attitude. There was

the ethnic element of course, yet Darren knew that to be too simplistic. He suspected that her dislike stemmed more from jealousy. Sanjay was Darren's friend. Added to that was Sanjay's apparent lack of ambition, which, in Amanda's book, was the ultimate sin. A sin that, Darren had a sneaking feeling, Amanda thought might be contagious.

The real kicker in all of this though was Sanjay's proven intelligence. That put a tin hat on things in Amanda's eyes. A hat made up out of a first-class degree in physics from Aston University. But he'd never capitalised on it, preferring instead to come home to Shunter Street to look after his dad, help run the business and do a bit of freelance development and website design on the side. Darren's take on it was that the desire to make his dad secure and comfortable in what little time he had left seemed a pretty good, and meaningful, ambition.

Compassion, however, wasn't high on Amanda's list of acceptable reasons. For anything.

'There are hospitals for that,' she'd said when Darren explained Sanjay's choice. And of course she was right. But in Sanjay's world, hospitals didn't feature. Mr. Bobal was more comfortable at home, thanks to his neighbours and Dealer Dave's cakes. Having been on the same journey as Sanjay, watching his mother fall ill like Mr. Bobal had, Darren had to agree. He knew that Amanda tolerated their friendship like one might a neighbour's old scarred and smelly cat. You had to respect it, but you didn't ever want to pick it up and cuddle the thing.

Darren got home a little after ten-thirty. He put the bins out, dried and put away the dishes, and was watching TV when he heard a car pull up outside. He did not get up, but he did hear a man's voice, followed by Amanda's throaty giggle and a singsong 'Thanks, see you,' followed by the metallic rattle of a key in the door.

'Hi,' he called out to let her know he was in the TV room.

'Why are you still up?' Amanda managed to make it sound like he'd been trafficking endangered species instead of watching a rerun of *Batman*. In reply, Darren did what he always did when faced with an unexploded Amanda bomb: tried defusing it with humour.

'Couple of films I wanted to see. Canine science fiction. *Bark to the Future II* and *III*. First was okay. Second was a bit rover-rated.'

If he was hoping for a smile, he hoped in vain.

'You been on the wine again?' Amanda asked, frown in place.

'Never. Did a cruise on the Danube once, though.'

Amanda shook her head and shrugged off her coat.

'Reuben give you a lift?' Darren asked, deciding that Amanda's humour detector was set on minimum. Again.

'Yeah, dropped me off on his way home.'

Darren said nothing. Reuben was on Amanda's business course. Though he and Reuben had not been formally introduced, from the odd glimpse Darren had managed on one of the few occasions he'd picked her up from the adult learning centre, he'd been struck by how Trey Lushton-like Reuben was. He wore his hair the same way and, judging by the shade of his unseasonal tan, probably used the same grooming products. Darren had asked around and found out Reuben lived on the other side of the ring road to the south. A direction diametrically opposite the one he'd taken to deliver Amanda to her home address.

Surprisingly, Darren was not much bothered by this fact. If truth were told he was more bothered by being not bothered. Maybe Reuben had the hots for Amanda. That, he understood, because Darren still did too—sort of. Amanda, though, seemed to show little sign of wanting a change of partner, not from the way she was forever wanting to shop for bathroom suites and curtains for the first floor 'project' she had planned once the garage was done.

'I'm exhausted,' Amanda said, sighing. 'I'm going straight up, okay?'

'Yeah, fine,' Darren said. 'I won't be long myself.'

She paused on the stairs, eyeing her forgotten coat with a frown. 'Damn. Darren, hang my coat in the wardrobe, will you?'

'No problem. If I'm not back by morning, knock three times and ask for Prince Caspian.'

Amanda shook her head. Tumbleweeds were drifting by behind her eyes. 'Try not to make too much noise in the bathroom, will you?'

'Got it,' Darren said. 'Porcelain not puddle.'

'And don't forget we're out tomorrow night. Auntie Pauline's fiftieth,' she said over her shoulder.

Darren stifled a groan. 'Is that tomorrow night?' he asked, hating himself for sounding so wimpish.

'It is. I told you weeks ago.'

'You did, must have slipped my mind.'

'What a surprise that is,' Amanda replied.

'Oh, and Sanjay and Mr. Bobal send their love.'

'Thought I could smell curry. Stinks the place out.' Amanda wrinkled her nose and turned away.

Somewhere deep in Darren's abdomen, his gut clenched. He squeezed his eyes shut to try and quash it but to no avail. No matter what he did, it ate at him. Why did she have to be like this? So…*Amanda*-like. Sometimes she could be tender and exciting, do something that made his heart sing. Other times, quite a lot of other times, she was unpleasant and moody and basically an implacable minx. He knew she was flirting with Reuben, for example. He'd watched them a few times, seeing the way she'd get out of his car, smiling, tossing her hair. He'd decided that it was something she needed to do and felt a little bit sorry for Reuben for having been given the Amanda treatment. She flirted with the men at work too, but her determination not to like Sanjay was something he found difficult to accept, and they skirted the issue like two hyenas circling a rotting carcass.

All a test of some sort, he'd concluded. One he did not want to contemplate for more time than it took to fleetingly acknowledge. Was she trying to make him choose? The knot in Darren's gut tightened a little more. Who were you supposed to ask about these things if you didn't have a sister or a mum? He sometimes flicked through Amanda's magazines looking for a section, usually at the back, where someone would answer readers' letters of the 'My great-looking girlfriend, whom I fancy to bits, is really a sociopathic cow' variety. Should he write to someone like that?

Ultimately, he knew he never would because somehow Amanda would find out if he tried.

She always did.

Darren sighed. God, this living with someone was so bloody difficult. No, not just difficult, it was a relationship bloody minefield. And she hardly ever laughed at his jokes anymore. But then, as Sanjay would undoubtedly point out, that was nothing to worry about since no one else did either.

He heard her in the bathroom, heard the water gurgle away after she pulled the chain, and with it felt his disgruntlement flow down the pan. Who was he trying to kid here? So what if Amanda had a few flaws? She was here, wasn't she? She'd chosen to live with him of all people, and when it came to the battle between gratitude and disaffection, there was only ever going to be one winner. Okay, she didn't like Sanjay. Did it matter since Sanjay didn't actually mind (or so he kept telling Darren)?

No, he was a lucky boy to have Amanda. Wasn't her dad constantly telling him that?

He made his way to bed in what had been his mother's sickroom, holding on to that thought. And though he felt his grip loosening a teensy bit as he sank into the old mattress, he clung to it as he turned over and shut his eyes. The very last thing he thought of before sailing off into unconsciousness, however, had nothing to do with either Amanda or Sanjay. He fell asleep thinking of the shot he'd taken in the garage of the menacing figure lit by light through the slatted blinds.

The spy.

## CHAPTER SEVEN

**Darren woke at** six, and after laying the table for breakfast, went to the studio armed with a cup of tea. He liked the early mornings, liked the quiet, the coolness of the air. He was at his best at this time of day; the luggage room of his mind cleared of the day before's dusty baggage by sleep. He liked to use the time to dissect his photographs objectively, and the morning brought a freshly critical eye.

Darren's interest in models went back a long way. His dad kept an old biscuit tin full of red plastic GIs and miniature cars collected over the years. Perfectly natural for Darren to follow in his footsteps. An innocent little boy's hobby, encouraged by the mega corporations whose admen wooed their target audience with Fun Meal toys and action figures planted at the bottom of tasteless cereals. It could be argued that he'd been primed.

After the event with the miniature man and his blood-besmirched briefcase, the psychiatrists surprisingly suggested Darren continue with his hobby. 'As good a way as any to desensitise,' was the phrase used. Combining an interest in photography was a natural progression and with time, said interest seemed to validate all the rest. The rationale was that every time he captured a two-dimensional image it would emphasise the model's lifeless, artificial, dumb nature. Though he'd acknowledged the vague awareness that what he was doing was somehow trying to recontextualise the models' existence through the camera, it worked very well, over the years, to reinforce the message.

The garage was cold this morning and Darren shivered. He flicked on the light over his workstation. Outside, a wind worried at the loose guttering, its low moan accompanied by a plastic timpani of vibration. He switched on a fan heater and settled in front of a high-resolution monitor hooked up to a MacBook, pulled up yesterday's images and studied them. What he saw confirmed his thought of the evening before. There was no doubt at all in his mind now that the last four photographs, taken just before he left for Sanjay's, were the best of the series. The third one might even do for the 'Vinyl Vignette' competition he'd entered for three years running, but in which he'd never placed. Well, time to see what they made of his spy.

Maybe this would be his year.

He glanced over at the set and smiled. Using the blown-up sepia print backdrop was a stroke of genius. He'd come across the negatives in an old album of his mother's, part of a set taken by his wild-spirited uncle in his younger days. Filled with youthful wanderlust, Uncle Tom sailed the world and lived in Tahiti, New Zealand, and even worked in an Australian gold mine. The images jumped out at Darren when he'd processed the negatives and had taken him completely by surprise. Of course, the details of his mother's account of the episode had long since faded, but he remembered enough. He remembered, for example, that the discovery caused much conjecture amongst the miners, especially the Aborigines. Quite how such a collection of items found their way to a spot accessible only via the mineshaft remained a mystery to the mine owners, but the Aborigines had their own theory.

The way his mother told the tale, when news of the discovery reached the local wise men, they'd suggested that the cave was a place where a Kutji—a shape-changing demon— had been trapped, and immediately insisted the cave be sealed off. None of the local miners would work near it and so the foreman, in the interest of expediency, sealed the entrance. But not before Uncle

Tom sneaked in and took his snaps. He didn't give a didgeridoo about Kutjis.

Darren accepted the story as apocryphal, but when he'd gone through his mother's possessions after her death and found the negatives secreted away behind the half-glued back flap of her old album, he'd known instantly what they were. Or at least what they were supposed to be.

The background, the figure, and the lighting all added up to macabre—at least he hoped they did. Darren glanced over at the set, a smile of satisfaction curling his lip. But the satisfaction drained away and the curl inverted into a bemused frown as a tingle of disquiet suddenly rippled through him.

The spy wasn't standing in front of the slatted blinds where he'd left him. Darren stood up and walked around to where he'd last adjusted the spy's stance, fully expecting to see the figure supine on the floor. But there was no sign of him. Intrigued, he scanned the other sets on display. A few yards away an urban setting for a piece involving primates that he'd wittily entitled *Gorillas in Their Midst* still had its lighting rig set-up, but there was no sign of the spy there either. He searched the floor and his camera box in case he'd packed the figure up without thinking. Nothing.

He found what he was looking for on the Homestead set, one of the few not already mothballed, ready for the move. Darren slid out the three-foot square hardboard base from under a trestle table, not believing for one minute that he'd find anything. This was a farmhouse set in an idyllic rural setting complete with a back meadow, copse, and rolling hills. It had nothing at all to do with spies, but what he saw caused his eyes to widen and his pulse to skip.

The spy stood upright, just inside the gate, facing the farmhouse. Yet it was the positioning of all the other figures that made the hairs on his arms stand to attention. All the animals—ducks, chickens, goats and dogs—were pointing away from the spy, not, as one might expect from animal curiosity, towards him. Meanwhile at the rear of the farm building, the farmer and his wife and two small children were heading for the back gate.

## CHAPTER EIGHT

FOR A LONG, very confused moment, Darren stared at what he was seeing. There was no explanation to any of this. He did not recall moving the spy. Even if he had, why would he move him to *this* set? And why move all the other models too? The old familiar sense of dread rumbled away deep in Darren's gut. He tried quelling it with a dose of good old-fashioned logic.

If he hadn't moved the spy, then someone else had. But who? Amanda? After he'd gone to bed? Was this her idea of a brain-frying curveball? If not her, then who else? Sanjay?

Of the two, Sanjay would be more clued up on how to play a prank like this because Amanda would not have known the spy from Adam. And yet, Darren couldn't bring himself to believe that Sanjay would do such a thing. Despite his propensity for appalling puns, he wasn't much of a practical joker and besides: he had too much respect for Darren's art.

Darren's gut gave another ominous gurgle. Another explanation sprang to mind, one that was so bizarre as to be instantly dismissible. And yet…Darren could go months without recalling the events of that bright spring morning and the bloody briefcase but they were always there lurking beneath the surface, ready to pounce, and pounce they did now, in stark detail, right into Darren's temporal lobe.

Blood drained from his face and the world tilted precariously.

He grabbed at a table edge to steady himself and sat, with a heavy thud, on a toolbox. He tried and failed to suppress the spiralling thoughts. There was no denying the facts: the spy had moved a dozen yards across a garage and was about to terrorise a group of inanimate objects on a completely separate plastic and cardboard set.

Sounded bizarre.

Sounded impossible.

Sounded insane.

The dam burst and the thoughts flooded him with a poleaxing force he was helpless to stop. All the old memories, the denials, the treatments, the ridicule. All flowing like a turgid tsunami into every corner of his common sense, overwhelming his carefully constructed barriers and washing away his defences to reveal that dark and battered thing cocooned in his mind. Cocooned like the larva of some grotesque insect waiting to hatch. Darren waited for the words to appear in his head, knowing he'd hear them rather than see them when they came. Whispered, in his imagination, by a toothless crone huddled over a bubbling pot. And though it was nothing more than a mere phrase, it possessed the same terror-invoking potential as, 'It's only the dentist', or, 'Just a small little jab', or, 'Oh shit, that's the wrong leg'.

*Please... The Porter... Hippos in Oxford.*

Six small, powerful, terrible words.

Who the hell was the Porter?

And there were no Hippos in Oxford, were there?

It was these words and this memory, one he'd tried so hard to suppress and forget, which struck fear into his heart now.

What if it was happening again?

What if this was Dolly Darren all over again?

He smelled burnt toast. Cold sweat sprouted on his forehead.

They'd told him he'd imagined it all. Told him that inanimate plastic figures couldn't speak. But he'd seen what he'd seen and heard what he'd heard. And he knew deep down inside that he had not moved the spy yesterday. The spy had moved himself.

Darren took some deep breaths and put his head between his legs. If he allowed that little squirming beetle out from under its rock, there was another much bigger one ready to follow, one with 'What-if-it-was-all-true?' written in big, bold letters on its back.

He lifted his head and stood, picked up the spy, and walked back to the set where he'd photographed him the day before. Shuddering at the snakeskin and the pale shaped bone images he'd used as the backdrop, Darren Switched off his monitor, went back into the house and stood under the shower for ten minutes. Then he dressed for work and went down for breakfast, pushing everything to the back of his mind. Half a pink grapefruit stared unappetisingly up at him from his plate. His fragile appetite dissolved into nausea, and he rushed to the toilet where he fell to his knees and retched.

In the kitchen a few minutes later, Amanda, freshly made-up, smelling wonderful, turned an appraising expression towards him.

'Morning,' he muttered.

'You okay? You look ill. Bad curry last night?'

Concern gilded with mild irony was what she'd aimed for, Darren guessed. But what he read in her expression was closer to a sneer.

He could have told her then, laid himself open, asked for understanding. But he could equally have skipped naked down the high street wearing only a sock as a willy warmer and singing 'Delilah' for all the good that might do. Truth was, neither was very likely to happen. Amanda didn't know about his past. Didn't know that for years in school his nickname was Dolly Darren. And whereas one day he might tell her everything, now was not the time.

'Nope,' he said. 'I'm fine. Woke up early and couldn't get back to sleep, that's all.'

'And thee noise I heard in the bathroom was you warming up for tonight's karaoke, was it?'

'Yeah, thought I'd gargle with whisky and swallow a fag. Do a Tom Waits cover.'

'Did he used to be with McFly?'

Darren suppressed a whimper and settled for a Kalahari

glance dry enough to turn any self-respecting flower to dust. 'Never mind.'

Amanda narrowed her eyes. 'Hmm, hope you're not trying to get out of tonight.'

'Tonight? No…I'm looking forward to it.'

The look Amanda gave him was sharp enough to cut an atom, but Darren had his innocent face on and the moment passed. He knew how to play this game, and so he should. He'd had enough practice.

Amanda drove them both to work. It took fifteen minutes by car to the gates of Dobson and Crank's where Darren worked in the stores—recently renamed Logistical Operations—and Amanda in the back office in Support Services. Amanda, as usual, did almost all the talking while Darren, preoccupied by the spy, struggled to assimilate half of what she said.

'…And Gillian says she got a council grant for setting up the gift shop. Oh, and Reuben says he knows someone who does nice salon furniture really cheap.'

'Yeah?' muttered Darren.

Amanda threw him a glare shot through with irritation. 'What's wrong with you this morning? It's like you're on a different planet.'

'Just tired,' Darren lied.

They pulled up at the side entrance of Dobson and Crank's to let him out. She was not smiling when she said, 'I'll pick you up at five sharp. We need to be at the Falcon by six-fifteen. No dawdling.'

'Right miss, yes miss,' Darren muttered as he got out.

Amanda shook her head as she pulled away.

# CHAPTER NINE

**WAREHOUSE PACKING DID** NOT SOUND ANYWHERE NEAR as impressive as Logistical Operations and had no place in the business ethos of Dobson and Crank's, even though that was exactly what it entailed. Darren filled boxes with a variety of hardware from power tools to three-inch nails and sundry other engineering and welding items, labelled them, and loaded them onto pallets for distribution. Sometimes the orders were large; sometimes they were small enough to put into a six-inch Jiffy bag. It was boring, undemanding work but Darren kept reminding himself that he was lucky to have a job there at all.

In the main, he kept his head down and had a reputation as a solid worker. He got on with his co-workers well enough, even if the continuous banter about girls, beer and football tended to leave him cold. He made sure he knew enough about all three not to seem aloof or disinterested. Since everyone knew he and Amanda were an item, it tended to excuse him from too many boozy nights with the lads because, on the one hand, they all knew what Amanda was like, and on the other, who wanted to fraternise with the foreman's daughter's boyfriend? Darren did not complain. The truth was that the mundanity of the job suited him very well since it allowed his imagination free rein as the hours rolled by. Hours in which he could lazily dream up new scenes or lighting angles or whole sets for his photography.

But this morning, the spy and Dolly Darren had hijacked his thoughts and were force-feeding his imagination amphetamines through the bars of its cage.

He'd partnered up with Big Jeff, a six-foot-three, overweight giant with a face like a moon squeezed between two panes of glass, large mournful eyes and a nervous stammer. Big Jeff drove the forklift, while Darren loaded the pallets that were then driven onto a parked articulated lorry. At a little after eleven that morning, Big Jeff let go a low whistle to attract Darren's attention.

'Heads up,' Big Jeff said, 'here cuh…cuh…comes Kaa.'

Kaa, as he was unflatteringly referred to by his work colleagues, happened to be Harry Cray, Amanda's dad. As Logistics Operations supervisor, he had an office against the back wall where he and a secretary named Edna monitored stock control with military precision. Kaa was ex-army, always wore a shirt and tie, had features ruddy from hypertension, and teeth that were unusually small and few in number, separated by large gaps. The most striking thing about him, however, was his stare. He believed in eye contact of the unblinking, psychologically challenging, look-away-and-I'll-strike variety. He also had a disconcerting habit of ending every sentence and punctuating every point with a little defying tilt of the head followed by a widening of his palpable apertures and a dare-you-to-contradict me glare. This challenging and quite frequently alarming trait had earned him a nickname based on Kipling's *Jungle Book* snake as seen in the Disney film adaptation; the one with the mesmerising eyes. But Harry Cray used his stare to good effect: a trick he'd developed as an NCO in the 150th Transport Regiment. Clipboard under his arm, Harry prowled the warehouse floor looking for discarded wrappers, time wasters, and trouble in general. And worse than the glare was the fact that Harry 'looked out' for Darren in what he considered a subtle way, but which was excruciatingly obvious to everyone else.

'Jeff, I say Jeff,' Harry sang out, marching over. 'Could you nip to the office and fetch the C64 for that load to Tilbury for me? Only I left it with Edna.'

'With Eh…Eh…Eh…Edna?' Big Jeff stammered.

Darren didn't bat an eyelid since this was how Big Jeff always spoke. But Harry couldn't resist. 'No, with the chuffin' Prince of Wales. Of course with Eh…Eh…Eh…Edna.'

Big Jeff said nothing, but his shoulders slumped, and he shot Darren a knowing what-a-prick look.

'Come on lad, I'm not asking you to scale the chuffin' Himalayas. About it.'

Big Jeff lumbered off, but not without a couple of scathing backward glances. Darren didn't try hiding the disapproving look on his face either.

'Don't look at me like that, lad,' Harry said.

'He can't help his stammer,' Darren argued.

'There's no such thing as stammering, Darren. It's just a screen for attention seeking. A way to invite sympathy and hog the microphone at karaoke nights.'

'That's because stammerers often don't stammer when they sing. They use a different part of their brain—'

'And if you believe that you'll believe anything.' Kaa's jaw tilted ominously upwards. 'Like I said, pathetic. Right, now Lur…Lurch is out of the picture, I've fixed it so you, Darren, are on car cleaning duty for the bosses when they come for their big powwow at three, okay?'

'You want me to clean cars?'

'Yes. And don't sound so chuffin' surprised. It won't kill you. There'll be three of them. Give them a once-over with a hose and sponge, you know the drill. Like I showed you the other Sunday when we found that sticker under all the grime on your boot lid.'

'I swear it wasn't there when I bought the car.'

'Yes well, if you kept the thing clean, you'd know if someone was vandalising your car with stickers, wouldn't you?'

Darren wilted under Harry's baleful glare. '*I Love Ladyboys* isn't quite the same as someone knifing my tires, is it?'

'Same principle,' Harry said. 'Anyway, make sure you're at the side entrance at three. I'll make sure they know who did it, so do a good chuffin' job, right?' The head tilted. The eyes bored.

Darren nodded. No point in complaining or protesting about how pathetic it all was to a man whose working life revolved around army bull. Spit and polish, neat and tidy, you wipe my arse and I'll wipe yours. That was the Harry Cray credo. It didn't matter in the slightest if you turned into an opinionated, nit-picking, self-righteous pillock in the process. 'Right,' he said, defaulting to his favourite word, trying to sound enthusiastic and failing.

'I'm putting myself out for you with this, I'll have you know,' Harry bristled.

'Yeah, I do know. Thanks, Mr Cray.'

'And I should think so. I promised Ron Millson I'd let his boy do some car cleaning soon. He's in the post room. He'll jump at the chance if you're not interested.'

'No, I'll do it. If you think it's worth it.'

Harry leaned in so that Darren caught a whiff of stale Aramis. 'Course it's bloody worth it. Bosses are like kids. They like shiny things. They also like initiative. You mark my chuffin' words.'

Darren nodded. Harry finally lifted his gaze away from Darren's face to glance at Big Jeff lumbering back from the office.

'All set for tonight then?' Harry grinned. Darren thought he caught a glimpse of dangling uvula through the gaps between Kaa's front teeth.

'Yeah, I think so.'

'It'll be brilliant. Compulsory karaoke and getting bladdered. Free bar till eight. It is killing my brother to pay for his wife's fiftieth and I want him to die a slow chuffin' death.' Harry grimaced in what Darren identified as a grin of pleasure, leaning forward to take the C64 Jeff had found, folding it, and putting it in his pocket with a belligerent, 'Th…th…thanks, Jeff.'

Darren watched him leave. When he was well out of earshot, Big Jeff murmured a single word.

'Git.'

# CHAPTER TEN

At about 3.00pm, Darren made his way to the side entrance where three black Mercedes and a Bentley were parked. A warm sun emerged intermittently between fluffy clouds drifting lazily across the blue sky. Despite himself, Darren embraced the task of shining up the cars, glad of the time to think. In so doing, he convinced himself that somehow, and without being aware of it, he'd placed the spy in the Homestead set. No other logical explanation fitted, because to accept any of the illogical ones involved scary visits to the funny farm for someone to open the lid of his head and check the contents. He'd had enough of all that.

He saw no one for forty-five minutes. How Harry was going to swing this to Darren's advantage remained a mystery. From where Darren stood, no one would be any the wiser that the cars had been cleaned at all. Perhaps he should leave a card:

***Cars cleaned by Darren from Logistics.***

But he needn't have worried. Harry had plans.

At three-fifty, a large truck pulled into the car park; a curious manoeuvre in itself since the loading bay was on the other side of the building. Even more unusual was the fact that the driver immediately honked his horn three times with a force nine startle factor loud enough to cause Darren to jerk murky water on the bonnet of an already cleaned Mercedes.

Loud enough to bring Harry Cray to the door.

Loud enough to bring faces to the windows of the boardroom above where Darren happened to be working.

Harry ran across to the truck driver, they exchanged a few words and then the truck, with a hiss of a brakes and the piercing bleep of the reverse warning signal, pulled out. The group of watchers above looked on.

'What was all that about?' Darren asked as Harry joined him.

'Pulled into the wrong entrance, didn't he,' Harry barked and made a great show of pleading apology to the faces above by holding out both hands palm up in entreaty. But when he reached Darren, he grinned and winked. 'Still, got the attention of the big knobs above, didn't it?'

'You set it up?'

'It's possible that I might have said second left instead of first when I spoke to the driver on the phone earlier. Lot on my chuffin' plate, lad. Come on, about it.' Harry gave Darren a gap-toothed grin. Above them, his snake eyes danced with a Machiavellian twinkle.

## CHAPTER ELEVEN

**THE FALCON WAS A LARGE**, faux-Tudor monstrosity on the edge of an outlying village. Laughingly termed a gastropub, it was the sort of place that served burnt food on wooden planks and got away with it by tarting up its menu with terms like 'Heritage Carrots' and 'Charred Leeks'. It was only safe to drink the beer from bottles and the locals often snapped the tops off with teeth, sometimes even their own.

Amanda's aunt and uncle had generously organised a couple of buses that were noisily disgorging their load of corpulent, clamorous Crays when Darren pulled into the car park. He endured the usual volley of ribald comments and hefty backslaps from the men, some sloppy kisses from the women, and even a tobacco-flavoured tongue from Amanda's nineteen-year-old cousin Kirsty, who'd been in the pub since five-thirty and was well on her way to becoming paralytic.

If a Trey Lushton concert was a tribulation for Darren, compared to a full-on night out with the Crays, it seemed suddenly as desirous and sophisticated as a Steely Dan reunion concert. Being a designated driver was no help either, since by nine-thirty everyone else was completely—to paraphrase Kaa—'bladdered'. Darren knew that he'd be made to sing and so gave a deliberately rubbish rendition of 'Back in the USSR' and was duly booed off with no danger of an encore. By ten-thirty, several cousins and an uncle had fallen over, and Amanda's aunt Lorraine, forty-two and predatory in a skirt masquerading as a pelmet, had disappeared into the car park with a member of the bar staff. The guy appeared ten minutes later, with his hair mussed and the shocked, queasy expression of someone who'd just stepped off the Oblivion roller coaster at Alton Towers.

Amanda spent most of the evening circulating, leaving Darren perched on a stool at the bar in sober observation. People came to talk to him, generally on their way to, or from, a fag break outside. The host, Amanda's uncle Joe, told him a rude joke about a dog with five legs, and her cousin Kirsty asked him if he wanted to go out to her car for a 'quickie'. An offer he declined without risk of offence since he was the fourth she'd propositioned in as many minutes while she lined up for the bar. At ten-thirty, Harry, on his way back from the loo, put his arm around Darren and oozed beery breath all over him.

'Great night, eh lad?'

'Yeah,' Darren managed to drag a grin up from near his boots.

Someone shouted something derogatory, and Harry told him to 'piss off' with a good-natured sneer, his teeth on show in a picket fence grin.

'What do you think of the family, eh Darren? Fancy being one of us?'

Darren winced. It was not the sort of question he wanted to answer because he'd been asking himself the same thing all evening. Darren quite liked the odd beer, but the Crays' manic determination to drink the place dry was breathtaking in its intensity.

'They certainly know how to live,' Darren said.

'Exactly,' Harry agreed, poking Darren in the chest with a hard finger. 'Yoyo, Dar. Yoyo. You're only 'ere once, it's not a bloody rehearsal.' He grinned again and let his voice fall to a lower range. 'Our Amanda likes you a lot, Darren. I think you two go well together and I know you're nice to her.' He swayed and let his voice fall even lower. 'Course if I ever found out you'd upset her in any way...' He let the sentence trail off.

Darren waited for the graphic explanation of what Harry

would do if the circumstances ever arose, but it never came. His guess was something involving long handled lopping shears, a lot of blood and Darren auto ingesting his own sautéed testicles. He'd heard it all before in gory detail. However, tonight, for once, alcohol-induced bonhomie won the day and Harry laughed uproariously.

'You should see your bloody face, Darren. Ha! You're a good lad and I don't need to chuffin' tell you that, do I?'

Darren shook his head and got an extra squeeze from Harry's hand on his shoulders in return.

'Right,' said Harry, turning to the barman. 'Six pints of lager and three double vodkas with orange if you please.'

At eleven, Amanda wobbled back to him on her four-inch heels and hung onto his arm whilst jiggling to something booming out of the disco.

'Less dance,' she demanded, cheeks flushed with drink, her words slipping and sliding into one another.

'I'm not in the mood, Mand.'

'Come on. Don't be sush a wuss.'

'It's "Mambo No. 5" for crying out loud.'

'You're sush a tight arse.' Amanda yanked hard on Darren's arm.

Sighing, Darren danced and had his tight arse pinched three times, twice by Aunt Lorraine. But when 'The Birdie Song' came on, he flatly refused to stay on the dance floor. And just as well, since all of Amanda's aunts appeared and did a synchronised version that ended only when Aunt Pauline, the birthday girl, fell over a table and crushed a railway worker from Leeds. The bloke had more tattoos than Edinburgh castle and got to his feet with a face like a baboon's backside. He looked furious and indignant, but one look at the assembled Crays fussing over Pauline brought on a sudden attack of survivalist common sense culminating in *him* apologising for being in the way and standing *them* a round of drinks.

At midnight the Crays spilled out of the Falcon into the car park in a drunken wave. Amanda's uncle Lou, Harry's older brother, a squatter cross between the Fantastic Four's Thing and The Incredible Hulk, had been spoiling for a fight all night.

Having his request for one last pint refused by the barman, Lou reached across and lifted the terrified man off his feet with one ham fist, dragged him over the bar and, with his face inches from the petrified youth's, said 'Think it's clever wearing a T-shirt with KFUC on it, sonny. Makes you look like a complete KCOC.'

It had been a seminal moment. As a result, Lou ended up being helped out of the front door of the pub by the bouncers, laughing uncontrollably and bleeding from a cut eye.

Stone cold sober Darren, one of a handful still able to stand without support, helped Lou to his feet and stared into his battered, pockmarked fifty-nine-year-old visage. The lapel of Lou's suit jacket hung by a thread. But he was still grinning. Darren counted lots of spaces where there should have been teeth.

'You've lost your plate, Lou,' Darren said.

Lou's hand flew to his mouth and an instant later was scrabbling on the tarmac, howling toothless urgings to his relatives to join in. It was Darren who found the dentures grinning up at him from an oily puddle five yards from where Lou had tumbled, cursing, out of the bouncer's grasp. Glad of the car park murk that hid his grimace and the fact that he'd used a discarded crisp packet as a makeshift mitt in order not to actually touch the offending article, Darren gingerly handed Lou's false teeth back to him and watched, in horror, as he slid them back in after a cursory trouser front wipe. Darren's reward was a crushing hug and a big, wet, sour-smelling kiss on the cheek.

'You're a good boy, Darren,' oozed Lou. 'Great night, eh? Now where's that chuffin' charabang?' He stumbled over to a nearby shrub and proceeded to relieve himself noisily and judging by the wildly varying tone of fluid striking tarmac, bush, leather and trouser material, none too accurately.

By twelve-fifteen the Crays had all but departed and it was with considerable relief that Darren finally scooped Amanda into the car and drove home.

'Thawasbrill,' Amanda blurted next to him.

'Right,' Darren said.

'Wassamatter? Dinyoujoy?'

'Sober,' Darren said. 'You know what it's like.'

'Nah. I-don,' Amanda slurred. 'Kitrsty, Kirtsty thinssyourcute,' she added.

'Kirsty thinks the elephant man's cute. The clue is in the 'man' bit. Or, knowing Kirsty, maybe it's the elephant bit.'

Amanda let out a deep guffaw. 'Yerfunny. Thasswha Kirtsty lies 'bout you. Anyoblackair, ncrinklyblueeyes. Cute, 'nfunny 'nweird—thassyou.'

'Thanks,' Darren said and glanced over at her. The last thing he wanted was for her to throw up in his car. But she was staring resolutely ahead, her lids at half-mast, trying, he suspected, to stop the world from spinning around.

'Amanda,' he said.

Mumbling 'Yessdarren,' her eyes slid slowly shut, though she did manage one deep nod in a half-hearted confirmation that she was still marginally awake.

'Something happened in the garage this morning. I'd done a shoot of this spy figure the day before and this morning, someone had moved it. The figure I mean. You didn't, by any chance—'

Darren's peripheral vision caught Amanda's head lolling forward, accompanied by a sudden loud snore. Her eyes were still disconcertingly open a quarter of an inch, but her brain had clearly set sail for sleepy shores on the good ship vodka.

'Thanks for being such a good listener,' Darren said and accelerated up the bypass.

He'd never been so glad he'd volunteered to drive, but the novelty was wearing pretty thin when it came to Uncle Lou and the others. Their bludgeoning insistence on ensuring that he got bladdered like the rest of them was going to be impossible to fend off forever.

Darren winced, and wondered, not for the first time, if being a Cray meant that he'd have to fork out to have his stomach lined with iron.

## CHAPTER TWELVE

He was already two cups of coffee in by the time Amanda made an appearance at mid-morning the next day. She was pale, eyes puffy, lips flaky from dehydration.

'Blimey. You need to go easy on that sumo wrestler night cream, Mand.'

She held up a warning finger without looking at him and shook her head.

'Grapefruit?' Darren asked.

Amanda winced and spoke in a slow and croaky whisper. 'Water.'

Darren filled a glass from the tap. Amanda drained it and put her hand on her chest in what looked like a brave attempt at keeping the liquid in its place.

'Good time last night?' Darren asked.

Amanda raised one eyebrow with difficulty. 'If you say so. Can't remember much.'

'No surprise there then,' Darren muttered.

'Getting legless at parties is a Cray tradition. Better get used to it,' Amanda said, her jaw jutting forward.

'Right.'

'Just because you were driving.'

Darren held up both hands in a gesture of innocence, but Amanda's disapproving glance told him she wasn't buying it.

And with the ease borne out of years of hung-over practice fuelled by a need for everyone else to share in her self-inflicted pain, Amanda flicked the switch marked 'deflected blame' and fired off an accusation at Darren.

'Why are you in here anyway? You should be sorting out the garage, shouldn't you?'

'Sanjay's coming in half an hour with a van. I'm taking my stuff to his.'

'Oh,' Amanda said, sounding more than a little surprised by this revelation. 'All of it?'

'Yeah, he's got a spare bedroom, so I thought, why not? I mean, even if I kept half the space in the garage, it would be way too cramped—' He did not get any further with his explanation as Amanda's croak cut him short.

'I suppose that means you'll be spending even more time at his.' It was a statement rather than a question, one that needed a tray beneath it to catch all the drips of vitriol.

'A bit…maybe,' Darren said, suddenly on the back foot. He'd assumed she'd be pleased. The sound of the doorbell was a welcome diversion. The postman stood with a bundle of mail in one hand and a battered PDA in the other.

'Need a signature for this one,' he said, waving a Jiffy bag.

Darren took delivery and scribbled his name on the scratched PDA screen with his finger. He went back to the kitchen and handed the bundle to Amanda. She flicked through the usual mix of bills and flyers until she came to the Jiffy bag.

'This is for you,' she said and tossed it to him.

'Really?' He hadn't bothered looking at the label. Amanda got parcels regularly from cosmetic companies, so he'd assumed it was for her. Frowning, he held the bag up and shook it. Nothing rattled.

'Who's it from?' Amanda asked, not bothering to look up, still busy with the envelopes.

Darren searched for the sender address, but it had ripped in half with the envelope. 'Hip something,' he muttered before adding, 'have you sent for anything?'

'Not that I can remember—' Amanda didn't finish the sentence as a squeal of delight erupted from her pale lips and she waved this month's copy of *Monail*, a bimonthly glossy for nail professionals containing industry resources and nail art galleries, and made big, excited eyes. She tore off the wrapping while Darren opened his Jiffy bag and reached inside. He took out a six-inch tall bubble-wrapped oblong and frowned. He couldn't make out much detail, but it looked like a vaguely human figure.

'What is it?' Amanda asked, not bothering to look up.

'A freebie, I think. Must be a new company. Probably got my name from a database somewhere.'

Amanda looked up and sneered. 'Wow, a free toy. I bet you can hardly contain yourself.' She shook her head. She let out a sigh that was audible in the next county.

Darren contented himself with peeling off the bubble wrap, but stopped when he caught sight of Amanda's stony glare.

'I'll put it with the rest of the stuff to go to Sanjay's,' he said, stuffing the figure back into the envelope.

Amanda snorted, pulled out a chair and began thumbing through her magazine.

'I'll get on with it then, shall I?' Darren asked after a long moment's silence.

Amanda did not look up, nor acknowledge his question. Darren had enough sense to take it as read that he'd been dismissed.

---

His curiosity well and truly piqued, Darren hurried out to the garage, the lumpy Jiffy bag in his pocket. The appearance of a new model manufacturer always gave him a buzz, since so many seemed to be going to the wall like every other small business. Once in his studio, he took out the bubble wrapped model and tore off the wrapping to reveal a female clothed in battle fatigues complete with helmet, camouflage trousers and jacket. Placing the figure on his desk next to the Mac, he carefully removed her helmet.

Pins and needles prickled his skin, and a small involuntary grunt escaped his lips. Under the helmet was a mop of caramel hair with blonde flashes framing an exquisitely modelled face, which sported startlingly blue eyes and a generous mouth. Carefully, Darren unbuttoned the combat jacket and removed it. His next intake of breath was tiny, but sharp. She'd been lovingly crafted, clean-limbed and straight-backed with a slight overemphasis on the curves. In all his years of collecting and photographing toy models, Darren had never seen anything quite like this. He was very glad she'd been bubble wrapped. With her obviously female figure on show under a resin hugging, sleeveless T-shirt, he wasn't quite sure what Amanda would have made of her revealed at the breakfast table. A surge of eager anticipation took hold of him, and he made a small triumphant fist.

*Yes.*

She'd be perfect for the Forest setting…

Then the irony of it hit him. Here he was, about to dismantle his world when through the post comes *the* most exquisite model he'd ever seen. But from where? Darren put his hand back into the Jiffy bag and came out with a folded compliments slip. There was no address or email or phone number. Instead, emblazoned across the top was the name Hipposync Enterprises. Underneath was a single word in ink:

### *Roxana*

Quickly, suppressing the pang of guilt that told him he should be packing, Darren pulled out the Forest set. It was one of his favourites, complete with real wooden fencing, conifer branches he'd stuck into soil, actual moss and blades of grass. He moved the spy's arcane lair onto a side table and put the Forest set in its place, left the lighting the same, and placed Roxana next to a large pebble, half covered with lichen. The branch of a fir tree hung down over the pebble. It looked like Roxana was in hiding, peering out at her enemies. Darren made a few adjustments to the foliage and stood up, satisfied.

He fetched the camera and took three quick snaps.

'Right. Let's see how you look through the lens, Roxana.' Darren turned towards his computer.

'Of what is this lens that you speak?'

His question was meant as rhetorical, so when he heard the mickey-take, he swung around fully expecting to find Amanda complete with crossed arms and disdainful expression.

'Checking to make sure everything works one last time before...' he began feebly, but his voice trailed off. There was no Amanda. No one at all in fact. Yet he could have sworn he'd heard a voice.

'Of what is this lens that you speak?' Small but insistent, the voice repeated its question, this time from behind him.

Something zinged through his spine on an adrenaline-charged barb. He stayed facing the door, his feet rooted, unable to turn around because if he did, he would have to acknowledge the voice. Admit it was coming from the vicinity of the Forest set. And accepting either of those two impossibilities would be opening a door he'd kept resolutely locked shut for twenty-odd years.

But there was nothing for it, because if he didn't confront this...*thing*, what hope was there for him? Trembling, he turned on wobbly limbs that threatened to give way at any second, stumbled to a chair and jerked the one remaining trestle table in the process. The Forest set shuddered and shook and a couple of small trees fell over.

'Shit,' Darren said.

## CHAPTER THIRTEEN

He got up on his shaky legs and checked the set, eyes primed for what he might find. Roxana was not where he'd left her. He got down on his knees to get closer, parted some of the foliage with shaking fingers and lifted a fallen palm tree. There she was: on her back under some long blades of grass. Two things struck him immediately. The first was that she wasn't moving. The second was that when she turned her head up to look at him, she had a very pretty face.

'The gods, it seems, are angry,' Roxana said getting up.

Darren jerked backwards, a strangled bleat of horror escaping from his throat.

*No. No. Not this. Not again.*

'There is little time,' Roxana said, concern in her voice as she got up off the floor.

Darren gasped. He couldn't quite place the accent. Nordic or Danish maybe? He let out a thin little giggle and knew it as a fanfare to the funny farm. But at least he had insight. Instead of calling for an ambulance so that they could put him into a padlocked straitjacket and throw away the key, here he was trying to place an accent.

The accent, moreover, of a six-inch high doll.

Meanwhile, Roxana, most definitely no longer resin, planted her feet and looked up at him.

'Are you hurt, giant?'

Darren whimpered but managed to shake his head.

'That is good, for we must hurry.' From a pouch on her belt she took a small hourglass. 'Minutes, no more. You have a name, giant?'

'Daaa…' mumbled Darren, the light-headedness of moments before threatening once again.

'Daaa. An unusual name, even for a giant.' Roxana shrugged.

Darren squeezed his eyes shut. This wasn't happening. Of course it wasn't bloody happening. But when he opened them, nothing had changed. Roxana was still there, standing with legs apart, staring up at him defiantly.

'You must listen. I am here to give a message to the Maker. Our land is in great danger. A monster is amongst us—a monster that kills and burns and lays waste for no reason other than he can.'

Darren swallowed drily. The voice that came out, when he eventually found it, sounded way too high. 'Where exactly is… your land?'

Roxana waved a very small hand. 'This is my land.'

'No, this is a set I made in my studio.'

'Daaa, giant you may be, but in this you are wrong. I know this land. I grew up in it. A mile to the south is a great sycamore. To the west, the silent lake.'

Darren frowned. He had stuck in a sycamore branch a couple of feet away and there was an old cereal bowl he'd used once as a setting for a patrol boat shoot. 'But…'

Roxana shook her head. 'Listen to me, Daaa. You must use whatever means you have to communicate this information to the Maker. The monster's name is Ysbaed and he has gathered an army of bottomless savagery. His cruelty knows no bounds. He has weapons of great power. We are here to ask for help.'

'Help?'

'You understand the message?'

'Yes. Ysbaed, monster, cruelty. But that doesn't tell me how you've turned from a plastic doll into, into…whatever you are?'

A tiny frown crossed Roxana's face.

'I know not of what you speak, giant. The Archivist asked for help and his belief was answered by the visitors. I took their draught and I slept. They told me when I awakened, I would be in a strange place full of wonders where I would have but moments to convey a message to the Maker. The visitors tell us that we need a Paladin and an Obfuscator. Please tell me you hear me, Daaa? Our survival depends upon it!' She glanced once more at the hourglass. 'The grains of sand run far too quickly. I beg you to do this thing. Ysbaed gets bolder. He raids and pillages to revel in the pain he can inflict, and we are defenceless against his dark weapons.' Darren heard her breath catch. 'Two nights ago, he captured my cousin and my betrothed. I doubt that either still lives. We need help, giant, we need hel—'

The words froze in the air at the same time as Roxana's expression of entreaty became fixed, her eyes lustreless, her complexion waxen. The fire in her cheeks paled to bland pink plastic. Darren, still on his knees, could only stare in disbelief. He stayed unmoving until the pain in his joints got too much and forced him stiffly to his feet. He reached out to touch the doll, but his hand shook too much to pick her up. He knew his breathing was too fast. He knew because his fingers were beginning to tingle. An involuntary bleat of denial erupted from him: it *was* happening again. All over *again*. Only this time he was twenty-nine, not nine. There'd be no childish excuses this time. This time, the horizon was dotted with labels like schizophrenia, delusions, barking madness. Yet he'd seen what he'd seen and heard what he'd heard. The Maker, the Obfuscator, Paladin.

What the hell did it all mean?

The noise of the door opening made him start badly. Amanda stood there, still no make-up, rake thin.

'I'm going back to bed for an hour. I wanted to see if you'd almost finished.'

'I'm checking lights,' Darren muttered, keeping his gaze away from Amanda's. 'No point taking duff light bulbs, is there?'

Amanda raised her one dubious eyebrow, shook her head and left. Darren didn't try to stop her. At this particular moment the less he saw of Amanda the better. He forced himself to breathe normally and sat down. He was still sitting when Sanjay arrived ten minutes later.

'What's up with you?' Sanjay asked.

Darren composed his face into an unconvincing smile. 'Nothing. But I can't do much more without your help. It'll take two of us to carry most of this stuff.'

'Had to sit down to work that one out then, did you?' Sanjay said. But when Darren's smile wavered, he added, 'You sure you're okay? You look a bit Himalayan.'

'Himalayan?'

'Yeah, you know, peaky.'

Darren forced another grin and dragged his thoughts away from Roxana. 'I'm fine. So, you got the van?'

'Yeah. VW. It's sweet, man. Tons of room inside. Thought we'd stack the trestles first. Okay?'

Darren nodded and stood, glad of the distraction loading the van provided. He went at it with vigour, wanting to spend as little time in small talk as possible. All the while his thoughts churned with the morning's events. It took almost five hours and four trips to get everything transported. Amanda appeared mid-afternoon and announced that she was meeting her sister in town to go shopping. But she tarried long enough to stride into the almost empty garage, scanning the space, unable to suppress a smug expression.

'This place is going to be so great,' she crowed. Her corneas gleamed through her slitted, calculating lashes. 'Can't you just feel it?'

Darren was saved from an incriminatingly negative mutter by Sanjay, who breezed through the door behind her. 'Hi, Amanda.'

Amanda turned on her heel, managed a cursory, 'Hi' and clopped off towards the car. Darren felt his face burn with embarrassment.

'Sorry about…'

'Don't sweat it. I think most girls are allergic to me anyway. Bit like nuts.'

Sanjay's good-natured dismissal of the snub made Darren feel even worse. Yet the truth was, around girls, Sanjay became almost pathologically shy. Of course, Amanda's take on his timidness had been typically Cray blunt.

'Shyness is just an excuse for not having to speak to people, Darren,' she'd declared. 'It's bone idleness and can't be arsedness masquerading as psychological bullshit. Besides, we both know Sanjay can't get a girl because he dresses like a five-year-old and smells of curry.'

In theory, Sanjay did have lots of female cousins and seemed to be fine with them. But when it came to matters of romance, much as Darren hated to admit it, Amanda was absolutely right. Sanjay was a tongue-tied wallflower.

## CHAPTER FOURTEEN

After they'd finally lugged the last few pieces of equipment up the stairs to Mr. and Mrs. Bobal's bedroom, Sanjay returned the van to his uncle and reappeared with a six-pack of IPA. They sat in the kitchen with the drone of Mr. Bobal's TV clearly audible through the walls.

'Thanks, mate,' Darren said and popped the tab on a Seven Brothers Juicy. He drank half the contents without stopping, only noting Sanjay watching around the curve of his can when he stopped for a required burp.

'What?' Darren asked.

'Wondering if you've decided to tell me yet?'

'Tell you what?'

'Whatever it is that's had you wound up all day. Your brain is on Jupiter, man.'

'Sorry, Sanj,' Darren said, and because he couldn't help himself, added, 'Is my red spot showing?'

'Very jovial. But I know what it is.'

'You do?' Darren shot him an incredulous glance.

'Amanda's spa plans, right?'

Darren half choked on a mouthful of beer. 'I don't even want to think about that, Sanj,' he protested, dabbing at his watering eyes.

'Is it that you've finally twigged that the nail spa thingy is just a blind and that what she really wants to do is set up a crystal meth lab?' Sanjay grinned.

'Trouble with that little theory is that Amanda's grasp of chemistry begins and ends with the sodium chloride she sprinkles on her chips.' Darren delivered all of this with an irritated little shake of his head.

'Come on. Surely you can visualise Amanda with a gas mask on, throwing a tray of aluminium filings into a vat of boiling chemicals out the back?'

Sanjay frowned. 'Oh, deary me. Someone got out of bed and left their sense of humour under the pillow today, didn't they?'

'Amanda doing a Walter White is not in the least bit funny.'

'Yes, it is,' Sanjay insisted.

Darren's brows beetled. 'Under normal circumstances, maybe.'

'What's making these circumstances so abnormal, then?'

Darren let his head drop. It was no good keeping this stuff inside. It was like trying to cage a noxious gas. He stood and walked across to a cardboard box in which he'd bubble wrapped his figures and models. For the second time that day, he unwrapped Roxana, holding her up for Sanjay to see.

'Wow. She's impressive.'

'Came in the post this morning.'

'You still subscribe to those magazines then?'

'The thing is,' Darren said, ignoring Sanjay's puerile riposte and his self-satisfied smirk, 'ten minutes after unwrapping her she was telling me how her world was being torn apart by something called 'Ysbaed', waving her arms and calling me 'giant'.'

The lager can froze halfway towards Sanjay's lips. He looked up, eyes wide and blinking rapidly.

'I know, okay?' Darren stood, palms forward in a don't-say-anything gesture. He started pacing, forefinger worrying at a go-to freckle on his cheek. 'I know how it sounds. Just like it sounded last time. Dolly bloody Darren who hears voices coming from plastic toys. I know how mad it seems, but I also know what I saw and what I heard. Jesus, Sanj, am I going bloody bonkers?'

Sanjay had a very odd look in his eye. He stood, put down his can and picked up the Roxana doll. 'I've never seen anything like this before. Who's the manufacturer?'

'No maker's mark. Nothing but a compliments slip in the Jiffy bag with a heading of Hipposync Enterprises.'

Sanjay glanced up from the model into Darren's troubled face. 'Tell me again exactly what you heard.'

And so Darren did. He relayed it to his friend, word for Scandinavian-accented word. After a short while, Sanjay held up a hand. 'Hang on.' He bolted through the door and came back forty seconds later with a pad and pencil. 'Go on, I need to write this stuff down.'

Darren frowned. 'Why?'

'Because we need to research this, don't we? Hipposync and stuff.' Sanjay scribbled something down on the pad.

Darren didn't speak for a long minute. Eventually Sanjay looked up again. 'What?'

'You mean you believe me?' Darren's voice, in his own ears, sounded like it was coming from a long way off.

'Of course I believe you. I believed you the last time, didn't I?'

A balloon seemed to burst inside Darren. It flooded him with a relief so overwhelming that he had to sit down and let his head fall between his legs. Though Sanjay was his friend, he hadn't known for certain how he'd react. And he hadn't laughed or accused Darren of a wind-up. For once, Darren could not find anything to say. He let his head hang further down and breathed deeply.

Sanjay watched him for a few seconds. 'Dar, if your nose gets any closer to your crotch, you'll be in danger of reinventing the word selfie. Though, from what I've heard, it would have to get a *lot* closer.'

'Sanj…' Darren shook his head and let a weak grin slide over his face.

'Hey, don't knock it.' Sanjay cracked a grin and then, holding up the Roxana model once more, asked, 'Tell me what she called these people you're meant to contact again?'

'Obfuscator and Paladin,' Darren replied, still reeling from not having been laughed at. He stared at Sanjay and asked, 'How come you're not calling the men in white coats?'

'Are you kidding me? Obfuscator and Paladin? You couldn't make those up if I locked you in a room with a thesaurus for a week. So that means something must have said those words to you.'

Sanjay wrote on a pad and then made Darren tell it all again. When he'd finished, Darren, for some reason, felt a lot better. Sanjay read through his notes and whistled. 'Man, can't wait to see the film.'

'It's not funny, Sanj. I thought I'd got over all of this stuff. Buried it in a steel chest forty feet under a concrete cap. Thought I'd got my life back on track.'

'What track is that you're talking about exactly?' Sanjay asked with eyebrows raised. 'The one where your hobby is ridiculed, you've been banned from enjoying yourself with your mates, and to top it all, chucked out of your own studio?'

'Look, I know I'm not exactly driving an Aston Martin along the Amalfi coast with a Chechen lap dancer in the passenger seat, but I'm not on the street or in the loony bin either, am I? By the time I was thirteen, I'd finally convinced myself that what happened was nothing but a touch of chemical imbalance in my head. And now…this.'

'I see,' Sanjay said. 'So now it's the same choice. Either forget it ever happened or do something about it.'

'Like what?' Darren said, knowing he sounded sullen but not wanting Sanjay to express what he'd already worked out for himself.

'Research, man. Someone sent you this.' He held up Roxana. 'And the stuff she said, Obfuscator and Paladin? Come on, it must mean something.' There was such childlike enthusiasm in the way his face lit up that Darren's misgivings wilted.

'But…'

'Come on. My MacBook's in the lock-up. Let's give it a whirl.' Sanjay held the Roxana doll out to Darren and he took it. It felt cold and plastic in his hands, but for a fleeting second, under his fingers, he swore he could sense the faint echo of a heartbeat.

They grabbed another lager and sat at a workstation under the railway tracks, firing up Google on the MacBook. Hipposync Enterprises came up as a seller of esoteric historical texts, established in 1385 and based in Oxford. There was no phone number and nothing more than an information email address.

'Worth a try?' Sanjay asked.

Darren shrugged and watched Sanjay type the query.

---

Dear Sir or Madam,

I recently took delivery of a resin figurine with your return address on the compliments slip in the envelope. I would be grateful for more information on why it was sent to me and for what purpose.

Yours sincerely,

Darren Trott

---

'Can't say fairer than that,' Sanjay said. 'Now what about those other names?'

With that, he typed in 'Obfuscator' and got a million hits. Wrinkling his nose, he turned and went to a bookshelf at the very back.

'Where are you going?' Darren asked.

'Old school. Sometimes it's got to be done.' Sanjay flicked open a thick dictionary. 'Obfuscate: to obscure, to make unclear or darken, to confuse or to bewilder. Obfuscator: one who confuses. Hmm.'

Sanjay opened up another search engine page and typed 'Paladin'.

'One of the twelve peers of Charlemagne's court. A defender of the cause or champion.' Sanjay turned to Darren. 'Not much information there. What about that last name?'

'Ysbaed.' Darren spelled out the name. 'Don't ask me how I know if that's the right spelling, but it's what came up in my head when she said it.' This time there were less than fifty hits when Sanjay punched in the name, and most of those were Turkish. Darren dismissed them with a shake of his head.

'Okay, so we know what two of the names mean. That last one may be just that. Someone's name. What now?'

'You forget the power of the Net. Now we search for people.' Sanjay hit the keys again.

Darren glanced at his watch and made a face. 'Sanj, I'd better get going. It's Saturday night. Amanda's getting a dine in for a tenner from M&S and I need a shower and stuff.'

'No problem, Dar. Leave this with me.' Sanjay grinned.

'Yeah, but I want to see this through, too.'

'Tomorrow?'

'Sunday lunch at Amanda's mum's.' An expression of pained anticipation flashed across Darren's face.

'Or we can take a couple of boxes back to yours, stow them in the garage and you tell Amanda that I could only get the van for a couple of hours today and that we'll finish it all tomorrow.'

Darren's eyes lit up. He punched Sanjay in the shoulder. 'You're a bloody genius, Sanj.'

They loaded a couple of unpacked boxes into Mr. Bobal's car and Sanjay drove back to Darren's. No car in the drive meant that Amanda wasn't back yet. Darren stuffed the boxes back into the garage, waved Sanjay off and had a shower.

Amanda served up grilled lime and coriander chicken breasts with potato wedges. For once she didn't want any wine and was unusually subdued during the meal. She didn't even object when Darren outlined Sanjay's plan, even though he deliberately chose to tell her while she watched the abysmal talent contest *Pizzazz!* on TV. Darren had no interest in the show, but Amanda insisted he keep her company regardless. And the first thing she always asked him was if he liked what Shanya Todd was wearing.

Ms. Todd had risen through the ranks from shop girl, via an abysmal pop band, to talent show panellist and Amanda idolised her. In fact, the new 'boobs' that Amanda intended to be paid for from the nail bar's profits would be modelled on those very orbs protruding with gravity-defying firmness from Shanya Todd's chest. And yes, maybe she was attractive in a made-up, vapid sort of way, and her propensity for tears was matched only by her propensity for slagging off her fellow band members and ex-boyfriends in the tabloids at every opportunity. But Darren found her about as attractive as warm fox poo.

Tonight, however, Amanda did not ask Darren to comment on Ms. Todd's attire. It was only as 10.00pm approached, and Amanda started yawning violently, that the reason for her conciliatory mood became obvious. From her position on the sofa, knees drawn up in a furry onesie, she dug out her little girl voice. 'Dar, listen, you know I said that if you moved your stuff out of the garage, we could start making Saturday nights our "practise night"?'

'Yeah?'

'Well, tonight's Saturday night.'

'It is?' Darren said. He had forgotten, what with everything else that had happened since he woke up this morning.

Amanda's indulgent little corner-of-the-mouth semi-smile told him that she'd interpreted his surprise as mere teasing.

'Well, the thing is, I'm knackered after last night and I really want to make Saturday nights special. So, can we postpone it for this week?'

'You were pretty bladdered,' Darren observed, not quite sure where all this was leading.

'I know. You should have stopped me,' Amanda sighed.

Sure. And leap tall buildings at a single bound.

'You don't mind do you, Dar?' The pout was back.

'Course not,' Darren said, and touched his nose to make sure it wasn't growing. 'You go and get a proper night's sleep. You're sure your mum won't mind if I don't come to lunch tomorrow?'

Amanda levered herself up from the couch and picked up her copy of *Monail*. 'Oh, she'll mind, of course she'll mind, but I'll explain it's for our project.'

'Thanks, Mand.' Darren held up his hand for her to touch. She ignored it and headed for the stairs. She'd taken three steps up when she swivelled her head around.

'You okay, Darren? You seem a bit out of it.'

If ever there was going to be an opportune moment for Darren to open up to Amanda, he realised that now would be it.

There seemed to be genuine concern in her voice. Enough to make him hesitate. Enough to make him ponder for a moment if she might understand. Enough to make him wonder, even, if she might have something to contribute regarding Obfuscator and Paladin.

He was on the point of opening his mouth when she added, 'I expect you're a bit disappointed aren't you? The deal we had was that the garage would be empty by tonight. I mean if it was empty tonight then I expect I wouldn't have felt quite so…tired.'

Darren frowned. 'But I have emptied it, almost.'

Amanda considered him, her eyes half lidded with her best lioness-watching-a-zebra look. 'Almost is one of those not good enough words, though, isn't it?' She turned away and continued up the stairs.

Darren knew his mouth was making an 'O' shape, but no words came out. He thought that the wiggle of her backside was a degree or two more exaggerated than usual. That wiggle, combined with what she'd said, left him speechless, but not entirely surprised. A minute ago, he was feeling sorry for her. Now he didn't feel anything other than numbness.

Talk about carrot and bloody stick.

Why had no one told him he needed to read the instruction manual at least ten times when he'd started this relationship?

He shook his head to try and reset his thoughts. No wonder he felt so much like a bloody kicked and beaten donkey most of the time. But then he caught himself. Who was he trying to kid, here?

Amanda was a Cray.

The daughter of a man who thought that charity armbands were nothing more than a way of tagging morons. The niece of a man (Lou) who, since his conviction for road rage, dealt with teenagers on public transport who played their music too loud by making them swallow their ear buds.

Amanda was, in her own way, very much a chip off the old Teflon block. Her stick was really a tempered steel baton, and her carrot…well he hadn't nibbled on that for quite a long time now. Darren shook his head. To think that he'd toyed with opening up to her.

His mother's wise warnings echoed across the years.

'Doesn't matter what she looks like, Darren, when you find her, just make sure she's kind and has nice round edges. Because the sharp ones don't make a happy home.'

But then, like most boys, he'd never listened properly to his mother.

## CHAPTER FIFTEEN

**The following morning**, Darren made Amanda breakfast in bed. At 10.00am, in reply to his cheery 'Good morning,' her response was to groan and turn over. He put down the tray and left her to it. By the time she'd showered and changed, it was almost midday. Darren made himself scarce in the garage. She popped her head in through the door at twelve-thirty.

'Want me to bring you back a plate?'

'Nah, I'll be fine. Not the same warmed up, is it?'

'Suit yourself.' She gave him a cursory wave and chirped, 'See ya,' before leaving in his car. The minute the door closed behind her, Darren was on the phone to Sanjay, who came round in the van within fifteen minutes.

They reloaded the boxes and by 1.00pm, Darren was at Sanjay's watching his auntie Anitha stirring a pot on the stove while Sanjay's dad sat at the kitchen table reminiscing.

'Just like the old days, you see. All of us in the kitchen on a Sunday before the football starts. Remember, Darren? Soon as it finished, you see, you and Sanjay would run out and pretend you were Man U versus Chelsea.' Darren nodded. 'So, what brings you here today? We haven't seen you on a Sunday for ages. Not since your lovely mum died.' Mr. Bobal bit into one of Dealer Dave's cakes. Never a shrinking violet when it came to telling it like it really was, the cakes' additional disinhibiting qualities were turning him into a real treasure.

'Well,' Darren said, 'Sanjay and I've got a bit of a project going on.'

'Scale models, you see.' Mr. Bobal shook his head. A gesture that Darren still found disconcertingly suggestive of a negative, when in fact it was a gesture affirming Mr. B's understanding. 'You two should have gone into business a long time ago. Buying and selling on the Worldwide Net, you see. I told Sanjay, what bloody good is having the theory of strings if you can't make money from it?'

Sanjay laughed. Darren grinned. Mr. B was on a roll.

'But scale models, they are something you can hold,' Mr. B made fists with his hands. 'Who would think that in these days of computers scale models would last? But it is their magic. They are 3D. You can touch them, you see. Not like bloody pictures on screen. And you two are experts. It's a shame you did not use your expertise.'

'Shut up, Dad. It's only a hobby,' Sanjay said, but it was a light-hearted rebuke.

'Ah, you see, Sanjay, that is where you are wrong,' Mr. B wagged a finger. 'People always need experts.'

Sanjay shook his head. 'Eat your cake, Dad. We'll come back for lunch in an hour. You coming, Dar?'

In the lock-up Sanjay apologised. 'Sorry about that. Those bloody cakes are turning my dad all mystical. Maybe you should try one?'

'Nah, cannabis can cause schizophrenia. I read that.'

'Yeah, but one in four people are affected by mental illness anyway.'

'Why are you looking at me when you say that?'

Sanjay giggled. 'I'm not. I'm just saying.'

'Yeah, well a split personality is the last thing I need, so it's no to the cakes. Me, on the other hand…' He let the sentence tail off and watched Sanjay shake his head sadly, trying not to smile. It was a forlorn effort.

'Ah, the old ones are the best ones,' Sanjay said with a sigh.

Darren was still thinking about Mr. B's wagging finger. 'But maybe your dad is right. Maybe we should have tried turning our hobbies into jobs.'

'Stops being a hobby then though, doesn't it?' Sanjay pointed out.

'Suppose.'

'Anyway look. Obfuscator and Paladin. I think I found them.'

'What?' The word came out wrapped in an incredulous laugh.

'It's weird. Every time I typed "Obfuscator" into Facebook, the same name kept coming up and exactly the same thing happened with "Paladin". What's weirder is that they both have addresses in this town. Can't be a coincidence. So, I thought, why not?'

Darren swung his head towards Sanjay, his expression wary. 'What do you mean, why not?'

'Why not try and contact them? I sort of fixed it up that we go and visit them this afternoon.' Sanjay said, with extra cheeriness.

'You made appointments for us?' Darren gaped.

'I can see your fillings,' Sanjay said.

'But…'

'Thought we'd invite them to a barbecue next week, too. Suss them out, you know?'

'No, I don't bloody *know*,' Darren protested.

'Look, it's the only way, man,' Sanjay insisted. 'Maybe they know something about Roxana.'

'I doubt it, since she's a six-inch plastic model.'

'Okay. You got any better ideas?'

Darren shook his head.

'Right. Come on, I'll tell you all about it on the way.'

They went in Mr. Bobal's car, a battered old Citroën 2CV Estate that sashayed around corners like a chicken coop on wheels.

'Should take us about half an hour,' Sanjay said, as they hit traffic. 'Go on, look Paladin up on Facebook, you'll see what I mean.'

Darren grabbed his iPhone and opened up a bookmarked Facebook page. When he found Paladin, what he saw was blokes with lots of facial hair, girls dressed as Goths, references to trash metal bands and Xbox games involving aliens, war and destruction.

'Nice,' Darren said.

'Yeah, I know. But this bloke, Paladin, he's a semi-pro gamer. He makes money by selling weapons on Second Life.'

Darren made a sneery face. 'What, a virtual business selling virtual weapons?'

'Oh, it's a real business all right. But in a virtual world.'

'Hang on, are you telling me that this bloke sells made up weapons to made up people and makes a living out of it?'

'Great impression of inhaling helium there, Dar,' Sanjay grinned. 'But yes. He does make a living from it. Welcome to the twenty-first century, Darren Trott. Halfway down that page is his avatar. Take a look.'

Darren complied and stared in astonishment. Up popped a stylised image of a pumped up, tattooed, shade-wearing jarhead.

'Does he know we're coming?'

'I texted and said we were interested in some weaponry.'

'Oh great. That mean we're arms dealers now?'

'Virtual arms dealers, Dar.'

Darren shook his head. 'What the hell are we going to say to him?'

'You'll think of something.'

Paladin's residence was an unprepossessing semi on an estate of Eighties houses. A white Seat with a red go-faster stripe on the roof and bonnet gleamed at the kerb. Sanjay parked behind it and got out. Darren stayed in the car.

'Come on, you pleb,' Sanjay said, jiggling the car keys. He looked like a little kid on his way to the fun fair.

But Darren didn't move. 'I've got a bad feeling about this. What's our strategy?'

'Strategy? How about winging it?'

When Darren still didn't budge, Sanjay let out an exasperated hiss. 'I just don't get you sometimes. Stop thinking about it so much. We're here now. The two of us, having a laugh, having an adventure. Like old times.'

Darren stared at him.

Sanjay stared back. 'Christ, if it was me that a six-inch doll had spoken to, I'd be knocking down walls with a sledgehammer to find out what the hell it meant.'

'You haven't got a sledgehammer, have you, Sanj?' Darren asked, with a wary look towards the back of the car to see if there was anything wrapped under a concealing blanket.

'No.' Sanjay growled a denial but with a little too much vehemence for Darren's liking. There was another deep sigh and when Sanjay next spoke, it was in a very measured, reassuring tone. 'Look, I know you think it's a curse, Dar, but have you thought that maybe it isn't? Have you thought about destiny, your destiny, man?'

Darren's face must have registered his horror. Sanjay's patience gave out with a shake of his head.

'How come you can take those brilliant photos of weird worlds and stuff, and yet you're worried about talking to a bloke who lives in just as weird a world as any of the ones you've made up?'

Objections were pouring into Darren's head like water through a broken bucket. 'He'll think we're genuine nutjobs for starters, have you thought about that?'

'I know you're a genuine nutjob, so I'm with him on that.' Sanjay grinned.

But on seeing Darren's lack of response to his damp firework of a joke, he slapped the car roof with a force that jerked Darren out of his glum reverie.

'Come on, man,' he urged. 'If it's all cowcrap, fine. At least we're out here doing something. Living a bit.'

That one stung like the scorpion king of painful truths it was. Sanjay was right. Internalising all of this was a bad thing. And what else was there to do?

Deny it ever happened?

Talk to Amanda about it?

Both of those options were about as attractive as roadkill sandwiches. They were not real alternatives for a whole raft of reasons. To deny it had ever happened was like signing an application form to the National Association of Fruitcakes. And as for Amanda, someone had sneaked in with a Tipp-Ex pen and crossed out 'sympathy' and 'empathy' from her dictionary, pencilling in their stead, 'disdain' and 'scorn'.

In capitals.

## CHAPTER SIXTEEN

Muttering to himself about wild geese and chases, Darren got out of the car. All his instincts screamed that this was a lousy idea. But no caveman would ever have left his cave if he'd relied on instinct alone, because instinct had a knack of adding up 'sabre teeth' and 'compete darkness' and coming up with 'stay very much put' as the total. It took logic and determination to cross that threshold, but they were in pretty short supply as a beaming Sanjay rang the doorbell.

The woman who opened the door to them was mid-forties with dark-rooted blonde hair and a faded black sweatshirt streaked with white cat hair. A cigarette dangled from the corner of her mouth.

'Is Paladin in?' Sanjay asked.

'You mean Malcolm?' asked the woman. Turning, she yelled up the stairs in a voice that was all gravel and dust. 'Malcolm, it's for you!' She looked back over her shoulder at Sanjay and Darren. 'As if he would be anywhere else.' A huge white cat brushed past her ankles, and she stooped to scoop it up. 'Say hello, Sooty.'

'Hello, Sooty,' Sanjay said with a nervous laugh. The cat hissed at him.

They heard the thump of someone running downstairs. A

short, heavyset man with long, frizzy red hair, beard and thick glasses approached.

'You must be Sanjay?'

Sanjay nodded. 'And you're Paladin?'

'You got it,' the man said.

Darren threw Sanjay a look and saw Sanjay shrug. They were both thinking 'extra from *The Hobbit*' seeing as Malcolm was about as far removed from the tall, shade-wearing, tat-sporting avatar they'd seen online as Timbuktu was from York.

'Thanks, Mum,' Malcolm said to the woman, then acknowledged Sanjay and Darren with a curt nod. 'Come on up.'

They followed him to a converted loft with walls of dark blue. The room was divided into two: one side had a bed and a fifty-six-inch TV; the other consisted of a bank of four monitors surrounding a stack of computer equipment, Xboxes, PlayStations, and all manner of controllers.

'So, you might be interested in some weapons?' Malcolm wore an AC/DC T-shirt that had not seen the inside of a washing machine since the signing of the Magna Carta.

'We might be,' Sanjay said. 'Depends.'

'On what?'

Sanjay said nothing and waited for Darren to explain. Darren swallowed.

'The thing is, your name came up in some…unusual circumstances, and…'

Malcolm flushed a deep burgundy under his freckles. 'Look if it's that webcam business, I genuinely didn't know it was on. And it was just the once.'

Sanjay made big eyes at Darren who did his best to ignore him.

'It's nothing to do with any webcam,' Darren said in a rush. 'Do you know anyone, real or virtual, called Roxana?'

Paladin frowned. 'Roxana? No, don't think so. Why?'

'That was the unusual circumstance. Roxana, she mentioned you by name. Seemed to know you.'

'Is she a gamer?'

Darren squirmed.

'Not exactly,' Sanjay said, stepping in, sensing that Darren had corpsed. 'But she may well be in the market for weaponry.'

'Oh, right.' Some of the wariness eased out of Malcolm's pale, pudding face.

'We wanted to check that you were kosher, right Dar?'

'Yeah, kosher.'

'I've got a whole page of testimonials,' Malcolm turned to a keyboard. His fingers flew and an instant later one of the screens filled with italicised quotes.

Sanjay leaned in. 'Impressive.'

'So, this Roxana?' Malcolm asked.

Darren looked at Sanjay, who nodded. Taking it as a cue, he said, 'Look, I know this is going to sound odd but Roxana, she is a bit…unusual.'

'Most of the people on Second Life are,' Malcolm said.

'Sure, but there's unusual and there is…*unusual*,' Sanjay said, tilting his head disquietingly.

Darren squirmed again. 'The thing is something happened yesterday. Something pretty off the wall…' And then he told Malcolm all about it. Watched as his expression remained neutral but a red flush spread up from his neck to cover his face. When he'd finished Malcolm looked from Darren's face to Sanjay's.

'Is this a wind-up?' he asked, a slow smile wavering on his lips. 'This is a wind-up, isn't it? Who sent you, Bartsie? Or that gimp, Rooter?'

'No,' Darren said. 'It's not a wind-up. I wish it bloody well was. No one sent us. Look, I can't explain any of this. I know it must sound mental.'

'No more mental than selling weapons in a virtual world,' Sanjay said, and Darren wondered, not for the first time, if amongst his many genetic traits was one for saying extremely unhelpful things at the worst possible moment. He sent Sanjay a withering glance for good measure.

'When we typed in 'Paladin' on the search engine,' Darren went on, 'Google, Firefox, you name it, your site was the first to come up.'

'I don't know any Roxana,' Malcolm said, his smile now gone. 'I've told you.'

'Okay,' Darren said. 'Sorry to trouble you. Thanks.'

'No, wait,' Sanjay said. 'Maybe if you saw her, maybe you'd know. Maybe you'd know her from a game, or…or maybe she's been an avatar in one of your online transactions. Come over on Friday and we'll give you something to eat. You like Indian food?'

'Gives me heartburn,' Malcolm said.

'Come on. Free food, booze, a chat and a little peek at Roxana, that's all we ask.'

'I'll think about it,' Malcolm said, but his eyes kept straying to the door.

'You'd probably like us to leave now, wouldn't you?' Darren said.

Malcolm nodded.

'So, Friday—it's a deal, yeah?' Sanjay said as Darren steered him down the stairs.

When they finally drove away, Darren muttered, 'I'm surprised he didn't call the cops.'

'Rubbish. I think he was intrigued.'

'Yeah, intrigued that there wasn't a posse of men in white coats following us.' Darren rubbed at the stubble on his cheeks.

'Come on Dar, what have we got to lose?'

'We're not going to meet this girl now, are we?' Darren's head dropped forward onto his chest.

'The Obfuscator? Yeah. She said she'd meet us in Costa Coffee in town.'

Darren groaned. He refused to look her up on Facebook and spent the entire journey almost wishing he were at the Crays', enduring Sunday lunch.

They ordered flat whites at Costa and sat at a bench outside.

'So, you looked this obfuscator up, right? You know what she looks like?'

'Yup,' Sanjay said.

'And?'

'See for yourself.' Sanjay picked up his cup, held it up to his lips and nodded over the rim to a point over Darren's left-hand shoulder. Darren swivelled around. The pavements were full of Sunday shoppers in the drab khaki and sage that was this year's uniform and consequently made the splurge of colour that was moving along the pavement even more startling. Darren felt his jaw slide open and was powerless to stop it.

Female, and of average height, the beehive hair and gull wing glasses would have made her unusual enough, but it was what she was wearing that really took the hobnob. Under a scarlet military style jacket, she wore a lurid pink and purple blouse. Swirled around her neck was something furry with black pom-poms dangling from it. Completing the ensemble were frilly hot pants over black tights that ended in pink ankle socks and teetering high heel wedges.

Darren turned back, praying that she hadn't seen him. 'Please tell me that isn't her?'

Sanjay had time to drop his eyes before the girl came to a halt in front of them. She scanned the pavement for signs of her rendezvous. Darren made eyes at Sanjay, but he knew it was hopeless. The Obfuscator was a girl and that meant that Sanjay had retreated into silent mode.

Cursing under his breath Darren stood. 'Excuse me, are you…'

'Obfuscated Fashions. Yes, Vivette Campbell-Fripp.' She held out a hand with lime green fingernails. Darren took it.

'Would you like a coffee?'

'Oh, absolutamous. A tall skinny cap would be great.'

'I'll get it,' Sanjay said and before Darren could stop him, he was off like a rabbit down a hole.

It was difficult to tell if Vivette Campbell-Fripp was attractive under the heavy make-up. That she was well covered was obvious even to the casual observer, but she had an open, intelligent face and a very direct gaze. Darren found himself wondering if she'd gone to the same staring school as Harry Cray.

'So, I hear you're interested in some of my designs?'

'Uhhh, yeah, yeah, we are actually.'

'Fantasticus maximus.' Vivette's face split into a huge grin.

'Well, a client of ours is,' Darren said, after accepting that she had just said fantasticus maximus and that he hadn't made it up. Having decided that the truth had not been a mistake where Paladin was concerned, he was not about to make the same mistake with Vivette Campbell-Fripp.

'And who is your client?'

'Goes by the name of Roxana—she's foreign—into natural products.'

'Faux fur I hope?' The Obfuscator smiled again, her scarlet lips retreating back over large teeth.

'Totally, yeah. You're not from around here then?'

In the five minutes it took for Sanjay to come back with the coffee, Darren learned that Vivette Campbell-Fripp had a degree in textile design from Goldsmiths and had followed her parents up to a smallholding on the edge of the Yorkshire Moors to develop her fashion house that presently was more of a fashion cardboard box. He learned that she was frustrated with the fashion world's inability to recognise what she was trying to do but, she assured him, it was only a matter of time. So here was a girl not lacking in self-belief.

'This is Sanjay,' Darren said a few minutes later. Sanjay put the coffee down in front of Vivette, looking like he was about to undergo open-heart surgery without anaesthetic. 'I was telling Vivette about our little get together next Friday evening. She'll get to meet Roxana and Paladin. She's very happy to come along.'

'Great,' Sanjay said, trying to impersonate a very small rodent.

'Brill. Want me to bring along something gluggable? Couple of bots of Dom Pee?'

Sanjay blinked rapidly. Behind her Darren mouthed '*Champagne*,' at him.

'Yeah, that would be…yeah…great.'

They stayed for fifteen minutes. The Obfuscator did most of the talking. In fact, she did all the talking. Darren and Sanjay sat and listened. In the end it was Darren who made a show of looking at his watch and stood. They shook hands and left her smiling outside Costa.

'That coat was visible from space, man,' Sanjay said. They

were on their way back to the car, full of coffee and giggles. 'And that accent. Where is she from?'

'A little county called Girl's Boarding School.'

'How can anyone talk so much?' Sanjay shook his head. 'I understood about one fifth of it.'

'How did you manage to get her to come to the thing on Friday?'

'I just…It was…'

'You lied, right?'

'Well…yeah. I mean look at what happened with Malcolm/Paladin when we told him the truth.'

'Sanj…'

'She's going to have one hell of a shock on Friday night when she finds out Roxana isn't a buyer for the Russian Harrods.' Sanjay said, grinning.

'Hey, it was your idea in the first place.'

'I know. Trouble is we can't be sure they're the right Paladin and Obfuscator.'

'Didn't I say that an hour ago?' Darren vented an exasperated sigh. 'Any joy with Hipposync?'

'Nah. They're a complete mystery.'

'Like everything else isn't?'

Sanjay shrugged and Darren felt a pang of regret. 'Sorry, Sanj. I know you're doing this for me. Come on—let's go back to yours. I fancy some *Mario Kart*.'

## CHAPTER SEVENTEEN

AMANDA WAS ALREADY HOME when Darren got back, and the cold car bonnet told him she'd been there a while. He opened the front door and was greeted by cackling laughter coming from the TV. Amanda sat on the sofa, barefoot in pyjama bottoms and a sweatshirt—her preferred TV watching garb—with a box of Maltesers open on the coffee table next to her.

'Hi,' Darren said. 'Sorry I'm a bit late.' He walked over to her and bent to give her a kiss on the cheek. Amanda turned her head away.

'Shh. This is the first episode of *Shanya Todd Gets Real*. She's got this job in a mega posh jewellers in London so that she can face the public just like an ordinary shop girl. Don't expect me to turn this off now because you want to chat. I thought you wanted to see it, anyway?'

'Not really my thing,' Darren said.

Amanda threw him an incredulous look. 'What is wrong with you?'

'I ended up chatting with Sanjay's dad. He's got these cakes…'

Amanda shook her head and waved him away. 'Wait until the adverts.'

Darren tiptoed out and made himself a cup of tea and a ham sandwich with the pappy white bread Amanda insisted on buying. It had the consistency of a used nappy, and much the same flavour—not that he'd ever eaten used nappy—but he could imagine. His mother used to buy crusty olive bread. When he was young Darren hated that bread. Now he drooled at the very thought of it.

Ten minutes later, Amanda came into the kitchen wearing her best petulant expression.

'Honestly Darren, you know how much I wanted to watch that programme. Barging in like that could have ruined it for me.'

'I didn't barge in, I wanted to say hello. If I didn't, you'd have said I'd been rude.'

'You're rude anyway. My mum and dad couldn't believe you missed Sunday lunch.'

'But you told them why, didn't you?'

'I told them you were at Sanjay's again.'

'And why was I at Sanjay's?' Amanda said nothing. 'We've emptied the garage, and you can now do whatever you like with it,' Darren said with feeling.

She didn't thank him. Instead, she helped herself to a glass of wine from the box in the fridge. It was German and sweet, and they drank it because her dad got it cheap from a wholesaler who had a line in chateau-off-le-back-of-le-lorry.

'My dad says Sanjay's dad was done for having illegal immigrants in his shop.'

'Yeah, I know. That was twenty years ago. And they were refugees from Tamil Nadu.'

She rounded on him. 'Well, I think that's terrible. Giving our jobs to people who shouldn't even be in the country! Did you know that there are three million people unemployed?'

Darren stared at her. This was Harry Cray talking. She was always like this after spending an afternoon with her family. It was as if she'd been given an angry pill with her dessert.

'Since when you did start canvassing for Reform?' Amanda didn't answer, so Darren tried again. 'Okay, so which bit of twenty years ago and refugees did you not hear?' He tried to temper his frown with a jaunty tilt of his head.

'That's not the point.'

'The point is,' Darren continued, 'that no one you or I know who is on benefits wants to work in the sort of business that Mr. Bobal and Sanjay used to work in. They ran that shop almost eighteen hours a day. No one in their right, nanny state mind would want to do it.'

Amanda's lips became thin and spiteful. 'See, this is what happens when you spend time with Sanjay. You always take his side.'

'Take his side in what?' Darren held his hands out in a peace-making gesture that he knew would annoy her.

'Come on, you'd much preferred to spend time with him than with my family.' The last word came out like shot from a gun.

'Sanjay is my oldest friend, Amanda,' Darren said with quiet patience. 'And his dad is dying. So yeah, I'm spending time with him. What is the problem?'

Amanda seemed to be stuck for a response and couldn't find much ammunition in the brickbat box. But she did manage one last little barb as she turned back to the TV.

'The oil thingy in the car keeps flashing,' she shot at him. 'You'd better do something about that.'

But for once Darren didn't climb down.

'Maybe you can lend me my car for a couple of hours to get it sorted, then,' he said and thought he saw a hint of irritation in the toss of her head.

———

It was the end of May. The weather was warm and dry, but it was arctic winter in Darren's house. He decided not to go to Sanjay's at all during the week, but emailed, Skyped, and texted instead. Unable to access his garage, he'd taken to occupying the spare bedroom and cataloguing his photographs on his laptop. It was something he'd been meaning to do for a while, and it presented no hardship. There were thousands of images, but he found the process of arranging, deleting, and indexing quite therapeutic. Yet truth be told there was an ulterior motive. Ever since the Roxana incident, he'd had the strangest feeling that he'd seen her somewhere before. The conviction stayed firmly lodged in his head, like a half-remembered tune, one that finally turned into a Hallelujah chorus when he struck gold.

A couple of years before he'd gone through a 'military' phase, spurred on, no doubt, by yet another disastrous political foray into some Middle Eastern despot's hellhole, and a debate about women troops on the front line. He'd set up a shoot of women in war settings, and the models he'd chosen were from a Japanese maker, verging on the anime and with a propensity for Western features. He'd purchased four from the dealer: a high cheek-boned beauty, a dark-haired Doppelgänger of the first, a chestnut-haired Asian and a stunning black girl. In a sardonic tilt at the feminist element of the discussion, Darren shot all four dressed in bikinis, armed to the teeth in an urban warzone, and contrasted that with another set with all four lounging on a beach dressed in full combat fatigues and sipping Bacardi Breezers.

The model with the high cheekbones had caramel hair with gold flashes. She looked exactly like Roxana.

He studied the photos and was pleased by how well the juxtaposition worked when viewed side-by-side. However, the combat dress he'd used for the shoots had been culled from GI Joe figures and did not look anything like the desert fatigues that Roxana had worn when she'd spoken to him from the Homestead set. In fact, the combat dress had not fitted at all well to begin with, and he'd used scissors and staples to make adjustments. Remembering all of that brought a curiously uncomfortable feeling floating to the surface and he felt himself blush. He'd dressed and undressed the caramel-haired model many times.

Why should that make him feel weird and uncomfortable?

'You're losing it, Darren,' he muttered to himself. 'Losing it big time.'

## CHAPTER EIGHTEEN

His week at work was no better. On Monday, he got in to find a choir of three workmates, one of whom was Big Jeff, singing an out of tune rendition of 'Car Wash' as soon as he walked in. The refrain, whistled or sung, followed him around for the whole of the week.

He managed to avoid Harry Cray until Tuesday. He was filling a retail order for a big DIY store, loading garden lights onto a pallet, when he looked up and saw Harry bearing down upon him, eyes blazing.

'Darren,' Harry said, and put a fatherly arm around Darren's shoulder. 'Missed you on Sunday. Ate all your Yorkshires.' Harry slapped his gut with the clipboard. 'The Mrs says I'm pretty lardy but she's no chuffin' Kay Moss herself, eh lad?'

Darren thought about correcting him but decided to let it go. It wasn't worth it. All it would do would prolong the moment. If Harry wanted to call the supermodel 'Kay' it was fine by Darren, even if it rankled. But the thought of pointing out the error rankled even more. Despite being 100% wrong with her name, Harry would end up arguing the point. Darren had lots of mental bruises from those encounters and didn't want another one, thank you very much.

'Mr. Hardcastle was very impressed with your car valeting

skills. Thinks we ought to make it a regular thing at the monthly chairman's meeting. How about that?'

If Harry thought it was a good thing, Darren wasn't about to disabuse him of that sentiment. 'Great, yeah, beats stacking pallets.'

'More than that, Darren,' Harry glared. 'It lets management know you're someone with chuffin' initiative. I wouldn't be surprised if you'll be in with a chance at promotion in a couple of months' time.'

'Really?' Darren tried to sound enthusiastic.

'Heard you enjoyed the birthday party. We were all chuffin' legless. Our Amanda says she had a head like a bucket for two days.' Harry chortled and shook his head. 'The good news is, Amanda's auntie Veronica has a fortieth next month, too.' He winked.

Darren tried for an airy laugh. A shrill, nervous giggle was what emerged.

'Tell you what, I'll fork out for a taxi for the two of you, eh? Give you a chance to tie one on too.'

Darren opened his mouth in clueless protest, but Harry was having none of it, interpreting Darren's speechlessness as abject gratitude in the way only the pachydermal could.

'Don't thank me, lad. You're almost family, you know that.'

Darren watched Harry 'Kaa' Cray walk away, and though the day was warm, he shivered.

Harry turned up twice at the house after work that week too. The second time he brought a boy wearing a baseball cap and trainers.

'Amanda's cousin, Wayne. Carpenter's mate, you know. Shouldn't set you back more than a couple of hundred to do the fixings, right, Wayne?'

Wayne nodded. The tattoo on his neck of a crab flexed its claw when he tilted his head. Darren couldn't take his eyes off the thing and the spell was only broken when Sanjay texted him.

Text from Paladin. CAN'T MAKE IT FRIDAY NIGHT. OBFUSCATOR SAYS OTHER ENGAGEMENTS TOO.

He made his excuses to the Crays and went outside to phone Sanjay.

'Okay, so they sussed us out. Let's forget it. Crap idea anyway.'

'No way, man. I've bought steaks and Mrs. R is making gohbi and fresh chapattis and tandoori lamb. We'll have the barbecue anyway. Work on a new strategy.'

Relief fought with disappointment in Darren's head. On the one hand it meant no embarrassing explanations to two strangers, on the other he'd be no further forward with anything. Sanjay took his silence for defeat.

'Come on, Dar, it'll be a laugh.'

'Yeah, why not,' Darren said. 'We can have Dave the Dealer cakes for afters too. At least then we'll go home feeling happy.'

'Yeah. Snow White deserves a night off.'

---

AMANDA, buoyed by her dad's visit, spent most of her spare time —which, after watching every single celebrity-based piece of tat on the TV, did not leave a great deal—poring over trade magazines. Darren kept finding glossy brochures with titles like *Beauty and Wax*, all of which had pages with the corners turned down. Apart from the small talk about work, and whose turn it was to buy the essentials this week, they didn't discuss Amanda's plans for the garage. Darren assumed this was to be an all 'Cray' enterprise. Okay, he was providing the premises, but to suggest contributing anything physical was a nonstarter; there'd be someone else in Amanda's extended family with an appropriate skillset who would do a much better job.

He should have realised something was brewing. On Friday evening, Amanda came downstairs bronzed, in heels and a skirt, smelling of something musky. Darren was putting away groceries when she entered the kitchen.

'Well?' She did a twirl.

'Very nice,' he said. 'Lot of effort for a business course.'

'It's not for the business course.' She sashayed across the room and pulled him to her. 'I've been thinking, Dar. It's been hard for you these last couple of weeks what with moving your stuff out of the garage and all. And last Saturday night, I was a bit mean. Why don't we bring everything forward to tonight? After I've been out for a drink with the girls, I know I'll be in the mood. What do you say?'

Quite a few things flashed through Darren's head at the speed of light, the main one being that he would now have to avoid Mrs. R's tandoori lamb.

'Sounds great,' he said. He went to kiss her, but she turned her head away.

'Fresh warpaint.' She excused herself. 'Save it for later. Oh, and there's some stuff on the bed for you to see. Just a few bits and pieces for the nail parlour—you know. Let me have your thoughts. I mean, I could have gone overboard but I'm trying to be reasonable. Stay within budget.' She smiled and brushed away something from his cheek. 'I gotta go. See you later.' She flashed her eyes at him and left.

Darren was quite often surprised by Amanda's behaviour. Her moods were mercurial at the best of times, but this evening, standing in the kitchen of what had been his parents', and was now his, house, he found himself speechless. The groceries remained on the work surface as he heard the car, his car, pulling away from the drive.

He walked upstairs.

On the bed was a blue ring binder. Darren flicked it open. Pages had been ripped out of magazines and placed in clear pocket files attached to the metal binders. Articles on the Vietnamese and US nail industry, advertisements for salon towels, candles, salon furniture, beds, chairs—all of it sparkling and new. At the back was a checklist. Darren let his eyes fall to the bottom line. There, highlighted in yellow, a figure in bold:

## £11,255 (including VAT)

He sat down heavily, his mind buzzing.

There had never been any real discussion, and no agreement, of his role in Amanda's project. He'd assumed that she, or her father, would be the ones fronting the venture. Yes, she'd mentioned it would probably cost a few thousand but…

Something cold and heavy rolled over inside him. He'd been

naive and dumb and totally misread the signs. She'd never asked him outright, but being Amanda and a Cray, she'd assumed.

He saw it all now. The times she mentioned the money had always been at moments when they'd been intimate—though intimate was a relative term when it came to Amanda. She didn't do post coital snuggling. In fact, she didn't do cuddles or hand holding or even whispered sweet nothings, and that suited Darren. Or so he thought.

Darren's recollections were sketchy. Those that did come to mind confirmed the fact that money always seemed to come up after Amanda allowed him into her (in truth, his) bed. Fact was he'd never taken much notice because on the one hand, in his head at least, it never applied to him, and on the other, like most men post-orgasm, his brain became cognitive mush incapable of registering any real detail.

A cold sweat broke out on his forehead and Darren wondered if it was forming the word 'MUG'. If he needed any further proof, all he had to do was think back a few minutes to the heels, the perfume, and the short skirt.

A little part of him was waving a flag for capitulation.

Did it matter? Why not give her the money? Anything for a quiet life, right? A month or two ago, that argument might have had some validity. But now, the mild horror of his naivety gave way to a cold, burning anger. Amanda had no right to assume anything. This was his mother's house, and his legacy they were talking about here. There wasn't much of it, but what there had been he'd invested and vowed not to touch until he needed it.

And a bloody nail bar in the garage was not what he needed.

He reached for the phone and called Amanda. It went straight to her answering service. That was odd. Amanda's phone was as much a sensory organ as her ears or her eyes. She never switched it off. But she had now. Darren shook his head and felt his mouth shape a wry smile.

'Nice one, Mand,' he said, tongue worrying the centre of his top lip as he composed a text.

NOT USING MY MUM'S MONEY FOR A NAIL BAR. WE NEED TO TALK. D

He deliberately left out the little postscript 'X' he usually added. He proofread his message and hesitated with his finger over the send button. She was going to be angry. It would scupper any chance of anything physical later on, but he knew Amanda was banking on him having this very discussion with himself. Well, he reasoned, this way at least he'd be able to enjoy some tandoori lamb. He pressed the send button, locked up and headed off to Sanjay's. Once he got outside, he switched off his phone too.

Two could play at that game.

## CHAPTER NINETEEN

**The smell emanating** from the back garden of Number One Shunter Street was a siren call to the three dogs sitting patiently outside the fence, looking in. A rare blistering day melted into a pleasant balmy evening. Darren walked through to the back garden to find Mr. Bobal waving at the passengers staring out from the windows of a passing, and rare commuter train.

'Sanjay has waved at thousands of people from this garden, you see. Just like I am doing.' The old man shook his head. 'He would sit here and wait for the trains to go by. And now he is here looking after his old, sick father. He is twenty-nine, Darren. He should have got onto one of those trains a long time ago.'

Mr. Bobal's face looked burnished in the sun, but there were deep shadows under his eyes.

'I don't know, Mr. B, it's a scary old world out there. You can't tell what's around the next corner.'

'But time waits for nomad, Darren.'

With admirable constraint, Darren waited a beat to let the slip sail by.

'Sanjay will be fine. I'd give anything to be able to work from home.'

Mr. Bobal turned and put his hand on Darren's elbow. 'You are a good friend to Sanjay, Darren. But he has no job, no girlfriend. I am afraid that Sanjay is drinking from the last chance spittoon here in this house.'

Wincing at the image Mr. B's nauseating metaphoric gaff conjured up, Darren nevertheless felt obliged to put him straight on one point. 'Well, we'll see what we can do about that. But you know, Mr. B, jobs and girlfriends aren't always all they're cracked up to be.'

Mr. Bobal tilted his head questioningly. 'Disharmony in the cohabitational home, Darren?'

'Not a bowl of cherries, Mr. B.'

Sanjay joined them with some lagers for him and Darren, and fruit juice for his father. 'What's this? The AGM of the National Optimists Society?'

'Darren has tissues,' Mr. Bobal said.

Sanjay's lower jaw flicked to the left and his eyes followed suit. 'You mean *issues?*'

'Only one,' Darren replied.

'You're referring to the one that lives with you, I take it?'

Darren nodded.

Mrs. Roopal appeared with a tray weighed down with bhajis and samosas, and a brown paper bag to break the tension.

'Dave from Number Six gave me this for you,' she said, handing the bag to Mr. Bobal.

'Ah, cake!' Mr. Bobal grinned.

'Shall I put them out on a plate?' Mrs. Roopal asked.

'Better not,' Sanjay said. 'Unless you want people bungee jumping off the chimney.'

Darren couldn't take his eyes off the mound of food on the tray Mrs. Roopal had put down on a trestle table. 'Jesus, Sanj, how many people did you invite to this barbecue?'

'Only the four of us, and my dad, but he doesn't count since he's become Marie Antoinette.'

'Marie Antoinette?'

'He only eats cake these days.'

Darren gave him an old-fashioned look, feeling the grin grow into a giggle. 'There's enough food here for the whole street.'

'Don't worry. I'll freeze what we don't eat.'

Mr. Bobal drifted away to the bottom of the garden. Darren

saw his hand sneaking into the paper bag. It emerged with a piece of innocuous-looking fruitcake that he proceeded to nibble.

'So, you've heard nothing from anyone since the texts?'

Sanjay shook his head. Darren took a long and hefty swallow from the sweating lager bottle. It did not go unnoticed by Sanjay, who echoed his father's concern.

'Trouble in paradise, Dar?'

Darren sighed. 'You could say that.' And despite all his misgivings about washing his dirty laundry in public and a self-made promise that he was not going to bore Sanjay rigid with his problems, Darren couldn't help but unburden himself over Amanda's financial shenanigans.

'That's one hell of a commitment,' Sanjay observed when Darren came out with the total.

'Tell me about it.' Darren sighed. 'I've only got myself to blame. We should have sorted this out right at the beginning.'

'What should have been sorted out was a business plan and a meeting with the bank.'

'Yeah.' He shook his head. 'And I thought that all Amanda wanted was a little bit of room to expand her horizons.'

Sanjay kept a straight face. 'When was the last time she let you expand her horizons?'

'What's that supposed to mean?' Darren feigned offence.

'You know what I mean. You've been sort of…frustrated for a few weeks now.'

'Has it shown?'

'A bit,' Sanjay said, grinning. 'Either that or you're in training for the world pocket billiard championships.'

'It's not funny. I almost have to make an appointment.'

'It is funny,' Sanjay said, 'because that's what my cousins do with Mr. Patel's daughter Dipty. You know, the one who works at the lap dancing club and does freelance work on weekends?'

Darren's horrified mind filled with the image of a willowy girl grinning shyly at him in her school uniform, as she walked home to Number Twenty-five a few yards away.

'You mean the pretty little schoolgirl?'

'Pretty yes, schoolgirl no. Not anymore. She got four A stars at A-level last year. She's doing all this in her gap year.'

'Work experience at Spearmint Rhino?' Darren laughed.

'That's illegal.' Mr. Bobal had walked back up the garden. Darren and Sanjay pivoted, Sanjay's mouth opening and closing as he searched for something to say by way of explanation.

'Why are you doing an impression of fish, Sanjay? No one should be spearing rhinos. They are endangered species, you see. Says so on Disney channel.'

The doorbell saved them both from having to unravel Mr. Bobal's convoluted leap of misunderstanding and explain to him why they were both trying not to giggle like idiots. 'I will get that,' Mr. Bobal said. 'You two stay here but remember, rhino spearing will get you in jail or your hands chopped off.'

'I have to admit,' Darren said, watching Mr. Bobal disappear into the house, 'your dad is better value than most of the stand-ups I've seen.'

'You should hear him on the phone to cold callers. He made the last one cry.'

'You ought to try recording—,' the words died on Darren's lips. Mr. B was returning with a squat man in biker boots, baggy jeans and a climatically inappropriate calf-length leather coat. Darren had a fleeting exchange of glances with Sanjay before Mr. Bobal announced, 'Mr. Paladin is here.'

'You, umm, made it then,' Darren said.

'Yeah, I made it.' Malcolm seemed to be struggling with something he wanted to say, but Mr. B was on a roll.

'I see that you are electrician, Mr. Paladin.'

'Pardon?' Malcolm said, unable to prevent himself from responding, but with the wary look of someone sensing he was going to regret the intercourse.

'AC/DC. On your T-shirt, you see. Very clever. Is that the name of your company?'

Malcolm's mouth opened but no words emerged. They were too busy searching for handholds on the slippery slope known as 'where to begin'.

'Let me get you a drink,' Darren said by way of distraction, and went to find a lager from the large trug that Sanjay had filled with ice and cold San Miguels. He snapped the top off one and turned back as the doorbell rang again. This time Sanjay went, while Darren listened to Mr. B warning Malcolm of the dangers of spearing rhinos. The latter's eyes had a wild, leery look. Fortunately, Sanjay hailing them from the passage spared them more of Mr. B's skewed view of the world.

'Look who's here,' he said, sounding smug. Everyone including Mrs. Roopal stopped to stare at what was coming towards them down the garden path.

'Hi, everyone,' the who said. No one replied immediately, due, Darren suspected, to everyone's speech centres being short-circuited by the sheer sensory overload that looking at the source induced. Vivette Campbell-Fripp was dressed for the occasion. Exactly what that occasion might be Darren had no idea, but it certainly was not a summer barbecue. The ankle-length beige and brown stripy sack that she wore had no sleeves, just slits for bebangled arms. It was almost ceremonial, in an off-world kind of way. Under a large, floppy straw hat she wore orange sunglasses, and dangling from one hand was a gigantic barrel bag.

Sanjay, who looked like he'd swallowed a large amphibian, made the introductions. Inevitably though, it was Mr. Bobal who spoke for all of them when he took Sanjay to one side and whispered in an accusatory voice that was meant to be confidential but was in fact audible to people on the long-departed passing train, 'You did not tell me it was fancy dress, you see.'

Vivette remained unperturbed. 'Thought I'd model some of my designs. I call this one Mocha Choca Reyeures.'

'Right,' Darren said.

There followed an awkward few minutes of stilted, polite conversation during which Sanjay offered the tray of samosas and bhajis, all the while exchanging questioning glances with Darren. Having accepted that Paladin and the Obfuscator had declined their invitations, seeing them turn up like this had thrown them both. Thankfully, Mr. Bobal was doing a great job of entertaining their guests. More entertaining still were the looks on their faces as they tried to follow his convoluted, but beguilingly philosophical, trains of thought. Trains that, compounded by an incomplete grasp of the English idiom and fuelled by cannabinoids, threatened to derail at any minute.

'What's the plan?' Sanjay whispered to Darren as they both went to replenish their drinks from the ice float trug.

'Plan? There is no bloody plan,' Darren hissed.

'Okay, well let's give them some food and then take them up to the first floor and show them Roxana.'

Darren shrugged and tried to quell the bad feeling that was bubbling inside him over just where all this was leading. But ten minutes later, with Mr. B left in charge of the barbeque, the others made their way up the stairs towards Darren's new studio. Sanjay kept up a running commentary, explaining how Darren's work was prize-winning and that he'd had a few pieces exhibited. Vivette, however, remained unconvinced.

'That's all well and wonderfullesque but I thought you said you were expecting a buyer? However, I see no *acheteurs*.' She finished the statement on an upward inflection. It made everything she said sound like a question, even when it wasn't. 'Yeah, I did say that,' Darren said. 'But it wasn't strictly true.'

'But I brought mucho samples,' she said in a tone ringing with disappointment. Next to her Malcolm's furrowed brow was beetling into a crevasse. Having escaped the exhausting mental hop, skip and jump that any conversation with Mr. Bobal entailed, he had not spoken for the last ten minutes, preferring to do an impression of a pot slowly coming to the boil. When his voice piped up, it took everyone by surprise.

'Sorry to break it to you, darlin' but these two are wind-up merchants for some bullshit YouTube scam. We're on camera. This will all be on the Net an hour after we leave,' Malcolm said, his expression sour.

'No, man, you've got it all wrong. There are no cameras,' Sanjay shook his head, sounding hurt.

'Then what are we doing here?' Malcolm demanded, the words exploding from his mouth in a belligerent gush.

## CHAPTER TWENTY

**They were in** the studio now. There at least they could see that what Sanjay told them about Darren's hobby was true. But it was not enough, and Darren knew it. They deserved an explanation and so, after a very deep breath, Darren told them. It wasn't news to Malcolm, except the bits about Dolly Darren, but Vivette kept blinking her large made-up eyes, looking utterly bemused by the whole thing.

'So, let me get this absolutely straight, you're telling us that a plastic model asked for your help and told you to contact us and that we would help you too?'

'More or less,' Darren said, knowing how insane it all sounded and suddenly glad he'd worn his old trainers. They had more room in which his toes could curl.

'That's the biggest load of crap I've ever heard,' Malcolm said.

'Moi too.' Vivette nodded.

Darren squeezed his eyes shut. Of course it was. They were right. He had no idea what Sanjay had been thinking of, inviting them here like this. Best they all go home and—

'So what are you both doing here, then?' Sanjay said, going for blunt and succeeding.

Silence ensued. The type that had so much weight on it that it bent in the middle. It was a very good question. The more

Darren thought about it, the more relevant it sounded, bearing in mind the fact that they'd both cried off by text. He looked up into the visitors' faces, his eyes quizzical.

'Let's stop playing games, shall we?' Malcolm blurted, his voice now a low growl.

'Games?'

'Oh please. This is bloody pathetic,' Malcolm shifted in his biker boots and threw down his plate. A plate that, Darren noted, he had hardly touched but whose clattering momentum now sent a samosa skittering across the floor and into a corner. 'You know damn well why we're here.'

'Look, I'm sorry but—'

'I saw it in a dream.' Vivette cut him off.

'Dream?' Sanjay asked.

'Yes. I'm a great believer in dreams and I had this bonko weird one where I was at this lushissimo catwalk show. I gave my coat to the cloakroom attendant and the thing behind the desk…'

'Thing?'

Vivette nodded. 'Yes, thing. Definitely *pas* human. Sort of four-foot tallish, orange skin with tufts of orangey hair and a head like—'

'A pumpkin,' Malcolm interjected in a disgruntled tone.

Everyone turned to look at him.

'How did you know that?' Vivette demanded.

'Because it's been in my dreams too.'

'Really? And did it remind you about the barbecue as well?'

Malcolm glowered. 'Remind is not the word I'd have used. More a graphic description of what might happen to me if I didn't turn up.'

'Oh.' Vivette put a hand on one hip. She looked ridiculous.

'Both of you sharing messages in a dream? Wow, that's…' Darren began.

'Unheard of? Effing weird?' Malcolm said, taking a step towards him. 'Let's not piss about anymore. Tell us how you did it and let's all go home.'

'What are you talking about?' Darren asked.

'Oh, come on,' Malcolm said, face flushed and leaking patience as quickly as the sweat running down his neck. 'You turn up at my place with some BS about a plastic bloody model that speaks and then I start getting nightmares about a tangoed goblin. And so, coincidentally, does she,' he threw a thumb towards Vivette, 'only she's so flaky she doesn't even realise it's a bloody nightmare.'

'Look,' Darren said, unnerved by Malcolm's accusations, 'I don't know anything about any nightmare—'

'I will admit that I'm intrigued about how you people do this stuff. Some sort of subliminal hypnosis, is it? Did you plant the idea inside my head when you visited me last week?' He pulled his lips back in a vulpine sneer.

'We didn't do anything of the sort.'

'So, why did you ask us here?' Vivette spoke up.

'Because of *her*,' Sanjay said. They turned to look at what he was holding up in his hands: Roxana in full combat gear. 'She is the reason.'

Vivette squinted at the figure; Malcolm meanwhile, could only shake his head. After a few seconds' silence Vivette looked at Sanjay, brows uplifted in one last vestige of optimism. 'So there's definito no buyer for a Russian chainstore?'

Sanjay shook his head. Darren sighed. 'We genuinely thought that you might know something about this. She said your names, Paladin and Obfuscator.'

'Rather a brill name for a designer, don't you think?' Vivette said.

Everyone ignored her.

'The only reason I'm here,' Malcolm said through gritted teeth, 'is for you to reverse whatever evil and illegal mind games you're playing. I want that orange thing out of my head and I want you to do it now or I'm going to the police.'

'What for? Breaking and entering your dreams?' Sanjay said. Malcolm took a step closer, his hands balling into fists.

'Shut up, Sanj,' Darren said. He didn't like what this was turning into, though exactly what he'd expected was anyone's guess. But Darren was genuinely disconcerted to find that *his* problems had become these people's problems, too. *That* bit he didn't understand at all. Still, he couldn't help but feel for these two innocent victims.

'Look, I don't know what's going on with this orange pumpkin headed thingy, really, I don't. I didn't expect any of this to happen. I'm sorry about the nightmares, but it has nothing to do with me. At least, nothing that I have any control over.'

Darren's apology, genuine and heartfelt, seemed to appease Vivette. But Malcolm was not so easily placated.

'Is that it?' he said with a teeth-grinding sneer. 'You have a hallucination about this doll, barge into our lives, screw us up so we have nightmares about orange-haired freaks, and all you can do is say sorry?'

'Well, yeah, I suppose it is.' Darren sensed that he could grow to dislike Malcolm without much effort.

'Thanks for nothing, mate,' Malcolm spat out the words. He turned and stomped out. Darren followed him to the landing.

'Wait, don't go like this. Maybe we can work it all out…'

'Yeah,' Sanjay added. 'I mean something this weird doesn't happen that often. We should talk about this.'

'Talk about it?' Malcolm spun on his heel. He held out both hands, eyebrows arched, a dangerous and derisory smile on his lips. 'I'd be delighted to. Let me get an hour's kip though, because I haven't had any for two nights. I've been too bloody scared to in case Pumpkin Head comes to call.'

'Is that why you're a teeny bit tetchy?' Vivette asked.

It didn't help.

'Tetchy?' Malcolm yelled. 'I'll show you what tetchy is!' He lifted his foot and looked as if he was going to kick down the bathroom door. Judging from the weight and size of his biker boots he would have succeeded, too, had the door not opened at that precise moment. At least it sort of opened, in that the actual door stayed closed, while another door, this one semi-transparent and superimposed on the original, swung in the opposite direction, out onto the landing.

# CHAPTER TWENTY-ONE

No one spoke. Everyone, even flamingo-miming Malcolm, was too busy staring at the door, trying to understand what he or she was seeing. A closed door that was open? It made no sense. And just to add to the inexplicably nonsensical, a woman stepped through. Not tall but carrying herself as if she was, dressed all in black, dark hair pulled back in a businesslike ponytail, sheathed knives in the belt at her waist. She looked around at the total disbelief on the faces staring at her and stopped when her eyes, which were the bluest Darren had ever seen, met his.

'Good evening. Darren, I presume?'

Darren tried to nod and swallow at the same time: a combination that ended in a gulp. The woman held out her hand. Darren shook it. It felt warm and dry.

'I am Captain Kylah Porter of the Department of Fimmigration.'

'Did she say Fimmigration?' Sanjay asked Darren in a wide-eyed, excited whisper, 'I think she said Fimmigration.'

From behind Kylah, a man stepped out of the bathroom. He was about the same height as Darren but a little bit older. He too wore black jeans but his was a white shirt.

'She did,' he said in a cheerful voice. 'Stupid name really, but then, it does what it says on the tin, as in, Fae Immigration.'

Kylah did a snail's-pace turn to look at him. The man mouthed, 'What?' back at her.

'How did you two…' Sanjay seemed to be the only one able to find his voice.

'Sanjay, it is Sanjay, isn't it?' Kylah asked.

Sanjay went into oh-my-God-I'm-being-talked-at-by-a-girl-mode and his open mouth clamped shut. He gave a mouse-like nod.

'Sanjay, I apologise for barging in like this. Sorry about the door paradox. It's a lot less messy than breaking the things down and saves a fortune in locksmiths. We only need a few moments of your time.'

'That doesn't include me, I presume,' Malcolm said, his face an advert for lemon sucking. 'Since I am here under false pretences, whatever this little charade is I'm sure you can manage without me.' He turned and took a step.

'Ah, the problem is, it does involve you I'm afraid,' the man in the white shirt said. He held a hand out to Malcolm on the cramped landing. 'The name's Matt. Matt Danmor.'

Malcolm glared at the outstretched hand and then back into Matt Danmor's face. The word 'belligerent' did not do the glare justice. 'Incandescent rage' probably came closest.

'We won't keep you long,' Kylah said. 'We've set a Krudian field around the whole first floor, so time, as you know it, will not actually pass at all. You'll have more than enough to go back downstairs and stop Mr. Bobal from overcooking the steak which, by the way, he is now convinced is rhino rump.'

'Dad,' Sanjay smiled, flicked his head up and down once and then shook it. The smile froze when he realised what she'd said. 'But, how do you know that?'

'That's why it's important you listen,' Matt said. 'Shall we go into the bedroom?'

'I'm going bloody well home,' Malcolm said through gritted teeth and turned to leave. He managed two steps before freezing midstride.

'Unfortunately, that will not be possible,' Kylah said with a little nod of gratitude to Matt, who stood behind her shoulder. 'We have the authority to detain you if necessary.'

Malcolm said nothing. He seemed to be fighting to breathe while his face was turning a nice shade of aubergine.

'Are you anything to do with Roxana?' Darren asked.

'We are,' Matt said. 'And it's going to take a bit of explaining, so —'

'What about him?' Sanjay pointed at a quivering Malcolm.

Kylah answered. 'My colleague, Mr. Danmor, has certain gifts. One of which has resulted in Paladin here developing intractable cramp, of the whole-body sort, in midstride. Extremely rare. Sheer bad luck it's happened now, of course. It's usually very painful, distressing and a bit frightening, since the cramp also involves the breathing muscles. However, if he agrees to cooperate…'

A muffled and desperate, 'Ysssss,' emerged through Malcolm's glued together lips.

Kylah smiled and nodded at Matt Danmor, who smiled in return.

The look of pleading on Malcolm's face was one that Darren would remember for a long time. And then the moment broke, and it was as if the marionette wires that were holding Malcolm up suddenly gave way. He slumped forward, almost losing his balance as the momentum of his forward step kicked in, sending him stumbling to his knees where he stayed, sucking in lungfuls of air on all fours.

'Hope you do better on the parallel bars,' Darren said.

Vivette stifled a giggle. Darren wasn't sure but he thought he detected a note of hysteria rippling through it.

'Sorry about that.' Kylah was apologetic but businesslike. 'A few brief moments of your time, that's all. I promise.'

Malcolm glared at her but made no attempt to move. They waited while he recovered and then, with Kylah and Matt at the rear, trooped into the crowded bedroom. Matt closed the door and stood guard in a laconic, lounging against the doorframe kind of a way.

'You must be wondering what the Department of Fimmigration is?' Kylah said.

No one moved and no one spoke. Kylah's eyes flicked up to Matt.

'Do you want me to do this bit?' he asked. Kylah nodded and stood back. Matt took a step forward.

'Sometimes it's best to hear this the first time from the human perspective.' Matt's smile was practised and held a hint of apology for what was to come.

Darren's pulse thrummed in his head. His brain zinged. Was this it? Was this finally an explanation for Roxana and Dolly Darren after all these years of waiting? Sanjay shot him a wary glance. But Darren didn't respond. He was too busy holding his breath.

'You're here, in this room, because your paths have all brought you to this point,' Matt continued.

Darren nodded. Sanjay's expression remained resolutely perplexed.

Matt acknowledged his confusion. 'You, Sanjay, are the one truly innocent bystander here, but on the other hand you are also a facilitator. You provide Darren with the commonsense streak he needs to succeed and a physical retreat where he can set his hobby back up.' He paused. 'Stop me if I'm going too fast.'

'You are going a bit speedishus,' Vivette said.

'Really?' Darren nodded, 'Okay. What if I told you the same thing happened to me once? There I was, minding my own business when, bang, I realise that there's something else out there, just beyond our understanding. And this was completely off the wall stuff. Mad religious fanatics from another dimension threatening world destruction; a visit to an interdimensional holding station for the dead.' Matt sighed and smiled. 'Ah, happy days. That's where I first met…'

Kylah coughed a genteel cough.

'Sorry, I digress.' He turned and smiled at Kylah.

She made eyes to the ceiling and muttered, 'Just explain to the people.'

'Course, sorry.' Matt cleared his throat. 'The F of Fimmigration stands for Fae as in fairy folk, nymphs, sprites, the supernatural. That's what this is all about. Difficult concept admittedly, but no more so than an eyeball tattoo. You don't believe it's possible until you see it for yourself. Basically, there are 'others' out there. All sorts of others. Multiple universes, full of all the mythical creatures you could imagine and a whole lot your imagination wouldn't dare come up with for fear of soiling its Jockeys. Believe it or not they do exist and occasionally they interact with our bit of the multiverse. Some even want to live amongst us. Hence the Department of Fimmigration. I will not bore you with the details of how it all works, except to say that it involves swapping dead human souls with live Fae. Sort of tit for tat. With me so far?'

Darren nodded. As existentialist concepts went it was not that difficult.

Matt continued. 'But sometimes really weird stuff happens. As it does in our world, the S.H.1.T. inevitably hits the F.A.N. Take Darren here.' Matt beamed at him. 'Nice enough, ordinary-type bloke with a penchant—and considerable skill I might add—for photographing humanoid figurines. Except that somehow or other, sometimes those figurines decide to talk back to him. Fact is, Darren: you're the fly in the Fimmigration ointment here.'

'Me?'

'You're the one.'

'He's certainly *a* one,' Malcolm muttered, clearly still sulking after being paralysed.

'It's something in your make-up, unique to you,' Matt went on. 'Think of it as a bit of rogue DNA, or a special extra bump in your temporal lobe anatomy, or maybe even a psychological gift delivered by genetic email. It's really very difficult often to get to the root cause of these things. But the fact is you've been given the ability to communicate with the very things you photograph. We think that somehow, and in your hands only, the process of your taking their image gives them an existence, a life force, a soul, you name it.'

'I'll name it if you like,' muttered Malcolm again. 'Eight letters, involves a male cow and rhymes with pulpit.'

Darren had to agree with him. He couldn't quite believe what he was hearing. It was as if his brain was in free fall and grasping for a mental rope in oxygen-thin fresh air. 'Sorry, I don't follow,' he mumbled.

Kylah stepped forward. She found Roxana lying on a bench

and set her to stand on the shelf so that they could all look at her.

'We run a monitoring service. Bit like MI6 or GCHQ, only ours is in the trans-dimensional way station.'

'Lovely spot, if you like asphodels.' Matt grinned.

Despite his confusion, Darren was already warming to him.

'Anyway, we picked up a distress signal from a little world called Moldarrenovia,' Kylah continued. Her delivery was snappy, no-nonsense. Darren could see her doing it in front of a squad of well-armed peacekeepers.

Malcolm, however, was not buying. 'Jesus,' he muttered.

'Curiously, the signal was also picked up by our station in Sydney,' Kylah continued. 'They think it was bounced to them from an old gold mine in the middle of the outback. In fact, there were two signals, both synched to the transmission from Moldarrenovia. Our investigation led us to—'

All the lights in Darren's brain lit up at once. 'My uncle's photographs!' he blurted.

'What?' Sanjay stared at him.

'My uncle's photos.' Darren spoke on the move. He rushed to a shapeless pile under a blanket and whipped off the sheet to reveal the flotsam of the spy set. The others crowded around with the exception of Malcolm, who leaned back, arms crossed, determinedly disinterested. Darren told them about Uncle Tom's wanderlust and his photographs of the weird chamber that had been discovered deep underground. He told them about finding the negatives in his mother's album and of how he'd had them developed to use as a backdrop for a set. He rummaged around until he found the images and held them up. Everyone, including Malcolm, stared at them, and him, in turn until Kylah, wearing an understanding smile, nodded sagely.

'That, my friends, is the final piece of the jigsaw.'

## CHAPTER TWENTY-TWO

'**But what's it** got to do with us?' Vivette asked, looking to Malcolm for support, but receiving a taciturn shake of a frizzy-haired head in response.

'Okay,' Kylah said in a measured tone, 'slightly more difficult to explain. Overall, in cases like this, it means that, like Darren, you both have skills that the Moldarrenovians recognise and—'

'Skills?' spat Malcolm, his index finger like the flesh barrel of a gun pointing at Vivette. 'Since when was dressing up like a clown wearing a deck chair a bloody skill?'

'*Excusez-moi*?' Vivette did a theatrical half turn and dragged her eyes across Malcolm as if she were examining a strange, bipedal alien.

A clown wearing a deck chair was not an image Darren was overfamiliar with, but one glance at a huffy Vivette was enough to confirm that Malcolm had scored a descriptive bullseye.

'Please, let's keep this civil,' Kylah said in a tone that added to Darren's conviction that here was a woman quite used to dealing with arguments. 'What I am trying to tell you is that the skills you take with you to other existences may not be all that obvious to you here.'

Malcolm was shaking his head. 'Is the bloke who writes your stuff on drugs?'

'Everything I've told you is true, Malcolm,' Kylah said, sounding surprisingly sanguine.

'Of course it is. All true. Darren here can talk to plastic models, you're Fae security, there are other worlds, I'm here on a trans-dimensional skills transference bloody course, and I'm apparently huge in Moldarren-bollocks-ovia. What is there not to believe?' He began striding about the room in a jerky way, scrutinising the ceiling, pulling back the curtains to peer behind them and muttering, 'There must be a camera here somewhere. More than one I expect.' He sent a look of entreaty to Vivette. 'Well come on, help me find it. It's the only way to out these bastards—'

'Why don't you tell me about your dreams, Malcolm?' Kylah asked with sudden and exaggerated calm.

He turned a suspicious face towards her, like he'd been hit with a slow-mo ray. 'What the hell do you know about my dreams?'

'Quite a lot, actually.'

Malcolm's suspicion flowed into a nasty little smile. 'You heard me talking earlier on, didn't you? Recorded our conversations covertly.'

Kylah shrugged. 'Believe what you want, but I am certain you don't remember telling anyone that your 'goblin'—and by the way he is a bwbach not a goblin and that is one semantic error you do not want to be making twice—was wearing a yellow and brown check waistcoat.'

'How did you know that?' Vivette gushed. 'It was some sort of tradelicious pattern and the most gorgeoso colour. I so desperately wanted to ask him where he got it. But it was, after all, nothing but a dream.'

Malcolm stared at her in total disbelief.

'Would you like to ask him now?' Kylah said in a voice that had gone very, very quiet.

Silence fell like a guillotine. It was broken by Vivette's hysterical laugh. 'Ha, ha. No way—'

The knock on the door made Darren jerk. Kylah opened it and stood back to let in a…pumpkin-headed thing that belonged fairly and squarely in a nightmare. The very nightmare shared by both Vivette and the now, goggle-eyed and cowering, Malcolm. It was four feet tall with red and very wrinkled skin covered by wispy tufts of orange hair. It wore black velvet harem pants and a yellow and brown check waistcoat. On its over large and pumpkin-shaped head sat a brown pork pie hat that, judging by its swagger, was clearly the cherry on the sartorial cake. It looked around at them with huge yellow eyes and, turning to Kylah, made a sound like someone with a heavy cold choking on a bit of phlegm whilst treading on a packet of crisps.

'I'm fine thanks,' Kylah said.

'Is it all right?' Vivette asked, alarmed, like the others, by the noises it was making.

Matt gave Kylah a stare and pointed to his ears.

'Oh, of course,' Kylah said and took out from her bag a large purple stone over which she poured some fluid from a small, stoppered bottle before setting the wet stone on the floor. 'Translational opal,' she said with an apologetic tilt of the head.

'Evenin',' gurgled the 'goblin' and Darren realised that although he could hear the guttural sucking and clicking that passed as its language still, the sounds now held meaning.

No one, however, felt inclined to reply.

'What…' spluttered Malcolm, '…is that?'

'That,' Matt said, 'Is George Hoblip, bwbach about town—well New Thameswick to be precise.'

The bwbach made a two-handed 'respect' gesture to Matt and grinned. At least Darren assumed that the sudden exposure of a row of gappy yellow teeth was a grin, though had a nostril flared it might just as easily have passed for a warning grimace of the type particularly favoured by a murderous orc. Especially one intent on turning a dwarf into a kebab the instant before an elvish arrow pierces its throat to save the day.

'And as you can see, he is most definitely not a goblin.'

Several faces swivelled back towards Matt, each wearing the expression of nervous desperation that always accompanies situations where knowledge of the obvious has been taken erroneously for granted. It was the look that patients gave doctors when the little lump on their elbow suddenly turned into a worryingly jargonistic inflammation of the subcutaneous synovial sac.

'You wouldn't believe how many people make that mistake.' Matt shook his head before adding, 'Though they tend only to ever make it the once if they want to keep all their facial features together, eh George?'

George Hoblip let out a thick laugh that sounded more death rattle than happy chortle.

Matt proceeded to make the introductions and when Darren nodded a hello, he thought he saw something glint in George Hoblip's lamp-like eyes as they lingered on his for a moment. But it was a fleeting, ethereal thought, because Malcolm's stertorous breathing was becoming intrusive. Kylah picked up a plastic bag from a table and handed it to him.

'Here, use this. Your legs are beginning to quiver.'

Malcolm took the bag and began to breathe in and out of it rapidly.

George Hoblip shook his head and turned to Matt. 'So, what's happenin', bro? They buyin'?'

'Haven't actually asked them yet,' Matt said.

'Asked us what?' Darren asked.

Kylah once again took her cue. 'Moldarrenovia is a preternatural construct, though, whether it's immanent or transcendental is something Matt and I were discussing on the way here…' She stopped. People were blinking at her with expressions commonly seen on volunteers forced to endure hours of mental torture or watch two party political broadcasts in a row.

'What I think my colleague is trying to say,' Matt explained, 'is that the Moldarrenovians are in trouble, and they need help.'

'But—' Darren said.

'And,' Matt continued, determined to deliver a little metaphysical nugget, 'through some capricious quirk of trans-dimensional fate, they managed to get a message to us. We duly relayed that to you via the Roxana doll because that's how these things work.'

'But…' Darren squeaked. He wanted to ask her about twenty years before. About 'Please…the Porter', but nothing came out of his mouth.

'I know. I know,' Kylah added. 'More questions than answers. Why you? What have you done to deserve this? You never asked for any of it. This is always the difficult bit. Truth is we don't know all the answers. We can only deal with what we find. But where it becomes interesting is where Malcolm and Vivette fit into Moldarrenovian cultural mores.'

'Mores?' Vivette asked.

'As in, when the leg that you feel tu-urns out to be eel, that's a-moray,' Matt said, or rather sang, looking very pleased with himself.

No one laughed, except for George Hoblip who high fived Matt and chuckled, or coughed up a bit of lung, it was impossible for Darren to tell the difference.

Kylah shook her head. 'If I may continue, the request was a genuine one. As Roxana explained to Darren, they are at war. We don't know how you, Ms. Campbell-Fripp—aka the Obfuscator, or you Mr. Burns, aka Paladin, can help. But the Moldarrenovian soothsayers obviously think you can.'

Sanjay threw a wary glance towards George Hoblip. 'And where exactly does *he* fit in?'

'Ah,' Matt said, 'good question. George happens to have some 'friends' in Moldarrenovia. A troll clan. He's developed a bit of a thing for their youngest daughter, Lulem.'

'Is that why he was so keen for us to come here?' Vivette asked.

Kylah nodded.

'And go over there to help them?' Matt added.

'Exactly,' nodded George Hoblip.

This time the silence was so thick it turned the air into soup.

'Go over?' Darren asked.

'There?' added Malcolm in an equally falsetto voice.

Kylah nodded. 'They're desperate.'

'But we have a choice, right?' the words burst out of Malcolm like a rattle from an Uzi.

'Absolutely,' Kylah said with feeling. 'Going over there will be dangerous. It'll be a very different existence space and time wise. Of course, Krudian physics and the Summerville paradox applies. For every hour you're there it's only a minute here, the usual stuff.'

Sanjay let out a weak little giggle. It was a physicist thing.

'And of course we're not at all sure how you would fare physically, whether you'd bleed if you were injured, etcetera,' Matt added.

'Oh well, that's all right then,' Malcolm said, his voice dripping sarcasm. 'However, I think I'll pass on that one, thank you very much. Not for me, not today, or ever.'

'Your prerogative,' Kylah said, nodding.

'So, I'm free to go and never see any of you again, is that right?'

'Absolutely,' Kylah said.

A wintry smile spread over Malcolm's face. He turned to Vivette. 'Right, I'm out of here. You coming?'

But she didn't move. She was looking instead at George Hoblip. When Darren followed her gaze, he saw that the bwbach's eyes had become tinged with scarlet and thin wisps of steam were drifting up from out of his large ears.

'Hey,' Malcolm said, 'you heard the Captain of Fimmigration. There will be no recriminations.'

'Certainly not. Well certainly not in this existence.' Kylah said.

Colour drained from Malcolm's face. 'What do you mean, not in this existence?'

Matt spoke up. 'While you're awake and going about your business, Kylah's promise holds true. You have nothing at all to fear from us…'

'There's a but at the end of that sentence, isn't there?' Malcolm said, with slits for eyes.

Everyone turned to the bwbach. 'My little Lulem wouldn't hurt a fly. In fact, she breeds 'em as pets. So if you walk out of here and harm comes to her because you chose not to help, I'll be coming to visit you every night to remind you of that fact. While you sleep, that is. We can share a little nightmare about me tearing your pimply head off and using your neck hole for an umbrella stand.'

Malcolm threw Kylah a fearful glance.

Kylah made a face. 'Fimmigration has no jurisdiction in dreamland.'

George Hoblip smiled. It was not a pretty sight.

'You bastards,' Malcolm said in words thick with emotion. His eyes were doing their best to pop out of his head.

'Right, now that's all cleared up, we need to say a few words about transportation, unless anyone's got any more questions?'

Vivette put her hand up. 'Just one. George, where did you get that waistcoat?'

## CHAPTER TWENTY-THREE

FOR DARREN, the next thirty minutes was akin to being in someone else's hallucination. Kylah did most of the talking, filling in all the little details, and every time he glanced at Sanjay he was smiling. Like this was all one great big joke.

'So, if you sent the Roxana doll,' Darren said after Kylah's explanation, 'You must be Hipposync?'

'We are. It's our cover for Fimmigration. Couldn't really have a Fae embassy, that would bring out all the weirdos.' Matt threw Kylah a sideways glance and smiled.

Darren resisted the urge to ask them to define weirdo, but it seemed a bit churlish, not to say dangerous, with George Hoblip in the room.

Both Kylah and Matt insisted they all eat while they hammered out the details, commenting, 'Never know when you'll get the next chance of a hot meal.'

Malcolm and Vivette exchanged silent looks.

When everyone had a plate—even a reluctant Malcolm whose beetling brows lightened once he'd had a mouthful of Mrs. Roopal's lamb—Darren found Kylah and asked if he could have a quiet word.

'The thing is, how did you know to send me the Roxana doll? How did you know she'd speak to me?'

Kylah shrugged. 'Your file. It showed that you'd had a previous episode.'

Darren blinked several times and then had to sit down. He exhaled, opened his mouth, shut it, swallowed, and then said, 'You mean you know about…about what happened to me before?'

'Not me personally, but yes, it's documented.'

'Then you know about the model with the briefcase and Dolly Darren?'

Kylah nodded. 'You're registered as possessing transfigurational communication skills, one documented occurrence. I don't know the details. What did the message say exactly?'

Haltingly at first, he recounted the episode and replayed, word for word, the message as delivered to him when he was nine years old.

Kylah's expression told him instantly that what he'd said rang a very loud bell. 'It wasn't 'Hippos in Oxford' you heard. It was Hipposync, Oxford.'

Darren nodded. 'I was only nine.'

'Wait until I tell agent Danmor,' she said.

'Tell him what?'

'That the very reason he's with Hipposync was foretold in a message to you a dozen years before it actually took place.'

Darren frowned. 'What?'

She nodded. 'Of course, it didn't really take place a dozen years before, the warning must have been caught in a Krudian helix and gone backwards instead of in a straight line, but still. You need to talk to Matt. Ask him about the vulture. You two will have an awful lot in common.' She glanced at her watch. 'Unfortunately, this is neither the time nor the place for that.'

Something in his face must have signalled his disappointment.

'You need to be strong, Darren. A lot of people are relying on you.'

Somehow, her words made Darren feel better. This stuff was crazy, completely insane, but then for years he'd thought he was. And now to hear that someone knew that it was all true was like a shot in the arm. Even more amazing was the fact that Kylah listened and accepted it as if all he'd done was casually mentioned a good film on the telly. He glanced over at Matt who was talking in earnest tones to Sanjay. He would like a chance to talk to him. He seemed like an okay bloke. But then Kylah touched his arm and broke the reverie. 'The thing is Darren, we don't have much time. Krudian anomalies being what they are, every minute we spend here now means hours or even days lost over there.'

Darren nodded. At Kylah's suggestion, they relocated to the lock-up, bypassing Mr. Bobal who'd taken up residence in front of the TV. Matt walked around Sanjay's magnificent landscape and model armies with unbridled admiration, but there was no time for questions. When everyone was inside, Kylah clapped her hands to get everyone's attention.

'This will be our point of contact. Please remember exactly where you enter Moldarrenovia. Since you'll be on a Krudian inter-dimensional visa, the portal stays open for a year and a day.'

'A year and a day?' Vivette said, horrified.

'I know, but don't forget the time anomaly. If you're away five days there, we're only talking a couple of hours here. Oh, and if things get at all bad there is an emergency extraction process, but hopefully it will never get to that stage.'

Malcolm cleared his throat and everyone turned to look. 'Can I ask what it is we are meant to do over there?'

'Of course you can.' Kylah smiled and it lit up the room. 'Unfortunately, I don't have any answers for you. I think however that it will all become pretty obvious once you're over there.'

'If it's anything like this it'll be a bloody shambles I should think,' Malcolm muttered.

'My money is on it being a quest,' Matt said. 'You know the sort of thing I mean.'

'No,' Malcolm said, 'I bloody well don't.'

'But I'm sure you do. Don't you spend at least six hours a day playing video games?'

'That's made-up stuff, for crying out loud. This is real.' He caught himself. 'Well, real-ish.'

'I'm still confused by why it is that we have to go? I mean

surely there are better trained people in Fimimigration?' Vivette asked.

'Fimmigration,' Matt said. 'And yes, there are. But the nature of inter-dimensional extradition requests—'

'Extradition?' Malcolm jumped on that one. 'Does that mean we're about to face charges?'

'No,' Kylah answered. 'More consequences of your actions here. It's an unfortunate term, but the best we could come up with.'

Matt continued. 'What I'm trying to say is that only the questers can fulfil whatever role is assigned them. You know, King Arthur and sword, Perseus and Gorgon, Diktik Seven and the Bludtremp—'

'That's supposed to be classified, agent Danmor,' Kylah said.

'Oh yes. So it was, sorry.' Matt let out an apologetic laugh.

Malcolm was shaking his head. 'But it doesn't explain how they know about us,' he nodded at Vivette, 'her and me, I mean. I only met him,' he sent Darren a scathing glance, 'a few days ago.'

'As I say, we don't have all the answers. Perhaps because most of them lie over there, in Moldarrenovia.'

'So, you're suggesting we wing it?' Darren asked.

'I am,' Kylah said.

Darren wasn't convinced. But Sanjay, who tried as always to be supportive, sensed his disquiet.

'Come on Dar, you have to admit this is bloody brilliant, mate.'

'Is it? Glad you think so.'

'But isn't this what you always wanted? I mean you spend all those hours making up places that don't really exist and photographing them. And we both know that this,' he dropped his voice low so that only Darren could hear, 'this is something you've dreamed about. You wouldn't even have to make it up. You'd be a reporter. It'd be a bestseller, man. I mean this is your chance to live that dream. You know, like a real adventure.' Sanjay let his wistful gaze drift over his lovingly crafted model. 'Man, I'd give anything to be able to walk along the banks of the Euphrates two and a half thousand years ago.'

'So why don't you come along?' Darren said.

But Matt overheard and shook his head. 'Sorry, it's invitation only at this point. You'd never get through the door.'

'Shit,' Darren said, seeing the disappointment in Sanjay's face. He glanced over at Vivette, who sat pulling a thread out of her deckchair dress and Malcolm, who was scowling like a gargoyle at the rear. Neither of them had taken the time to read the *How to Be the Life and Soul* handbook, it seemed.

But then George Hoblip was coming towards him, arm outstretched. 'Do your best, Darren. We'll be rooting for you.'

'Thanks,' Darren muttered. He shook the proffered hand. It felt papery and warm.

'Be aware that the transition can cause a bit of light headedness,' Matt warned.

'Okay,' Kylah said, with enough volume to grab everyone's attention. She took out a polished blue and purple doorknob and placed it on the lock-up's door where it sat glued by some invisible force.

'What is that thing?' Sanjay asked. 'Plastic explosive?'

'An aperio. It's a device for opening doors,' Matt explained. 'Any door to any place, so long as you know where you're going.'

'Yeah,' Malcom said with a sneer. One that turned quickly into wary anxiety on seeing neither of the DOF agents joining in the joke.

'See you then, Sanj,' Darren said and moved towards the door.

Malcolm, face like thunder, pushed off the wall and joined Vivette behind Darren.

'Shame my dad didn't see this. It's better than half a dozen Dealer Dave cakes,' Sanjay said, and Darren heard the hollow tone in his friend's words. He forced out a smile and cursed the God of irony. Sanjay would give anything to come with him, while his 'squad' members looked like they were being asked to eat rat meat.

Kylah turned the aperio and pushed. The lock-up door swung open the wrong way and, with a little shake of his head, Darren stepped through into another world.

# CHAPTER TWENTY-FOUR

Darren registered several things at once. It was warm, they were at the edge of a clearing, lush foliage surrounded them, and cicadas provided the background noise to which the calls of exotic birds added a periodic melody. And two bright suns rode high in the sky.

Two suns.

What the absolute F, thought Darren.

They emerged from behind a lichen-covered boulder. Above them dangled the overhanging branches of a large and incongruous sycamore that had no business at all being in such a subtropical setting. But Darren had no time to ponder the botanical implications because someone was calling to them from within the undergrowth.

'Hail, strangers!'

Darren put a hand over his eyes to look but could see no one.

Vivette and Malcolm seemed understandably bewildered at finding themselves in a strange land, but Darren, forewarned by his private chats with Kylah and Matt, stepped forward and held up both arms in a wave.

He sucked in some jungle air. It tasted…good. Full of the warm odour of exotic perfume from the flowers sprouting everywhere. But it was not simply the smells. There was something else. Something intangible yet highly invigorating. And then it struck him.

He felt alive here. Much more alive than he had moments before in Sanjay's, where the millstone of his uncomfortable domestic arrangement weighed constant and heavy on his soul. Here his soul felt as light and airy as one of Amanda's cardboard-textured fat-free rice cakes, but one heavily flavoured by some delicious spice. He felt wonderful and…yes, Cray-free. It was as if someone had sneaked in and changed the batteries without him looking. As if it were the first time ever his senses had seen or heard or tasted anything. Something rustled in the undergrowth nearby and he sensed that it was a python. He didn't know how he knew, he just…knew. He felt the heat of the two suns beating down upon him and turned his face up towards them, relishing the light.

'Wow, the colours are so…colourful,' Vivette said.

'I bloody hate jungles,' Malcolm grumbled. 'Plays havoc with my psoriasis.'

But Darren barely heard them because four people were emerging from the trees opposite. Four women dressed in combat trousers and sleeveless vests with dark bandanas keeping their hair back, each carrying something long and dark that looked like some kind of weapon. Immediately on emerging from their cover, two of the girls ran to the flanks. Of the two that remained on a direct line, one turned to walk backwards so that she could watch the treeline behind. But the other, with the turquoise-eyes, marched straight towards Darren.

Roxana.

She wore no hardhat today and her hair was cut short, the sun reflecting off the lighter streaks so that it appeared halo-like against the dark green jungle backdrop. Her features were delicate, almost childlike, but there any semblance of adolescence stopped. She had slim well-muscled arms and the rest of her was as he remembered. Darren's legs trembled. God, what was wrong with him? If she was anything to do with the model he'd bought all those months ago, he'd dressed and undressed her, photographed her a dozen or more times, but somehow, seeing her like this—life-size and real—threatened to blow all his mental circuits.

Roxana threw a final wary glance right and left before trotting the last few metres to stand opposite Darren. She walked behind the boulder and, satisfied that no one else was hiding or following, whistled for the others to join them. In seconds they'd made a tight knot with the other three facing outwards, on guard.

'Welcome, warriors from across the divide,' Roxana said, and a fire seemed to burn in her eyes.

'Umm,' Darren said.

'I am Roxana, and these are my sisters. We are soldiers of the Moldarrenovian Freedom Force.' She held out her hand and Darren took it. Like Kylah's, it was warm and dry, whereas sweat sprinkled the back of his own. When he let her hand go, she threw her arm across her chest in a kind of salute. 'The people of Moldarrenovia thank you for coming.'

'That's no trouble,' Darren said, before remembering who was with him. 'Oh, and this is Paladin and the Obfuscator.' He had no idea why he chose to introduce them as such. It simply seemed…right.

From behind him, Vivette waved hello and Malcolm glowered.

Roxana shook her head, a smile of delight playing on her lips.

'This is news that we dared not hope for. To have you all here…' She choked back a sob. 'A light has been kindled in the darkness.'

One of the other girls put a hand on her arm in a gesture of support.

Roxana smiled. 'This is Maeve,' the girl who leant support raised a hand. She was the tallest, ebony-skinned with thick dark hair and a flashing smile.

'On my left is Bron and on the right, our baby sister, Una.' Roxana continued with the introductions.

Both girls turned and revealed the same, traffic-stopping smiles. Bron was coffee-skinned with intense hazel eyes and auburn hair. Una, a younger version of Roxana, with bunched muscles under her eyes and caramel wisps under her bandana.

A noise, animalistic and angry, erupted from somewhere not too far away. It made Darren start and Vivette whimper.

'Come, we must leave this place. It is too dangerous to remain exposed like this.' Maeve said.

Vivette grabbed Darren's arm. 'Why are they speaking like that?'

'Like what?' Darren said.

'Like they're in a sword and sorcery script?'

'I've got no idea. But I quite like it.'

'Really?' Vivette looked Maeve up and down. 'Maybe you're right. It has a certain kitschagoogoo.'

Malcolm sighed. 'Kitschagoogoo? Jesus. You ever tried taping yourself?'

A thin vertical line appeared between Vivette's eyebrows above a disapproving pout. But before she could answer, another roar, much louder than the last, boomed nearby.

'Follow me,' Roxana said, her eyes darting over the jungle. 'Maeve will take the rear.'

They crossed over the clearing in a half trot and within a few minutes were passing under the dense jungle canopy. Within seconds, Darren was lost. But Roxana forged ahead, surefooted and confident of the way.

'Where are we going?' Darren asked, bending back a branch as thick as his arm in order to follow Roxana.

'Our encampment in the hills. We have evacuated the farms. It is not safe.' She paused and looked at him with a troubled expression. 'I must apologise. I called you giant.'

'In the studio? Yeah, you did. But then I was a hundred times taller than you. Don't worry about it. I've been called much worse things.'

She smiled a thousand candela smile.

The saliva froze in Darren's throat.

'You are not as…as I expected,' Roxana said, slowing down to let Darren catch up and swat a couple of hundred insects away from his face.

'Really? Were you expecting someone in a cape and a mask?'

'I was expecting a world-weary warrior.' She looked back at the others. Vivette especially was finding the heat oppressive and was doing a great impression of a parboiled beetroot.

'We have waited long for this day. A chance at last to strike a blow against the unassailable foe that Ysbaed has become. It fills my heart.' Roxana's eyes shone.

Darren's pulse accelerated to a gallop. What the hell was wrong with him? He flailed around for something intelligent to ask her because he wanted to hear her great throaty voice again, but his brain had zeroed in on the words 'unassailable foe'. As confidence boosters went it was up there with some of his well-meaning mother's best such as, 'At least it's just the one pimple Darren, even if it is a beauty.' and, 'Don't fret, there are plenty more fish in the sea. And besides, she was way too tall for you.'

The path narrowed to a single-file trail between an honour guard of massive trees. The vegetation was diverse; he could reach out his right hand to the crocodile hide bark of one vine-entangled trunk, while the fingers of his left caressed the skin smooth branch of another. His feet rustled through an inches deep layer of soggy debris as above, glimpses of blue sky through the verdant canopy grew increasingly rare.

Finally, they broke through into another small clearing, this one on higher ground that afforded a view of their surroundings. Roxana stopped to give the others a chance to catch up. She perched a hip on the edge of a petrified toppled beech and offered Darren a leather water bottle. He declined and watched her drink from it.

'So, uh, what exactly has this Ysbaed bloke been doing, then?' Darren asked.

Roxana took two healthy swallows and said, 'Ysbaed grows stronger every day. He recruits mercenaries from afar. Heartless savages.' Her voice seemed to lower a notch before she added, 'And he has beasts.'

The roar of earlier on took on a new, sinister significance and Darren's throat suddenly constricted. Through the tiny gap left for air he managed to ask,

'What kind of beasts?'

'Monsters from a child's nightmare. Some breathe fire. Others spit acid. Some tear their victim's limb from limb.'

Darren knew his eyebrows were already arching and he could feel the muscles of his brow straining to lift them even higher. He could also feel another muscle much further south straining with equal force to keep Mrs. Roopal's tandoori lamb in its rightful place. He motioned towards the flagon Roxana still held. She passed it over and he took a swallow. It tasted cool and refreshing and rejuvenating. He wiped the excess from his lips with the back of his hand and searched for his normal voice.

'Before Ysbaed and the monsters, what was it like here?'

A smile pushed the serious, troubled expression from Roxana's face. 'We wanted for nothing. The suns shone, children laughed and played openly in the meadows and streams.'

'Mobile phones? iPads?'

Roxana frowned. 'You are injured? You require a dressing?'

'Not an eyepad…it doesn't matter,' Darren said.

Roxana tilted her head and narrowed her eyes, trying, it seemed, to answer Darren's question; a gesture he found disquietingly erotic. 'After Ysbaed came, we tried to fight.'

'With bullets and guns?' Darren nodded towards the automatic weapon slung around her shoulder.

'Bullets?'

Darren peered at the gun more carefully. It had a stock and a gun-like barrel, but it also had an elaborate arrangement of leather and cord wound around the chamber and trigger guard, and a metal crosspiece sitting where the sight should have been. The gun was, in fact, nothing more than an elaborate crossbow. Roxana tilted up a quiver from where it hung on her hip.

'Our darts are poison-tipped. But against the beasts they are useless.'

Darren nodded. He wasn't surprised. Judging from her description of the things you'd need some heavy artillery at the very least, and preferably an air strike. 'Your only real option has been to hide?'

Roxana nodded. 'Hide the families and children.' She shook her head. 'Many men left to fight. Pride led them to believe they could march against him. None has yet returned.'

The men. He could see it all in his inner vision. The need to protect spiralling after a couple or ten fermented coconut juices, first into bravado and then into bloodlust. They were generally a peaceful people and so would have been motivated, enthused by alcohol, and militarily naive. A deadly combination that allowed warlords over the millennia to hurl aggression at their foes. What they would not have had was a strategist, or even a leader with the sense to say, 'Hang on boys, let's think about this for just a moment…'

His voice, or rather her voice, would have been totally drowned out by the rattling of the sabres.

'But what does he want, this Ysbaed bloke?' Darren asked.

Roxana's expression hardened. 'He wants to see us suffer, like a cat torments a bird. He has no reason. He is a demon.'

They were chilling words. It was clear that Roxana believed them wholeheartedly. Darren was glad when first Malcolm, followed by Bron and then Vivette and Una, caught up with them. Malcolm looked even sourer than he had ten minutes before.

'Everyone getting to know one another, then?' Darren asked.

'Apparently, we have to meet the Archivist to find out what we're meant to do,' Malcolm said, not trying to hide his disdain.

'Is there a loo anywhere nearby?' Vivette asked.

Darren let his mouth fall open and did a theatrical 360-degree swivel before looking at Vivette and blinking, which was better than expressing the thoughts that were running through his head in block capitals.

'You wish to relieve yourself?' Bron asked with admirable perspicacity.

'I shouldn't have had that litre of Evian on the train. Bladder burstio syndrome.' Vivette added an apologetic smile.

'Pick a bush, I will stand guard.' Una waved her hand to the edge of the clearing.

'A bush?' Vivette laughed, but seeing no reciprocal chortle in any of the Moldarrenovians' faces, added, 'Really?' She looked to Darren and Malcolm for support. Darren shrugged. Malcolm scowled.

Muttering to herself, Vivette walked off to find appropriate cover with Una close behind. 'At least turn your backs,' she snapped when she realised everyone was watching.

The break provided an ideal opportunity for Malcolm to launch into a fresh tirade. 'Not even a bog. What sort of bloody fourth world hellhole doesn't even have a bo—'

He was cut off by a sudden loud crack, as a stone the size of a tennis ball ricocheted off a boulder three feet away from his head.

'Incoming!' yelled Maeve from behind them. Una sprinted across and lunged at Vivette, yanking her down and disregarding the fact that her knickers were around her ankles. Bron did the same with Malcolm. Darren didn't need any help. He threw himself under the dinner plate leaves of a nearby plant.

'What the hell was—' Malcolm protested. Once again he was cut off, but this time by the cracking, slapping noises of stones falling like granite hail all around them. It lasted a few seconds and was followed by a leaden silence.

'I've heard of heavy rain,' began Vivette, who'd crawled back to their position 'But…'

'This is not rain,' Bron muttered, 'Ysbaed's troops greet us with their love.'

They sat for another two minutes in silence. 'Think they've gone?' asked Malcolm.

The words were no sooner out of his mouth than he got his answer. An unearthly, horrifying roar rent the air. It was a cross between a baritone camel with a thorn in its hump and someone with the mother of all bubbly colds.

'Can someone please tell me that's someone's dodgy sound system and not something that walks and has eyes?' Vivette asked in a very shaky voice.

She did not have to wait long for an answer. A noise like a heavy damp blanket rushing through the air filled the clearing.

'Get down!' yelled Bron. Everyone went foetal. Seconds later there was an almighty splat and a wheelbarrow-sized splodge of something gelatinous struck the side of a boulder ten yards to their right. The stone began to smoke and appeared to be blistering.

'Regurgor,' Una said in a way that made Darren think of something unpleasant lurking in a toilet bowl.

'We have tarried too long,' Maeve said, staring about her.

'Dare I ask what a Regurgor is, when it's at home?' Vivette asked.

'There is your answer,' Maeve said and pointed towards the jungle to the south. Coming through the undergrowth, using its powerful neck to bulldoze a way through the tall trees and snapping them like twigs in the process, was the most horrifying and disgusting thing Darren had ever seen, and bearing in mind that he'd been to many a Cray party, that was really saying something. Its head sat low on its shoulders, squat and blunted like that of a turtle, its eyes rolling on the side of a bullet head. Below that head was a second mouth, this one puckering and working constantly. Behind it, smaller shapes seemed to be moving, but Darren only had eyes for the…thing.

# CHAPTER TWENTY-FIVE

Emerging from the cover of the trees, it dropped its long forearms and used them to lumber across the ground. A line of figures broke cover either side of it like infantry behind a tank. Except that these were unlike any infantry Darren had ever seen. They were a sort of muddy blue for a start, on two squat legs, wearing leather helmets over heads sporting pointy ears that stuck out on either side. They wore leather tunics with beaten metal armour on their wrists and shins. All in all, if Darren had to describe them, it would be more scrawny upright monkeys than anything else. But monkeys that carried clubs and slings and were baring lots of pointy teeth.

'Dankboer,' Bron said.

'Not quite the UN peacekeeping force I was hoping for,' Darren said.

'Kidnapping and cannibalism, that's their speciality,' Malcolm said, his eyes narrowing.

'Not funny,' Vivette said. She threw Malcolm a beseeching look and Darren saw within it a desperate desire for him to capitulate and admit he was joshing.

When he didn't, Darren fired off his own question. 'How the hell do you know that?'

'Lucky guess,' Malcolm said, one wary eye on the monsters. 'You know.'

'No, I don't know,' Darren replied, not sure whether to be alarmed or intrigued. 'Humour me.'

'I just know,' Malcolm said. He sounded distracted, looking around at everything afresh with a calculating look that wasn't there a moment before.

'That's not an answer,' Darren said. 'That's just patronising codswallop.'

Malcolm's distracted expression suddenly hardened, and he seemed to make his mind up about something. He looked up, eyes locked on Darren's face. 'I've seen this stuff before. In a game called Death Planet Hub: The Avenging. Old game. A classic. Still has loads of online followers.'

'A game? But that rock that nearly hit us was real. How come—'

'Don't bloody ask me,' Malcolm said, his words heavy with sarcasm. 'You're the one who brought us here.'

Darren frowned. A little fragment of insight was struggling to free itself from the heavy weight of fear and confusion under which it was trapped. Another gobbet of something disgusting from the Regurgor hit a tree three yards away, causing it to erupt into flames, and the momentary spark of insight that flared in his inner vision passed. Yet when Darren looked up again, he noted a strange look on Malcolm's face. A wry, almost excited smile crept over it and Darren heard him mutter, 'Just a game.' The smile then became a pursed lip expression of grim determination and before anyone could stop him, Malcolm stood up.

'Just a game!' He taunted the enemy, who, on seeing him, jumped up and down, made grunting noises, pointed and adjusted their slingshot weapons. Malcolm turned to the others, his face now wearing an arrogant sneer. 'It's only a stupid bloody game. Can't you see that?' He turned back to the line of Dankboer. 'You can't harm me because you're all just a stupid bloody game.'

The Dankboer waved their arms in defiance. Darren looked at Roxana and realised that her expression must have mirrored his own perplexity. Maybe Malcolm was right. If he recognised these things, then maybe this was some weird manifestation of a computer-generated world. Perhaps they were all wearing total immersion suits and were plugged in to something akin to a steroid-fuelled Avatar script.

Another fist-sized rock tore through one of the huge leaves of the plant he hunkered under. If this was a virtual world, the rendering was pretty special. He hoped for Malcolm's sake he was right, because if he wasn't, it looked like he'd stirred up one hell of a hornet's nest.

A noise like a hundred nails being dragged over a dozen blackboards filled the air. Darren clamped his hands over his ears. But Malcolm stayed on his feet, smiling broadly. The Dankboer let fly with their slingshots and for a moment Darren thought that Malcolm might be right. The rocks seemed to fly right past him, clattering into the foliage beyond, taking out branches and punching holes in the huge leaves they struck. Malcolm, drunk on his conviction, yelled a challenge and put up a hand to try and catch one of the missiles. A sickening slap was followed by a howl of pain as Malcolm's hand met with flying rock. Crimson blood arced skywards and spattered against the leaves of the bushes. Malcolm fell to his knees, worryingly silent and clutching his injured hand, staring at it in disbelief and shock.

Darren groaned.

So Krudian visas did not make you invincible, and Malcolm was a hundred percent wrong about the game. Worse, his right hand now had two fingers less than his left.

Another disgusting noise emanated from the Regurgor's throat. Darren dragged his eyes around from where they were glued to Malcolm's hand and registered the fact that the Regurgor was forty yards closer than it had been moments before. He watched, spellbound, as the thing hesitated, hawked up another nauseating bucket full of goo and sent it unerringly in their direction.

'No!' Maeve shouted and lunged upwards. She tackled Malcolm and pulled him down as the Regurgor's poisonous spit flew past him. It missed Malcolm by a foot. But it didn't miss Maeve's left arm.

Malcolm slumped against a boulder and Darren crawled over to him. Vivette got there before him.

'Tourniquet,' she said and ripped at her dress. But before she could complete the tear, Una pointed to Malcolm's arm.

'Look,' she said in breathless astonishment.

The air shimmered around Malcolm's hand. The blood was slowing and two ghostly fingers were appearing where moments before had been stumps. Within seconds, two new flesh fingers solidified in front of Darren's gawping face.

'Grossolio,' Vivette said in a voice that was both amazed and sickened in equal measure.

Malcolm went from agony to hysterical relief without passing go. 'See that?' he sang. 'See? I told you they can't touch us here. Krudian watchumacallit applies like Kylah said. Look,' he waved his hand around, turned to show Maeve and froze. Triumph leaked out of him like air from a slashed tyre. The whole of Maeve's left arm from the elbow down was blistering and bubbling.

'Water!' screamed Una. 'We must dilute the acid.'

Quickly, the sisters began emptying their leather flagons onto Maeve's arm. Darren, trying his best to be helpful, started scooping off the thick gloop with both hands.

'No!' Roxana yelled, but Darren took no notice. His hands tingled and then started to burn. The Regurgor's fiery phlegm smelled of lighter fluid. He got most of the gloop away from Maeve's blistering skin and then felt the excruciating pain kick in. Darren wiped his hands on the earth and then stared at them. Huge red blisters appeared, the fluid ballooning up, his banana fingers swollen and throbbing. But after a few seconds the pain eased and the air about his hands seemed to shimmer in exactly the same way it had over Malcolm's fingers. Half a minute later, the redness faded back into normal flesh-coloured pink.

Darren giggled. He looked up at Vivette. 'Did you see tha—' But his words died as he followed her gaze. Whatever protection Krudian whatchamacallit was giving them, it seemed to have bypassed the indigenous troops. Similar blisters had formed on Maeve's arm and her hand, swollen to twice-normal size, was turning a lurid purple. She looked pale and sweaty, and the grimace of pain on her face needed no soundtrack.

'Shit,' Malcolm whispered, distraught, 'I'm so sorry.'

'We must get away,' Roxana said. 'We are easy targets here.' She seemed to be fighting an inner battle. 'We will take you back. You will be safe if you leave us.'

'No,' Darren said. 'We can't. We can't leave you here to face those…things.'

'We have no choice,' Bron said. 'We are outnumbered.'

Malcolm was frowning in concentration. His foolish, selfish act and its consequences seemed to have sobered him, concentrating his mind on their predicament. 'Death Planet Hub: The Avenging,' he muttered. 'Dankboer are hard to kill. They have body armour and two hearts.'

'Great,' Darren said glaring at him. 'Thanks for that. Ever thought of taking up motivational speaking?'

'Hard to kill by conventional means,' Malcolm went on, his eyes sweeping the adjacent jungle. 'But there are weapons you can use and they're usually hidden.'

'What the hell are you talking about?' Darren asked.

'Wooden crates,' Malcolm said, his eyes burning. 'Look for wooden crates.'

'What for? To lock you up in?' Darren said.

Malcolm rounded on him. 'Trust me, I know what I'm talking about. Look for pieces of wood, nylon string from an air drop, anything.'

They began scouring the vegetation at floor level. Everyone except Una who was ministering to the injured Maeve. They pulled back leaves and stalks, kicking at likely shapes with their feet, yanking back shrubs and bushes to peer behind.

It was Vivette that finally shouted in triumph: 'Here! Think I've found something.' She was squatting beside an oblong boulder, pointing at the shards of a piece of shattered wood jutting out from a tangle of vegetation. Malcolm tore at the greenery. But Roxana had a better idea. She took out a foot-long machete from a leather sleeve in her belt and slashed the jungle clear with practised ease to quickly reveal a thin piece of wood sticking up from the edge of very broken crate. Nestling at its ruptured base was an elongated black plastic case with a bulbous bulge at its centre.

'I knew it,' Malcolm said with grim triumph and pulled the

case free. Bits of earth and leaves flew everywhere, but Malcolm was oblivious to them as he snapped open some metal clasps and lifted the lid. Inside was a gleaming black and silver gun the exact shape of the case, with a curved ammunition carousel in front of the trigger guard. It reminded Darren of the old Tommy guns from black and white gangster films.

'That looks more Al Capone than Death Planet Tub,' Darren said.

'Hub,' Malcolm corrected him, explaining, 'in the game, they're the legacy of an ancient ammo drop.'

'Think we're actually in the game?' Darren asked.

Malcolm shrugged. 'Dankboer are definitely Hub nasties, but I don't remember any jungle levels in The Avenging.'

A muffled peel of bells rang in one of the deepest caverns of Darren's head and sent a jarring tremor through his spine. He remembered borrowing one of Sanjay's game covers for a shoot. Its lurid sci-fi design appealed to him instantly and he'd modified it to be an off-world holiday destination poster, pasted on the inside of a bus stop, for authenticity. But that had been years ago...

'What's the matter with you?' Malcolm asked, reading the guilty look on Darren's face with stark shrewdness.

Darren flushed. 'Nothing. Weird thought, that's all.'

'Save it for later,' Malcolm said, flicking bits of metal open on the gun.

Darren risked a glance up at the approaching line of Dankboer and the Regurgor. They were no more than twenty yards away, the monster in the lead, lumbering its way through the undergrowth, the soldiers in a line behind it.

'We must move.' Roxana said. There was urgency in her voice.

'Yes, we must,' Malcolm agreed. 'But let me give them a little blast from this little beauty first.' He stood up again. The beast in front of him roared and Darren could smell death and pain on its ketone breath. But Malcolm didn't seem fazed in the slightest. In fact, he seemed in his second-life element.

'Right, you bastards. Have some of this.' Malcolm hoisted the gun to his shoulder and pulled the trigger.

The air in front of the gun distorted and a pulse of light energy flowed outwards. Not so much a beam as a sparkling ball. Darren watched it shoot across the space. Saw it hit the beast first and then the Dankboer. The Regurgor staggered as if struck by a sudden wave of invisible water. It remained standing and so did the troops behind. Their outlines distorted in front of Darren's eyes, but then snapped back and they continued to advance even more quickly. The beast let out a screech of anger and charged. Roxana yelled and Una grabbed Maeve, ready to run for it. But Malcolm wasn't moving.

'Stand your ground,' he said softly.

Everyone stopped and so did the beast. It came to a wavering halt and stood where it was, as if in response to Malcolm's quiet order. It let out a final roar, and then quivered and shook until it was vibrating uncontrollably. Behind it, the Dankboer were suffering the same fate. The shaking became more and more chaotic until, with a sickening splash, beast and Dankboer exploded, showering everything within a fifty-metre radius with red, dripping gore.

'Eaagghh,' Vivette said, picking some Regurgor intestine out of her hair. 'This is disgusterous maximus.'

The girls, Maeve included, were less critical. At least, judging from the way they all stood up and began whooping with unmitigated delight at the total destruction of their enemies, they were.

Malcolm, meanwhile, looked very pleased, if a little shocked, by what his gun had achieved. 'Bit more dramatic than on the screen,' he said, with an expression more suited to something covered in wool and bleating. Una displayed no such reticence. She ran forward, plucked the Regurgor's disgusting head from the branch it had landed on and held it up in both hands above her head.

'This is a great day for the Tirerenans,' Roxana proclaimed. 'A day when the tide of our suffering may, at long last, be turning.' Her face, both terrible and beautiful in its triumph, beamed at Darren. Bron and Una and even a pained Maeve went to Malcolm to congratulate him, while Vivette continued to remove debris from her clothes with an expression of someone asked to skin a plague rat.

'Thank you,' Roxana said, but she had eyes for no one but Darren when she said it, and they gleamed with pride and gratitude.

Darren would have said something glib but his tongue turned to wood in his head. Instead, he grinned like a ventriloquist's dummy and shrugged. Roxana stood with her weapon held high, blood-smeared and sweating and triumphant.

For years, Darren had striven to portray the hyperreal in his art. But he knew that no amount of careful lighting and staged imagery could come close to what he was seeing in front of him at that moment. Roxana had been a magnificent and fierce warrior queen in the viewfinder of his camera. But in the flesh, she was something else altogether.

He was aware that he'd been in a battle, aware that adrenaline must be coursing through him. But no amount of neurochemical stimulation could explain the way his heart was banging at the bars of his rib cage. It was mad, it was inexplicable—it was infatuation. But while he tried to calm the maelstrom inside, he couldn't manage so much as a clearing of his throat to reply to those burning eyes.

Instead, all he managed was a nod. In return he got the Roxana salute and another brain-melting smile. And in that moment, Darren realised that here was a smile a hundred times more dangerous than a whole vat of Regurgor acid.

## CHAPTER TWENTY-SIX

**THEY WRAPPED some** special medicinal leaves around Maeve's arm and followed Roxana out through the jungle, ascending quickly through dense vegetation so that Darren again lost all sense of direction. But Roxana seemed to know the narrow path, stopping whenever Malcolm spotted what he thought might be another weapons cache, and bagging four more 'sonic cannons'. They saw no more Dankboer and heard no more beasts, though there were jungle noises all around them of things that squawked, growled, slithered and grunted. And since he knew from watching the Natural Geographic Channel with Mr. Bobal that the things that made these noises came with a selection of claws, fangs and teeth as standard, complete with a default mindset of 'kill and eat', he kept his head down and walked. After what seemed like hours of relentless climbing, which would have been unbearable but for the fact that the temperature fell as they ascended, they emerged out of the jungle onto a high plateau surrounded by verdant hills. In the far distance, white-tipped mountains rose to the sky.

'There,' Roxana pointed towards a craggy bluff to their left, indicating, Darren assumed, their next checkpoint, judging by the beeline way she set off for it. Three of the girls now carried a sonic cannon, while Malcolm insisted on supporting the injured Maeve, his broad shoulders her crutch. From the concern written all over his face, he'd clearly assumed responsibility for her well-being.

They walked for what seemed like most of the day, travelling along a steep gorge, its riverbed wide and arid apart from a thin, trickling mud-brown ribbon at its very centre. After what seemed like hours, Roxana turned and scrambled through a narrow ravine to emerge in a bowl-like meadow. Beyond, the land fell away towards rolling hills dotted with low buildings surrounded by patchwork fields and hedgerows. Grazing animals moved slowly over the greenery. Darren stood, spellbound. He was willing to bet that if he were able to prise up the earth, he'd find a nice selection of Belgian pralines in the shape of seahorses, or shinily wrapped chocolate coated fondants (with a predominance of orange creams if anyone had been there before him) in a plastic tray. This was exactly the sort of landscape he'd imagined he'd like to end up living in. A cosy farmhouse nestling in the shelter of a hillock somewhere, the animals all well-tended and free ranging, some rosy-cheeked children and a beautiful…

'Darren,' Malcolm called his name and dragged him back to the present. The others turned sharply towards a tented yurt compound surrounded by wooden palisades at the centre of the meadow. Una cupped her hand to her mouth. Her animalistic yodel was answered immediately. Moments later, they were surrounded by chattering women and grinning children, all pressing the girls for details.

Maeve was led away, much to Malcolm's concern. A concern that remained unassuaged by Bron's reassurance that all would be well, while Roxana led Darren, Malcolm and Vivette to a large and ornate yurt at the far end of the compound.

'You are our guests,' she announced. This stronghold is not as well provisioned as we would want, but it suffices. Please refresh yourselves. I will return in a short while and we will meet the Archivist. There is fruit and fresh water inside.' She smiled and Darren's pulse did a jig.

The yurt was large, a cheerful fire burning at its centre. Drapes had been hung as partitions for the bunks that lay against the wall. Vivette went in search of a 'proper' toilet, leaving Darren and Malcolm alone.

'Okay,' Malcolm said. 'I admit it. I was wrong. This is not a YouTube wind-up and yes, I'm a total wanker for getting Maeve hurt like that.' He sat slumped; dejection etched on his face.

'All new to me too, if it's any consolation. Kylah and Matt didn't say anything to me about Dankboer and bloody Regurgors.'

'Didn't sound like they knew much of anything themselves either, did it?'

Darren shook his head.

Malcolm's voice dropped to a whisper. 'Did you see her arm?'

'And the smell? It was like burning—'

'Plastic, yes. But how can that be? I touched Maeve; you've touched Roxana. They feel…normal.'

Darren nodded. Roxana certainly did feel normal. And all the girls' skin looked flawless too.

'But we are assuming that this place, wherever it is, plays by our rules, which, judging by the *Death Planet Hub* baddies, it obviously doesn't,'

Darren nodded again. These were wise words, and he got the impression that though they were all trying to find their feet, Malcolm had already spotted his and was well on the way to fitting them and removing the stabilisers.

Vivette came back in. 'That's better, not exactly Molton Brown accessories but it'll do. So, anyone worked out what the hellisimus is going on yet?'

Darren exchanged glances with Malcolm and they both shook their heads.

'Fruit,' she said and grabbed an apple from the bowl. 'Want one?'

Darren nodded and caught the tossed apple. It looked like a real apple and felt like one, complete with a tiny little green leaf attached to a stalk. But when he bit into it, he knew instantly that it was not real. At least not in the way that he'd experienced apples previously. The flesh was solid, but not crisp. Like biting into an apple-flavoured boiled potato. The texture was waxy and firm, the flavour exquisite.

'Any good?' Malcolm asked.

He got no reply from either Vivette or Darren. They were both staring at their apples in delighted surprise.

'I'll take that as a yes, then,' Malcolm said and reached for one.

They ate two each and Darren felt the weariness drain from him. He was wide-awake and alert. From the look of them, the apples were having an identical effect on the other two as well.

'God only knows what the pears are like,' Malcolm said, eyeing a separate bowl.

They were even better. The water, too, was superlative. Cool and clear, the stone jar containing it sweating with condensation; though how it kept so cold was anyone's guess as Darren saw no ice anywhere.

A bell rang near the entrance flap. Darren threw back the material to find Una standing there, but no longer in combat fatigues. Instead, she wore a brightly-coloured sarong.

'The Archivist awaits your presence.'

No one objected. Una gave them the guided tour as they walked through the village. After a few yards the yurts gave way to more substantial wooden buildings.

'Looks like you've been here a while,' Darren commented.

'Our shepherds bring their families up here during the summer. Sheep and goats use the high pastures. It was not built to accommodate all of our people, that is why we have also needed tents.'

They entered a small square and Una explained how the larger buildings doubled as communal dining areas, a school and male and female instruction centres. Malcolm picked up on that.

'And what goes on in there?'

'All our children, once they become of age, enter for a period of instruction. We are a hard-working people, Paladin. But we also pay attention to our pleasures. Every man and woman of age is taught the art of pleasuring their partner in the same way they are taught how to fight.'

'Really?' Darren said, his voice higher than he wanted it to be. 'Any instructor jobs going?'

'Of course. I volunteer occasionally. So does Roxana. Do you have a particular skill?'

Darren waited for her to laugh. She didn't, which meant that she was serious. A thought that sent Darren off on a wild water ride of the imagination that threatened to make him lose the ability to stand up. He managed to let out a little guffaw and a dismissive shake of his head that seemed to satisfy her. If she noticed the way he kept glancing at her sideways after that, she said nothing.

'And here we have our library.' Una pointed to a larger wooden building set apart on a small rise. Elaborate symbols were carved on a great arch above the entrance. Darren studied the symbols and frowned. He recognised some familiar shapes there. At least he interpreted them as familiar since they looked very 21st-century. But he had no chance to ask because a figure was emerging from out of the shadow of the building. A man, dressed in a white coat with flyaway white curly hair and a lugubrious expression, his jowls heavy beneath a bushy white moustache.

'Ah, welcome, welcome.' The accent was Germanic and Darren exchanged an amused and knowing glance with Malcolm. Neither of them would have been surprised to hear the man announcing that E equals MC squared, such was his resemblance to an iconic 20th century physicist whose name began with E and ended in N.

'I am the Archivist of Moldarrenovia. Please come in.'

They followed him into an antechamber in which a chaotic assortment of items was stacked on ceiling-high shelves. The sheer variety of the things Darren saw kept him blinking in amazement, but for some reason he could not for the life of him work out why they were so tantalisingly familiar. But the Archivist did not allow them to linger. He continued through to a larger room, lit from above by large openings in the roof. Huge oak trusses held up the walls and ceiling, but it was the room's contents that made Darren's eyes goggle and his mouth drop open. A spider's web of rope and string crisscrossed from one wall to the other, each joining some artefact or another to the centrepiece raised on a dais. And it was to this altar-like structure that the Archivist led them. There, on a stout wooden table, set up and surrounded by a metal frame to which all the strings were tied, stood a giant, ancient and battered-looking mobile phone.

'What the…' Malcolm said.

'Behold: the Oracle,' the Archivist announced, his gaze reverential.

'Looks more like an old-school Nokia to me,' Malcolm whispered.

'I am the keeper of the Oracle. I am the Archivist. Every item, every artefact, is brought to me and I add it to our knowledge base.'

'May one ask why?' Vivette asked.

'So that we may learn. TYhee Oracle speaks to me.'

'Really?' Darren said.

'These miracles are rare, but when one does occur, the words and images projected are prophetic and profound.' The Archivist's voice quavered with emotion. It reminded Darren of a vicar who used to visit his mother. His sermons were always tasty, peppered with words he virtually sung whenever he got excited or upset. Words like 'temptation', or 'Samaritan', or 'some-bugger-has-nicked-the-lead-from-the-roof-again'.

Darren let his eyes roam the room. For the first time since entering he took in the items connected to the old Nokia on the dais properly. He hardly used the word 'eclectic' much, but in this case, he couldn't think of a better one. Not even hotchpotch or cornucopia came close. It was like someone had upended a rubbish bin at home, photographed the contents and then made a collage of the separate items.

Darren's brain flipped from astonishment to panic in a fluttering heartbeat.

The memory of one of his experimental shoots swam to the surface of his consciousness and circled with one dorsal fin showing, while a two-note stalking motif played in the background.

Could it be? Was it even possible? Because he'd done exactly that once. On a whim, he'd upended a bin full of refuse and stuck a model of a discarded, one-eyed teddy bear in amongst the rubbish. Then he'd photographed the result, trying to capture the pain of an abandoned toy. He could even remember seeing a broken mobile phone lying in the debris. Now, looking up at the Archivist's collection, his gut spasmed.

'So, is this what told you about us?' Malcolm asked, breaking in on Darren's unpleasant musings.

'It is.' The Archivist nodded. 'It spoke the words Paladin and Obfuscator. Of course, we knew of the Maker, but it has also showed us the source of Ysbaed's power.' His voice faltered and dropped to a lower register, as if he feared that in speaking the words they would somehow be overheard. 'The Votives.'

No one spoke for a moment, but Darren suspected that of the three of them, Vivette would be the one whose curiosity broke through first.

'And what exactly are votives?' she asked.

'Offerings. Powerful objects full of arcane energy. Ysbaed hides them in his stronghold. We believe that if someone were to take them, break his connection with them, Ysbaed's power would be shattered.' The Archivist shot them each in turn a feverish glance, his eyes deep set, full of unspoken meaning. Darren waited for a clap of thunder. It never came.

'And is that what we are expected to do?' Malcolm asked.

'It is your destiny,' the Archivist said. 'Your paths have led you here. You have been chosen from the words the Oracle has spoken.'

Malcolm expelled air in a loud exhalation. Gone was the truculent gamer convinced that he'd been punked by Darren and Sanjay. Maeve's injury had changed all that. The man standing in front of Darren now, eyes to the floor, pondering the Archivist's words, was no longer Malcolm the whining gamer, it was Paladin, the people's champion. And the thing about being a people's champion was that it didn't always come with a badge, but it did always come with a conscience. And that was fair enough since most of the people you were a champion of couldn't be bothered with one, had one buried under several tons of manure called justification, or had one they could easily switch off when it came to taxes and money. In general, the people preferred instead to let their champion be their conscience for them. But the trouble with having a conscience was, like glittery make-up on that pretty secretary from HR's hair, it rubbed off if you got too close to it and was an absolute bugger to get rid of. Darren could feel it already creeping over his skin and he was at least ten yards from the 'champion'. Malcolm glanced up and caught Darren looking at him.

'What do you say?'

But Darren couldn't find any words. He was too caught up in the hundred-mile-an-hour race his brain was having with itself.

'Darren?' Malcolm asked again.

'Perhaps the Maker would like to meditate for a vile,' the Archivist said.

'Maker?' Vivette said, frowning.

'Of course,' the Archivist said with a little smile and a nod to Darren. 'The Maker is amongst us.'

Darren cringed. Seeing the Oracle was bad enough. Being called the Maker was something else altogether. He didn't want to be put on a pedestal by these people because from what he knew of pedestals, the quickest way off one was to fall flat on your face. He knew bugger all about these people or what was going on—well, nothing apart from the growing conviction that somehow his involvement with all of this went deeper than he could possibly imagine, and in a way that was weird and scary and that he could not control. A little acorn of insight had fallen off a tree on the hilltop of his consciousness and was rolling downhill, cartwheeling and gathering snow as it rolled, threatening to trigger a full-blown avalanche. He spoke for no reason other than to stop himself from thinking any more.

'When…' His words creaked and stalled in his dry throat. He cleared them out and tried again. 'When did Ysbaed come here?'

'It has been many months. The Oracle forewarned of a great pestilence to be visited upon us.'

'Is this what you used to ask for help too?' Vivette asked, pointing towards the giant mobile phone.

'It is, Obfuscator. The Oracle has been our deliverer.'

'Darren, you alright?' Malcolm asked.

Darren had gone the colour of something found under a very heavy rock that had not seen the sun in an eon. Many months in Moldarrenovia would be but a few days in Yorkshire money. Though he'd photographed the spy a matter of 'days' ago, even without a Krudian calculator, he'd put an each way bet on those two things being no coincidence. 'Yeah,' Darren muttered by way of reply to Malcolm. 'Yeah, I'm fine.'

'What exactly do these votives look like again?' Malcolm asked, one wary eye on Darren.

The Archivist nodded. 'Images appeared to me in the Oracle. I drew what I saw.' He walked to an easel and pulled off a thin drape.

Shock brought forth an inward groan in Darren, but it escaped into the outside world as a stifled whimper. He managed to keep from moaning out loud by a whisker, but swallowing it back brought up a fit of coughing so bad it made his eyes water. The sketches were crude but not so crude as to be unrecognisable.

'There are three: a knife, a coiled rope, and some kind of rock…'

'Pyrite. Fool's gold,' Darren said before he could stop himself.

Everyone turned in amazement. Everyone except the Archivist, whose eyes still burned with fever.

Malcolm and Vivette were staring. The Archivist, however, smiled broadly. 'Your wisdom is vell received, Maker. We are justified.'

Inside, Darren squirmed. There was no way back now. 'And the knife isn't a knife, it's a shard of sharpened bone. The rope isn't a rope either—it's a shed serpent's skin.'

After that, things happened very quickly. Una, Bron, and Roxana were summoned, and the Archivist explained what Darren had told them.

'Are they large objects?' Roxana asked.

Darren shook his head. 'No. They could easily be carried.'

Vivette, who'd worn a quizzical frown ever since Darren's revelation about the pyrite, but who'd remained determinedly silent, finally spoke. 'How do you know they can be carried?' she asked.

'I just do,' Darren said. 'And they're right. Without them, Ysbaed is nothing.'

Both Malcolm and Vivette eyed him suspiciously.

Roxana, eyes gleaming, turned to face them all. 'Then our task is clear. We must capture or destroy the votives. We suspected as much but now, with your knowledge…'

'Ah yes, your knowledge,' Vivette scoffed. 'Tell us a bit more about your knowledge, Darren? Bit hard to fathom, that one, Darren. Or should I call you *Maker*?'

Darren didn't answer. He was saved from Vivette's Rottweiler glare by Malcolm, whose newfound feet were already treading the path of a suggested way forward.

'Is that it? Our quest?' Malcolm asked. 'Capture the votives?'

'Since when did you become Rambo?' Vivette sent him a peevish look.

'I deal in virtual weapons.' Malcolm said patiently. 'If that's all he's got, the spitting beast and those Dankboer, we're sorted. Those sonic cannons will cut through them like a knife through butter.'

A thick silence congealed around them.

The Archivist finally whispered something to Roxana, to which she nodded.

'Come,' she said to Darren. 'We must get you suitably attired.' She led the way, and they walked outside into the sunlight. Squinting against the glare, Darren cringed at the assembled, and expectant, crowd of women and children.

'They have come to greet you, Maker,' Roxana said. She gave him another one of her thousand candela smiles. 'Many were working or asleep when you came. They have come to hear you speak.'

'Speak?' squawked Darren. 'But what should I say?'

Roxana was still smiling. She had every confidence in him, whereas Darren felt about as confident as a short-sighted ostrich in a minefield. 'Say what comes to you naturally.'

Darren turned to look at his eager audience.

'Boy, am I looking forward to this,' Vivette said in a voice loaded with so much schadenfreude, Darren was surprised she could walk.

'Ummm…' He cleared his throat. People of Tirerena. When…life is a rollercoaster…you need to search for the hero inside so that you…can climb every mountain. If you do, then… things can only get better and…you'll never walk alone.'

A tumult of applause followed, led by Roxana and the girls. The crowd looked pleased, but Vivette shook her head and rolled her eyes. 'What was that? The gospel according to *Now 22: The Soccer Anthems?*'

'Best I could come up with,' Darren said, looking pained.

Malcolm, though, was less critical. 'Leave him alone. I've heard a lot worse. I want to check in on Maeve if that's alright.'

'She will like that. Do you know where the hospital is?' Una asked.

Malcolm shook his head.

'We can all go,' Roxana offered. 'It is on our way.'

'We'll follow,' Vivette said. 'I need a *mot tranquille* with the Maker here.' There was no mistaking the sarcasm that weighed down her words this time.

Darren hung back while Malcolm and the girls headed off. Once they were alone, Vivette motioned him back inside the Archivist's hut.

'A word,' she said, her eyes like gimlets.

Darren watched Roxana's departing back for a couple of seconds longer and then turned to follow Vivette into the cool darkness, feeling like he'd been summoned to the headmistress's office.

# CHAPTER TWENTY-SEVEN

**As soon as** they were alone, she lunged at him, fists flailing. He ducked and tried to restrain her, but she was beside herself, punctuating the slaps and punches with, 'You absolute *sod*. You total *bugger!*'

Though none of her blows connected with enough force to cause him actual harm, the surprise and vehemence of her verbal attack made him fall back until he met with the wall.

'Wait,' he protested, dodging her pummeling fists. 'For Christ's sake…'

He grabbed a chair and managed to brandish it, lion tamer-like, and in a fleeting moment of epiphany, he clocked another transformation. The flaky designer who'd walked naively into Moldarrenovia had disappeared. In her place now stood a berserk, violent she-cat.

'Jesus, Vivette, calm down.'

His words were lighter fluid on a lit barbecue.

'Calm down,' she seethed. 'CALM EFFING DOWN?'

Darren poked the chair at her, and she flinched, but only for a moment.

'It's you, isn't it?' she spat at him.

'What?'

'All of this. It's all your sick doing, ISN'T IT?'

He recoiled. Her words were worse than the blows; more

painful than any of the ineffectual slaps she'd aimed at him moments before.

'I saw the way you looked at the Oracle. You recognised it. You did this. You're the reason I'm in this disgusterous hellhole. You're the reason Maeve got hurt. The reason Ysbaed is persecuting these poor people. It's all down to you, you…sick, evil… MONSTER.'

He didn't answer. Couldn't answer, because he knew it all to be true. It was all down to him. Okay, there'd been no malicious intent, but nonetheless, it was he who had built the sets, he who had photographed the models and, in all probability, he who had recruited Vivette and Malcolm. Even the Archivist came from an iconic image of Einstein he'd used for a scene he'd dreamed up. And now, thanks to some Aboriginal bloody demon, the bogeymen were all out of the toy cupboard and innocent people had been dragged out of their comfortable existences and were being maimed and hurt. Darren let the chair drop and slumped against the wall, the enormity of it all suddenly draining all the resistance from him.

'Yes,' he mumbled. He didn't look at her. Didn't care anymore if she picked up her own chair and smashed it over his head. But all she did was stand there in front of him, out of breath from her exertions, pinning him to the wall with her angry glare.

'What are you going to do about it?'

'I…I don't know…'

'You don't know,' she repeated very slowly. 'I am stranded here with Mr. Charisma from Nerdlington who thinks he's stumbled into a PlayStation game and a bunch of Amazons who fire crossbows at thirty-foot tall Godzillas and you don't know what you're going to do about it? Not goodenuffski, Darren, you total bum-wipe.'

Darren could only shake his head.

'I'm a designer,' she wailed, 'Not a sodding secret agent.'

Darren had a fleeting realisation that 'sodding' was the nearest Vivette would ever come to real profanity. It would have been funny if she hadn't been so furious.

'I'm sorry,' Darren said. There was nothing else to say.

'Oh well, that's all right then,' Vivette's words were bright and brittle. 'So long as you're singing the sorry song, we're all in happyville.'

'Look, I didn't ask for any of this either.'

'I don't care if you applied in triplicate, or if it was dropped unbidden into your lap from a great height by a dysentery-ridden albatross. The fact is you *are* responsible. For all of…*this*. I want to go home and not be haunted and bullied by something called George Hoblip. I want closure and my old life back, the *touter* the *suiter*. I don't care if people laugh at my designs or the way I speak. I'd rather be called names than have my head smashed by a rock thrown by a freak with a sling. So, *Maker*,' she used the word the same way a seven-year-old might, 'stop making excuses and *make something happen*.'

'I…I don't know what to do.' He heard the desperation in his own voice but was powerless to stop it.

'What are you good at?'

'Pub quizzes. I'm the music expert. I listen to anything from heavy metal to teenybop stuff.'

'Even Girls Aloud?'

'It's an inclusive pub.'

Vivette's expression went rigid. 'How can you make jokes? Why are we here? Why, of all people, are you here?'

The answer burst from him in a frustrated shout: 'I don't know, okay!'

'You don't know?' Vivette frowned and, to Darren's horror, anger morphed into misery. Big dollops of fluid began cascading down her face and her lips started to quiver. 'That's not the answer I want to hear,' she sniffed. 'It isn't fair. You said that someone wanted to see my designs. That someone was interested in…'

Darren stood up and reached out a hand.

'Don't you dare touch me,' she flared. 'Don't you dare.'

His hand fell away.

'You're a liar, Darren Trott. Rotten and stinking and…and a freak.' She turned on her heels and stormed out.

# CHAPTER TWENTY-EIGHT

HE DIDN'T GO after her. Instead, he stayed slumped against the wall, contemplating her words. Guilt hung anvil-like around his neck, weighing down his thoughts. No matter which way he twisted it; there was no denying the incontrovertible truth of Vivette's words. He'd got them into this mess and somehow he needed to get them out of it. The sycamore in the jungle? The cover of *Death Planet Hub: The Avenging*? Yurts? Even Einstein as the bloody Archivist? It wasn't only that he'd been gifted with the random power to speak to plastic figures, somehow or other; judging by what he'd seen, everything he'd ever photographed had been transformed into this living, breathing, monster-ridden landscape.

He dragged his eyes back to the Oracle room. Darren walked forward and stood on the threshold, his eyes following one of the strings until it found the image he sought.

It was there between a ticket stub and a pencil sharpener. Nothing more than a mere scrap of torn photographic paper showing a posed image of the family Trott on holiday. There was his mother looking happy in a floppy hat, his father lithe and tanned before the heart attack got him, and Darren with an ice cream-smeared mouth and sand all over his hands and arms. He couldn't even remember where it had been taken.

'Is this what it's all about?' he muttered, not expecting an answer, but still half hoping that one of them might talk to him. 'Is this why there was all that striving, finding work, Dad dying, you struggling with two jobs? All so that I could make my own world and watch it being torn down again?'

His mother and father kept smiling back. They were still smiling when he heard footsteps behind him.

'I am sorry to disturb your meditations, Maker.' It was Roxana, her voice hushed and husky. 'Maeve is asking for you and Paladin is anxious we meet to discuss strategy.'

Darren nodded.

A frown creased her face. 'Excuse me for asking but are you unwell?'

'I'm fine.' The lie came easily. 'Just a little tired.'

'There will be time for rest after we have eaten,' Roxana said.

He forced a smile. 'Okay. So, where is this infirmary?' Darren followed her out into daylight.

———

THE INFIRMARY REMINDED Darren of an old-fashioned military hospital with a bank of beds, dormitory style, and women in white uniforms and headscarves ministering to the infirm. Maeve sat up, her arm still bandaged, in the middle of exchanging a little laugh with Malcolm and Bron. The ward buzzed with conversation until Darren walked in.

It was as if someone threw a switch labelled 'mute'.

His stomach shrivelled inside him.

All heads turned his way and he wished, with all his might, that a crack would open in the floor and swallow him. Not because of anything he saw—though there were many terrible injuries on display—but because of the expressions on the faces of those looking back at him. He saw hope and expectation in the main, but in more than one he saw awe. And awe was the last thing he wanted or expected at that moment.

He blinked away his desperation and concentrated on Maeve. She looked much better than the last time he'd seen her. There were bandages on her arm and high colour in her cheeks.

It could easily have been mistaken for a fever, were it not for the way that she kept glancing at Malcolm.

She turned towards Darren and smiled.

His stomach made another rapid descent.

She was glad to see him when in fact she should be livid. All of this was his fault, and he did not deserve any of her gratitude. It was wrong. All so wrong.

'How are you?' Darren asked.

'I am much improved, Maker. The healers do good work.'

Darren nodded.

'They assure me I will be ready for any expedition you decide to mount. Ready and willing.'

'Glad to hear it,' Darren said and was suddenly relieved Vivette wasn't within earshot. Come to think of it, why wasn't she? He posed the question.

'Vivette is with Una, visiting the children.' Roxana answered. She'd tied her hair back and it surrounded her face like a gilded frame.

Stop it, Darren said to himself. But her smile made it difficult to think of anything else.

'Let me show you.' She walked a few yards to a door halfway along the dormitory. Darren did his best to keep his eyes away from the split in her skirt that kept folding open to show a glimpse of thigh. His best, however, was proving to be far from good enough. He followed her to the door, drinking her in, and stepped into a cool, high-ceilinged room filled with smaller beds and cots, and felt his Roxana fuelled lust turn into a mushroom cloud of horror.

In the middle, sitting amongst a group of at least thirty children, was Vivette with Una at her side. The Obfuscator was telling them a story about three bears and a girl who liked porridge. She was doing all the voices, and her audience was lapping it up. When she saw Darren, she stopped and glared up at him, her eyes hardening.

For a moment he could not interpret her expression, but then thirty small heads turned towards him and an iron band clamped around his heart. All of the thirty small victims wore brave faces in the presence of horrendous injuries. Whatever weird anatomy and physiology applied in Moldarrenovia; it was a very different anatomy from that which Darren accepted as the norm in York. He remembered the strong smell of burning plastic and petrol in the Regurgor's venom during the attack on Maeve. These children had been subject to an identical fate.

And, as with Maeve, the venom caused dreadful injuries. Or rather, melts. One little boy in particular seemed to be most cruelly affected. Half of his face had crumpled in on itself, one eye a good two inches above the ruined other. Darren was aware of Vivette watching him with a ferocious look of condemnation. She didn't need to say anything. Her face said it all. And something compelled him to respond to that look, though he had no idea which clueless and idiotically optimistic part of his conscience pulled the trigger. But pull it did and the muscles of his face all colluded to form a group of silent words that he mouthed in her direction. '*I'll work something out.*'

Darren turned and walked away, suddenly desperate for fresh air. He, like everyone else, watched the news and its bulletins of war and famine. They were the two apocalyptic horsemen that generally turned up at six and ten every evening as compulsory guests for the newsreader and reporter. Darren saw the pictures and heard all the words, but rather like the vast majority of other people, mentally tuned them out whenever refugees or desperate victims suddenly robbed of every small possession they had by a missile or a barrel bomb, appeared. He knew there were wars in places he could only vaguely point to on a map. Knew that murder and mayhem took place every day in the name of politics or religion or money, and also knew that he had become inured by the sheer frequency of the images and newsreels so that, much to his shame, the faces and the severed limbs seemed all to have run into one, harrowing, misery-filled, blood-soaked fact of bloody life.

But when you saw it for yourself, when you were in the same room to see and smell the pain and suffering, it was very different. Very different in a way that you could never explain. Particularly when you were the root cause.

Guilt wrenched at his insides and threatened to bring up the apple and pear for inspection. He leaned against the infirmary wall and swallowed back his bile, and wondered how long it might take for someone with a flammable secret to self-immolate since '*I'll work something out,*' seemed to be branding its way through his skull and threatened to boil his brain.

When he turned around, Malcolm was waiting for him.

'Any plans?' Malcolm asked.

Darren didn't answer.

'Don't you think we should at least discuss the situation instead of you moping out here staring into a big black hole of I-haven't-got-a-clue?'

And there it was. Delivered in a throwaway remark by a frizzy-haired man in biker boots. The answer to '*I'll work something out,*' all nicely wrapped up and waiting for someone to tie on the bow.

'Yeah,' Darren said pushing off the wall. 'I do. When would be a good time, you reckon?'

'How about right now?'

## CHAPTER TWENTY-NINE

**They convened in** a low wooden building Roxana termed the 'war room'. Hand-drawn maps hung on the walls next to shields and morning stars and daggers and swords. It didn't take Darren long to realise that they were a pretty accurate reflection of sketches in his studio, but on a much bigger scale.

'So,' Malcolm said, studying the maps, 'looks like they've been busy. Where are we? More importantly where is this Ysbaed?'

Roxana did most of the talking, gesturing to the most elaborate and colourful of the maps.

'Tirerena,' she announced before walking a quarter of the way around the room to a much darker map and pointing to a red dot. 'Ysbaed launches his raids from here. It is a place we call the Barans. Three days' hard riding will get a good horseman to within crossbow range, and yet Ysbaed seems able to travel quickly to anywhere in Moldarrenovia.'

'It is part of his dark art,' Bron said, and the other girls nodded.

'Have you ever been to the Barans?' Malcolm asked.

The girls looked at Roxana. Darren got the impression that Malcolm had brought up a taboo subject.

'The men set off on an expedition, but Ysbaed knows our movements. He sees us even in the dark.'

'Some believe there are spies,' Una blurted out.

'It has nothing to do with spies. Ysbaed has powers beyond our understanding,' Bron argued.

'So with the men all gone, what's been your strategy?' Malcolm asked. Darren realised that Paladin was in his element here, viewing the situation from the lofty heights of the expert.

Squaring her shoulders, Bron replied, 'If we decide to confront Ysbaed, it will be as proud Tirerenans. We would march to face him. The rules of battle require this.'

*I hope someone has read those rules to the Regurgors and the Dankboer*, thought Darren. But Malcolm, who was quite happy to volunteer, saved him from voicing his despair.

'Nice one,' Malcolm said. 'Honour in battle, which, roughly translated from that dialect known only to despots and World War I generals as shite wrapped in tripe, means young sheep to the charnel house.'

Bron and Roxana were both looking at him as if he'd suggested that the world was, ha ha, a disc floating on the back of half a dozen rhinoceroses or a clay and plastic landscape stuck on the surface of a wooden palette.

Malcolm's stare flicked from one girl to the other, his face incredulous. 'Do you think Ysbaed respects any rules? You've seen the tactics he uses.'

'Nevertheless…'

'Nevertheless, you're all going to be wiped out unless you change the way you think,' Malcolm shook his head. 'Now, list your weapons.'

Darren listened to the run through of armaments and their tactical use, risking the occasional glance at Vivette. Though he thought he detected less outright hostility in her expression, there was no lessening of her disgust, judging by her expression, the like of which he'd last seen on the face of someone lifting a toilet seat in a student flat and realising that the cistern had broken several days before.

Darren had watched her at the infirmary. Seen her total acceptance of the children's horrifying disfigurement, allowing each of them to clamber onto her knee in turn. He'd thought her a self-absorbed, spoiled little madam; a feeling reinforced by her outburst in the Archivist's library. But since the infirmary, something seemed to have changed within her too. She'd even taken off the sofa cover that had masqueraded as a tunic and he watched her expression soften as Una picked up the garment and commented on its cut and quality.

'What do you think, Darren?'

The question jerked him back to the moment. He swung his gaze back to Malcolm and Roxana who were peering at him, keen for his opinion.

'About?'

'Deploying the cannons?'

Darren heard the question, but the words seemed to be coming to him from a long way away and in Portuguese. He knew not very much about cannons and even less about their deployment. So, with the deferral skills of a man well aware that he was ill-equipped for leadership, Darren said, 'You're the expert, Malcolm. We should do as you see fit.'

Everyone nodded. Malcolm took out a sketchpad and began sketching. Bron and Maeve, who'd joined them from her hospital bed, peered over his shoulder at what he was drawing. Roxana, however, walked over to Darren. 'Maker?'

Darren shook his head. 'Please don't call me that. My name is Darren. Would you mind?'

Roxana gave an easy shrug. 'I see that you are troubled, Darren.'

*Of course I'm bloody troubled*, thought Darren. *Who wouldn't be? The germ of an idea is poking through the cack that's been spread all over my brain, but I don't know if it's a good one or if it'll get trodden on and wither before it gets a chance to sprout.* But then he caught himself. Roxana and her people were the victims here, not him.

'My mum used to say that unless you have something to say, why waste words.'

'A wise woman.' Roxana smiled.

'Tell me,' He asked, letting his eyes stray again to the maps so that he wouldn't have to look at her when she answered, 'how many people have you lost in this war?'

'We, the Tirerenans have lost over two thousand. Our neighbours, the Audia, many more.'

Darren nodded, trying to imagine what two thousand people looked like in one place. How deep and long would a trench have to be to bury them all… 'The Audia, are they like you?'

Roxana shook her head. 'They are a small race. Cave dwellers mainly.'

'Lots of spikey hair?' Darren asked. He was thinking of George Hoblip and his girlfriend, Lulem. It brought to mind the collection of trolls he'd bought on a market stall in Birmingham and of how he'd used them in an ironic shoot about High and Mighty clothes.

Roxana said, 'They are a colourful people. They farm the steeper slopes. Shepherds like us. They took the brunt of Ysbaed's first attack.'

He risked another glance at her. She was regarding him with such reverence he thought his skin might erupt in its fierce glow.

'I would have liked to have seen this place before Ysbaed came,' he said to try and deflect her.

'I believe it will once again be beautiful. Ysbaed is a pestilence, and yet such poisons always pass, and we will be whole again. Now that you are here, I feel it.'

Darren's blood became a trickle of thick, cold molasses. Roxana spoke with the utmost conviction and yet, he, the Maker, had no idea how he was going to help her and her people. He was a stranger in a very strange land wandering blind and ignorant. Malcolm's voice broke through to give him a moment's respite from Roxana's zealous gaze.

'So, guerrilla skirmishes I think are the way forward. We go by stealth rather than brute force. Once there, we create a diversion to allow a small group to infiltrate.'

'Sounds like a plan,' Darren said.

'We are seventy fit and able. I will arrange for horses.' Roxana turned to leave.

'It'll take too long.' Darren's voice called her back.

'But how are we to get to the Barans without horses?' Maeve asked.

Darren shrugged. 'I think I know a way. The same way Ysbaed travels.'

There were gasps from the girls.

'But the Archivist has spent months attempting to find—' Una began.

'Oh, but Darren has special knowledge,' Malcolm said, cutting across her.

Darren shot him a questioning glance, but for once, there didn't seem to be much in the way of scepticism in Malcolm's neutral face. The same could not be said for Vivette.

'Yes, good old Darren. He is indeed very…special,' she piped up, her words dripping with sardonic vitriol.

Darren did his best to ignore her. 'I think there are conduits connecting all these different places.'

Of course, he didn't know for sure. How could he? Yet he was willing to bet on it, since this world was a construct of the sets he'd built.

'And where exactly would we find these conduits?' Maeve asked.

'Ah,' Darren said, 'that's the tricky bit. Haven't quite worked that one out yet. I suggest we all sleep on it. I'm pretty certain that a few hours' rest would do us all some good right now.'

'Hoblip?' Malcolm asked.

Darren said nothing but he did drag up a tight smile and a shrug. That combination had got him out of all sorts of tricky spots in the past since it left the observer with the enigma of not knowing if the gesture hinted at meaningful hidden knowledge, or vacuous desperation.

Malcolm nodded, but out of the corner of his eye Darren could see Vivette regarding him with outright hostility and suspicion.

'A wise suggestion,' Roxana said. 'We will eat and then rest and rise with the dawn.'

Darren smiled, relieved that they'd bought into his ideas. Respite was all that mattered. One night of sleep was all he needed to put an end to all of this.

They ate together: a spicy, rich goulash with hard black bread that tasted nutty and delicious, and reminded him again of the loaves his mother used to buy. They drank water that tasted of coconuts and was as refreshing as melted snow. The Tirerenans laid on entertainment in the form of a children's choir and a band that played traditional-looking instruments made of animal horn.

There was a dance too, where several teenage girls, fur-clad and body painted to resemble a variety of animals, cavorted around the Archivist, who seemed to be enjoying himself quite a lot. The dance appeared to be a variation on musical chairs, only with drums as background music and with a pole that the animals had to touch in lieu of a chair. Last one to the pole dropped out. The winner, a stunning beauty, faithfully mocked up to look like a cheetah—complete with spots and a tail—ended up with a hug from the delighted Archivist.

Darren, caught up in the moment, clapping along with the rest of them, couldn't resist leaning across to Roxana and nodding towards the unlikely pairing.

'I hope he's not trying to pull a fast one, there,' he said.

Roxana blinked at him. 'All of the dancers are his daughters,' she replied.

Darren choked on his coconut water and spluttered, 'Oh…I didn't mean…I wasn't implying…'

Roxana frowned for all of two seconds and then laughed. It was a great laugh, slow and deep. One that began somewhere low down in her throat and emerged like a gently mewling donkey, not harsh, more a jenny's lullaby to its foal than a bray. And it soon became wholly uncontrollable. She dabbed at tear-filled eyes, her face contorting as she tried and failed several times to speak.

'They are not…' she said, corpsing and pointing a fork at Darren. She corpsed again, curling up on her seat, almost losing her plate in the convulsive giggling.

Darren watched with bemused delight as his faux-pas found a target, even if that target wasn't exactly a bullseye, or even on the board. The Tirerenans didn't do puns but they did do irony. At least his humour was a hit with Roxana. Which was a lot more than could be said when it came to…

*Amanda.*

He hadn't given her much thought since they'd arrived. But she was there now, in his head, scowling, disapproving of…well, everything.

Despite the laughter and the joy of the celebration, from that moment on, Darren found it difficult to relax. He nodded and clapped politely, but he was relieved when Roxana, mistaking his lack of enthusiasm for exhaustion, called a halt to proceedings before leaning in close.

'Forgive them, Mak…Darren. They wish only to please.'

'They've been great,' Darren said. Close up, Roxana smelled exotic and heady. Her eyes held his without flinching. He saw the flickering orange light of the fire reflected within her pupils and knew that it would be very easy to burn up in that heat.

He dragged his eyes away and made an effort to talk to the kids and shake hands with the dancers. It helped his heart slow to a mere gallop. The Tirerenans were warm and tactile. They smiled and laughed a lot.

It made him feel welcome.

It made him feel like royalty.

It made him feel like a fraud.

## CHAPTER THIRTY

**HE MANAGED to** avoid Vivette's glares as they made their way back to their yurt, not wanting to be browbeaten by any more accusations. At her suggestion, Vivette's bed had been moved across to the far side and another simple curtain hung to provide them with a little privacy. He grunted an acknowledgement of Malcolm's, 'See you at daybreak,' and lay down on his bed.

Darkness fell like a stage curtain. Almost like someone had flicked a switch to turn off the power, or turn off two lamps illuminating the sets in his studio. And then Darren thought about how the food was like the Hungarian menu he'd once used in a pastiche of a fast-food restaurant, using a sumo wrestler model to imply the consequences of gluttony. Everything in this place, every single thing he looked at, smelled, tasted, breathed or touched was all something he'd photographed.

All a part of his frivolous pursuit.

Vivette was right. It was up to him and him alone to sort it all out.

He didn't sleep. He lay awake listening to the others breathing. Finally, at 2.00am, Darren got up, grabbed a fur-lined jerkin that Roxana had given him, pulled up the tethered canvas wall of the yurt and slipped out into the night. He crept towards the stream he'd noted on the map earlier. A sickle moon threw silver light over the village, making it easy to spot the sentries. But their concern was watching for interlopers; Darren had no difficulty slipping out.

Outside the confines of the village, the going got slower and more than once he thought he saw a pair of yellow eyes looking back at him through the undergrowth. They were not human eyes, but neither was he frightened of them. Somehow, he knew that being eaten by a jaguar in the jungle was not in this script.

The streambed was narrow in parts, overhung with low branches, the stones slippery beneath his feet, but once he'd descended into the valley, it opened out into a riverbed that wound its way through the lush countryside. He could see the dark humps of hills ahead of him and after an hour of walking, the lustrous glint of a lake came into view.

When he made his sets, the lighting was all-important. Sometimes he'd need running water too. He'd learned early on that cables and pipes simply got in the way, and so he'd constructed a system of conduits attached underneath the palettes on which the sets were built in order to carry the cables and pipes he'd need. His gut told him that they must also exist in this world in some shape or form. And since the lake was the most obvious place to have pipes, it was here, by his reckoning, that he'd be most likely to find such a thing.

The water, when he reached it, was a huge expanse. He could just make out the murky silhouette of an opposite bank in the moonlight. He walked along the shoreline and, despite his depressed mood, realised that it was stunningly beautiful. What was the temperature? Twelve, or perhaps fourteen, degrees? It was very warm in his jerkin. His senses drank in the grey scale world around him, the silver-tipped waves lapping gently on the pebble beach, cicadas and the odd screech of an owl his chorus, the breeze carrying on its warm breath a hint of mysterious jasmine. It would have been very pleasant, in another life, to stroll along this shore, perhaps throw a line for a fish, light a fire and drink some cold beer. Or even bring a girl here and enjoy the night…he stopped himself right there.

He'd thought girl, not Amanda.

Okay, she was in another world, another existence: one where nail bars and boob jobs and getting completely and regularly ratarsed with a bunch of boorish louts was the norm. It was not surprising that he hadn't thought of her, was it?

God, what was the matter with him? He'd give anything not to have to do what he was contemplating doing at this very moment. Even sitting watching one of her crap TV programmes would have been better…He stopped walking and let out a huge sigh as the truth of his pathetic argument sank home. Who was he trying to kid? This place was a paradise. Walking along this lake at three in the morning beat at least seven different shades of guano out of *Shanya Todd Gets Real*.

But Moldarrenovia's attractions were not all geographical. Some of them walked and breathed and had blonde flashes in their hair and—

Stop it. This was fruit of the most forbidden kind.

He tried to push all thoughts of Roxana to the back of his mind and pressed on. It didn't matter anyway. If he didn't sort things out, none of it would matter to anybody.

It was at the very head of the lake: a yawning gap at the top of a small rise like the open mouth of some giant petrified animal. It was at least fifty feet across and as tall as it was wide—a cavernous opening in the rock that sat silent and dark. But it looked like it was full of debris. No wonder the Tirerenans had not taken it for a conduit of any kind. But a faint cool breeze wafted out from between a couple of large rocks at the very base, suggesting something else beyond. Darren squeezed through and found himself in a wide opening. It brought to mind some of the older underground stations in London when he'd taken his mum to The Smoke to see a show.

He swivelled around to look behind him. There was no sign of any pursuit. With luck, no one would miss him for another three hours. He felt in his pockets for his keys. Attached to them was a small LED fob light. He suppressed a hysterical giggle. Here he was, doing an impression of Orpheus staring into the gates of the underworld and all he had with him was an inch-long torch and a phone with no signal. Still, the phone had plenty of battery power left and it would do for a torch at a push. He switched it on, looked at the clock and laughed. Unlike his watch, the phone was linked to a satellite signal that determined its time display. And according to it, only fifteen minutes had elapsed since he and the others had left Sanjay's barbecue. Such, he concluded, were the wonders of the Summerville paradox. He shook his head to stop it from boggling, pointed the torch forwards and stepped into the pitch-blackness of the conduit.

## CHAPTER THIRTY-ONE

**THE TORCHLIGHT ILLUMINATED** the roof of the tunnel—because that was what the corrugated cable tidy had become in this simulated situation—high above.

There were glints and sparkles up there, whereas the walls were curved and grey, the floor below rough dirt. Most of the time he walked in total darkness, abandoning the phone torch, sensing that some internal gyroscope was keeping him in the middle of the way. And after a while he couldn't even feel his feet on the floor. It was more like being in sensory deprivation than a walkway. Other than a faint warm wind rippling over his body, silence was his only companion. He wasn't frightened of the dark, but he was scared of drowning in the roiling sea of self-loathing in which his mind was marinating. By dint of human nature, his logic circuits swirled the available information around in a sieve of existentialism, threw away the dirty water and picked out the one remaining nugget.

'Why me?'

He thought of accidents he'd had when he was a child. The day he'd come off his bike and hit his head on a fence post. Of possible bouts of illness that might, in truth, have been encephalitic infections that banjaxed his brain. He wondered if his mother and father had in fact been aliens and this current existence was a natural part of his rite of passage into adulthood on Borhantor 7. A bit like Hamar cow jumping, or your first pint of Stella Artois with a Jägerbomb. But each new idea that he held up as a key to unlock the truth would not fit—no matter how hard he tried.

Oh, there were reasons enough to play the 'Why me?' game many times throughout his young life. But he'd never *wallowed* like this before. Previously either someone had surreptitiously fed him stoicism pills, or he'd had the sense to know that there were no answers to any of this.

Matt Danmor had come closest with the suggestion that he was just a genetic quirk, or someone with an extra knob of tissue on his temporal lobe with a little arrow pointing to it, labelled *Freak*.

Fate had dealt the lousy cards. Nothing to do but play them.

His mother had helped at the start. Kind and supportive, she'd been with him during the whole of the Dolly Darren phase, helping him through the batteries of psychological tests they'd put him through. And in the aftermath of his dad's death, she'd been a rock.

Later, when the tables were turned and his insistence on accompanying her to every hospital visit ate into his own school attendance, costing him exams and jobs, there'd been no remorse. Sanjay had been a brick too, copying school notes and helping out with homework. Not one self-pitying thought had entered Darren's head throughout it all. Not even when everyone else in his year went off to college and he spent his days at home caring for his mother, armed only with an eclectic smattering of poor qualifications that bore no relationship to his intelligence or potential, and were about as useful as a PVC umbrella against a Regurgor's spit.

Part-time jobs with no prospects had been his lot until he met Amanda at a pub and she'd listened to his story with real interest. Well at least as much interest as three Baileys and Sambucas —colloquially termed a Slippery Nipple—would allow. From there, Harry Cray wangled him a spot in Logistics at Dobson and Crank's, and before you could say, 'claws' and 'in', he was part of someone else's plan.

Amanda's plan.

Hardly the blazing trail he, or his mother, had wanted. But a job and a girlfriend, nevertheless.

Throughout it all, his hobby had been a crutch. And in the secret locked cupboard of his heart, where his innermost hopes and desires were filed and stored, he knew that not going away to university and missing out on boozy Saturday nights with his adolescent mates were no obstacle to his dreams. His art was the canvas of his imagination. One day, he would fill that canvas with words to flesh out the photographs. He wanted to write books about strange places and stranger occurrences and had contented himself with knowing that all he needed for that was time and patience and a pencil and paper.

He'd scribbled down some thoughts already, but they were for his eyes only. It would take time, he knew, to develop his voice and craft. And to that end, he looked on everything that happened as fuel for his imagination. Even dull dreary days at Dobson and Crank's would somehow, he told himself, come in useful—though his memoir of Logistics would, if he ever wrote it, be a very short one, and fashionably miserable to boot.

But a book based on several Krudian days spent in Moldarrenovia? Now that was a different proposition altogether.

Yet in the conduit, his hopes and dreams seemed to belong to someone else. This was a different reality. And here, the large boulder of self-doubt he was burdened to carry pressed down on him incessantly. In his relatively short life, he'd already shouldered enough responsibility to backfill a crater the size of the Aitken basin. But this ludicrous position of being a whole world's creator was an unasked-for googly. And so, the question kept hammering away like a demented woodpecker at a sore point somewhere behind his eyes.

Why me?

He walked for hours, neither hungry nor thirsty. There was only the blackness, the soft breeze, and his tumbling, rolling, unresolvable thoughts.

Amanda popped up quite often, her angular, unsmiling face full of its usual derision and disapproval, tutting and telling him to grow up. But disconcertingly, Amanda did not appear as often as someone else did. Someone with short hair and blue eyes, who looked delectable in a sarong.

He told himself not to be stupid, that he'd known her no longer than a day. It was imbecilic of him to even begin to think of her in any way other than the leader of a disaffected people desperately clinging onto the idea that he was their salvation. It would be a folly of enormous proportion to think anything else. And yet his mind would not give up on her, no matter how often he led it to a mental cold shower. With no distractions in the void, and with only his soft footfalls providing timpani, his imagination did a very good job indeed of ignoring his warnings. Especially when it came to full colour reconstructions of her in said sarong, or worse, without it.

His memory of her in a bikini stemmed from when she'd been a six-inch tall plastic model that he'd photographed for his feminist anti-war set, but Darren's mind found no trouble in putting the flesh Roxana and the plastic model together and coming up with something that made him gasp in the darkness.

And then, to cap it all, there was Una saying that Roxana volunteered in the adult pleasuring tutorial sessions. That set his knees quivering. What, he wondered, did she specialise in? Girls or boys? Did she read them stories in that smoky voice of hers? Draw naughty diagrams on a board? Or did she supervise practicals? Darren's imagination, untroubled by external stimuli in the solitude of the tunnel, went into overtime on double pay. He fervently hoped it was the practical because she looked more than capable of being 'hands on'…

Alone in the darkness, Darren groaned.

The light, when he saw it, was a mere pinprick. And for several minutes he thought it was some trick his mind was playing on him. When it didn't fade and grew bigger, changing from a dot to the size of a five pence piece, he knew it was real. At least, Moldarrenovian real. He glanced at his phone. Twelve minutes had passed since he'd entered the conduit. That equated to twelve hours of solid walking in Moldarrenovia. Yet he did not feel in the slightest bit tired.

Bloody good, this Krudian anomaly stuff.

About a quarter of a mile from the mouth of the tunnel, the

floor started to rise. It was strange to see detail begin to appear again. What it showed him was bright daylight and beyond it, moorland and fell. He was high up. High enough to look down onto the rolling landscape below with its lakes and rivers, mountains and villages. There was no jungle here. Impossible though it seemed, it appeared he'd travelled to a different place in another country. But then, that had been his aim. A recce. So that he could go back to Roxana and the others, tell her that he was right about the conduit, even steal a march on the spy. It would be worth it just to see that smile and the light in her eyes. But the truth was, after returning to the Tirerenans in triumph, there was no plan, except to hope that Malcolm had some weapons and ideas up his sleeve, or even in a battered, half-buried crate.

Darren stepped out from the tunnel onto the high flat moor, turning a quick 360. A few miles away, behind the mouth of the conduit, he saw a town. It sat hunched, dark and brooding, with buildings of stained brick, and factories with towers like spears thrusting up into a milky sky. Darren stared and tried to think. It looked so familiar. And then it came to him. How could it be anything else? After all he was from Yorkshire: a county well known for its dark industrial heritage. Brooding satanic mills were a staple for any self-respecting photographer and Darren had snapped dozens of them. But where was his bow of burning bloody gold with the added modification of titanium-strengthened poison-tipped arrows when he most needed it?

Because he knew too, that this is where he would find Ysbaed.

Where else?

In confirmation of his instincts, a stone the size of a cricket ball fizzed two feet over his head to thud into soft grass three yards away. He looked up and saw a lone Dankboer standing on the cliff top above the escarpment to his left.

Probably a scout.

Within seconds, a dozen identical figures joined the one. He counted twelve then twenty, and then thirty before giving up. Not just a scout then, more a Scout *troop*. But one that had not stood in a circle that morning and promised to do their duty to God and queen, nor, he suspected, to help other people. Two very long-range slingshots landed nearby, the second whistling past his left ear. Obviously, their ballistic proficiency badge was a work in progress, but it was an exercise too close for Darren's comfort. He ducked back into the cool dark entrance of the conduit, retreated fifty yards and waited. He saw the same squat Dankboer silhouettes appear in the mouth of the tunnel. But no one entered. A few speculative missiles were lobbed inside, but they ricocheted harmlessly off the walls with an echoing clatter. It was obvious that his sentinels were happy to keep him, as they would a rat, trapped. They were happy to wait.

But for what?

Darren sheltered in the conduit, trying to work out some way of getting past the sentinels. Now that he was here, he wanted to find out what he could, rather than start the long journey back with nothing more than a tantalising glimpse of what lay ahead. What he needed was some sort of major distraction. But after an hour of mulling over every single way he could think of to get past the guard, something happened that made him realise how naive he'd been to assume that they'd been content to drive him back into the tunnel and await *his* next move. The real reason for their siege activities lumbered into view at the tunnel mouth.

# CHAPTER THIRTY-TWO

**AFTER THE INITIAL** SHOCK, Darren actually smiled and indulged himself with a little shake of the head. Whoever wrote this script had done their homework and carefully prepared a file entitled *Appropriate Monsters for Each Occasion*. The fact that he, Darren, had provided the cast was something he decided could wait until he had time to invite that inconvenient little truth out to lunch for a cosy chat over a nice beer before he took it outside and beat the living daylights out of it. And probably the dead daylights, too.

It was reptilian, of that there was no doubt. One with a long lizard-like body and several scaly spines running Mohican-style along the centre of its back. The only thing that made it not an actual dragon was its lack of wings. In all other respects it did indeed look very ophidian. It stood in the tunnel entrance flicking out a long, forked, lurid yellow tongue before scrabbling forwards on four legs in an alarming burst of speed.

Darren's stomach lurched, yet he didn't move. His legs had become piles of frozen ice driven yards into the ground.

The reptile/dragon kept coming. After ten yards it made a noise like a motorbike with a sore throat and sent a gout of red fire exploding into the conduit. Heat soared towards Darren. His legs thawed enough for him to dive face down to the ground. The thing's breath, redolent of petrol and tar, blew over him in a searing wave. With a roar, the thing lumbered forward again, its heavy head swinging from side to side as it trotted.

Darren scrambled up, turned and sprinted along the conduit, back into the darkness. Behind him he could hear loud, excited yells from the Dankboer as they followed their living flamethrower into the tunnel.

What had he been thinking, showing himself like that, allowing the Dankboer to call up the scaly cavalry? The behemoth's engine roared once more, and a fresh tongue of flame jetted into the conduit. Darren felt his back get very warm and smelled singed hair. He glanced behind him. The reptile's legs were carrying it along the conduit at a faster pace than Darren could run. He'd been taken by surprise and was now going to fry in this tunnel like a piece of Mrs. Roopal's tandoori lamb. He knew he couldn't outrun it. The thing was far too quick.

He threw back another wide-eyed, over-the-shoulder glance. It was now less than thirty yards away and even if it didn't catch him, its next flamethrower burst would surely turn him into instant kebab. Sprinting for his life, he heard its engine revving up again and braced himself for…

'Get down!' a voice, male and familiar, yelled from out of the darkness up ahead.

Darren reacted and dived to the floor. Something powerful distorted the air above his head and the behemoth's revving ceased. There were three seconds of utter silence before a huge WHUMP rent the air and bits of black and yellow dragon rained down all around him, slapping the walls and floor, the air suddenly full of the smell of fireworks.

He pushed up from the floor. Yes, all his limbs were intact. The shirt had not been burnt off his back. He wasn't a kebab.

'Darren, are you all right?' Vivette was kneeling at his side.

He got up on one knee and looked into her face. Concern and disapproval in equal measure stared back at him.

'Yeah, fine.'

'That was bloody close,' Malcolm said.

Darren, gasping from his efforts, looked up and saw Malcolm grinning. He'd never felt so glad to see an AC/DC T-shirt in all his life.

'But…how?'

'The girls tracked you. After what you said about the conduit, it was pretty obvious you were going to check it out. We followed.'

Darren exhaled loudly. 'I'm bloody glad you did.'

Vivette helped him to his feet. Darren looked about him. 'Where are the girls?'

'They're not with us. We told them to stay put,' Malcolm explained.

Darren nodded and the only noise for several seconds was his heavy breathing and the sound of dragon brain dripping from the ceiling.

'Are you going to tell us what your great plan was?' Vivette asked. 'You know, the one involving you sneaking out of the tent in the middle of the night without telling anybody?'

Darren shrugged. Most of the behemoth was on fire. It filled the tunnel with a flickering yellow light. Reflected in it, Malcolm's unamused accusatory expression was plain to see.

'I didn't want to involve you…'

'Really?' Vivette said.

Darren winced, deflated once again by her scepticism. But he made himself speak.

'Okay, I didn't want to involve you any more than I have already.'

Vivette frowned.

'Oh, come on,' Darren said, feeling like he'd swallowed a piece of rancid humble pie. 'You were right. It's all down to me. You said so yourself. Everything. Monsters, disfigured children, whole villages without any menfolk. All down to me. And it should be *me* that sorts it all out.'

'What about us?' Malcolm said.

'What about you? You're only here because sometime, somewhere over the last two years I've taken a random snap and you're in it. I take loads in and around town. You were probably passing by and it's nothing more than sheer bad luck and trouble. But I am not asking you to do any more.'

'Seeing as you were doing so well by yourself, you mean,'

Malcolm said, watching a piece of burning dragon land with a plop a foot away from Darren's head.

'You don't understand,' Darren said, needing to explain. 'All my life I've dreamed of somewhere, some fantastic place drawn up to my specifications. I even managed to achieve a little bit of that doing what I do with my camera. But this…' Darren shook his head. 'I never meant for any of this. It's insane. People are dying and it's all because of me.'

'Finished?' Vivette said.

'Yes.' Darren said.

'Good,' Malcolm added. ''Cause I've never heard so much complete pigswill in all my life.'

Darren felt his brows furrow. 'Hang on, aren't you the one who wanted to walk out five minutes after arriving at Sanjay's barbecue?'

'Yes, I was. But that was when I thought this was all a scam. It isn't. There are people here…of a sort. And I can help them.'

Darren turned to Vivette. 'What about you?' He was astonished to see her face flush a bright pink. It looked as though she wanted to speak but Malcolm beat her too it.

'We had about four hours after dawn at the village,' he said. 'Vivette here made herself busy,' he paused and then added with a smile, 'very busy in fact'.

'How?'

Vivette shrugged. 'An accident. I was *très* interested in the material that the yurt was made of. It was reflective but sometimes, if you held it against the light in a certain way, it seemed to have a matte finish. Una was with me. She's *mucho* enthusiastic about some of the things I'd brought. She'd never seen nail varnish before, for example. So while I was inspecting the material, she was playing with my Cherry Chutney…' There was a short pause while Darren and Malcolm tried to stifle inappropriate but helpless giggles and failed. 'It's a nail varnish,' Vivette explained with an upward inflection at the end that would have given the Olympic ski jump ramp at Lillehammer a run for its money. 'And…' she added, '…it spilled.'

'Sounds enthralling,' Darren said, sending Malcolm an exasperated look as he dabbed his eyes.

'Wait for it,' Malcolm replied and flashed a knowing grin.

'Una was upset. Real lacrimosia. I told her to freak-not and that nail varnish was *très* cheap, and that it might even wipe off. The problem was, we couldn't find the piece of material.'

Darren looked from Vivette to Malcolm and back again. 'Am I missing something here?'

'Only the fact that painting nail varnish on the yurt material turned it into what I can best describe as chameleonic.'

'It turned the tent material into a lizard with eyes on the side of its head?' Darren frowned.

Vivette rolled her eyes. 'What can chameleons do? And please don't say extend their tongues two feet in front of them.' She sent Malcolm a look with 'old hat' stamped all over it.

Darren thought. He hated trick questions. 'Aren't they supposed to change colour to suit their background?'

'Exactly. So can certain types of octopus. It was supercamouflageristic. The material took on the exact same colouring and markings of the table we were working at.'

'And the good news is that one tiny drop of nail varnish can treat a whole yurt's worth of material,' Malcolm said, his features glimmering a coppery gold in the flickering light of the burning dragon.

'So I made them some camouflage suits,' Vivette went on. 'I would have made a lot more only Rambo here said we had to leave and come looking for you.'

Darren was staring at her, nodding. 'The Obfuscator. It all makes sense now.'

Malcolm grinned. 'Then we found this tunnel and kept on walking. We saw the flames and…'

'Don't. I know what happened after that. I was in that scene, remember?' *And it was almost a bloody deleted scene*, he thought, but wisely didn't say anything. Instead, he tried swallowing, but his spit tasted of barbecued lizard, and he hawked it back up and deposited it on the floor.

'*Decorus maximus*,' Vivette commented, impersonating someone who'd found something the dog had once eaten under its bed. 'All that's left for you to do now is to pick your nose and scratch your bum and you'll have a hattrick. It's so disgusting being surrounded by men.'

Darren sighed, deflecting the innuendo grenade. 'I was never very partial to the taste of charred Gila monster, if you don't mind. I mean, which bit of me almost being bloody rotisseried did you miss?'

'All your own fault, if you ask me,' Vivette said folding her arms.

'Well, I didn't ask you, so—'

'Look, will you two stop arguing for two minutes and listen to what I have to say so that we can execute Plan B—'

A noise from somewhere in the tunnel ahead made Malcolm pick up the sonic gun and peer into the darkness.

'Plan B?' Darren could not have sounded more nonplussed if he'd been made to add a zero to a zero.

'We go back, make the girls about a hundred suits, attack Ysbaed's lair, grab the votives, go home,' Malcolm explained.

Darren looked at them both. The air was still full of the pungent smell of oil and burning flesh. But gone were the miserable, recalcitrant gamer and the flaky, whining designer. In front of him now stood two motivated, indignant, righteous individuals. Darren felt a sudden pang of gratitude and yes…almost affection. But more than anything he felt an expanding sense of relief that he no longer had to do this all on his own.

'Okay,' he said.

'Right, well—' Malcolm's words were cut off by a scream. As one, the three of them turned to look at the entrance to the tunnel and a chilling sight. Silhouetted against the milky sky was a figure.

'Is that a…' Vivette's question hung in a dense silence, swaying drunkenly like a squeaky gibbet on a crossroads: everyone knowing what it contained but no one rushing to confront it.

The figure in silhouette was wearing a white apron—identical to the ones worn by the nurses in the hospital back at the village. A moment later, the lone figure was joined by several others, many of them smaller in stature, some of them limping.

'Hostages.' The word seemed to ooze out from Malcolm's clamped together teeth.

And, just for good measure, to ensure that they were in no doubt as to the implications of what they were being shown, they heard the sickening, bubbling bray that signaled the presence of Regurgors.

They ran, negotiating the lumps of steaming dragon flesh and pools of flickering gore. Once past the lizard the activity at the tunnel mouth became more obvious. Three nurses and half a dozen damaged children stood huddled together, shivering at the mouth of the tunnel. Behind them, a Regurgor, wearing a heavy leather harness on its head, was stationed at the top of a hillock. Four Dankboer held the harness attached to a large steel bit between the monster's teeth.

'No,' Darren moaned and sprinted forward. But his sudden appearance out of the darkness of the tunnel mouth spooked the Regurgor. It reared back, yanking its head up and dislodging the leather strap from one of the Dankboer handler's hands. The bit fell forward and the Dankboer scrambled frantically to recapture the reins. But the Regurgor, spotting an opportunity, started hawking up its foul venom.

The other three Dankboer were pulling hard to try and keep it controlled, but without the fourth anchor, their yanking succeeded only in making its head tilt at a weird angle. With an expulsive strike, the Regurgor spat. Mercifully, from the hostages' viewpoint, the fluid emerged at a steep and acute angle, down towards the ground and well away from the tunnel mouth. But for the hapless Dankboer handler scrabbling for the flailing tether, there was no such luck, and it took a bullseye strike.

The effect was instant. Covered from head to foot in Regurgor spit, it screamed. Darren skidded to a halt, unable to tear his eyes away from what he was seeing. The Dankboer flesh began to melt in seconds and run like melted wax down over its leather tunic. He saw with sickening clarity that the head was now a stream of ochre, running like a boiled over pan of beetroot. Shuddering, the figure fell, its screams cut off as the flesh melted away, its torso crumpling as the acid ate through the limbs.

From the gathered ranks of Dankboer guards above came a peal of incongruous laughter. Obviously, they considered what had just happened a sign of incompetence, rather than tragedy. One of them ran forward and picked up the fourth tether and soon, the Regurgor was back under control.

'Bastards. Bastards!' Malcolm yelled, bursting through into daylight, not even attempting to find cover. He brought the cannon up to his chest, but the Regurgor retreated to behind the hillock from where it brayed its protests.

Vivette emerged a few seconds later, panting and red in the face. 'What did I miss?' she demanded. 'Where's that thing?'

But when Darren turned back towards the hostages, the reason for the Regurgor's initial presence and now its retreat, was starkly obvious. When he, Vivette and Malcolm emerged, Dankboer had run in to make a line across the tunnel's mouth. Three of them had also moved forward to the nurses and were holding knives to their throats.

Darren cursed. They'd been suckered out like mice offered a piece of Camembert.

'What the hell is this?' Malcolm said.

'A trap,' Darren said. 'A lure…'

Before he could say anything else, a man stepped out from within the ranks and addressed them.

'Excuse my incompetent, but obliging, minions,' the man said. 'Still, as a demonstration of my capabilities, it could not have been better staged, don't you agree?'

Darren recognised the full lips and cruel mouth instantly.

Ysbaed grinned.

## CHAPTER THIRTY-THREE

'**AND PLEASE, stay** precisely where you are and lower your weapons,' Ysbaed continued, his voice devoid of emotion.

'Who the hell are you?' Malcolm shouted.

'That's him,' Darren said, his gaze boring into the spy. 'That's Ysbaed.'

'Who, or indeed, *what* I am is irrelevant. What is important for you to know at this moment is that if you make any attempt to fight or resist, my imbecilic but enthusiastic colleagues will dispatch the nurses…first.'

The damaged children, shivering in front of the ranks of Dankboer, whimpered.

'What do you want?' Darren asked.

'Ah, that is a question I often ask myself…' Ysbaed smiled, and Darren saw Vivette flinch next to him. '…because to want something implies that there is a desire that can be satisfied. Unfortunately, I have long ago concluded that my particular appetite is seldom, if ever satiated.'

He was dressed in the clothes he'd worn when Darren last photographed him as the spy; plain black trousers and shirt, but he'd added a black bearskin cloak for effect, the arms of which still bore six-inch long claws. His voice was dungeon deep and devoid of any accent.

'Let them go,' Vivette said, in a voice shrill enough to claim

Ysbaed's attention, though all it earned was a contemptuous glance.

'What I do depends on you,' he replied, evenly.

'What is it you want from us?' Malcolm asked.

'For now, cooperation,' Ysbaed said. His tone was light and non-threatening. Instead Darren heard an amused detachment that was somehow much more unsettling. 'Leave your weapons on the ground. Lie face down.'

They did as they were told. Half a dozen Dankboer moved forwards to yank their hands behind their backs and tie them together.

'Good. Now.' Ysbaed stepped forward and began walking back and forth in front of Darren, who, still face down, strained to follow his footsteps. 'Though my army's weapons may not be fatal when applied to you, they have no such limitations with regard to the indigenous population. Any attempt at violence will be met with the painful death of these *cattle*.' He nodded towards the captives. Darren had no doubt that he meant it. A moment later he was yanked roughly to his feet and made to march, flanked on both sides by a line of Dankboer.

To begin with it was easy, flat going along a trail that took them across the spine of the hills and eventually to the high moorland. But there the wind was a constant force that made every step an effort.

*No wonder the sodding trees look like they've been trodden on*, thought Darren, blinking away the gale-induced tears that were streaming down his face. *Why couldn't Ysbaed have chosen something subtropical rather than this blasted heath?* It was so blasted that it didn't even have any blasted sheep or cows on it. In fact, there'd be more shelter on the dark side of the blasted moon.

Eventually they descended and the moor gave way to walled-off fields with broken gates and tumbledown walls. The few farmhouses they passed were empty shells. Soon they came in sight of a town, but there was little sign of habitation here either. The streets they walked along echoed to their footfalls. The houses were cramped and dark, their stone walls stained with soot and grime.

Deeper and deeper into the bowels of the town they trudged.

The only evidence of any occupation behind the grimy facades came in the form of an occasional slammed door, or a twitching curtain in one of the gloomy houses.

'Looks like we missed the ticker tape parade,' Darren muttered.

'And the marching bands,' added Malcolm.

Darren filled in the blanks without difficulty. The occupants of this town had long ago learned to hide themselves for fear of attack or worse. And for worse read being *taken*. Because being *taken* implied a destination and Darren would bet a month's Dobson and Crank's wages that it was a destination from which not many returned. Fear was what drifted up from the gaps between the cobbles; terror was what tainted the thin smoke drifting up from every chimneypot.

They marched for another thirty minutes, crested a rise and came to a halt on top of a hill. The building that loomed in front of them was massive; a huge soot-stained factory under a vast saw tooth roof, its enormous brick edifice punctuated by six floors of dark and grimy windows. Above, two gigantic brick stacks extended skywards from the roofs, both belching thick sooty smoke into the heavens.

If there'd been a competition for darkest and most satanic mill, this one would have finished in the audience's top three and was probably a shoe in for the judges' first prize.

Ysbaed turned to his captives and waved an arm, raised an eyebrow and said, 'Welcome all. Welcome to my humble abode.'

A shudder warped through Darren with such force that he lost his balance and took a step to steady himself. Lack of food and water after his long trek through the conduit perhaps? Or the thought of having to enter this godforsaken building? His rational brain told him it was hunger, yet his every instinct zinged with piano wire edginess. It was as if someone was tugging on the anchor chain of his soul. And if he felt like this, he could not imagine what the captives must be experiencing. He threw them a glance and saw desperation and helplessness etched into every drained, grey face.

They knew that this was journey's end.

The Dankboer pushed and prodded and paid particular attention to the children being herded towards the massive doors of the factory. They seemed to be taking great pleasure in taunting, leaning in close to make their already ugly faces even uglier by baring teeth and making gestures meant to terrorise, subdue, and generally induce maximum misery. Darren watched with growing anger before he felt someone jab him in the back and he was shoved unceremoniously towards the doors.

They entered a huge space that once would have been full of machinery for the weaving industry. Now, fires roared in several large pits, the smoke billowing upwards to be sucked out through the massive stacks. Darren saw a cart trundling in from the rear of the factory. It overflowed with books. Ragged groups of filthy people were unloading the carts to feed the fires.

Ysbaed stood on a raised dais behind a lectern, grinning his approval.

'What are you burning?' Darren demanded as he and the others were herded in front of Ysbaed.

'Knowledge. That most dangerous of properties,' Ysbaed said.

'Why?'

'We burn four hundred and fifty-one books every day.' He stood in front of the trio, his mouth parted in a gloating smile.

'Four hundred and fifty-one?' Malcolm asked.

'He's trying to be clever,' Darren explained mirthlessly. 'Bradbury's classic, *Fahrenheit 451*. It's the temperature at which paper spontaneously combusts.' Ysbaed nodded.

'And that is why we need to burn three hundred and twenty of these Tirerenan abominations,' Ysbaed offered up his mad logic. 'The melting point of polyvinyl chloride.'

A cold sickness gripped Darren. 'Let them go,' he said, watching the group of terrified Tirerenans huddling together.

'No,' Ysbaed said.

'What do you want with them?' Malcolm asked through his teeth.

Ysbaed let out a dismissive laugh, letting everyone know that the reply to Malcolm's question was so obvious as to be hardly worth the effort of answering. 'To see them melt and bleed. To hear them scream. To inhale the heady aroma of burning Tirerenan.'

'What is wrong with you?' Vivette asked shrilly.

Ysbaed tilted his head in contemplation. He pondered for a moment and then shrugged, his black eyes gazing out over the hellish scene. He seemed completely at ease.

'I am what I am. Would you ask a rattlesnake what it is? Or a rabid dog?' He stepped forward and looked without blinking into Vivette's face. She defied his stare for several seconds, but then looked away.

Ysbaed turned his gaze on Malcolm. 'What I want from you are answers. Why are you here?'

'To see you rot,' Malcolm said.

Ysbaed smiled and an icy hand closed around Darren's heart. There was something terribly familiar about that smile. Imperiousness was not an attractive trait, but hardly surprising in a demonic despot. Yet what drained the blood out of Darren's face was the thought that he'd seen that exact look in Amanda's face the day he'd tried to explain about…all of this.

'Brave words,' breathed Ysbaed. 'We'll see precisely how brave when the entertainment begins.' He turned back to Vivette. 'And you? I am curious about you, feckless seamstress. How can *you* be a match for *me*?'

'Your *visage* my *derrière*,' Vivette said.

Darren threw her an open-mouthed glare tinged with admiration. She shrugged. 'Best I could come up with *dans le* circumstances.'

Darren nodded. If ever he needed to hear anyone say, 'Your *visage* my *derrière*,' anywhere other than a school yard, it was here and now. *You'll do*, Darren thought, *even if you do dress like a barber's pole*.

'And then there is this *Maker* I have heard so much about.' Ysbaed turned to the crowd. 'Behold,' he jeered. 'Tethered like an animal awaiting slaughter. And what is it to be? The fire? Or something a little more exotic?'

'I know what your power is, Ysbaed. I know about the votives,' Darren said.

'Ah, is it at this point that I am supposed to cower at your superior knowledge? To feel afraid? I, who have lived longer than you or your kind have existed?' He smiled again and it was awful to behold. 'But I must not seem churlish. After all, it is you that has given me my freedom.'

'You can't stay here. I won't let you,' Darren said.

'But you cannot stop me. You let the genie out of the bottle, Dolly Darren, but even if you could…Even if your puny friends could help you, it is far too late. Here the votives have taken on a new existence. Even more powerful than in your pathetic little world. Look.'

Ysbaed stepped back. Behind him, massive doors rolled back, pushed by a crew of some twenty straining Dankboer. Darren turned to stare into a room the size of a hangar. Three huge items hung suspended in mid-air, each surrounded by colourful pulsing light. He stepped forward in awe to look at the nearest: a long shaft of bone sharpened at one end, the other crenelated and bulbous. The thing was huge, at least forty feet long and buzzing with an arcane power. The doors continued trundling open to reveal a glistening coiled snakeskin, now returned to its magnificent green and black pattern. And still the doors rolled until they reached the end of their travel and the final votive came into view: a glittering multifaceted stone gleaming and sparkling in a golden halo of light. It exuded power, like the moon to the tides.

With a drowning heart, Darren knew that Ysbaed had been right to gloat. They'd found the votives. But the harsh truth was that even if they were in a position to do anything, it would be impossible to move them without cranes or heavy plant. Each one must weigh tens of tons. Whatever plan Darren harboured about somehow removing them died with the final rumbling clank of the doors coming to rest.

'And now some entertainment, I think.' Ysbaed raised his right hand. A phalanx of Dankboer moved in response. They drove into the terrified huddle of captives and pulled out a young girl. She could not have been more than nine or ten, dark-haired, limbs stick-thin. Even from thirty yards away Darren could see the abject terror in her face. The screams and pleas of the others were met with jeering blows from the studded clubs the Dankboer carried in straps around their shoulders. They dragged the girl to the biggest of the open fires, goading her forward with sharp spears, making no attempt at being gentle about it.

# CHAPTER THIRTY-FOUR

Darren saw Malcolm strain to break free, wrenching ineffectually at the bonds around his hands. He was driven to his knees by a blow to his back. And then, from within the group of captives a single shout emerged.

'Hewar!'

The effect it had on the girl was instant. She stopped struggling. Her sudden stillness threw the Dankboer and they stepped back to leave the girl standing alone and calm a few yards from the fire. Darren threw Vivette a questioning glance.

'It's their word. It means pride and bravery,' Vivette answered, her voice tremulous.

Darren's hammering heart cantered up to his epiglottis. He swallowed it back with difficulty. 'But she's just a kid,' he said.

Malcolm shook his head.

'Stop it,' Darren turned to Ysbaed. 'Stop this.'

'Why?'

'It's me. It's me that you want. Burn me. Let her go.'

'So noble,' mocked Ysbaed. 'But Maker, it is you that has made all of this here for me to play with. Why would I want to damage you?'

Darren heard a scream begin from somewhere deep inside his own head and reverberate around the caverns of his skull.

Ysbaed was evil; there was no doubt about that. Skin you alive as soon as look at you, evil. There was no point appealing to a better nature because what nature there was in Ysbaed was wild and unpredictable, and capable only of mass destruction. There was no calm after the storm because the storm never ended. Darren had seen the same unfocussed glimmer in some people's eyes, well in two people's eyes if he really put his mind to it. Both Lou and Harry Cray shared that exact same thousand-yard glare where the glassy eyes were the only things separating you from the tornado behind them. Of course, with the Crays there was motive and consequences to consider and, Darren realised, that made them a thousand times worse—because with both motive and consequences came *choice*. Ysbaed, on the other hand, had no choice because he was a thing, and things had all the decency of an atomic warhead.

The child moved toward the fire. She was close enough for Darren to see the tears running down her face. Some fresh wailing emanated from the crowd. Then came the word 'HEWAR!' a second time, this one louder and firmer. The crowd fell silent.

Darren couldn't breathe, couldn't swallow, couldn't drag his eyes away from the girl. These people were incredible, magnificent, undeserving of any of this.

'Ready for some barbecued plastic?' Ysbaed asked, his tone Sunday lunchtime airy.

He raised his arms and four Dankboer stepped forward and grabbed the girl by her arms. She offered no resistance. Darren shut his eyes. He could not bear to watch. But before Ysbaed could give the order to cast the girl into the fire, another voice broke into the horror-filled anticipation that cast a pall of silence over the factory. A single loud, shouted, order.

'DOWN!'

Darren's eyes snapped open. He saw the young girl fall to her knees, head bowed. Elsewhere, the Tirerenans all did the same. A second later came the high-pitched whine and sucking noise of sonic cannon.

There must have been a thousand Dankboer inside the

factory. Ten seconds later, they were Dankboer jam, coating the inside of the roof and the walls in a sticky, gory mess. Darren swivelled his eyes towards Ysbaed, saw his face contort with fury. He looked down and spat, 'So you want to play dirty, Maker?'

With desperate fury, Ysbaed depressed levers on the raised lectern-like structure before him and instantly, the huge gates of the votive room began to trundle shut. At the same time, other gates were opening at the other end of the factory floor. Darren heard the beasts before he saw them. At least half a dozen Regurgors and the fire-breathing lizards responding to the noise of their cage doors opening with monstrous screams and trumpets of their own.

Roaring and clawing the earth, they shouldered their way through the barely open gates, zeroing in on the still tethered group of Tirerenans. But Darren's eye caught something else. There was a movement against the walls. He looked hard but saw nothing until…yes, there *was* movement of sorts, as if a large droplet of water was running horizontally, distorting the wall behind it. Moving between Darren's line of sight and the brick wall of the factory. And now that his eyes knew what to look for, he counted four blurring, moving distortions that were gone the moment his retinas registered them. But then, from the point at which he had last seen the blur, three sonic cannons appeared out of the smoky air.

The beasts didn't stand a chance. They didn't even have time to hawk up their disgusting acid phlegm or vomit out their fire before they started to shudder. Within seconds, yet more Regurgor and lizard innards joined the Dankboer gore running down the walls.

Darren heard Ysbaed gasp, but not because of what he'd recently witnessed. The spy was grappling with something, some invisible force that was making him partake in a sort of wild dance. For a moment it looked like he might succumb to the zephyr that he battled, and he fell to his knees. But then he threw Darren one final sneering look and became a column of yellow smoke that seeped into a crack in the stone floor and was gone.

From somewhere a female voice protested with a word that

he was not familiar with but could grasp the meaning of nonetheless. And then, to his utter astonishment, he saw Roxana's face appear from behind the mask she peeled off her head. From her neck down all he could see was the same water droplet effect of distortion on her lower body. Only this one was very much Roxana-shaped.

'What the…'

Roxana shot him a mirthless smile. Darren knew his mouth was gaping open, but he was helpless to stop it.

'The Paladin has taught us well, Darren. We are guerinjas.'

'No. It's either guerrillas or ninjas,' Malcolm corrected her, 'not guerinjas.'

'Let them be guerinjas if they bloody well want,' Vivette glared at Malcolm. 'Judging by what they just did, I see no one arguing with them.'

Malcolm shrugged and nodded. 'Fair point.'

Darren only half heard. He was too busy being flabbergasted. Roxana continued peeling the shimmering droplet off to reveal her combat fatigues beneath.

'The Obfuscator is skilled in legerdemain, is she not?'

Darren looked at Vivette.

'I did try and explain to you,' she said, unable to hide the grin. 'Turned out a tad better than I expected, I admit.'

Near the captives, three more heads appeared out of thin air. Maeve, Una, and Bron immediately began releasing prisoners. Roxana took out a machete and proceeded to cut Darren's, Malcolm's, and Vivette's bonds.

'You almost had Ysbaed,' Darren said, massaging his wrist.

Roxana's expression hardened. 'I know. But he is a trickster.'

'Wonder where he went?' said Vivette, voicing all their thoughts.

Darren swung around. The doors to the votive room were trundling shut with gathering speed. Through them, he saw a wisp of yellow smoke harden into a shape.

'I think I know. Come on.' Darren put his head down and sprinted. He was vaguely aware that it had taken a large number of Dankboer to open them, yet the doors seemed to be closing under their own power and very quickly. Beyond them, in the huge room, the votives pulsed with power. Roxana matched him stride for stride, Malcolm a few paces behind with Vivette panting at the rear and crying, 'Wait for me, wait for me!'

But they could not wait. The gap was narrowing by the second. When they were within a yard or two, Darren slowed to let Roxana through and then threw himself inside the huge room. He heard Malcolm's grunt of protest as he, too, squeezed through to collapse onto the floor, gasping for breath as the doors shut with a reverberating clang, shutting out Vivette and her cry of protest. And then there was nothing but a surreal silence into which Darren cast an enveloping glance around the room.

'Wow,' Malcolm said, staring up at the glistening serpent's skin. 'Wonder what sort of snake that belonged to?'

'No thanks,' Darren said, shivering. Now that that he was standing next to them, the votives were even bigger than he'd estimated. Reality crashed in with a vengeance. There was absolutely no way they were going to be able to transport these anywhere.

'You cannot touch them. Cannot destroy them. Cannot steal them.' Ysbaed's mocking voice echoed in the huge chamber.

Darren looked around, but there was no sign of the spy. His voice seemed to come from everywhere and nowhere at the same time.

'You brought them here and now they are a part of the fabric of this world. Your pretty little Tirerenans can play soldier until I melt every last one of them. It will be a highly pleasurable diversion in this tedious immortality. Of course, they cannot touch me because I am smoke and wind and something much, much more. Let us see how much you like your world, Darren.'

There was a sudden loud crack above and they looked up to see plaster and dust descending down from where a jagged gash had appeared in the ceiling. Through it, Darren could see the milky sky fade into a dense black dotted with small glittering lights. His ears popped and there was a hissing wind. But one look at Roxana's hair becoming vertical told him that this wind was blowing upwards, and he knew what Ysbaed had done.

The 'wind' was, in actual fact, the atmosphere inside the room escaping through the roof. Through a hole that led to somewhere else, some other world, or dimension, or universe. Darren gasped and then gasped again, the second time as an oxygen grab. There was hardly any air and what little there was stung his chest with cold. He turned to see Malcolm on all fours, sucking in the thin atmosphere through an open mouth. Roxana, eyes popping, coughing and choking, scanning for an enemy she could physically fight. But it was no use. What good would cannons do against someone who could conjure holes in the very matrix that held the world together?

And it was all Darren's fault.

All because some capricious god had blessed him with the gift of bringing inanimate objects to life. But at what price? Like Dr Frankenstein before him, Darren had given birth to a heartless, unfeeling monster. And somewhere in his oxygen-starved brain, he was aware of the monster laughing at him for creating all of this with his camera. Mocking him for his impotence and the fact that with the genie out of the bottle, he was powerless to do anything about it.

Or was he?

The idea, almost dismissed as a quirk of his hypoxic imaginings, appeared fully formed in his head and with startling clarity. His chest heaving, desperate for every last molecule of oxygen, Darren fumbled in his pocket for his phone. But something was wrong with his vision. It was like he was looking at the numbers through a long dark tunnel.

'There is no signal…you idiot…' Malcolm panted. But Darren knew that. He didn't need a signal. Ysbaed's laughter redoubled.

'You fool! Your devices are useless here.'

'Really?' Darren hissed and held the phone up at arm's length, eyes on the screen, willing the integral camera to focus in on the snakeskin. It was a good camera, too. Ten megapixels and an anti-shake mechanism. The camera clicked, and with a snap, the snakeskin disappeared. Or rather shrank back to something small and grey and rotten on the floor.

Ysbaed screamed.

The hole in the roof began to close up and the hissing wind dipped a couple of notches. There was air in the room again.

Darren sucked it in, and it tasted sweet and wonderful. The sweetest, most wonderful air he had ever tasted. But he wasn't thinking about that, he was too busy swinging his camera around to the bone. He framed it, pressed the switch and with another snap it too shrank to its normal size. One more to go.

Yet even as Darren swung around to focus the camera on the pyrite, Ysbaed responded. With a terrible rumble, the floor beneath Darren's feet began to shake violently.

'Earthquake!' Malcolm yelled.

Bits of the floor were starting to fracture, gaps were appearing, and large slabs of stone were poking upwards like gigantic broken teeth. Darren was thrown off his feet and started to slide down a smooth slab the size of a house. He threw out his free hand and grabbed an edge and managed to stop the slide. Beneath him, the floor beyond was darkness. It might even have been Stygian.

'Come on,' Malcolm urged.

Roxana had already moved. A chunk of masonry the size of a motorbike clattered to the floor next to Darren's head. The walls were cracking, and the rumble grew into a roar.

'Out!' screamed Roxana.

Staggering, leaping onto the more stable slabs that shuddered and shivered and broke apart the instant he stepped on them, Darren scrambled for the doors. Ysbaed's votive room was coming apart at the seams and with it, the huge metal doors were buckling. With a whip-cracking snap a gap appeared between the two. But still Darren hesitated because he had a job to finish. He needed to take a picture of the pyrite.

Turning, bracing himself against a momentarily upright slab of juddering floor, Darren found the massive gleaming rock. It was still rotating, but in it he thought he could see the shape of a man with full cruel lips.

'Look out!' Malcolm yelled and wrestled Darren to the floor in time to avoid a brick chimney from crushing them both. The noise was now deafening, and Malcolm's shout barely broke through the cacophony. Darren dragged himself forward, scrabbling for purchase on the tilting slabs. He caught a glimpse of the huge wheels that supported the metal doors and then he was tumbling through, yanked by the collar into smoky warmth. There was another noise, this one like a knife zinging through the air and then silence. The cataclysmic crashing of the votive room was gone, and he was on a cold, wonderfully unmoving, concrete floor.

# CHAPTER THIRTY-FIVE

**Panting, Darren got** to his knees, looked around and was glad to see that, somehow, he was back in the huge factory outside the votive room with its massive doors once again intact. His chest heaved and his head thumped as his mind registered the fact that, as improbable as it seemed, whatever had taken place on the other side must have happened in a different reality. He stood up, walked to the doors and thumped the thick metal with his palm. He'd almost taken a picture of that fool's gold. He'd almost done to the pyrite what he'd done to the snakeskin and the bone. How or why that idea had come to him he had no idea. But there was a strange logic to it. If he truly was the Maker, then why shouldn't he un-make as well? Darren leaned his forehead against the cool metal, limbs shaking, unable to fight the terrible feeling that he was going to severely regret not finishing the job. Then he heard Malcolm's fuzzy voice as if though a wall of cotton wool.

'Darren, take a look at this.'

Slowly he turned and froze.

The huge factory floor was teeming with people. Hundreds and hundreds of them all buzzing with relief in the heady joy of freedom. Tirerenans—tall men with beards and women like Roxana and her sisters—were mingling with other, smaller, snub-nosed people with brown skin and astonishing multi-coloured, gravity-defying hair. Darren guessed that these were the Audia.

A breathless Maeve ran across to them. It did not escape Darren's notice that she went directly to Malcolm and threw herself into his arms.

'Paladin, I thought that…when the doors closed and…'

'I'm fine,' Malcolm said. 'I'm fine.'

Darren looked for and found Roxana and, for that brief moment, the sheer exuberance of having escaped certain death was a heady concoction. Darren wanted to say something, but he didn't get the chance as Roxana pulled him to her in an embrace, her mouth close to his ear.

'Thank you,' she whispered. 'Thank you.'

She was crying, sobbing in his arms with, what he assumed, was relief. He felt her smooth skin beneath his dirt-stained fingers and felt the solid firmness of the bones within. If she was made of some sort of plastic, it was bloody good stuff.

'Don't cry,' Darren said. 'We're all safe, aren't we?' He tried to pull back, but she wouldn't let him.

'They are all free,' Roxana breathed. 'All the people. All the men. All free.'

'Yeah,' he spoke into her hair. 'Lottery bonus ball. Look, when everything calms down a bit, is there any chance…'

She sobbed some more. A deeper gulp. This time Darren did pull back and, in the momentary glimpse he got before she buried her head in his shoulder a second time, he saw that the sob wasn't entirely driven by joy. There was something else in there, fighting with the relief. Something regretful and tinged with sorrow. 'They are all free, Maker. Do you understand?' Still, she wouldn't look at him.

'Well yeah, of course I understand.'

She pulled back then, her face distraught. 'If only…' The words died on her lips and were replaced with another convulsive gulp. For a moment Darren feared she might even throw up. He would have forgiven her that, but instead Roxana turned and ran off towards the milling crowd, leaving Darren standing there like a dog at a birthday party after the song, realising that something important had happened but not having the faintest clue as to what it was. Except that inside was a terrible, agonising emptiness where moments before had been swooping tingles of anticipation.

Away to his left, Maeve and Malcolm were holding each other's hands, talking animatedly. From out of the crowd Vivette and Una came running.

'We thought you were gone.' Vivette said, and there was no trace of rancour in her expression.

'So did I,' Darren mumbled, distracted still by Roxana's reaction.

'What happened?'

With one eye on the crowd trying to pick her out, Darren explained what took place inside the votive room. In return, he listened while Una told him all about Roxana's decision to strike out as 'guerinjas' at the heart of Ysbaed's lair.

'But how did you get in?'

Una looked across at a suddenly bashful Vivette. 'The Obfuscator is well named.' Once again and much to Darren's astonishment, she took Vivette's hand and squeezed it. Though he tried not to let it happen, Darren felt his eyebrows shoot up and was quite glad there was a hairline there to stop them from taking off altogether. Vivette caught his glance.

'Look, neither did I,' she said in response to his unasked question. 'I've been pretty much a hetero metro up to now. But if this is a closet I'm stepping out of, then goodbye Narnia, hello Una. Apparently, the school of pleasure does AC *and* DC.' She threw Una an appreciative glance. 'I volunteered.'

Darren nodded with a fixed smile. 'Right. But you still haven't answered the question. How come they were almost invisible?'

Vivette shrugged. 'The nail varnish. Something chemical at the molecular or nanotech level, I would guess. I don't know. You do the maths.'

The crowd was funnelling out of the factory. The great doors were trundling open, shafts of golden sunlight flooded in. Bron detached herself from the crowd and joined her sisters and the others.

'Are there many dead?' Una asked.

'Very few. It is truly miraculous.' She gave Darren a perfunctory hug.

'So all your menfolk are—' Darren meant to say 'all right' but Bron stepped in to finish the sentence for him.

'Idiots. They walked straight into Ysbaed's trap, thinking they could vanquish his army.' She shook her head. 'We need not have lost any lives if our leaders had planned. This cannot be allowed to happen again. We need strategists.'

'Right,' Darren said. 'Shame you can't meet my friend Sanjay. He's a real whiz when it comes to all that kind of stuff.'

Then they were joining the thronging crowd hurrying out into the warm sunshine that was already burning off the grey clouds. It was over. They'd done it. *Okay*, thought Darren, *so I didn't get all of the votives on camera but nevertheless my hunch was correct.* Photography was what brought things to life, so photography had to be able to take that life away, too. He blinked in the sunlight. Una and Vivette were getting on like a house on fire. So were Maeve and Malcolm. So where was Roxana? More importantly, how come she still smelt of fresh paint even after a hard day's conquering despots? The thought made him smile as the enormity of their achievements sank in. Amanda and Kaa and his old life were like a strange, half remembered dream. And it looked like the Audia were all okay too, so George Hoblip would be happy.

Movement on his left caught his eye. A blonde streaked head gleaming in the sunlight. He looked up, the smile already halfway to his lips. She was there, but she was not alone. Behind her was a man. Darren blinked. There was something familiar about him. Something that made Darren's testicles crawl.

It was at that point that his insides turned to icy slush. The man emerging from the crowd behind Roxana, gazing at her with adoring puppy eyes (after fiddling with the parting in his hair) was a trim, tanned version of none other than bloody Trey Lushton.

'Darren,' Roxana said, as she neared the point at which Darren's feet had taken root.

He barely registered the fact that her voice warbled with

some unnameable emotion. 'I'm…I would like you to meet my…fiancé. Trelish.'

A bit of Darren's brain wanted to let go a hysterical scream. Trelish? What sort of a bloody name was Trelish? Darren saw the hand come out. Saw a million teeth in a deeply smiling mouth. He felt his hand being gripped and saw Roxana turn to wipe away a tear. His ears were hearing a male voice saying, 'Thank you,' but his brain was laughing like a hysterical hyena at the total, chocolate-coated, digestive-taking insanity of it all.

'It was nothing. All in a day's work.' He was spouting platitudes like the luckless idiotic berk that he was for thinking that he'd had any chance at all with this wonderful, loyal, warrior goddess. And then, to put the manky dried-out glacier cherry on the stale old threepenny cake, the crowd started to cheer. He knew they were cheering him and so he arranged his mouth into a smile made of teak and acknowledged their applause, all the while wanting nothing more than to crawl away and lick his wounds, the mother of which was the awful ache from the spike that had been driven through his hopeless heart.

After several excruciating seconds, the adulation ended abruptly when a horseman galloped down the cobbled street complete with urgent but inarticulate shouting and a flailing arm. Foam flew from the horse's mouth and the rider, when he dismounted, looked exhausted and on his last legs. He went straight to Bron.

'A company of Dankboer with a dozen beasts in retreat five miles to the east. The beasts appeared to be carrying a huge golden stone.'

'Shit,' Darren said. He'd never realised how fond he'd been of that word. Small and succinct, it summed up everything he felt about the situation.

'Might be worth us going after them,' he said. 'I might be able to get a long-distance photo of the stone. That would finish Ysbaed off forever.' Everyone, apart from Malcolm and Roxana, stared at him blankly. The truth was Darren was glad of the distraction. Maeve responded first.

'We will need fast horses.'

Bron nodded. 'I will take Darren,' she said.

Something passed over Roxana's face. Darren dared to hope that it was a final skirmish in the battle that was raging in her head between devotion and what could never be. After several long seconds of troubled glaring, she nodded. A reluctant little movement, her mouth a wafer-thin slash that said loyalty had won as, of course, it would have. He would expect nothing less of someone like her.

Bron was shouting orders. Malcolm hadn't moved. He was staring at Darren, just like Vivette was, wearing an awkward expression.

'Do you want us to come, mate?' Malcolm asked.

'No. Stay here. Enjoy.' It earned him a frown from Malcolm, but he meant it. He walked a few paces away, pretending to look back at the Barans, needing to be away from Roxana and everyone else's pity. The horses appeared a minute later: large, strong-looking animals. Darren had never ridden a horse in his life. But it didn't matter. If he fell off, he couldn't look more of a prat than he felt at this particular moment. And he owed it to these people to make them safe once and for all, didn't he?

Bron held his mount for him. 'If we head north to the pass, we should…'

It happened without warning. The huge explosion to the south turned the hill into a flat field. Two more followed in quick succession. The sky became a dark canopy in an instant, both suns blocked from view in a dual eclipse. People were screaming. The earth shook. This was much worse than what had taken place in the votive room. The ground rattled and rolled once more.

Was this more of Ysbaed's madness? If it was, he was doing this on steroids, because the very landscape was crumbling around him, the sky boiling with dark menace.

Darren stumbled and as he fell, he looked up and saw something that rocked his sanity like a trawler in a force ten.

A huge shape fell through the sky. Something massive, an asteroid of some sort, pitted and brown and cigar shaped. Yet even in his terror, his darting eyes zeroed in on something written on the side of the comet. He read the word 'Slogger' in huge letters along its length, registering it with utter bewilderment in the two seconds before the missile struck a direct hit on the crowd. Screams mingled with the sickening noise of flesh being crushed against hard ground. Bleating Audia and Tirerenans ran in every direction. This was a scene straight out of Brueghel or Bosch, but without the weird medieval faces.

Hell was visiting Moldarrenovia.

Then something yanked at his midriff with an unstoppable force. Like he'd reached the end of a very elastic bungee cord that was now recoiling with tremendous force. He shot upwards, or was it backwards? He couldn't tell. It was the strangest feeling of leaving without actually moving.

Moldarrenovia receded. He was being pulled at impossible speed along a long, dark corridor, his breath shoved out of his chest by a giant hand. The last thing he saw before everything changed was Roxana's diminishing face, pale and rigid with fear. An image branded into his retinas, never to fade. She looked at him, her expression desperate, her eyes, before the darkness enveloped them, brimming with unbearable heartache and anguish.

It was the last recognisable piece of Moldarrenovia he saw.

## CHAPTER THIRTY-SIX

**It was like** being in an elevator travelling upwards at high speed. From the first floor to the hundredth in five seconds flat. His stomach lurched so badly that it French kissed the roof of his mouth and threatened to void its contents. A kaleidoscope of destruction flashed past his eyes for ten vertiginous seconds before the blackness. And then, incredibly, he was falling out of nowhere onto grass, landing on his back with a grunting thump. He lay still, listening to two other thumps and grunts close by.

Stars glittered above in the night sky and a half-moon hung low on the horizon in the west. Light spilled out from a room nearby. Darren pushed himself up, disorientated. The aroma of chargrilled tandoori lamb hit his nostrils.

He knew where he was.

He was in the Bobal's back garden. Through the kitchen window, he watched Sanjay making tea a dozen yards away. But there were voices behind him at the rear of the garden too, interspersed with the tinny, static hiss of a shortwave radio. He glanced across to his right and saw Vivette and Malcolm brushing themselves off next to him.

'What the hell just happened?' Malcolm asked.

'I don't know,' Darren said, grimacing against another spiral of dizziness. 'But I don't think we're in Moldarrenovia anymore.'

'We can't leave them. Not like that…'

'How come one minute we were there and now we're… here?' Vivette looked perplexed.

'And why is there a blue light flashing over the roof?' Malcolm added.

Darren glanced up.

'I don't like the look of this,' he said and hurried to the back door. Sanjay was pouring hot water into a mug. He looked up on hearing the door open and almost dropped the kettle.

'Jesus, Darren. Where did you just come from?'

'Long story, Sanjay.' He took in his friend's careworn expression and the two steaming mugs in front of him. 'What's going on? You look like—'

'Don't say it.' Sanjay's plea was beyond earnest. Tears welled in his eyes. 'It's Dad. They've taken him to hospital. I would have gone too but the police are here and…'

An echoing static burst crackled from a radio somewhere in the house, and suddenly the flashing lights and voices all fell into place.

'Shit, Sanj,' Darren said. 'What's happened?'

Sanjay exhaled loudly. There was a lot of pain in that exhalation. 'We had a break-in and Dad tried to fight…' He stopped, composing himself.

Darren opened his mouth to say something but stopped because a man in a uniform with three stripes on his sleeve walked through into the kitchen.

'Who are these three?' asked the policeman.

'Just some mates, Sergeant Vine. This is Darren and that's Malcolm and Vivette,' Sanjay explained.

The policeman gave a perfunctory nod as Sanjay handed over the two cups of freshly made tea.

'Thanks for this. Much appreciated.' The policeman took the cups by the handles. He was very businesslike. 'We've checked the rooms downstairs. Been a bit of disturbance but nothing broken. Upstairs it's the bedroom that's been done. And of course, the lock-up.' He took a sip of tea and gave Sanjay an appraising look. 'Got any enemies, you or your dad?'

Sanjay shook his head. 'Everyone knows my dad. Everyone…'

'Yeah, sorry. Have to ask. Trouble is there are some vicious bastards around. Probably junkies looking for drug money. My theory is your dad disturbed them and they legged it.' Sanjay nodded. 'We're dusting for prints up in the bedroom and then we'll be off. To be honest, the chances of us finding them are pretty slim. I hope your dad'll be all right. If I hear anything, I'll let PC Sharma know. He wanted to come, being related to you and all, but there's a dawn raid in the offing and he's their armed response guy.' He glanced at Malcolm and Darren. 'Take care.'

'Thanks again,' Sanjay said. They watched the policeman disappear back into the house in silence and then Sanjay spoke again. 'Cup of tea anyone?' He reached for the kettle with a trembling hand. Darren stepped forward, grabbed his arm and guided him towards a chair.

'Why don't you let us make you a cuppa, mate?' Darren said. 'I'm sure we could all do with one.'

Malcolm and Vivette stepped forward and busied themselves. Darren was glad of something to do too, because his head was still spinning, twisting with images of the horrific destruction that he'd witnessed moments before and trying to reconcile that with the bleak situation they'd now stumbled into. Tea made, they sat down at the kitchen table, everyone with a story to tell. Sanjay went first.

'So, I'm out in the lock-up. Hannibal is advancing, but the weather is lousy so there are delays. That allows the Sumerian divisions to move up on the sly.'

'Non comprendosimus,' Vivette said.

'Scale model of the Babylonian Empire,' Darren explained. His voice was terse, like a piece of thin ice, threatening at any moment to crack unless he unburdened himself. But he needed to know about Sanjay's dad first.

'It's about one in the morning and I hear this noise. Like someone having a row, stuff breaking, you know. I ran in. The light was on upstairs. Then I heard my dad shouting and the next thing I know there's this black shape in front of me and before I know it, I'm flat on my back. Someone flips me over and sits on me. I hear some more shouting. Muffled like through a balaclava. 'In here, in here. There's more stuff in here.' Then I hear them in the lock-up…' His voice faltered. 'They went into the lock-up, Dar.'

'What's in the lock-up?' Malcolm asked.

Sanjay's head fell forward. 'Nothing much.'

'What are you talking about, San? There's nothing to steal in the lock-up unless you're heavily into papier mâché and clay, is there?' Darren grabbed his arm.

'See for yourself,' Sanjay said.

Darren got up on heavy metal legs. He dragged himself down the garden to the door under the railway arch. It hung at an awkward angle and through the gap, light spilled out into the night. From the doorway, Darren looked in and felt his bladder flop like a pillowcase in a stiff breeze.

What he beheld was a picture of utter devastation. Sanjay's wonderful, intricate landscape was nothing more than the aftermath of a tornado. Puddles on the floor made watery graves for the small plastic animals, and Hannibal's army lay scattered everywhere. Whoever did this had succeeded in causing maximum vindictive destruction. His mind flew back to Sergeant Vine's question about Sanjay and Mr. B having enemies. He could not think of one person who would want to do them harm. His eyes raked the room, flitting from one scene of willful vandalism to another, but after half a minute, Darren had seen enough. He turned and hurried back to the house. Sanjay was still sitting there in earnest conversation with Vivette.

'Why?' Darren interrupted. It was a hopeless question, he knew.

Sanjay shrugged.

'Did they do anything to your dad, Sanjay?' Vivette asked.

Sanjay shook his head. His eyes were dark hollows. 'I don't know. He'd collapsed on the landing. Couldn't speak. They think it's a stroke.'

'That's awful,' Vivette said in a whisper.

Sanjay didn't answer. He merely nodded. Darren read it as shock and read it wrong.

'I'm sorry, Darren,' Sanjay said.

'Sorry? What have you got to be sorry for?'

'The bedroom…' Sanjay's words died on his lips. A light

seemed to go on in Darren's head at that moment. Mr. B had interrupted intruders. They'd found him on the landing and that implied a fracas upstairs…

Darren ran. He took the steps three at a time to the landing. The door to Mr. and Mrs. B's old bedroom was open and instantly he wished that it wasn't. The scene was one straight out of the IED testing site handbook, on a page marked 'Aftermath'. It made the damage to Sanjay's lock-up look like a spilled drawer. Everything, every single thing, had been systematically decimated. The sets were not only disrupted, they'd been smashed to smithereens. His models, some of them collectors' pieces, mashed underfoot or cut into pieces by something sharp. As far as he could see nothing had been spared. His cameras, lenses, tripods—all crushed. A sudden dreadful image of a huge wooden baseball bat with the word 'Slogger' written on its side loomed once again in his head. He grabbed the wall to prevent the vertiginous swirling taking hold and barely managed to keep whatever was left in his stomach where it ought to stay. He slumped to the floor, eyes shut, not understanding any of it, fearing all of it.

Malcolm and Vivette must have come and found him and taken him back downstairs, because that was when unwelcome reality once again reasserted itself into his jumbled thoughts. He looked down to find that he held another teacup in his trembling hands, full of a dark brown liquid that was, as everyone knew, the panacea for all ills of the mind. Especially with a half-inch of Jameson swirled into it. He downed the drink and welcomed the fire of it along his oesophagus as it took away the pain for the briefest of moments. Somewhere, a long way away, he could make out Malcolm explaining to Sanjay what had taken place since they'd left the barbecue.

Disjointedly, he and Vivette related the events of the last forty-eight Moldarrenovian hours (the eight or so since they'd left the barbecue). And the horrific retelling of what they'd left behind compounded the shock of the burglary. Somehow, the look of desperation in the Tirerenans' faces and the apocalyptic events they'd been plucked from had been displaced by the mundane criminality of vindictive burglars. But Darren relived it again now in Malcolm's narrative, and a dam holding back the dark waters inside him broke.

He pushed his chair back and stood abruptly. 'We have to go back,' he said. 'We have to help them.'

'How?' Malcolm said sourly. 'Do you happen to have one of these aperio things on you?'

'Poor Una,' Vivette whispered. She looked like a woman waking up from a nightmare, only to realise that it had all been real.

Mention of Una brought Roxana's image into Darren's head. That last, reluctant, remorseful little nod she'd given him. He shut his eyes to force the image away and turned to Sanjay who remained quiet, as through the whole of Malcolm's relaying of events. But the look on his face was now one of incomprehension and despair.

'Christ, Sanj, you must think we're all bloody mad. Your dad is in hospital, this place is a mess and all we can talk about is what we've been doing in a world that may not even exist outside of our warped imaginations.'

'Sounds pretty real to me,' Sanjay said.

'It is,' Malcolm said, leaning forward, eyes staring and desolate. 'It is real. Maeve's real. I know that for definite.'

'But why were we brought back?' Vivette demanded. 'I thought we were meant to help them?' Her voice took on a disconsolate, accusatory tone.

'You were,' a male voice said from behind them. Darren swung his head around. The door had opened the wrong way, yet, at the same time, still seemed to be shut. Matt Danmor and Kylah Porter were walking through, both wearing the same wary, unhappy expressions.

'What we hadn't bargained for was a dimensional destabilisation secondary to structural breakdown,' Kylah explained.

'In other words, having your model sets smashed up here made Moldarrenovia fall apart too,' Matt explained.

Despite the despicably wheedling tone in his voice, Darren asked, 'But I took it all apart and rebuilt it last week. How did it survive that?'

Matt's eyebrows went up in apology.

'Don't tell me,' Malcolm said, wearing a sour expression. 'Krudian anomaly?'

'I think I must have stepped in some Krudian once,' Vivette muttered, her eyes flashing ominously.

Matt winced. 'I know how it sounds. Nevertheless, it is the case. Darren dismantling it and putting it back together wouldn't matter since he is the Maker. We're not sure how. Perhaps it only even existed in that form since he put it back together. I don't do metaphysics, but I know a Fae that does,' he nodded towards Kylah before adding, 'but anyway, the major instability caused by being smashed up—not by Darren—tripped the emergency recall.'

'Like someone hitting the ejector seat button?' Malcolm asked.

Kylah nodded.

'But the people?' Vivette said. 'We've left those poor people—'

'There are no more poor people,' Matt said in a low voice.

'What you mean?' Malcolm was staring at him.

'The whole population has been wiped out.' Matt nodded. 'No world can withstand that much destruction. Something to do with critical tectonic destabilisation.'

'Oh my god!' Vivette said shrilly, her hand up to her mouth. Malcolm was shaking his head.

Darren, for once, was speechless. Those last few moments of horror were burned into his memory. The screams, the destruction and before that, Trelish, and Roxana turning to wipe away a tear. He wanted to howl out his anguish but didn't. All those years watching his mother wasting away had hardened him to mental pain and now a strange and stifling stillness came over him. Perhaps it was shock. Perhaps it was the difficulty his brain was having reconciling the arcane with the here and now and the harsh reality of Mr. Bobal's predicament. After several long seconds of a stagnant silence, Darren said in a dry rasping voice, 'So, what now?'

'Now we get you lot back to some semblance of normality,' Kylah said.

Everyone stared at her.

'Just like that?' Vivette protested. 'Just walk away from it? After all we've been through?'

'We have ways of making it easier,' Matt said, and Darren couldn't help noticing how his eyes wanted to slide away and didn't through sheer force of willpower.

'Like what?' Malcolm asked, his eyes narrowing with scepticism.

'Well, we can fully debrief you with our pentrievant…' Matt hesitated, seeing the looks he was getting. 'It's like a memory recorder. Lets you get everything off your chest, or off your mind —same thing in effect—without opening your mouth.' He tried to smile, but it withered on the vine and turned into a rictus.

'Once that's done, it's back to your old lives, I'm afraid,' Kylah said.

'But what about that bastard Ysbaed?' Darren demanded.

'Much reduced, I'm pleased to say,' she replied. 'Stroke of genius using your camera phone.'

'But I didn't get them all. The votives, I mean.'

'No.' Matt nodded. 'But he can't do much on a world that has fallen apart and where there's nothing to terrorise. We think he's in limbo at the moment. Awaiting events.'

'But…' Malcolm frowned in confusion.

'He can exist in a variety of forms,' Matt explained, 'but his votives need a semblance of physical reality in order to function.'

Kylah reached into her shoulder bag and took out an opalescent green stone the size of a fifty pence piece, attached to the middle of a leather strap. 'Perhaps if we could use the living room? And one at a time would be best.'

Darren, Malcolm, Kylah and Sanjay looked at each other in silence. Surely they hadn't been through all of this for nothing?

Sanjay seemed totally confused and Darren saw that same bemused horror etched on the other two's faces. He suspected, too, that his own expression was doing a pretty good impression of theirs.

People quite often misused the word 'shock' to describe what they felt when something unusual and disturbing happened to them. Like the shock of, 'Oh dear,' on getting home from the supermarket to find that you'd bought the wrong brand of sardines. Or the shock of, 'Oh crap!' on realising that the ketchup you'd just slathered over your scrambled eggs had a sell-by date that expired three years before. And then there was the shock of, 'OMGnnnnhhh!' on opening that old chest freezer in the outhouse of the isolated cottage you'd just rented for the weekend to find it contained items that were no longer functional because they were:

1) Frozen.

2) Only really of any use while still attached to a warm body with a still-pumping human heart.

(And all this while the smiley owner, who'd turned up unexpectedly to welcome you, was helping your girlfriend upstairs with the luggage.)

The point being that there was a spectrum. And at that moment, Darren was positioned much closer to the cottage freezer end than the sardines to the extent that he couldn't think straight, or argue straight, or even see straight to truly appreciate what was going on.

*Vivette went first. The Obfuscator. Very aptly named, thought Darren. Designer of a fantastic chameleon camouflage suit. The guerinjas' saviour. Who'd have thought it?*

The others sat numbly at the kitchen table, and it was then that Darren realised that there was no reason for Sanjay to be there anymore. And a very good reason for him to be somewhere else.

It was then that practicality came to Darren's rescue and elbowed shock out of the way. For a while at least. 'God, Sanj. I'm a bloody idiot. You need to get to the hospital.'

'What about Matt and Kylah?'

'They'll keep. God knows what sort of time loop system they're on anyway. May even be going backwards for all I know. Come on, I'll take you.'

They left Malcolm waiting for his debrief and Darren went with Sanjay to the General in his dad's old Citroën. Doing something helped. Distraction meant he didn't replay Roxana turning away like that in his mind's eye; at least not every other second.

# CHAPTER THIRTY-SEVEN

**The city hospital** was small hours quiet. A smattering of unsmiling relatives whose reasons for being there, like Sanjay's, had chiselled their features into hard masks of worry, stood around clutching Styrofoam cups of liquid, or surreptitiously smoking near the entrance. Sanjay enquired at a reception desk manned by a jowly porter and was directed to the second floor via an empty lift. An efficient West Indian nursing sister met them at the nurse's station and showed them to Mr. Bobal's bed.

He looked like the cliché victim in a low-budget TV movie. IV lines ran into both arms, and he was being ventilated. The breathing tube ran into his mouth, distorting his lips and revealing his tobacco-stained lower teeth. Mr. B's eyes were closed and the only noise in the room was the rhythmic ebb and flow of the respirator pumping oxygen into his lungs.

'Shit,' Sanjay said, his voice raw. 'The paramedics said he'd had a stroke. This looks much worse than that, doesn't it?'

Darren nodded. He didn't know what to think. He'd seen stroke campaign adverts on TV. Obviously they'd worked because Darren could remember the mnemonic they'd used. FAST had stuck in his head. F for fallen face, A for unable to lift arms, and S for slurred speech?, and T for time to call an ambulance. As far as he could remember there was no 'C' at the end for Completely Gone—which was what Mr. B looked like he was.

The nurse who'd brought them into the room came back with a twelve-year-old in a white coat who turned out to be the duty registrar responsible for looking after Sanjay's dad. They listened to her explain that Mr. Bobal had suffered a haemorrhagic stroke. The CT showed massive bleeding into the brain, probably from a pre-existing aneurysm.

'Can he feel anything?' Sanjay asked.

The doctor, whose badge read Dr Britton, shook her head.

'He hasn't regained consciousness.' She hesitated and then said, 'At some stage we will be turning off the machine to see if he can breathe by himself.'

Sanjay nodded. 'And if he can't?'

'We'll do some other tests to assess brain function, but…'

Sanjay nodded again. Darren was astonished at how calm he was. There seemed to be an instant understanding between him and Dr Britton. An understanding that was cruising at high altitude, way over Darren's head.

'Wait a minute,' Darren said, 'are you saying that Mr. B isn't going to get better?' He knew it sounded doleful, if not downright childish, but he couldn't help it.

'With the amount of bleeding on the scan, a vegetative state is very likely. If the respiratory centre is affected too, he will not be able to breathe on his own.'

'Vegetative state?' Darren repeated, an edge to his voice now.

'It's okay, Dar,' Sanjay said. 'I understand.'

Dr Britton smiled a tired, grateful smile and bowed out.

'Jesus, Sanj, I am so sorry,' Darren said. He was having difficulty looking at his friend.

Sanjay nodded. He wasn't looking at Darren either; his eyes were firmly fixed on his father's face. 'He's not in pain. Looks right out of it, doesn't he?'

'Yeah,' Darren agreed.

They didn't speak for almost a minute. But then Sanjay said, 'It could be a lot worse, you know. What with the cancer and all, Dealer Dave's cakes weren't going to work forever. This way, if he doesn't wake up, he's going to hold up two fingers to the whole thing, isn't he?'

Darren thought for a long moment and then nodded. He marvelled at the way Sanjay was able to rationalise all of this, even find a trace of argent in a dark and dismal cloud. But he was right. There was no other way to look at it. Sanjay had already explained to Darren that palliative care was going to involve hospices and morphine syringe drivers and a whole load of unpleasantness if not in the next post, then pretty soon for Mr. B.

'It's a sort of blessing, really,' Sanjay said again.

*No it isn't*, screamed the voice inside Darren's head. But that was for his own consumption. It had no place here and now sitting next to Sanjay, watching Mr. B's chest rise and fall, watching the nurses keeping his lips moist, watching the clock and not understanding one tenth of what had happened in the last three days. After half an hour of it, Sanjay told Darren to stay where he was and went off to find a nurse. When he came back, there was a new expression of resolve on his face.

'Come on, let's go.'

'But…'

'It's okay. They're going to watch him. They'll contact me if anything happens. I want to get home, start sorting things out.'

They drove back to Shunter Street in a self-absorbed silence, broken only by the buzz of the car's tyres on the road. Darren's thoughts flitted between Mr. Bobal and Roxana and in both instances, they left him weak and feeling sick. He guessed that Sanjay's were much the same. Worse, a terrible sapping tiredness came over him and he could barely summon the will to follow Sanjay into the house. Kylah and Matt were there, but Malcolm and Vivette were nowhere to be seen.

'Didn't see much point in them hanging around,' Matt explained.

'Oh, and we've done some clearing up,' Kylah added. They followed her upstairs. The bedroom and its contents had indeed been tidied, in that the broken and smashed sets, models and cameras had all been neatly collected and stacked onto the trestle tables in labelled boxes.

'Wow,' Sanjay said.

'She was very well brought up,' Matt said.

Kylah ignored him. 'We've done the same in the lock-up. Far less damage there.'

'Thanks, I'm really grateful,' Sanjay said.

'We are very sorry about your father,' Kylah said.

Sanjay nodded.

'Oh, and some of your relatives called. Your auntie Anitha is coming to stay the night, and your cousin, and your uncle, and your other uncle.'

Sanjay squeezed his eyes shut and nodded in resignation.

'Darren, can I have a word?' Matt beckoned to him while Kylah took Sanjay out to show him the lock-up.

'Umm,' Matt said, studying the interesting fan-shaped patterns of Artex on the ceiling, 'this is all a bit awkward, but we're going to have to modify your friend's memory. The Moldarrenovian bits anyway. After all, he wasn't involved.'

'Wasn't involved?' Darren balked at that. 'How can you say that? This is his house.'

'Yeah, but, you know…'

Darren felt a surge of anger. 'No, I don't know. I don't know anything. Talking models, a world that has two suns, votives the size of jumbo jets and now *this*.' He waved his arm about like a crazed bookie.

'Yes, it can be a bit overwhelming,' Matt agreed. 'But it might be kinder if Sanjay was relieved of the burden of remembering any of it.'

'And what about me? You going to relieve me to?'

Matt shook his head. 'Couldn't even if you wanted us to. You were the primary source. Without you there'd be no Moldarrenovia past, present or future.'

If Darren heard the word 'future', it didn't register. Not then. 'I thought you said it had been destroyed?'

'It has.'

'What about Roxana?'

Matt glanced at his feet before looking back up. 'I'm sorry, Darren.'

'*I'm sorry Darren*' seemed woefully inadequate. She'd been

alive, smiling, laughing, warm. And yet….and yet she had also been just a plastic figure he'd imagined into life, hadn't she?

Swallowing with difficulty, Darren said, 'What about the photos I took of the votives?'

'Ah, right. Excellent point. I was going to ask a favour. Could you email them to this address?' Matt reached into his pocket and pulled out a piece of paper on which was written an email address. 'Use votives as the subject. They'll find it that way.'

Darren attached the photo files and pressed send. As well as the usual rushing noise of mail leaving his phone, the whole handset glowed silver for ten seconds and then beeped.

'That's a reciprocal sweeping program that's made sure all traces have left your phone,' Matt explained.

'You mean the images aren't there anymore?' Darren asked.

'No. And they weren't just images, just so you know.'

Seeing Darren's perplexed stare, Matt added, 'It's for your own safety, you know that.'

Bewilderment combined with a bone-aching fatigue suddenly made Darren yearn for his own bed. 'Whatever,' he said. 'I'm too tired to even think.'

Matt gave him a reassuring little smile that ricocheted off Darren's Teflon-coated misery.

There were noises coming from the ground floor. People were arriving. Darren walked halfway down and then turned to ask Matt something else. He wasn't there. But Sanjay was in the kitchen meeting people as they came in, shaking hands and fielding questions. Darren waited in the hall until he came through, laden with coats.

'What did Kylah have to say for herself?' Darren asked.

'Who?' Sanjay said.

'She of the tight black trousers and amazing eyes, you know?'

Sanjay shook his head. 'You okay, Dar?'

Realisation hit Darren like a tsunami. That was why Matt had waylaid him. They must have done the memory thing to Sanjay already because it was clear he had no idea what Darren was talking about.

'It's okay,' Darren mumbled, 'Been a long old day.'

'Yeah.'

'So, listen, I'll shoot off. I'll give you a ring in the morning, okay?'

'Cheers, Dar,' Sanjay said.

Darren left him to it, hoping that weird panic suddenly engulfing him wasn't showing in his face. All he knew was that he suddenly needed space, and some time to walk alone and let his jumbled, tumbling thoughts settle.

## CHAPTER THIRTY-EIGHT

Darren awoke slowly on Saturday morning, swimming up through layers of awareness with reluctant strokes, his mind clinging, clam-like, to the coat tails of unconsciousness. Confusion reigned. Was he in his own bed under a tog 10 duvet or lying under the fur covers of a cot in a yurt? For several seconds, the computation necessary for anchoring and orientation got stuck in safe mode. He registered, with eyes shut, daylight beyond his lids and the distant noises reaching his ears might equally have been a car horn or a bleating goat. Then memory rushed in and catapulted him into full consciousness.

His eyes snapped open and took in the familiar floral-patterned curtains hung by his mother ten years before. The curtains were almost her last act of redecoration before illness struck. He knew then, with a strange mixture of relief and dread, that he was home. Images from a few hours ago were burned into his memory, and yet here he was in his own house, in his own bedroom. Was it possible that he'd dreamt the whole thing?

The tinny beats of a radio drifted up the stairs from the kitchen. He got up with difficulty. His whole body ached like he'd done ten rounds, the oily taste of garlic in his mouth from Sanjay's barbecue a reminder of what he'd done the day before…before Moldarrenovia. He padded to the bathroom to relieve himself, brushed his teeth in the shower and almost bit the toothbrush in two as the jets of water washed out the many cuts covering his body. He found a clean T-shirt and jeans and went downstairs.

In the kitchen, the radio segued into an inane pop song while Amanda watched some eggs boiling.

It must be Saturday: her protein fix.

'Morning,' he croaked. She turned and gave him one of her good smiles. Not the usual terse greeting: this one was full on, welcoming and broad.

'Hi, handsome,' she said. She wore a short dressing gown. The one that rode up to the little crease at the bottom of her buttocks when she threw her arms around his neck and kissed him. 'Mmm,' she said. 'Freshly showered, too. Is that the Ibex shower gel mum bought you for Christmas?'

*Make an effort, Darren*, he thought. *Pave the way.*

'I expect so,' he said, 'explains the sudden urge I had in the shower to gallop vertically up the side of the house and stand on the chimney.'

She did not smile, but neither did she frown. Neutral was a good omen. She reached up to a bruise blooming above his eye, frowning. 'What have you been up to?'

'Good question. Need a cup of tea first, I think.' Darren busied himself with boiling a kettle while Amanda transferred her eggs from stove to sink and ran cold water into the saucepan. Darren stirred in a teaspoon of sugar, went to the kitchen table and sat cradling the cup, wondering again why hot sweet tea was such a Band-Aid for the soul. Amanda already had a cup of coffee on the go. She retrieved it from the edge of the stove, sat opposite him, and arched her eyebrows.

'Right,' Darren said. 'I know all this is going to sound off the wall mad, but I want you to hear me out and no interruptions, okay?'

Amanda nodded, genuine intrigue in her expression.

'First things first. I was late last night for several reasons; the most important one is that Sanjay's dad had a stroke and I ended up taking Sanj to the hospital.'

'Is he okay?' Amanda asked.

For a second Darren wasn't sure if she meant Sanjay or Mr. B. 'No. It was a massive stroke. He's in a coma. '

'Shit,' Amanda said, frowning with what Darren took to be genuine concern.

'Yeah,' Darren nodded. He took another sip of tea and it helped. 'But that's not what I wanted to tell you. This next bit is going to sound more than a bit crazy, but…'

'Come on, Darren. You can tell me.'

*Really?*

Darren winced, took a deep breath, exhaled through his nose and reached for the off switch on the radio. He then told Amanda the story right from the beginning. Several times she looked as if she was about to interrupt him, but each time Darren held up his hand to stop her. There was no noise other than the hiss of cold water trickling into the saucepan and Darren's voice. Amanda sat and listened to him tell her about Ysbaed, Matt and Kylah, Malcolm and Vivette, Regurgors and the Armageddon that visited Moldarrenovia. When he'd finished, she sat looking at him, saying nothing for thirty long, silent seconds.

'Obviously you believe that, otherwise you wouldn't have told me, right?' Although Amanda's mouth was going for a beatific *Mona Lisa*, her eyes were more Mount Etna; smouldering under the surface with a potential for eruption at any moment.

'Yeah, I believe it. I've got the bruises to prove it, as you can s—'

'Only…I know Sanjay is your mate and all, but haven't you told me that he gets cannabis cakes for his dad?' Her voice remained reasonable and even.

'Yeah,' Darren said, wondering where this was leading.

'Well it sounds to me like Sanjay might have spiked your drink or given you some cannabis cake, or cannabis bread or even cannabis naan if you had another curry.'

'Barbecue,' Darren said automatically, but then shook his head. 'No, listen, I saw what I saw. I was there.'

'Darren,' Amanda sighed his name. 'We both know things like that can't happen. You were in a house where they use illegal substances like I use make-up remover.'

'We didn't…I didn't…' protested Darren.

But Amanda's lips morphed from *Mona Lisa* into one of her special, knowing, irritating little smiles. 'What's the alternative, Darren? It's obvious that none of this really happened.'

'But Sanjay's dad is in hospital.'

'Okay, that bit's true. I can live with that. I mean, having a stroke I can accept.'

Darren stared at her, wondering if she realised how unfeeling she sounded. But Amanda remained unfazed.

'And burglars I can buy into too, but as for the rest of it…' She let out a little laugh. 'You're seriously telling me that this Ysbaed bloke is some sort of Aboriginal demon and tortures people with bits of snakeskin and bone, these…*vetoes?*' She shook her head.

'Votives,' Darren said, but he heard the lack of conviction in his own voice.

'Whatever,' Amanda said. 'That's all nonsense. It's all made up. Something my cousin would call a bad trip. He had a couple of dodgy Es once and he ended up in hospital for a week. Thought all the nurses were poodles for the first two days.'

'I didn't hallucinate any of this, Amanda.'

'Of course you did, Darren.' Her voice bore a cold edge and her smile was fixed. 'And if you ask me, it's been on the cards for a while.'

'What does that mean?'

'It means that Sanjay, in my opinion, is a very bad influence.'

'Look, I know you've never liked him,' Darren said.

Amanda got up and turned off the running water. What she said next was spoken to the drowned eggs in the saucepan, not to Darren. 'Maybe not, but then I'm not the one seeing twenty-foot monsters that spit acid, am I?'

Darren stared at her back. She could be so irritating when she was like this. So cocksure of herself. He'd wanted a sympathetic ear, not a slap across the face with a wet fish.

'Amanda, I swear it's true. All of it.'

She turned to face him. 'True, is it?' She nodded. 'Okay, let's see the proof. What did you bring back with you?'

'Nothing,' Darren said. 'I told you, we had to leave in a hurry.'

'Photographs? You said you took photographs.'

'Matt made me send them off and that caused an automatic deletion…'

Amanda stayed quiet but let her eyebrows do the talking.

'Look, it was as real as this table.' He rapped his knuckles on the wood.

She walked towards him, undoing the sash of her dressing gown and letting it fall backward off her shoulders. It fell to the floor and she stood before him wearing nothing but a pair of very thin and strappy panties. 'No, Darren.' She ran her manicured hands down the length of her torso an inch away from the flesh. '*This* is real. And if you want to get anywhere near *this* ever again, you're going to have to stop talking made-up rubbish, because if my dad hears one word of this…this *fairy story*, he's going to get you locked away somewhere that does a nice line in padded cells. This is it, Darren. I'm not taking any more crap. I thought we'd got rid of all that pathetic toy photography stuff, and I hoped,' she let her lids fall to half-mast and dropped her voice to follow, 'I really hoped you'd take that chance to grow up and decide.'

'Decide?' Darren said, knowing that his voice was reflecting the confusion he was feeling. Though there was no mistaking Amanda's drift, which was ten feet high and impassable even in a snow plough.

'Yes, decide. It's your toys and Sanjay and his bloody weed cakes, or me.' She put both hands on her hips and glared at him, her lips doing an impression of a freshly drawn ruler line. Her figure was boyish and lean, but with all the right bumps in all the right places, especially the perky ones at the front. Despite himself, Darren let his eyes fall to take in the view. He shook his head. It still hurt when he did that. He was still dog-tired, but his brain buzzed like a wasps' nest that someone had poked a stick into. Amanda was implacable. Everything he'd told her was true, and yet as he stared at her firm body a part of him, the part of him that stuck with her even when her manipulative psyche had become something he'd feared, was inveigling him to see it from her point of view. And despite everything, that viewpoint seemed suddenly, contrarily, attractive.

Why the hell couldn't he be like everyone else? Not be the bloody *Maker*. Not be weighed down with horrors and guilt at what had happened to all those people. Not feel sickened and torn. Why couldn't he get regularly pissed with the Crays and throw up and brag about getting paralytic with the men at work on Monday mornings? Watch crap on TV and actually enjoy it? It wasn't so bad, was it? He felt the numbing attraction of it begin to seep into him like a slow poison. And, after all, Kylah and Matt didn't seem to care that much. Despite all their talk they'd walked away, leaving Darren the only one with a memory.

Suddenly, Darren felt a little sick.

Amanda picked up her dressing gown, threaded her arms through and tied the belt with a satisfied smirk. She went to the sink and came back to the table with the two hard-boiled eggs firmly in one hand, still smirking.

The irony of her clutching those eggs was not lost on Darren, but he didn't care. He knew he should have; the little skirmish that Amanda had just won hands down was more evidence, if need be, of the way the Crays did personal business. All the alarm bells should have been going off in his head, but they weren't. A sudden pang of guilty pleasure jolted him, like that first explosive taste of a forbidden fruit. What had that bloody Matt said?

*'We have ways of making it easier.'*

And there it was. This was his ticket out of jail. This might be the best, the only Trott coping mechanism. All he needed to do was to lie to himself a little bit. Convince that part of him that was too smart for its own good. Cajole himself into believing that the Cray way was how people lived and that there was no shame in it.

Sanjay didn't need him now, he'd be overrun with auntie this and cousin that. He could always keep in touch by text. Perhaps it was best to stay away from his smashed-up equipment and broken dreams for a while. And if anyone (Sanjay) asked, he'd say that Amanda needed him. They were busy with the project in the garage. And who knows, once Mr. B was back at home again, he'd go around, tell Sanjay to get someone to empty the crap from the bedroom and chuck it in the skip. Maybe, with time, he might even come to believe that Roxana and Ysbaed were all a Dealer Dave cannabis cake trip that took a wrong turn at Jupiter.

Maybe.

Amanda used a spoon to crack her eggshells. The noise made Darren look up.

'What time is your cousin coming?'

'About ten-ish,' she said, concentrating hard on peeling off the shells.

'Right, I'll put on some old clothes and give him a hand.'

Amanda looked up. 'Does that mean we've got a deal?'

Darren nodded. 'If deal means that I promise not to mention Moldarrenovia again, then yeah. It's a deal.'

She flashed him one of her special smiles. 'It's about time,' she said. She pushed herself away from the table, grabbed his T-shirt and pulled him down with such force that, caught off balance, he fell to his knees in front of her.

'And, if you're a very good boy today for mummy,' Amanda breathed, 'we'll reward you later, eh?'

Darren looked up into her eyes. Something moved behind them, a little spark of excitement. But that spark had nothing to do with the anticipation of the intimacy she was hinting at. This was something else, something Cray-like that he'd seen in Kaa too. And in a flash he knew what it was. How could he have missed it all this time?

Power.

That was what turned Amanda on.

Being in control.

He stood and she let him go. But something fundamental had changed between them. Something that he'd unconsciously fought for months, but that he'd relinquished for the sake of two boiled eggs. He walked upstairs to find an old pair of tracksuit bottoms and a sweatshirt. He slid them on and heard an annoying, accusatory voice in his head saying, '*Now you've done it, you berk. Welcome to the dark side, Darren.*'

The voice sounded very much like George Hoblip's.

# CHAPTER THIRTY-NINE

**WAYNE CRAY WAS** a man not overburdened with sparkling repartee. But what he did have was a voracious appetite he assuaged with regular swallows from a two-pint container full of something called a 'tuna shake'. This was a dubiously lumpy concoction the colour of calamine lotion that smelled like a broken urinal on the hottest day of the year. Wayne also had a lot of tools. Before Darren knew it, the garage filled up with long lengths of four-by-twos and sheets of plywood, all transported in complete silence from the large white van parked in the drive by Wayne, with a physique hewn from the base materials of barrel chest and long arms that were trademark Cray physiognomy, and modified by long, repetitive hours in the gym. Darren couldn't think of any other word to describe the almost Neanderthal appearance that Wayne had developed, aided by various hormonal stimulants designed to coax muscle growth into the bulges and swellings that rippled alarmingly when Wayne moved.

But watching Wayne work was a distraction that Darren welcomed. Of course, a part of him was protesting at his willing participation in the systematic reconfiguration of his erstwhile studio, but the larger part of him was glad to have a tedious job to do. And Wayne's taciturn approach to life meant that for long stretches of time, the whine of a drill or the smack of a hammer was the only noise in the garage. And that left space for Darren to think. It was like having a lesson in carpentry in a Benedictine monastery but without the promise of a nip of herbal liquor at the end. When Wayne asked for a glass of water in a curiously high voice after two hours of slog, Darren almost dropped his hammer.

He texted Sanjay mid-morning to ask about his father. He got a *NO CHANGE* reply. Wayne left sometime late afternoon and before Darren knew it, it was Saturday night and Amanda had brought home another dine-in for a tenner from yet another supermarket. They ate chicken with cheddar gratin and roasted vegetables, followed by chocolate pudding, all washed down with Pinot Grigio. Finishing that bottle, they opened another while Amanda settled in front of the TV to watch talentless wannabes being jeered at by a baying audience. Darren kept hoping that if only the celebrity chairman of the panel gave a thumbs down, a lion would come out and tear the contestants to pieces. When it was over, Amanda switched the TV off and turned to Darren.

'So, you ready, Trot?' she said, overdoing the husky voice a bit and shifting in her seat so that quite a lot of thigh was showing.

'For what?'

'You know what. I told you, it's practise night tonight.'

'Oh right, upstairs you mean?'

'I do. And I've got something special lined up for you.'

She'd put on a black dress and heels and a bit too much make-up. Her voice slurred slightly as she leaned in to kiss him, her perfume jasmine heavy. Darren hadn't thought much about his 'reward' for helping in the garage, but now he felt the first stirrings of desire. If he did wonder why it had taken a kiss from her for him to feel anything, he managed to suppress it as she pressed her body into his.

'Give me five minutes,' Amanda said, and walked out of the room. He waited downstairs, swirling the wine in his glass before swallowing it down. It tasted curiously bitter, but he poured another half glass and threw that back too. He went to the window and looked out. Rain and mist made the streetlamps glow with a fuzzy halo and the pavements were emptying as people retreated to the warmth and safety of their homes. Darren wondered why he could no longer achieve either of those emotional states in the house he'd occupied his whole life. He dragged his thoughts around to contemplating what Sanjay might be doing at that moment. On a normal Saturday night he'd be at home karting on the Wii, or maybe doing something else ending in –ing at his lap dancing cousin's. But tonight he'd probably be at his dad's bedside.

Then he heard Amanda call.

'You coming up or what?'

Darren felt his gut twist and expelled some air in a sigh.

Despite Wayne and the physicality of dry walling, he'd spent the afternoon trying, and failing, to push Roxana to the back of his mind. After all, she didn't exist. He was not ever going to bump into her in the checkout at Tesco. No point even thinking about her again. It had been nothing more than a very vivid—and possibly cannabinoid-fuelled—dream. The real world was the here and now, and she was already upstairs beckoning to him.

And that was the trouble.

What the hell was wrong with him? Although there'd been quite a lot of misgivings since the first time he'd met Amanda, doing *it* with her had always been conducted in the dark under the cover of sheets and darkness. But nonetheless satisfying in a non-visual sort of way. And he was on a promise here with a real live girl and he should have been bouncing with anticipation. Blimey, he'd been made to wait long enough. He tried to examine his anxiety and when he did, he realised that it wasn't anticipation that was making his palms sweat. It was the 'something special'.

Was there someone else up there waiting to make it a party? He told himself not to be stupid. Hardly Amanda's style or inclination, not that such a thing was even on his suck it and see list, as Sanjay liked to call his male fantasy top ten. Something he usually did with a cheesy eyeroll.

He squeezed his eyes shut, opened them again, wiped his palms on his jeans and went upstairs. When he walked past the open door of the bedroom, he wasn't surprised to see the only light coming from the sodium lamps in the street outside. He went to the bathroom, brushed his teeth, slipped off his clothes, showered and then joined Amanda under the covers.

'Dar?' Amanda said in the dark next to him.

'Yes?'

'Will you do something for me?'

'Sure,' he replied, not sure at all and swallowing loudly as a result. He felt a hand on his bare chest and a manicured nail run down his belly.

'Will you put something on for me?'

'Like what?' he said, suddenly anxious. Her hand reached a point where her fingernails could do some real damage if she pressed that little bit harder. As it was, though, he wasn't about to ask her to stop.

'Will you put on a mask?' she whispered.

'A mask. What, like Zorro?'

'No, not like Zorro. A head mask. A Trey Lushton head mask.'

Darren froze. He stopped both breathing and moving. A hundred thoughts stampeded through his head. Right at the front carrying a banner was *No way, never! A bloody Trey Lushton mask, of all things? You must be kidding.* But then another thought trailing on the heels of that one galloped right over it: *Hey, why not? If it pleases her, why not?* After all, she was doing a pretty good job of pleasing him right at that moment. And people did worse things in the name of intimate pleasure. Much worse things with ropes…and cucumbers.

Sometimes, indeed, with both.

This second thought surprised him as much as it would Amanda. Why wasn't he stamping up and down and telling her to go to hell? Why hadn't he laughed at her and got up and walked away? And then the answer came like a fresh bit of sewage on the incoming tide.

If he wore a Trey Lushton mask he would be pandering to Amanda's fantasies, but he would also be appeasing his own doubts. Because it was doubt that caused the sweaty palms downstairs, he realised that now. If he wore the mask it wouldn't be Darren Trott any more in this bed. He could pretend that he was someone else. Like he'd been doing all the long day.

'No problem,' said Darren, and in the darkness he heard Amanda's breath catch in her throat. And then something floppy was pressed against his chest. Darren took it and slid it on over his head. A minute later, he felt Amanda reach up for a pull switch and the lights came on. This time she squealed. The mask was light and snug fitting. The only bad thing was that it stank of synthetic rubber. Amanda was kneeling on the bed, staring at him, her cheeks pink, lips moist. She wore a short T-shirt and nothing else. She took off the T-shirt and…after that the details all blurred because somebody had thrown a switch turning Amanda from 'off' to 'on'.

What happened in the next hour-and-a-half had never happened before between them. Trott/Cray interactions were, by and large straight, in the dark, functional. Now it was no holds barred, feet, hands, mouth, something that buzzed, the works. Darren did what he was asked to do and threw in a few things he wasn't. And it was easy, because he wasn't Darren anymore. And that helped a lot. Because he knew that as Darren he would not have been able to do any of them. At least not that night.

And definitely not with Amanda.

At midnight they fell into an exhausted sleep. Amanda took off his mask and stored it carefully away with a murmured, 'For the next time.'

She even cuddled him.

Yet, even in his exhausted state, Darren knew that her hands were cold and her grip half-hearted. After two minutes, she turned over and went to sleep, leaving him wide awake in the dark, wondering about how easy it had been to comply with Amanda's little game and knowing too, that perhaps tonight might be a template for future life in the bedroom with her. A night that he'd been a willing participant in, but that now left him feeling cheap and unhappy. Was this how it would be if they ever got married? Would he be asked to put on a mask every time they made love?

Amanda took the Fig Newton all right. A contradiction

melded with enigma in a wrapping of hypocrisy. How could she happily play fantasy doctors and nurses with him, while at the same time castigate him for photographing plastic models in made-up situations?

The irony of it was exquisite.

But Amanda was back to her normal harpy self on Sunday morning. Darren got up later than usual, walked to the shops for a paper and by the time he got back she was up.

'Listen, Mand, about last night,' he said in an opening salvo, but all she did was smile at him.

'Brilliant, wasn't it?' she said.

'I—'

'That can be our special Saturday night. Something to look forward to, eh?'

'I suppose—'

'You be a good boy and we'll see.'

Darren looked at her and again he saw that odd light flicker in eyes that had become large questioning ovals. 'You enjoyed it too, didn't you? Least, I didn't hear you complain.'

'That's because my mother told me never to talk with my mouth full,' Darren said, cringing mentally at the way he automatically tried to please her.

She laughed and once again Darren saw her father in that laugh, and it chilled him. Harry Cray had no right to be in the same thought bubble as the one surrounding what he and Amanda had done the night before. In fact, Harry Cray had no right to be in any of Darren's thought bubbles at all. It was like letting a hungry fox into a battery hen enclosure: horror and carnage were the only possible outcomes.

But Amanda was right. He hadn't complained the previous night, even though he'd put on a bloody Trey Lushton mask. And why? Because something inside him had enjoyed it in a vicarious, sordid kind of way. Like people who outwardly profess to be literati but secretly read the odd schlock thriller on their eReaders so no one else would know. But he knew it was wrong, he knew he was lying to himself, knew, too, that it was all part of the self-deluding subterfuge he needed to get through all this without going completely and utterly insane.

# CHAPTER FORTY

**At lunchtime, they** took a taxi to her mother's, or rather to the pub nearby first. Harry came to meet them, together with Amanda's uncle Lou and auntie Pauline, as corpulent as each other and equally thirsty for their Sunday ritual. Darren bought the first round. He came back to the table with a tray laden with drinks, including a pint of lager for himself.

'Hello,' Harry said, eyeing the lager. 'What's this then, lad? Darren Trott drinking on a Sunday lunchtime? Has the world gone chuffin' mad?'

Darren shrugged. Being Amanda's designated driver, Sunday's poison had always been innocuous orange juice and lemonade.

Lou fixed him with a leer. 'What you been doing to make you so thirsty then, eh Dar?' He winked and nudged Harry. Darren couldn't quite believe he'd actually done that and waited, in the brief but very pregnant pause that followed, for the guano to hit the weathervane. But Harry, in Sunday lunchtime happy-mood, embraced the joke and pretended to chide his brother-in-law. 'Oi, steady Lou, that's my daughter you're talking about.'

The two men creased up. Amanda shook her head with her eyes skywards in an indulgent, 'what-are-they-like' way. Though she did throw Darren a knowing glance when she thought the men weren't watching.

Darren drank his lager. If it did feel like he'd been cast into a bad Seventies sketch show, the feeling quickly faded as the level of beer in his glass fell with startling rapidity. By the time they sat down to lunch at Harry's house, Darren was three pints in and laughing uproariously at the crass jokes. When conversation, which revolved for the most part around family members' ditch water anecdotes, got around to Darren, it somehow or other ended up with him recounting Sanjay's dad's stroke.

Most people sympathised, but Harry Cray was less impressed.

'Come on, Darren, talk about raining on the chuffin' parade. Lighten the mood a bit, will you?' he said with a mock horror glare.

Darren frowned. 'He's in a coma.'

'Christ, so will we be if you keep talking like this.' That brought a guffaw from uncle Lou that triggered laughs all around.

A voice, not often heard in the Cray house, piped up.

'No Harry, don't be unkind. The boy is upset by it.' They all turned to look at Janice Cray, Amanda's mother. She was not renowned for her conversational skills, other than a perfunctory 'You sit here,' or 'Want some more?', and Darren struggled to recall hearing her say anything of any weight in all the time he'd known Amanda. Of course he wasn't surprised; being in Harry Cray's shadow she'd found solace in quiet observation, red wine and tobacco, which showed in the coarse, ruddy skin of her face.

'Bloody hell, Darren. Now see what you've done?' Lou said.

Harry nodded. 'The kraken chuffin' wakes.'

'All I'm saying,' Mrs. Cray said, passing the gravy around and not rising to the bait, 'is that you shouldn't make fun of the ill.'

'We're not making fun, Janice. All I'm chuffin' saying is that it was hardly a champagne bloody story. If Mr. Bombay decides to have a stroke, it's nothing to do with us.'

Uncle Lou stifled another giggle.

Harry turned to Darren. 'That reminds me, my auntie Edna had a stroke when she was in the park watching a cross country race. She tried to have another one, but the buggers were too fast for her.'

Everyone laughed. Darren, fuelled by the cheap red table wine on top of the pub Stellas, bought into it and laughed too, fending off the queasy, uneasy feeling it gave him with another slurp of the cheap wine. After lunch, the men decided to go back to the pub for the football televised on a big screen, and Darren staggered off with them. He remembered the first fifteen minutes of the game, but after that, it all became a fuzzy alcoholic blur.

One thing did stand out in his memory like an ominously brown stain on a cream carpet. Outside the pub afterwards, Harry put his arm around Darren's shoulders and, with his face inches from Darren's ear, said, 'You're a good lad, Darren. Nice to see you enjoying yourself like this. It's been a long time coming, but it's great timing because I wanted a special word with you.' His voice dropped to a whisper, beery breath hot and moist in Darren's ear. 'There's a job going in Health and Safety. Assistant to Rog Fielder. You know Rog, big bloke. Drinks at the chuffin' Globe.'

Darren shook his head. His wavering eyes focused in on the large veins on Harry's nose. They formed a purple pattern reminiscent of a coiled serpent looping between the open pores. Having found it, Darren could not drag his eyes away.

'They've shortlisted two people. I've put a word in for you. Better hours and you'll be off the warehouse floor. Not bad money too. Job's a doddle. Checking stuff, ticking boxes for the ministry. That sort of bollocks. Fancy that?'

'Yeah, but I…I never applied,' Darren said.

'Don't you worry about that, lad. I've got you down on the chuffin' reserve list if one of those blokes fails to turn up…'

'Why shouldn't they?'

'Maybe they'll get lost. Maybe someone in the office might send them the wrong chuffin' directions.' He tapped his nose and the venous snake writhed.

Darren grinned. He couldn't help it. Suddenly Harry was the funniest man in the world.

'I'll let you know, Darren. Mum's the word.'

They wandered back down the road to Harry's house. On

the corner of Bethlehem Street, where the Crays lived, Harry said, 'Right, who's having one for the road?'

Judging from the tone, the word 'no' was not an option.

Some hours later, after the taxi dropped them off, Amanda made Darren drink a pint of water. He woke up during the night to throw up. He slumped over the toilet in misery; lager and bits of carrot, lamb and gravy spattering all over the white bowl like mud thrown up by a speeding car. Some broccoli got stuck up his nose, but vomiting released the pressure on his bloated stomach and at least granted him a few hours of anaesthetised sleep. At 7.00 am he awoke with a headache of gargantuan proportions but managed to keep down some cereal and a couple of paracetamol. Amanda held them out, smiling with ceremonial delight, only to snatch them back at the last moment.

'Get through to him then, did you?' Amanda said with a smirk.

'Who?' Darren replied, wincing against the light blazing in through the kitchen window, sending laser arrows straight to the pain centre of his head.

'Whoever you were shouting at on the big white telephone last night.'

'Don't,' Darren warned.

Amanda enjoyed his pain for a few moments longer. 'This is the first Monday hangover I think I've ever seen you with. About time if you ask me.' She popped the pills into his mouth, still smiling. 'Don't fancy a fry up this morning then, I take it?'

Darren groaned.

## CHAPTER FORTY-ONE

AMANDA DROVE THEM INTO WORK. He listened to her tell him how everyone said what a nice bloke he was, and how her influence had obviously rubbed off. She'd added the second bit with a little tinkling laugh. Darren sat like a still warm corpse, nodding and praying that the paracetamol would kick in soon.

He'd meant to phone Sanjay, but his phone was dead, and his brain was following the same fate. Monday went by in Hangover Hades, punctuated by Harry giving him the nod that all was well and set up for Wednesday's potential interview, reminding him to wear a shirt and tie, just in case. Darren refused lunch and tried to snooze in a quiet corner. When he got home, he went to bed at seven and slept for twelve hours.

He forgot to text Sanjay the following morning too, and to charge his phone. At break Harry called him up to the admin office and introduced him to Rog Fielder, who was a barrel-shaped fifty-year-old in a suit that probably last fitted him twenty years before. His comfortable plastic grey shoes had badly worn heels, and at his last visit to the barbershop, they'd forgotten to use the nose hair trimmer.

'I told Rog you'd clean his car lunchtime, okay Darren?' Harry said with a hypnotic glare once the introductions were over.

'Could do with a bit of valeting too,' Roger said. He had a

sallow pockmarked face that didn't smile too often, and small sluggish eyes.

'Oh, okay,' Darren said, trying to quell the irritation squirming inside at being placed in a position where he couldn't say no.

'Dab hand at valeting and car cleaning is Darren. If he moved up here, Darren could do that car of yours every week, couldn't you Darren?' Harry said, smiling his gap-toothed smile.

'Suppose,' Darren said. Harry kept smiling but threw Darren a warning glare.

'Probably be able to wax it a couple of times as well,' Darren threw in, trying to inject a little enthusiasm now.

Roger played his fingers on the desk surface and said nothing while he weighed Darren up. 'Let's see how it goes then,' he said with finality.

Satisfied, Harry stayed in the office to continue soft-soaping Rog, but dismissed Darren back to the warehouse floor. Darren meandered back, wondering why on earth cleaning a car was so vitally important to middle management.

He passed some of the other lads from the warehouse and heard someone shout, 'Hey Darren, got something on your nose, mate.'

'Yeah, 's all brown and smelly from where you been sticking it up Kaa's arse.'

He gave them the finger. All meant to be in good fun, he told himself. But then why wasn't anyone laughing?

He ate too much at lunchtime on Tuesday. He wanted to go for a walk, but lassitude combined with a lasagne and fries bloat won the day and he ended up spending ten uncomfortable minutes in the toilet. He blamed the weekend's overindulgence, at the same time glad of the solitude the cubicle brought. No one in their right minds used the toilets at lunchtime—except in dire emergencies—because it ate into 'restroom' time. Employees at Dobson and Crank's were allowed a statutory ten minutes per three hours loo break during the working day and never were six hundred seconds more treasured or religiously adhered to. Darren wondered about patenting the Dobson and Crank method as a potty-training manual. But then going for a Dobson and Crank had all sorts of suggestive rhyming connotations that might not endear it to mothers.

On the factory floor, however, the consensus was that spending a precious lunchtime straining unnecessarily was crass incompetence.

Darren washed his hands and then wrung them together under the dryer. As he turned away to leave, he heard a familiar voice.

'He's dead, you know.'

# CHAPTER FORTY-TWO

**Darren started badly.** So badly that he was very glad he'd just finished what he'd gone in there to do, because hearing that voice out of the blue would have very likely precipitated events. As it was, he thought he might need a bit more toilet paper. He swivelled around, eyes darting everywhere, but there was no one in the room.

'Hello?' he said in a small voice.

'Yesterday, midday,' said the voice. It came from behind him, but there was no one there.

'The mirror,' said the voice in exasperation. 'Look in the mirror.'

A small one-foot square reflective square hung on the wall next to the dryer. Darren swung his eyes up and saw, at first, only his own face. But then, by shifting his head, there, lounging against the door was a small figure with red skin and orange tufted red hair, dressed in black velvet harem pants and a yellow and brown check waistcoat.

'George?' Darren said.

'Who the hell else would it be, the tooth fairy?'

'But how come I can understand you? Is Kylah here, too?'

'Nah. Decided to go intestine for this.'

Darren pondered that little gem for several seconds, toyed

with scatological, but finally plumped for over-confident use of big words as an explanation. 'You mean clandestine, don't you?'

'Exactly what I said. Anyway, don't need her. It's Krudian, this language thing, innit. After you've heard it once, it's permanent. Like opening a valve. And I would have been here ten minutes ago, bro, but I thought I'd better leave you to it. Strewth, what've you been eating?' George shook his pumpkin head. 'Oh, and when I say dead, I'm talking about your friend's dad, BTW.'

Something deflated inside Darren's chest. 'Mr. B?'

'Yeah. Sanjay's tried texting you, but your phone is dead.'

'Yeah, I know…I…'

'"Been meaning to charge it up" is the sentence you're looking for,' George said.

Darren nodded and slowly looked behind him again into the room. It was empty. Yet when he turned back, George Hoblip was still leaning against the door.

Darren searched for something meaningful to say and came up with, 'Umm…. How are you?'

'Pissed off,' George said. His voice was more clipped and irritable than normal, which was going some.

'Why?'

'Girlfriend troubles,' George stared out of the mirror with eyes that seemed to bore into Darren's brain.

'I'm sorry to hear about Mr. Bobal,' Darren shook his head.

'Really? Got a funny way of showing it if you ask me, bro. From where I'm standing, looks like you prefer screwing around with your girlfriend and getting pissed than giving a toss about Sanjay or his dad. Funeral's tomorrow, BTW.'

'Look, Mr. B…that wasn't my fault. Everything else was, but not Mr. B. I'm not taking the flak for that one.'

'No? Well think again, Darren.' Sarcasm dripped off George's delivery like the gelatinous gravy off Mrs. Cray's Sunday lunch plate.

Guilt fuelled by anger at having his failings pointed out to him so bluntly lit a flame in Darren's gut. 'What exactly is that supposed to mean?'

'It means that you are the one and only bloke in this world that can make this right, you tart.'

Hot blood rushed to Darren's cheeks. 'Make it right? How can I make it right? I watched all those people die. Watched them smashed, their world torn apart by that bastard, Ysbaed. Watched it and couldn't do a thing about it.'

'Well maybe what you saw, and what you think you saw are two very different things,' George said with narrowed eyes.

'I don't understand.' Exasperation sent Darren's voice up an octave.

'You are still the Maker, you tosser. There are people that can help.'

'People?'

'Yeah,' George's belligerent tone dipped a little. 'But you need to want it. You need to want to make things right. If you do, help will be given, Darren.' George spat out his name as if it was something floating persistently in one of the toilet bowls, despite a flush.

Darren clamped his eyes shut, fighting a sudden urge to smash the mirror with his fist. 'You…people. Waltzing in and out of my bloody life. I wish you'd stop faffing around and tell me what to do,' he said through grinding teeth.

George pushed off the wall and walked forwards in the mirror. 'I think you're a good bloke, Darren, despite what they all say. But you need to stop being such an effin' dishcloth, yeah? You know the right thing to do, don't tell me you don't. But if you want some help, okay. Just remember to eat your cereal.'

Darren's brows furrowed. 'Cereal?'

He heard someone try the door. It didn't open but the sudden noise drew his attention. When he looked back into the mirror, George Hoblip had gone. The door rattled again. As far as Darren knew, there wasn't even a lock on it.

'Oi, open up.'

Darren stepped across and pulled at the handle. It opened at once. He looked up into Big Jeff's anxious face. 'Jesus, Dar, got a torpedo in the tube and it's about to launch. What you lock the door for anyway? You in here with a customer or what?'

But Darren wasn't listening. He turned back into the mirror. Looking for a sign.

'Alright,' he said to his own reflection. 'I'll do it. I will. But I need a little help, okay?'

Big Jeff took three steps into the room heading for the cubicle, each one slightly slower than the last. He finally stopped to watch Darren talk to his reflection with a wary expression.

'Dar? Who the hell you talking to?'

Darren ignored him and kept talking. There was desperation in his voice now. 'Please. Help me.'

Big Jeff shifted into reverse gear and retraced his steps backwards out of the door. 'I'll just…the other…I can hold it for…' He turned and bolted.

Big Jeff's panic barely registered in Darren's head. He was looking in the mirror, waiting for something or someone to respond to his plea. But all he now saw was his own face, full of troubled confusion and misery. Any thought he had of ever understanding what the hell was going on seemed as distant as the stars.

Darren muddled through the rest of the day, almost misdirecting a forklift truck into a sixty-foot-high wall of assorted gardening tools, the collapse of which would have made the climax of *300* look like a pillow fight. Big Jeff shouted twice before Darren took any notice. When Harry came to fetch him to get on with cleaning Roger's car, all he could do was nod automatically in response to the issued set of unnecessary car-cleaning instructions.

'Elbow grease, lad. Spit and polish. That's all you'll ever chuffin' need in this world.'

He sponged and rinsed, hoovered, polished and buffed, but all he could think about was George Hoblip's words. Of course, there was the faint possibility that he'd imagined the whole George Hoblip thing, too, but even if he had, the imaginary words were impossible to dismiss. The obvious thing to do would be to ring Sanjay, but having ignored him for two days, Darren felt horribly embarrassed and chose, now that he'd charged up his phone, the impersonal route of a text. After ten minutes he'd received no reply. Suppressing his angst, he phoned, and his call went straight to a generic messaging service. By the time he'd finished with the car it gleamed, but the same thing could not be said of Darren's mood. He looked down at the filthy water in the bucket and emptied it into a drain. It slopped away with a gurgle, and it felt like he was pouring it into the chambers of his own hollow heart.

## CHAPTER FORTY-THREE

Amanda drove them home from work in a buoyant mood. Darren didn't speak, feigning a migraine as an excuse, though that didn't stop her from talking. Later, he waited until she'd buried herself in one of her mandatory TV soaps before slipping out. He'd decided to go straight to Sanjay's, but when he turned the corner into Shunter Street there must have been a dozen cars parked outside Number One. Once more Darren found himself hesitating, watching a steady stream of visitors come and go, and cringed inwardly at his own rubber-spined weakness. The last thing he wanted to do was interrupt a family's grieving to explain…to explain what, exactly? That he hadn't bothered visiting Mr. B over the weekend because he thought it might be for the best? As pathetic excuses went, that was a beauty. Worse even than the truth of being too caught up in his own self-absorbed tribulations to bother about his best friend's dying father.

Darren had insight. He knew he was a procrastinator. He'd said as much to Amanda once. Without missing a beat, she'd shrugged and said it didn't matter because she was Church of England too. But Darren had taken the advanced dithering course, which meant perfecting the art of acting immediately, so long as that act was an excuse for not doing the thing he really ought to do. However, when it came to Sanjay, the more he thought through his excuses, the worse it all sounded. After half an hour of mental handwringing, in a decision that put the buttercream icing on the Victoria sponge of his self-loathing, he turned and trudged back to his own house without speaking to Sanjay, feeling lower than a snake's gonads.

Amanda hadn't even noticed his absence. He drank half a bottle of cheap wine, tried watching a TV programme about two female detectives, who looked about as capable of solving a crime as Big Jeff was of doing the high jump, and at ten went to bed. Had he really seen George Hoblip in the mirror of the toilet at work that morning? Or was his insufferable guilt triggering increasingly fantastic delusions?

Sleep remained tantalisingly elusive. He tossed and turned, wondering yet again if all that was happening was that he was going completely mad. He heard Amanda go to bed, heard dogs barking, heard his own heavy heart pounding away in his temples. What, he wondered, would his poor mother have said if she could see him now? He fell asleep thinking about her and woke up at six-thirty in the morning, groggy and with a brain like cotton wool, feeling like he hadn't slept at all.

Amanda was already up. His best shirt and his good tie were already folded on the kitchen table. She looked bright eyed and very bushy tailed in her shorty dressing gown and Darren chided himself for wondering if she had anything on underneath. Half an anaemic grapefruit sat looking woebegone in a bowl at his place setting. Amanda was already halfway through hers.

'You look awful,' she said.

'Didn't sleep too well.'

'Nerves?'

'Nerves?' He sent her a vague, questioning look.

'Because of the interview?' She held up her hands in a 'duh' gesture.

Darren knew his expression gave away the fact that he'd forgotten all about it. 'No, just...stuff on my mind.' He pushed away the grapefruit, much to Amanda's stony-faced disapproval, opened the cupboard and took out a cereal box. It felt light and when he looked inside, it was indeed empty.

'Mum gave me a new box of cereal for you to try, if you

must,' Amanda said, in a huff. 'I don't see anything wrong with grapefruit myself.'

'I need something more substantial this morning,' he said, his stomach rumbling its approval.

Amanda got up and fetched a carrier bag still laden with purchases. Darren took out an unfamiliar orange and yellow box with *Brand Flakes* written in bold black letters. He opened it and poured out a helping. Something clattered into the bowl along with the cereal. Darren fished it out: a three-inch high orange plastic figure with a pumpkin-shaped head and a brown and yellow waistcoat over voluminous black trousers.

Amanda's face was a picture. Just like the ones you got of tourists in the Amazon who'd just witnessed an anaconda eating a tour guide. 'If that's supposed to be a kid's toy someone ought to be shot. That is sick, and definitely not in a 'yay' way,' she exclaimed.

Darren studied the scale model of George Hoblip in his hand and laughed. He laughed so much he couldn't stop. Not even when the front doorbell rang.

'Answer it then, Darren,' Amanda urged, her irritation showing. But he was doubled up, helpless to respond, tears streaming down his face. Seeing her storming out to answer the door made it all the worse. When she came back to the kitchen with her mouth like a squeezed lemon, his laughter redoubled. She waved the parcel at him.

'It's for you. And I'll have you know the postman said I'd made his year.' Her eyes flared and she threw the envelope down on the table.

Darren was groaning now, holding his stomach to stop it aching. Finally, he managed to control his breathing. And when he did, he announced, 'I'm not going to the interview.'

Amanda, grapefruit-laden spoon almost to her lips, said softly, 'What did you say?'

'I'm not going to the interview. Sanjay's dad's funeral is this morning. I'm going to that instead.'

'Oh, Darren,' Amanda said, irritated but not too concerned. 'You're being silly now.'

'No, I'm not.'

'Yes, you are. My dad worked really hard to get this interview for you—'

'Yeah, by scuppering some other poor bastard's chances.'

Amanda frowned. 'So? What difference does that make? Still no reason to blow it because of Sanjay's dad.'

Darren gawped at her. 'Sanjay is my friend. And I've been a piss poor friend to him. Being there for him today is the least I can do.'

'God, you sound like a pathetic little boy.' She spat the words out.

Darren shrugged. 'Sorry about that. But you know what? There'll be other interviews, but there'll never be another funeral for Mr. B. I am going to be there for Sanjay.'

Amanda's face blanched with seething anger. She slammed down her spoon and grabbed the hair on the side of her head, pulling at it with both hands as she growled in frustration. 'Effing Sanjay again! I swear if I hear his name in this house once more, I'm going to scream. Jesus, I wish I'd let my uncle Lou brain the little nerd when he had the chance the other ni—' Her words seemed to freeze in the air on the way out of her open mouth to match her expression of eyes and mouth stuck open as three horrified ovals.

Darren stiffened like a cat mistaking the rattle of a tin roof for thunder. It took several seconds before he could bring himself to speak. When he did, he was astonished at how calm he sounded. 'What did you say?'

'Nothing,' she muttered, dropping her eyes and her hands to attack her grapefruit.

But Darren wasn't having that. He leaned over the table. 'What did you mean, Lou and the other night?'

'I didn't mean anything.' Amanda pushed the grapefruit away in disgust, got up and cleared away her things, clattering cutlery with unnecessary force. Darren stared at her. He couldn't move. His limbs were paralysed by the disgusting, shattering truth of what he'd heard from her lips.

'It was *you* and your bloody psychopathic family, wasn't it?' Darren whispered.

She had her back to him. Kept her back to him.

Darren persisted. 'It was you that smashed up my stuff at Sanjay's. You that caused Mr. B to have a stroke.'

'They never touched him!' she screamed, spinning back around to face Darren, her face contorted with rage. 'He went for them with a lamp. All they did was take it off him. He collapsed, all right? He blew a gasket and—'

'Blew a gasket? Are you serious?'

Amanda fists were balled at her sides, her eyes deviated up and to the right as if she was searching the ceiling for the right words to use in explanation. The sudden blaze of white sclera made Darren wonder if she was having a fit, or attempting, and succeeding, in doing a passable impression of that girl in *The Exorcist*. After several deep breaths her gaze drifted back down, straight into Darren's stunned face. She slunk towards him, reached down and took one of his hands into both of hers, her eyes half-lidded as she wet her lips with her small pink tongue.

'Oh, Dar, we had to do something. I had to do something. I can't be with a loser. Playing with action figures? Spending all your time with a nerd like Sanjay? Locking yourself away with a pathetic little hobby? I couldn't stand it.' She shook her head. 'I couldn't let myself be made a laughingstock anymore. Can you imagine me married to someone who took pictures of toys? Dad and Uncle Lou agreed with me. It should have been simple—'

Darren snatched his hand away as if he'd been scalded. 'You're sick, the lot of you. A load of bloody psychos.'

Her pleading, conciliatory expression disappeared, and her mouth became thin and ugly. 'It's not me that's sick. And don't think for one minute you've got anything on me. I'll deny everything. And we've all got cast iron alibis.'

Darren could only shake his head. 'Why?' he breathed.

'Because you're mine now, Darren. You're a Cray, and Crays don't play with toys,' she hissed.

When Darren said nothing, stupefied by what he'd heard, she turned on a slipper and stormed out, leaving him sitting at the table alone, heart thumping, temples pounding. He tried to assimilate what she'd said and failed. It was all so…so monstrous. But it also confirmed what he knew in his heart of hearts, and he felt his soul do a nosedive.

Amanda was one of the many fed a diet of ludicrous celebrity and mendacious longing, taught to grab what they could. One of the 'precious' generation convinced that society owed them a life and were angry at a world run by old people with money…or any people with money, intelligence or talent that they did not have. Sometimes that frustration boiled over into social unrest of the 'Let's throw things at the police and nab that forty-inch TV while I'm at it,' variety, as long as it wasn't too cold outside. But Amanda was subtler than that. She was like a crow spotting a shiny trinket on the bedroom dressing table and wanting it there and then. And, like a crow, she didn't care who got splattered with crap while she fluttered to and fro, trying desperately to get at it.

After a while Darren's eyes focused on the thick envelope in his lap. He picked it up. The sender's address read Hipposync Enterprises. Darren ripped it open. Inside was a bubble-wrapped bottle with a screw top no more than two-inches tall. The label read:

**SOUPERGLUE. For Mending Anything and Everything.**

He looked at it for a very long time, was still looking at it when he heard Amanda come downstairs and stand on the threshold of the kitchen. She didn't say anything, and he didn't look at her. After several seconds of .30 calibre, safety-off silence, he held the model of George Hoblip up above his head for her to see and heard a muted grunt of frustrated anger before she turned away. The front door slammed, and the car roared away, but Darren didn't budge. An idea was beginning to form in his head and he daren't move for fear of it evaporating like mist on a summer's morning before it was fully formed.

When he'd thought it all through, he put the model George on the table in front of him and said, 'Okay, I'm a king prat. Happy now?'

The model did not move or speak.

'But I am going to the funeral, and I think I'm going to sit Sanjay down and have a long chat.'

Still there was nothing from the model.

'You could at least give me a sign that I'm on the right track here.'

Nothing.

Darren got up and rinsed his bowl under the tap. To no one in particular, he said, 'You can go off goblins, you know.'

There was a noise like falling cutlery from the dishwasher. Darren pulled open the door to stick in his cereal bowl and almost fell over. Seven of the plates in the lower rack had 'fallen over' to lie flat. On each plate, the cutlery was arranged into letters. In sequence, left to right and back to front, the cutlery read *bwbach*.

Darren replaced the dishes, did a gangsta finger snap, smiled and, for no rhyme or reason, said, 'Respect.' He shut the dishwasher and heard more crashing cutlery noises. When he opened the door cautiously to peek, the plates had fallen into exactly the same pattern, but the cutlery was spelling out a new message.

*BELLEND.*

'Very funny,' Darren said.

From out of the plughole in the sink he thought he heard a deep, gurgling, definitely inhuman laugh.

## CHAPTER FORTY-FOUR

**DARREN KNEW ENOUGH** about Hinduism to realise that Mr. B would be cremated. He made some phone calls to the local crematoriums and found out that the service was at 11.00 am. He wore the Amanda-ironed shirt, his best tie, and a grey suit but he needn't have worried; hardly anyone wore black. Too many mourners were milling around outside for him to make his way through to the small chapel. Instead, so he stood with Dealer Dave who looked morose. Darren wanted to believe it was because he was genuinely sad to have lost a friend, but in a cynical corner of his mind he suspected it might have something to do with having lost one of his best customers.

After the service, which Darren saw nothing of because he was outside, Sanjay got stuck in a handshaking, hugging, mourning procession. Darren was one of the last in a long queue and when Sanjay saw him, much to Darren's relief and eternal shame, there was no sign of the anger he feared would greet him.

'Sanjay, mate...' Darren shook his head.

'Thanks for coming, man. How did you get time off work?'

Darren shrugged. That was Sanjay all over. Worrying about someone else, not even mentioning his absence for the last four days.

'Sod work. I should've come and seen you yesterday *and* the day before. It's unforgivable.'

'Been like a madhouse, man, I tell you. Still, it's done now. You coming back to my auntie Anitha's for some food? My dad didn't want people back at ours.'

'Yeah, if you want me to?'

'I'd be glad of the company, man,' Sanjay looked genuinely relieved. 'Didn't know I had so many bloody relatives.'

An hour later, Darren knew exactly what Sanjay meant. His aunt's house was like a Dulux advert: brightly coloured saris were the order of the day, and he lost count of the number of delicious spicy finger foods he ate. But Sanjay's younger cousins needed entertaining, and Darren gladly donned the mantle to play football and hide and seek and, managed to keep the five to ten-year-olds out of the adults' way. In reply he got an instant fan club and about a dozen dazzling smiles.

At four-thirty, Sanjay found him in the garden trying to get a football down from the middle of a huge laurel bush.

'My auntie Meena is asking how much you charge for kids' parties,' Sanjay said with a wry smile.

'Thousand an hour,' Darren said, in a strained voice as he reached up for the football. 'Hardest work I've ever done.'

'Is it?'

Dan shook his head and smiled. 'Nah, They're a great bunch.'

'Don't let them hear you say you enjoyed it.'

They both looked back at the house. The crowd was at last thinning out but there were still almost thirty people talking and eating.

'Tell you the truth, I've had enough now,' Sanjay said. 'I can only retell it so many times. And if I hear another story from when my dad was a kid, I'm going to scream.'

'So, what do you want to do?'

'I fancy going back to mine and having a few beers.'

Darren smiled. 'Let's do it.'

'What about Amanda?'

'What about Amanda?'

Sanjay's eyes were showing lots of white. 'What are you saying, Dar?'

'I'm saying nothing until we're out of here.'

While Darren bade farewell to a group of very disappointed kids, Sanjay said goodbye to his relatives. They decided to walk the mile-and-a-half back to Sanjay's. It felt good to be away from the claustrophobic atmosphere of the house. The rain stayed off, and despite a stiff breeze, it wasn't unpleasant to be outside.

'So, you and Amanda then?' Sanjay asked. 'Bit of a tiff?'

'It wasn't just a tiff, Sanj.' They passed the entrance to a pub called The Ten Bob Note. Darren hesitated. 'Fancy one?'

They sat in a quiet corner of what was still a drinker's pub. A couple of teenagers were playing pool in one corner whilst a group of older men played dominoes in a snug. Darren bought the drinks, sat down next to Sanjay, and let out a long, resolute, exhalation through his nose.

'If that's an impersonation of a horse, it could do with some work, Dar.'

Darren allowed himself a wry smile and then launched into his apology. 'First of all, I'm really sorry about not being in touch. It wasn't cool and I've been a total pillock and an arse, and all I can say is that I've been in a bad place, Sanj.'

'Uzturnsitstan, you mean?'

'Where's that?'

'Dunno. Just came to me.'

'I'm trying to be serious here, mate. But I do know how shit my 'bad place' sounds compared to what you've been through.'

Sanjay sat back and folded his arms. 'Okay, let's have it, then.'

Darren eyes slid away. 'I don't even know where to start.'

Sanjay frowned. 'As my dad used to say, 'Why the long faeces?''

'Thing is you know all the stuff I'm going to tell you, but you don't know you know it. Because your memory's been wiped by Kylah and Matt.'

The drink that was six inches from Sanjay's mouth remained where it was. 'Whoa, slow down there, Usain. Are you talking a 'Hermione's parents' deal here?'

Darren sighed and decided to begin at the very beginning. By the time he'd regurgitated everything and answered Sanjay's very pertinent questions, they were three rounds in. When he finished speaking, Darren took the three-inch model of George Hoblip out of his pocket and placed it on the table.

When Sanjay had recovered, he picked it up and examined it with an expression of wary distaste.

'Well, you're right about one thing. They must have wiped my memory because there's no way I'd ever forget meeting something like this.'

Darren stared into his glass. 'I wouldn't blame you if you didn't believe me. Sounds mental. Maybe it is mental. All I know is that it's all my fault.'

Sanjay frowned. 'How come? You just told me it was Amanda and her psycho dad and uncle.'

'They did the burglary, yeah, but if it wasn't for me, they would never have met you. None of this would have happened. Your place being smashed up, your dad having a stroke…' Darren choked up. 'We ought to ring the police.'

'I thought you said they'll have alibis?'

'They will.' Darren shook his head.

A little silence crept into their corner of the pub and settled. Sanjay looked pensive and unhappy.

'You do believe me, don't you?' Darren asked after a while.

Sanjay sighed. 'I do believe you, man. Trouble is, will the police? Amanda and her psycho dad breaking in is a no-brainer, and it sounds like my dad went down fighting, but that thing in his head would have given sooner or later so the way it turned out might even have been for the best. Weirdly, that makes it a bit better somehow. But the rest is a bit of an ask. I mean— Aboriginal demons and stuff?'

'Yeah well, I was ready to believe I'd dreamed it all up myself. I even thought of buying a season ticket to the funny farm. But then this came through the post this morning too.' Darren reached into his pocket and brought out the souperglue.

'Someone can't spell,' Sanjay said.

'I think they can spell just fine. I've got a funny feeling this isn't the sort of stuff you can buy in B&Q.'

'What do you mean?'

Darren stood up abruptly. 'Only one way to find out. Come on.'

Almost every surface in the house at Shunter Street was laden with bouquets, many still in their paper wrappings. The smell of stocks, sweet peas and pinks followed Sanjay and Darren up to the bedroom where the flotsam of Darren's sets lay in boxes, all neatly labelled by Kylah.

'I was wondering who'd done all this?' Sanjay said. 'I mean tidy and organised don't feature on your job description, do they?'

'Chaos is the natural state of the universe, Sanj.'

'What does that make Kylah?'

'Mistress of her universe, I'd say. I bet her toilet at home has gleaming surfaces and no limescale.'

'Yeah. I went to a house like that once. My auntie Meena's. You could do operations in her bathroom.'

'I hope you resterilised the bowl after your lower bowel procedure.'

Sanjay giggled. 'I was too scared to *ever* do that, man. I only had a pee the once. Trouble was, there were so many shiny surfaces to distract me, I took my eye off the ball—'

Darren smiled. 'An excellent metaphor, if I may be so bold. In fact, one of your best.'

'—and managed to spray the wall.'

'Well at least her cat knows whose territory it is now.'

They grinned at one another.

'Where should we start, man?'

# CHAPTER FORTY-FIVE

Darren let his eyes roam the mess and settled on one of his first constructs. 'Let's give the village a go.'

They cleared a space and poured out the contents of a box. Staring at the smashed and broken pieces, their faces filled with despondency.

'You any good at jigsaws?' Sanjay asked.

Darren shrugged and fished out the broken sections of the roof. What should have been a nine by six-inch moulded piece now consisted of at least thirty fragments, some no bigger than his fingernail. Sanjay laid out bits of fence, while Darren pieced together the bits of roof. He arranged them in position, fetched the souperglue and carefully unscrewed the top. A strange aroma that could best be described as an amalgam of almonds and old leather drifted up. He wondered what it might reveal if he sent it off for forensic examination. The bottle had a long, thin nozzle and when he applied it to an edge the single drop seemed to flow around of its own accord, coating the surface. When he held two pieces together, the adhesion was instant and solid, and the fragments seemed to almost align themselves. It took him fifteen minutes to put the roof together. Then he started in on the farmhouse walls. By nine, they'd done the fences, the farmhouse and some trees before Darren turned his attention to the models.

He searched for and found Roxana and her sisters, swallowing back the weird thickness that appeared in his throat. She was in bits, missing an arm and with her head twisted off. Carefully, and doing his utmost to control his trembling fingers, Darren put her back together. But he was getting tired now what with the beer and the long day entertaining Sanjay's relatives. He yawned wide enough to swallow a microwave and told Sanjay they'd better stop.

'Mind if I crash here tonight, Sanj?'

'Make yourself at home,' Sanjay said. 'You going to text Amanda?'

'No.' Darren stated. No argument. 'About the cops…'

'I reckon we should sleep on it. I'm just thinking how Amanda and her dad might spin this on you. Lover's tiff turns into spiteful accusation, you know the drill.'

Darren stared at him. Once again Sanjay stunned Darren with his emotional intelligence and…intelligence full stop. Whereas he, Darren, could see nothing other than through the red mist of revenge, Sanjay had thought it through logically and saw nothing but a potholed road ahead. Even in his grief, Sanjay was prepared to protect Darren from an embarrassing run-in with the authorities.

'Fancy a quick game of *Mario Kart* before we bed down?' Sanjay asked.

Darren was tired, but not that tired.

'Totally,' he said, grinning. He heard his phone buzz and realised he'd left it upstairs in the bedroom. He ran up. It was on a trestle table next to the repaired farmhouse. He couldn't help glancing at the glued buildings as he picked up his phone. They seemed not that bad at all. Then he looked again. They really weren't that bad. In fact, they looked almost brand new. Darren bent to inspect the roof he'd patched together. Even squinting, he could not see any lines of fracture where the glue had been. Then he remembered why he'd come upstairs. He picked up his phone and frowned. There was a message from Amanda.

WHERE ARE YOU? WORRIED!

'Yeah, I bet you are,' Darren muttered. He was about to switch the phone off—he could do without any more messages from her—when the idea light flickered into life in his head. He used the phone's camera to take a picture of the farmhouse, meaning to show it to Sanjay. On the way back downstairs Sanjay texted him.

BRING OUT SOME BEERS AND CRISPS.

Darren, being a bloke, knew how to prioritise, so long as there weren't too many items to rank, and that ironing wasn't on the list. Unfortunately, he also had a brain that was easily distracted. By the time he'd remembered to fetch four bottles of beer, find the crisps and some dry roasted nuts for himself from the upstairs storeroom, he'd forgotten all about the photo on the phone.

Sanjay was in the lock-up, *Mario Kart* already up and running. 'All right?'

'Yeah,' Darren said.

Sanjay nodded. 'Thanks for the company, mate. I appreciate it.'

'Wait until I smash you on *MK*, you'll regret saying that,' Darren said with an evil laugh.

'You wish.' Sanjay grinned.

Without thinking any more about it, Darren switched off his phone and settled down to do battle. They played *Mario Kart* and it was fun, like old times, and Darren guessed that it was exactly what Sanjay needed. They talked a lot about their school days and Mr. B's hilarious and eclectic use of a language he loved, but always managed to mangle. They drank a little too much, swore and generally behaved in the puerile way slightly drunk late twenties males do.

But after an hour, the day's events caught up with them both and Darren's fitful sleep the night before was turning his brain to Gruyère. They switched off *Mario Kart* at a little before 1.00am. Darren slept in the same 'spare' room he'd slept in countless times since he was nine years old. It felt comfortable and familiar. Sparsely decorated, Sanjay's mother had chosen chocolate and blue striped wallpaper, and Sanjay's old *Star Wars* duvet cover was still on the bed. Darren felt pleasantly inebriated, but it was with a moment of clarity that sometimes only comes with the correct amount of alcohol on board, that he realised he also felt more at home in this bed and in this room than he had in his own house for the last twelve months or more.

Since Amanda had moved in, if truth be told.

Darren let his mind wander back over the days when he and Sanjay were kids. When they were being particularly boisterous and annoying, Mr. Bobal would let the two of them grab a pick and mix from the shop and usher them out from under his feet with an order to go and throw up in the woods. They'd go willingly, overdosing on chocolate and crisps and fizzy pop. On Saturday afternoons they'd watch rubbish westerns on TV and play *Age of Empires* and be nerds.

Neither of them was into sport. TV and video games were what preoccupied them the most. They both knew that their parents loved them, and Darren never felt sorry for himself or Sanjay for not being a jock or a heavy drinker. When he thought of the Crays and their booze and fag lifestyle, their self-serving, insular hedonism and their complete disdain of the world at large, he knew that he could never do that weekend after weekend, and would never want to.

Later, he would wonder if that final Cray-hating thought was what triggered the journey he took that night.

# CHAPTER FORTY-SIX

DARREN FELL ASLEEP, alcohol induced, without any trouble. Almost immediately he found himself in a dream. At least he thought it was a dream. At first, it was pretty standard; a funfair complete with scary clowns and off-key barrel organ music, both of which were *de rigeur* in his nightmares, but it quickly morphed into a house of mirrors. In his dream, Darren stood outside, but he could hear the people in there laughing at their own wide reflection, beanpole reflection, just-shoot-me-now-and-be-done-with-it reflection. Darren went inside and found himself, thanks to the arcane logic of dreams, in a large empty room with one mirror. There was nothing very remarkable about that mirror either, except for the fact that a single red arm was poking out of it. At the end of said arm an orange-tufted finger beckoned. Darren walked towards it and peered in.

There was, of course, no reflection, only a life-size George Hoblip glaring at him.

'You took your time.'

'Is this a dream?'

'Sort of, yeah.'

'I can wake up at any time I want?'

'Yeah, 'course. Any time you want. After we've finished.'

'Not really a dream, then,' Darren said.

'Don't be such a ponce. C'mon, time for you to go back to school, Darren me boy. Ready?'

'Ready for what?'

The answer came in the form of George's large, clawed fingers grabbing Darren's dream blue and white striped polo shirt and yanking him through. He felt the strange sensation of being in a cold, very dark place for all of two seconds—not unlike what he'd felt when he'd been yanked unceremoniously from Moldarrenovia—and then he was in the same room except that there weren't any mirrors anymore. Instead, there were windows. Hundreds, if not thousands of windows arranged on walls along a never-ending corridor. George Hoblip stood next to him.

'What is this place?' Darren asked.

'It's a sort of between place. Between being asleep and awake. Between here and there.'

'Then, why are we here?'

'It's a way for me to talk to people. Or scare people shitless, depending on what mood I'm in. It used to be away for me to talk to Lulem.' George's face darkened.

Darren's shoulders slumped. 'George, I'm sorry about that. Absolutely nothing I could do.'

'No?' George let the word hang in the air and Darren knew there was a sharp hook on the end of it that made it an accusation as well as a question.

'Why are you looking at me like that? And why does your 'no' come out sounding like 'You didn't even try'?'

'Look, Summerville wossname means we haven't got that much time here. It goes quick, opposite to what it's like in Moldarrenovia 'cause you're technically asleep, see?'

Darren shook his head. 'No.'

George's shoulders slumped in exasperation. 'Follow me and everything will be fine, bro, okay?' He started walking.

Darren followed. The corridor led to another, and another. After a few minutes of labyrinthine turns, George slowed down. He kept looking through the windows, searching for something. As did Darren. What he saw were people. Lots and lots of different people doing all sorts of different things. Quite a lot of them were in baths. Many of them were taking part in bath time pursuits. Several of them appeared to be enjoying themselves an awful lot, especially the teenage boys. There were also large numbers of young girls in diverse fancy dress, doing twirls. Darren surmised that the linking factor had to be mirrors. It would explain the propensity for bathrooms and bedrooms. But there was the odd living room too. And somehow he and George were on the other side of those mirrors looking back into the rooms.

Ahead of him, he heard George let out a triumphant, 'Aha! Right, you stand here and watch the show. I've seen it all before.'

'How come?'

'It's not real time. This happened this afternoon.'

Darren wanted to press for an explanation, but George was pointing through the window. Darren peered in and let out a little gasp. He recognised the room, though seeing it from this angle made him feel a little off kilter and it took a couple of double takes for understanding to sink in. There was his TV set and his settee. Amanda, her dad and her uncle Lou were all there, and though it took a moment, Darren twigged that he was seeing the room from the mirror over the mantelpiece. Lou was sitting in the chair Darren's father had favoured, drinking from a can of Special Brew. Harry decanted his into a glass. Amanda wasn't drinking anything because she was too busy pacing.

'I still don't know what all the fuss is about,' Lou said. 'He stayed out with some mates and missed an interview, so chuffin' what? He'll be back with his tail between his legs soon enough.'

'You're missing the point, uncle Lou,' Amanda said, or rather shouted.

'Amanda,' Harry said in a warning tone. 'Now calm down…'

'Calm down? Calm down? This is my dream we're talking about here.' Amanda stamped her foot.

'Dream?' Darren glanced at George.

'Yeah.' George shook his head. 'You know, as in the 'all our dreams can come true if we have the courage to pursue them' twaddle her dad has been drumming into her for years. Trouble is she's not 'special' even though that's what every sodding adult's been telling her since she was four. What is the matter with you people? You're always lying to kids about them being 'unusually wonderful'. They're not all unusually wonderful otherwise nothing would be ordinary. And there's a lot to be said for ordinary, Darren. Doesn't cost anything for starters, bro. And security ain't to be sniffed at neither. Ask a Moldarrenovian.'

Darren shuddered.

'Keep watchin',' George added. 'Best bit's yet to come.'

Lou took a swig from the can and belched into his hand. 'Hang on, I thought we'd sorted all that. I thought you got him to sign on the dotted.'

'I did. You know I did,' Amanda went over to her voluminous handbag and took out an envelope. She removed its contents and handed the sheets to Lou. He fixed some glasses on his nose and scanned the pages.

'And this is all kosher, right?'

Amanda nodded. 'Got some of the boys at work to witness it. They thought it was my will.'

'And how did you get Darren to sign this again?' Lou asked.

Amanda shrugged. 'I told him it was a licence application for change of use from the council. Garage to nail studio.'

'Didn't he read it?'

'He gave up after the first page. I stuck the will bit at the end. He signed it without looking. I was wearing a very short kimono at the time, and he is a bloke after all.'

Lou shook his head. 'I like old Darren. He's a good lad.'

'That's not the chuffin' point, Lou.' Harry said.

'What is the chuffin' point?' Lou's brows reflected the battle for understanding that was raging inside his skull.

'This isn't like him,' Amanda pleaded. 'Something's happened to stop him coming back home.'

Lou shook his head. 'He's showing a bit of defiance. Like I say, he'll get over it. Use some of those female charms of yours.'

'That's just it,' Amanda said, her lips downturned. 'I don't want to anymore. He's twenty-nine, uncle Lou, way too old for me. And time is passing. I've booked my boob job for July. Singing lessons the month after that. I've applied for *Pizzazz!* in

October and I will be ready. If everything goes according to plan, I'll be swinging from a wrecking ball in the altogether by Christmas.' She turned to her father, sniffed, and in a petulant voice, added, 'tell him, Dad.'

'All right love, calm yourself,' Harry stood, put a fatherly arm around his daughter and led her to a chair, then turned a serious face to Lou. 'I don't like seeing my little girl upset like this, Lou. We're moving on to Plan chuffin' C.'

Lou scowled. The cogs were all going round, but clearly needed oiling. 'Plan A was when we were going to let Darren and Mand get hitched and then arrange a little accident…'

'Exactly.' Harry nodded. 'Then Amanda decided that getting hitched was too chuffin' expensive…'

Lou's scowl deepened. 'We forged the will and the plan was to bring the little accident forward to when Darren and Mand went to Wales on holiday in the summer. Plan B, right?' He looked very pleased with this feat of memory.

'That's right. On the coastal path. Wait for a slippery day on a high cliff and off we go to the races. But look at her, Lou,' Harry's eyes welled up. 'Look at her. Those are almost tears in her eyes. Me and Amanda have had a chat and we've come up with Plan C.'

Lou waited.

'We go back to Bombay's house, finish the burglary, and arrange a nerdy accident.' Amanda said, sounding pleased with herself.

Lou's frown deepened. 'But we only just burgled the place—'

'No we didn't,' Harry said, 'we smashed some stuff up, remember?'

'Yeah, but—'

Amanda was leaning forward now, her eyes glittering with excitement. 'It's perfect timing because no one will be expecting it a second time. We break in, nick some stuff to make it look different, get them both in that silly lock-up and…'

'Bosh,' Harry said.

'Bosh?' Lou asked.

'Yeah, I'm still working on the details of the exact bosh with

Mand, but it will have something to do with the equipment Darren pinched from work yesterday.'

'Did he? He's a dark horse that Darren,' Lou grinned, but it froze on his face when he got a look of deep disdain from Harry.

'He didn't nick it, I chuffin' did, you clot, but I made sure it looked like he did. All so that he could do stupid experiments with his mate.'

'What?' Lou asked, now totally flummoxed.

'Darren's forever watching things on *Discovery* or *Science Stars* or whatever other childish rubbish he finds on TV. Things like putting propane canisters in microwaves, or freezing tennis balls, or building steam powered nail guns from kettles,' Amanda said.

'Is Darren going to build a nail gun?'

'No, you prat,' Harry said. 'Experiments. Amateur science. It's chuffin' dangerous. And we all know what happens when you play with fire, don't we?'

Lou looked blank.

But Amanda leaned further forward, her eyes wide with feeling. 'It can be fatal.'

Lou's glazed gaze slid from his brother to his niece. Finally, he shrugged. 'So long as it don't involve heavy lifting. My back's been playing up something rotten.'

'No lifting. I promise,' Amanda said.

Lou took another swig from the can. 'But what makes you think he's not going to turn up this afternoon? Breeze in and carry on where he left off yesterday? You know how much of a wuss he is.'

'Because something's definitely changed. There was this toy that fell out of the cereal box this morning and then Darren got a parcel and then…he sent me this.' She took out her phone and held it up for Lou to see. He stared at the image, frowning.

'But we smashed everything…'

Amanda nodded. 'See what I mean?'

'Needs to be taught a lesson I reckon,' Harry said and the little laugh that accompanied these words sent a dream chill right through Darren from the top of his head to his heels.

Lou finished his can of Special Brew, burped and stood up.

'Okay. What time?'

'Tomorrow night. Let's say midnight?'

'Good for me. There's a quiz on at the Three Horseshoes at eight,' Lou crushed the empty can in one ham-like fist. 'Can't miss that.'

## CHAPTER FORTY-SEVEN

THE SCENE FADED, but Darren kept staring into the darkness that took its place. His brain was spinning, his heart was thundering. He blinked and then blinked again, but no matter how many times he did, the image of Amanda leaning forward, her eyes glittering as she said 'It can be fatal' burned in his retinas. He wanted to scream with rage. He wanted to crawl into the smallest, darkest place he could find and hibernate for a thousand years. Anger and humiliation fought for supremacy in his head and left him sweating and shaking on the canvas.

How could he have been such a completely moron?

How could he not have twigged?

How?

'Bloody shits,' Darren said, the words forced out through a mouth clamped shut with fury and aimed at himself as much as the Crays.

He couldn't lash out at them, so he did the next best thing. He brought his fist back and struck the wall with a reverberating crash.

The noise helped, as did the pain that followed. He paused for a moment only to try and understand how he was feeling pain in a dream, but it passed quickly. He was breathing too fast, holding his throbbing hand, feeling the pins and needles start to spread up from his fingers. He tried swallowing but there was no saliva in his mouth. He was too bloody useless to even conjure up spit in his dreams.

But someone read his mind. Darren felt a nudge on his arm and, through the fog of his anger, looked down to see a glass of water in George's hand.

'Expect you'll want this.'

Darren took the glass. His hand shook so badly, half of it spilled. But what was left was ice cold. He brought it up to his lips and drank too quickly. It sent a wave of searing pain up into his head. Darren groaned.

'Bit of a shock seeing them, was it, bro?' George asked.

'Bit,' Darren groaned, wincing still from brain freeze.

'But not so much as maybe it should have been, eh?' George tutted. 'Money does weird things to people.'

'Not everything is about money, though, is it?' Darren heard the querulous note in his own voice.

'That's just something people say, Darren. Fact is, with that lot, it's always about the money and being a spoiled princess.'

Utter silence followed, pierced only by Darren's express train breathing slowing to a mere trundle interspersed with loud swallows as he gulped the water. He wiped the excess away with his sleeve and looked up at his companion.

'What should I do, George?' Darren asked, after a long pause.

'Whatever you come up with,' George said, glowering. 'I want to be a part of it.'

Darren had to admit that a darkly enigmatic George was good value for money. But his own stupidity ate at him. 'I've been such a bloody idiot.'

'You'll get no argument from me there, bro. Though she's a good actress, I'll give her that.'

Darren could only shake his head. 'They need to be put away.'

'Or put down. Less cost to the taxpayer.'

Darren stared at him.

'Only kiddin', Darren' George's grin was straight out of the *Hammer House of Horror* archive. 'Chill bro'. We'll get it sorted, oh, and about them souperglue repairs? Remember them old crisp packets, the ones that they relaunched about ten years ago?'

Darren shook his head. He couldn't think straight. George made a disappointed face.

'Hang on,' he left and came back with a blue striped packet of Cripe's crisps. George popped it open with a bang by clapping it in his hands. Inside was a small blue twist of paper. George fished it out and untwisted it. Darren peered at the pinch of salt it contained.

'It's real old school. You open the salt, pour it on, shake the bag and wazoo! Complete recipe for obesity, hypertension, and dental decay in a handy eighty pence packet. Want one?' George proffered the bag.

Darren shook his head.

'It's smoky tree venk flavour,' George said.

Darren shook his head a tad more vehemently.

'Anyway,' George said, 'that's the key.'

'Sorry, you've lost me.'

'Your repairs, you tart. You don't have to vbe a tight arsd. It's uncool and bloody painful to watch. The souperglue comes from a little place in New Thameswick. Specialist shop. Bee and queue. That glue is well powerful. Remember the crisp trick the next time you're trying to use it, that's all I'm sayin', okay?'

Darren nodded, though he had no real idea what George was trying to tell him. This was, after all, a dream, if not an out-and-out nightmare. And dreams were quite often allegorical, weren't they?

'No, not allegorical,' George said, much to Darren's alarm. 'And stop using big words you don't really know the meaning of, bro. Do exactly what I showed you and no messin'. Right, that's enough entertainment for one night. You need your beauty sleep. Big time. And I need to get back to the office before I'm missed.'

A hundred questions begged to be answered, but Darren decided on the obvious one first. 'What sort of work is it you do, George?'

George's hips seemed to dip a tad more than usual when he walked. 'Troubleshooting. Sourcin' vittles. Bit of this an' that; duckin' an' weavin'; bobbin' an' bouncin'; you know.'

'I'm feeling seasick just thinking about it.'

'But mainly I help my mum in the kitchen. She reckons I could be a chef.'

'You've certainly got the profane vocabulary for it,' Darren muttered.

'Wassat?'

"Umm, you can talk the talk alright and, judging from that swagger, walk the arthritic walk, too.'

'Yeah, got my eye on one o' them Michelin tyres.'

'You mean stars.'

'One of them as well, yeah.'

'Right,' Darren said, and surprised himself by not even tittering. 'Can I ask how old you are, George?'

'Matt says I'm about fourteen in your money.'

'Well on the way to maturity then,' Darren said, trying and failing to keep the irony out of his voice.

George stuck his chest out. 'Exactly.'

Darren followed George back along the corridor, his brain still reeling from what he'd seen. 'Is there an endpoint to all of this, George?'

George's huge eyes narrowed into very large eyes. 'Apart from putting three psychopathic prospective murderers away, you mean?'

Darren nodded but persisted anyway. 'Your concern for law and order is touching, but I have to ask, what's in it for you?'

'I already told you about my girlfriend, Lulem. And then, of course, there's your fulfilment.'

'And what, dare I ask, is that supposed to mean?'

'Ah,' George said in a way that suggested he'd said a little too much in his enthusiasm. 'That's another instalment for another dream day. Let's just say you'll know it when you see it and it will be well cool.'

The enigmatic finish. Well, it wouldn't be a dream otherwise, would it?

'One last question. That message on Amanda's phone?'

'Yeah,' George muttered. Again, he looked uncomfortable, as if something slithery was moving around in his trousers and had to be wriggled away from. 'I…sent a photo from your phone.'

'What photo?' Darren asked.

'The one you took of the model farmhouse you and Sanjay repaired. Did a good job on that even if it was painfully slow in a non-crisp-packet kind of a way. Oh, and I added a teeny, little message.'

Darren stopped walking. 'What little message?'

George waved away his concern with an orange hand. ''S all right. Nothing offensive.'

'What message?' Darren repeated.

'All I said was: *Wish You Were Here*. Oh, and I added a little smiley face.'

Darren grinned. 'Amanda hates those.' It all made sense now. Except for one thing. 'Hang on, I thought you said that what we saw in the mirror took place this afternoon. I didn't take that photo until gone ten tonight.'

'Yeah,' George nodded happily. 'It's the bees knees this Krudian/Summerville wossname, innit?'

Luckily there were no flies around to buzz into Darren's mouth, which, at that moment, was doing a prizewinning impression of a goldfish.

## CHAPTER FORTY-EIGHT

**Darren woke up** with the dream fresh in his mind. He had no doubt that George Hoblip had revealed the truth. And, as unpalatable truths went, it was a diced raw blowfish on a bed of lightly braised thistle leaf entrée. He'd been played like a hungry mackerel and, what was worse, kept striking at the lure despite knowing it was a false and shiny thing without substance. Anger at his own gullibility gave way to an absolute determination to put things right for Sanjay, Mr. B, and George, if it was at all possible. A small part of him wanted to include Roxana and her sisters in the promise, but there was no point aiming for the stars when the only transport you had was a clapped-out old bicycle.

He and Sanjay ate a breakfast of cereal and jam-smothered toast sitting in front of Mr. B's massive TV, like they'd done as kids, watching a reality show about trawler men catching Alaskan King crabs on *Discovery*. Sanjay commented that his dad spent hours watching this show and when Sanjay asked him why, he said, 'Because it reminds me of your grandfather fishing in Mormugao Bay, you see.'

When Sanjay pointed out that the warm Arabian sea didn't quite throw up the same challenges as the freezing ocean off the Aleutians, Mr. B retaliated with, 'I went out on the boats with your grandfather many times. I know what these men go through, you see. I have been there, done that. I know the T-shirt and I have also got the ropes.'

Sanjay did an excellent Mr. B impression as he recounted this tale of his father torturing idioms with tender good humour and without any trace of being maudlin. While the men on TV battled huge waves to land the spindly-legged sea creatures, Darren told Sanjay about his dream date with George Hoblip. And, yet again he was astonished by his friend's ability to put aside his own, quite justified, ire at being targeted by association and instead offer genuine sympathy.

'Bummer, Dar. What a way to find out that your girlfriend is a bad egg.'

'I suppose. Trouble is, I've been smelling bad eggs for months and ignoring it. Okay, I didn't think that she was that extreme, but she's always been a cow when it came to you. And to be honest, though I've been too scared to admit it to myself, I've known for months that it wasn't going anywhere.'

'That's not what she thinks, by the sound of it.'

Darren smiled a bitter little smile. Sanjay'd hit the well-manicured nail on the head there. But being a part of someone else's plans provided plenty of scope for scuppering, no matter how well laid they were. And when it came to the Amanda and Darren equation, well laid was most definitely not a function that applied, notwithstanding the bloody Trey Lushton mask.

'How do you think we should play this?'

Sanjay shrugged. 'I could tell my cousin the armed policeman.'

Darren mulled the thought over for a moment and then shook his head. 'Thing is, if we tell them officially what we think is going to happen, we'll have to explain why.'

'And that way lies basket weaving and the waistcoat with lots and lots of buckles,' Sanjay said with a wary look.

'Yeah, but even if we left out all the weird bits and said we'd had a tip-off, it would never happen, would it? I mean, there'd be safety issues and stuff. They wouldn't allow the bastards to come anywhere near us.'

'You're right,' Sanjay said. 'But what's the alternative?'

'What would be really good is if we caught the Crays red-handed.'

Sanjay nodded. 'What have you got in mind, man?'

Darren tilted his head. 'How well do you know your cousin, PC Sharma?'

'We played poo-sticks together when we were kids.'

Darren explained his idea and watched a slow smile of approval spread over his friend's face.

―――

They spent the afternoon separately: Darren up in the bedroom with his sets, Sanjay in the lock-up sorting his landscapes and setting things up for what they had planned for that evening. Darren still hadn't quite grasped what George Hoblip had been trying to tell him with the twist of salt and the crisp packet analogy. He was still repairing stuff with painstaking slowness because he couldn't see any other way of using the glue. After spending a little time on one of his industrial sets, he turned his attention to his cameras. His expensive Olympus had a badly dented body and buggered electronics. The lenses too were all smashed. He glued the housing on one of the zooms to stop the glass from falling out, but everything else looked beyond repair. He fetched a carrier bag, put all the bits in and decided to take it along to a camera shop to see what they could do. He was not hopeful, but what did he have to lose?

They drove into town late afternoon. Sanjay stocked up on essentials while Darren went to the camera shop. He chose a long-standing family business that specialised in good second-hand cameras and repairs, the sort of place that was sadly becoming a rarity in most towns, and where they knew him by name and had always been more than helpful. When he got inside, however, he did not recognise the young man behind the counter today. He looked like a temp and a few years younger than Darren.

'Good afternoon, what can I do for you?'

'I need to see if anything is repairable from this lot.' Darren held up the bag.

'Can I see?'

'Easier if I tip it all out, I think.'

The bloke, Richard according to his badge, created a space on the countertop. Darren upended the bag and let the contents spill out. And spill out they did.

All three pieces.

There are moments when the universe conspires to surprise you, genuinely and indubitably. Though he didn't hear the shifting of gears denoting the realignment of a few stars, or the shuffling of the seats of the gods, there was no doubt that this was one of those conspiratorial moments as Darren stared at the camera body, the 80-120 zoom, and the 35mm telephoto, trying, and almost failing, to stop his brain from frying.

*All three pieces.*

There'd been a damn site more jangling, cracked bits of camera when he'd put them in the bag.

'So,' Richard said looking down at the items. 'What exactly is the problem?'

Darren tried speaking but all that came out was an incoherent blurt. 'Nnnndddon't...nnn...I...'

Richard peered at him. He was too young to have seen many people having dyspraxic seizures, but if he had, he'd have worn the exact same expression that creased his face now.

'Would you like to sit down, sir?' Richard asked with great concern.

'I...I...umm,' stammered Darren, looking up into Richard's face. 'There seems to be not so many...there were a lot more...'

Richard at last seem to grasp what Darren was saying. 'Have you lost something?' He reached for the plastic bag and felt inside.

Darren didn't reply. He picked up the camera body and examined it. It looked normal. In actual fact, it looked pristine. All of the scuffmarks that came with months of use had disappeared, the lenses shone with not a finger mark anywhere near them. He picked up the zoom and snapped it into position on the housing, held the camera to his eye. The image was clear, the zoom mechanics slid and twisted smoothly and perfectly. When he turned back and picked up the other lens, he saw that Richard was examining that.

'I can't actually see any damage,' he said.

'That's because of the salt,' Darren said.

'The salt?'

Darren nodded. 'Yeah. In the crisp packet.' He snatched back the empty plastic bag and took back the lens from the bewildered Richard. 'I'm sorry for wasting your time.' Without another word, he put the spare lens and the camera back in the bag and walked out.

'You okay, mate?' Sanjay asked, joining a white-faced Darren next to the car a few minutes later. 'You look a bit pale?'

'I feel a bit pale.'

They got in and sat. Neither of them spoke for several seconds.

'Is it the cost of the repairs?' Sanjay asked.

Darren shook his head. 'Weren't any. It's fixed.'

Sanjay turned his head very slowly to look at Darren who kept his face straight ahead. 'That was bloody quick.'

'Thing is, they didn't need to fix anything, Sanj. It fixed itself.'

Sanjay weighed up these words for some time before asking, 'What does that actually mean?'

Darren pulled out the camera and lenses for Sanjay to inspect.

'What the—'

'I know,' Darren said in a voice laden with sympathy. 'I think we need a couple of beers, don't you?'

They drove to The Ten Bob Note and sat in a quiet corner that smelled only faintly of disinfectant where, over a pint and some fish and chips, Darren told Sanjay about George Hoblip's crisp packet advice—a bit of the dream he'd previously withheld since it had not made any sense whatsoever up to now.

'You're saying we need lots of packets of unsalted crisps?' Sanjay asked in the voice of a man struggling with a theoretical concept that needed a practical demonstration to make it clear.

Darren shook his head and glanced at his watch. It was 8.00pm already. 'Come on, let's go. We don't need crisps, but we do need some blankets. What I want you to do is to roughly put the bits that go together where you want them and find some duct tape so that we can cover up your landscape. Three blankets should do it if they're joined together.'

'O…kay,' Sanjay said very slowly.

'While you're doing that, I'm going to experiment with the souperglue.'

When they got back to Sanjay's, Darren went straight to the bedroom where his sets and models still lay scattered in boxes about the room. He tipped one out and placed the shattered remains of the trashed industrial plant set into the plastic bag he'd used earlier. Then he took some souperglue and let one drop fall onto the bits. He closed the mouth of the bag, shook it gently and, heart in his mouth, counted to thirty and then, gingerly peeled back the bag's opening and looked in to see…a fully reconstructed, reformed building.

'Yesss!' Darren punched the air. 'Thank you, George.' After that, it was a question of making sure all the right bits were in the bag together. But he needn't have been too concerned about that either, he soon found out. Kylah had done an excellent job of separating everything. Pretty soon he was emptying the contents of the boxes that Kylah had carefully labelled into the bag, adding a drop of glue, waiting a nonchalant ten seconds and then pulling out intact and complete items. Within an hour, he'd fixed every single broken thing. Not only fixed but returned each one to its original state. He put Roxana, Una, Maeve and Bron to one side and they stood watching proceedings inanimately. All that was left was to arrange everything in sets. And of course that was the bit that took the longest time. He still hadn't even got halfway when Sanjay texted him at eleven-thirty from the lock-up.

ANY JOY?

Darren texted back: MUCH JOY. DOWN IN MO…

He hurried down to the lock-up to find Sanjay struggling with three taped together blankets, trying to throw the thing over the broken bits of his rearranged landscape. With Darren's help, they taped down one side and after that, things became much easier.

'Right,' Sanjay asked, when everything was taped up, 'now what?'

'Well since we don't have a crisp packet big enough, the blanket will have to do.'

Sanjay grimaced. 'Okay Darren, me speak English, you speak Poop of bull.'

'No, seriously. If you'd seen what I've just seen upstairs…'

'You been in my magazine stash again?'

'Make sure the blanket touches the floor, covering everything.'

'It is.'

'Right, if I lift up the corner and chuck some glue in…' Darren did exactly that and let the blanket fall, took a step back and waited. Twenty seconds later, he heard Sanjay gasp and followed his gaze. Something was happening under the blanket. There was a strange writhing movement right in the middle, as if some large sea animal were moving under the cotton waves. He was on the point of commenting when the door burst open behind them to reveal four balaclavaed figures all in black. All of them armed. Darren saw a couple of baseball bats and a crowbar and, disconcertingly, a kitchen knife.

'On your knees!' someone shouted. 'On your knees.'

Darren saw Sanjay lurch to the side and stumble towards the array of equipment on one of the benches before one of the balaclavaed figures hurried over, grabbed him and forced him down on the floor. Darren was aware of a blur of movement and felt rough hands on the back of his shirt. Then he was lying face down on the floor with someone's boot on his head. His racing brain registered the fact that the floor smelled of diesel—probably a legacy of its position under the railway—and that one of the figures was carrying a baseball bat with the words 'Ole Slogger' written upon it, before he heard another voice; this one all too familiar.

'Hello, Darren.'

'Amanda,' he said, his voice distorting through his squashed mouth. 'Nice of you to call.'

'Shut up. You stupid, pathetic idiot.'

A clanging sound like a cylinder clanking against a stone and concrete floor reached his ears.

'Such a nice place you two have got here. Proper little love nest.' Though he couldn't see her, Darren knew she was delivering all this snark through a nasty grin.

'And you'd know one when you saw one, right?' His riposte was less than needle-sharp, but it found its mark.

'Shut up, Dolly Darren. Look at this place. Nerd Central. You two deserve each other. Maybe we could have a joint burial, would you like that?'

'Come on, Amanda. No chuffin' chitchat.' Even through the balaclava he could make out Harry's military tone. 'Leave him to Lou. You set up that stuff like I told you.'

She leaned in and hissed, 'You've been in my way for months, Darren. Time I decluttered.'

Above him, Darren felt the pressure ease on his head, after one final grinding boot thrust. Someone grabbed his hands and pulled them roughly behind him. Amanda said, 'Hold this.' Something was pressed into his palm and his fingers forced around it for a second before the thing was removed and the footsteps retreated. Almost immediately he felt a different, heavier boot in the middle of his back.

'Lou? Is that you?' Darren asked. 'Don't do this, Lou. You don't have to, you know that.'

'Shut up,' snapped Lou. Though the snap didn't sound all that convincing. But Cray blood was thicker than water. Darren had several years' worth of night out examples to prove that.

Out of the corner of his eye, he saw two people over at the workbench. The smaller one poured something into a steel bowl. Steam immediately rose from it, flowed over the rim and then downwards as gravity took hold.

Were they mixing something explosive?

Darren guessed that the smaller of the two figures must be Amanda. She was holding something wobbly in one hand. It looked a bit like a rubber tube. Very much like the sort of thing he'd been made to grasp moments before. Amanda dropped the tube into the bowl and then, wearing thick gloves, used some wooden tongs to take the tube back out of the bowl. It was now rigid and white with frosting. With a sudden blow, she smashed the thing down against the workbench and Darren heard a tinkling noise, like glass shattering.

'That'll do,' he heard Harry say. 'Snapping rubber tubes in liquid nitrogen sounds right up these two's street.'

Darren's stomach contracted into a tight ball and his skin tried to crawl in after it.

He knew all about liquid nitrogen. His brain was screaming at him for being such an idiot. For not thinking things through. For underestimating how diabolical the Crays were.

There was going to be no explosion here. They'd planned something far worse, far more devious and far too quick for the police to be effective unless they turned up in the next few minutes.

'What's the spec, Harry?' he heard Lou ask.

'Get them together. Chuck the tarpaulin over them to trap the gas.'

They dragged Darren across the floor, the concrete suddenly rough against the skin of his face. He resisted and got a kick in the ribs for his trouble.

'Don't worry, Darren,' Amanda said. 'They tell me pure nitrogen is quite a trip. No pain, no choking, just a very, very, very long sleep.'

The boot mashed into his back again. He tried to struggle, but it was no good. A different boot mashed his face into the floor, pinning him. Out of one eye, he saw Sanjay being dragged across to join him. Their faces were now only a foot apart. By straining his eyes upwards he could see the figure that sounded like Harry tipping out the liquid nitrogen. It boiled on impact; the liquid so cold the concrete floor was like a hotplate sending billows of gas wafting towards him. Darren knew that nitrogen vapour was heavy and would cling to the floor. He looked across to Sanjay. His friend's eyes were large and frightened. This was definitely not going according to plan.

'Sanjay,' Darren hissed. 'I thought you said you sorted this.'

'I did, man. I did, honest.' Sanjay's eyes went up to the corner of the lock-up. Darren glimpsed a small black rectangle with a blinking red light. 'Skype linked to my cousin's phone. I've put in a call —'

Sanjay was cut off as the tarpaulin plunged them into darkness. Another knee was added to the weight on his back, forcing out his breath.

'Hold your breath,' Darren ordered. He tried to struggle but the pressure from whoever knelt on him was too great.

'Yes, that's it, Darren. Struggle a bit. Go on. Good for the lungs,' Amanda urged.

Darren wished more than anything that it wouldn't be her voice that he'd hear at the last.

'Sod off, you bitch,' he said.

'Four minutes, Darren. That's all it takes. Four minutes and then what's yours is mine.'

'Let Sanjay go, for God's sake. He has nothing to do with you and me,' Darren said, and he didn't care if it sounded like begging.

'Collateral damage, Darren. Life, as you know, is tough.'

He hated her then. With a vengeance that was palpable. A clock in his head ticked away the seconds. It was a clock on speed because the seconds were ticking very fast, and he couldn't hold his breath for longer than a few of those sickeningly swift seconds. The pressure on his chest from Amanda's weight was crushing, forcing him to pant as the vapour kissed his flesh with icy lips.

'That's it. That's a good boy,' Amanda said. 'Suck it up.'

'That audition on *Babe TV* finally paying off then, eh Mand?' Darren groaned. Next to him, in the darkness, Sanjay snorted. Unfortunately, his humour had no such effect on Amanda.

'Shut up,' she snapped. 'Always the stupid smart remark. Even now, you just don't know when to keep your bloody mouth shut.'

'That's because you bring out the very best in me, Mand.' Darren tried to roll. He did his utmost to shift Amanda's weight. He didn't want to give her the pleasure of going quietly. At the same time, he was acutely aware that his activities were making him use up what little oxygen was left.

'Listen,' Sanjay whispered in the darkness.

Darren stopped wriggling.

A noise met his ears. A wonderful noise carried on the wind. Sirens in the distance. Darren didn't dare guess how far.

Someone shouted, 'Cops. Shit, let's go!'

'No!' Amanda shouted 'Not yet. It'll take another couple of minutes. Wait!'

'Amanda, come on love. There's no time,' Lou said.

'One MINUTE!' Amanda screamed. There was real hate in that scream. Hate and something much worse. Not only did Darren hear it, he could feel it emanating from her: blacker than the darkness under the blanket, colder than the liquid nitrogen that was inexorably killing him, more frightening than Ysbaed's insane mayhem.

'Give me that bloody knife,' Amanda said.

'No, Amanda,' Harry replied. 'Too messy.'

Gas enveloped Darren's head now, odourless and deadly. He tried not to suck it in. Tried until he felt his lungs might burst. How could this be happening? Where was bloody PC Sharma? He wanted to thank Harry for keeping the knife from Amanda. Darren giggled. The knee thrust further into his back.

He gasped from the pain, sucked in pure nitrogen.

Amanda's knee dug in again.

Two breaths.

The truth was, it wasn't too bad. Especially now that everything was turning blue with little pink flowers bursting everywhere.

Three breaths.

A small corner of Darren's consciousness knew that this was it. Another three or four breaths and his brain would shut down. He'd read somewhere that nitrogen did that. Suppressed the suffocation reflex, the one that made you fight and struggle for air. They used it sometimes to dispatch chickens in abattoirs. He and Sanjay would sail calmly towards oblivion, and even if PC Sharma arrived with the cavalry, it would be too late. Nothing he could do, nothing he wanted to do because he was floating towards a nitrogen-induced high. They were going to die in Sanjay's lock-up because of a few puffs of gas and he was going to dream away his last few moments of life not caring a jot.

Because you couldn't do anything in a dream.

Unless you wanted to spy on people through a mirror.

And you could only do that if you knew a certain…certain… it was difficult to marshal any kind of lucid thought now and Darren strained to remember the name. It began with an H, didn't it? Hubert maybe, or Hermione, or Hobson, or…He was so pleased when it finally came to him, he whispered the name out loud.

'Hoblip.'

'What did you say?' Amanda asked, her voice grinding out deep and feral through her teeth. She dug in her knee one last time.

'Christ, come on Amanda, let's—' Harry Cray's urgings were interrupted by a strange gurgling cough.

Then someone screamed. In fact, several people screamed.

And who on this earth would blame them.

# CHAPTER FORTY-NINE

Darren learned later that it was Wayne and that the scream had been accompanied by involuntary bodily functions, front and back.

The pressure eased but Darren didn't move. He didn't want to anymore. What he wanted to do was look at the little pink flowers in his head and wonder at the way the darkness crept in on both sides.

Yells broke in on his reverie.

'Jesus H Christ—'

'What is it?'

'It's a CHUFFIN' ALIEN!'

And then he was sitting up against the wall next to Sanjay. And this wall wasn't blue with pink flowers, it was whitewashed brick. Someone slapped him hard.

Slowly, his eyes came back into focus. Opposite him, four balaclavaed people were sitting facing the wall, hands on their heads, trembling and whimpering. Between them stood a four-foot-tall George Hoblip in a yellow and brown check waistcoat. Darren felt a calloused finger lift his upper lid.

'Yeah, you'll be fine. You and your mate. But Darren, bro,' George tutted loudly. 'Talk about cutting it fine for callin' me in. My assessment? Nice plan, shit execution. A minute more and you'd have been slab-meat.'

The door rattled. 'POLICE. OPEN THE DOOR.'

'Right, I'm off,' George said with a grin. 'Got a surprise for some old friends.'

The wonky door burst open and, five seconds later, the lockup filled with very shouty, very large, and very armed police officers, including Sanjay's cousin who'd seen the whole thing—well almost the whole thing bar the last minute when the Skype link that Sanjay set up went all dark and fuzzy for some technical reason no one would ever be able to quite explain.

Darren labelled it the 'bwbach' factor.

Didn't matter. They had enough on tape to put Harry, Lou, Amanda and cousin Wayne away for a good while.

It didn't take long for all the evidence to be collected. The Crays left quietly, except for Wayne who was crying. Darren didn't speak or look at Amanda. But then human waste didn't stimulate much interest in anyone other than night soil men or parasitologists.

Darren and Sanjay, being neither, were able to give statements in the kitchen over cups of sweet tea after the Crays left and Sergeant Vine told them they only needed to come to the station the following day to finish it off.

By 1.30am everyone had gone, leaving Darren and Sanjay exhausted, elated and bewildered. They both had mild frostbite on their cheeks from where they'd lain on the garage floor but were otherwise remarkably unscathed.

'Sorry about my cousin Sharma, man,' Sanjay said. They were drinking a beer now that the police had gone. 'I told him we'd heard some idiots were out stealing roof lead, like you said, and that I'd Skype him if we noticed anything, being that he was on nights, and we were usually up late. He said he'd be close by, but he was four bloody miles away in an all-night burger bar. The lard ass.'

'Still, they made it,' Darren said.

'Yeah, but we wouldn't have if it hadn't been for your mate, George.'

The police explained away the Crays' fantastical story of how a horrendous orange 'thing' appeared and moved with lightning speed to disarm and physically constrain them, by suggesting leaking nitrogen had got the Crays too. But Darren knew the truth.

There was a knock on the back door. Sanjay yelled, 'Come in.'

The door didn't open. At least the real door didn't. Instead, a different door swung inwards to reveal Matt Danmor standing there, looking more than slightly sheepish.

Darren stood. 'Matt?'

Matt walked in and offered his hand. Darren shook it. 'Where's Kylah?'

'Upstairs. Doing some tidying up.'

Darren nodded. Sanjay looked totally confused. 'You two know each other?'

'Yeah. Sanjay, this is Matt. You've met before.'

Sanjay's brows thickened. 'Have we?'

Darren explained once more. Though he'd been through it all before, he found it immensely helpful to have Matt there to corroborate his story. Sanjay's bewilderment doubled and then trebled.

'Difficult to take it all in, isn't it?' Matt said with a sympathetic smile.

Sanjay nodded.

'But there is something that may help. If we could go back through to the lock-up?'

Sanjay followed Darren and Matt outside. Yellow police tape was all over the place, but Matt ignored it. The taped-up blankets were as they'd been left, covering Sanjay's smashed-up Mesopotamia.

'Ready?' Matt asked. He and Darren grabbed hold of the taped-together blankets and pulled them off together. Underneath, the souperglue had done its stuff. Sanjay's amazing landscape of the Babylonian empire was completely restored, even if it was devoid of any elephants or Hannibal in the vanguard.

'Wow,' Sanjay said in a wobbly voice. 'That's not possible.'

'Don't ask. Well, okay, ask, since I don't know the answer either.' Darren said.

'It's far too complicated to explain,' Matt said. 'Let's just say that it shouldn't have been this difficult. George forgot to put the instructions in with the souperglue and he's in Kylah's bad books. Oh, and in case you're wondering, the troops are all neat and tidy in their boxes underneath.'

Sanjay was like a kid on Christmas morning. He walked around the model, picking things up gingerly, inspecting, peering. 'But it's even better than before,' he managed to breathe finally.

Matt put a hand on Darren's arm. 'We could leave him here if you like. I know Kylah wants a quiet word.'

Darren looked at his friend. He'd been through an awful lot over the last few days. It might be better to leave him out of things, but he'd tried that before, and it hadn't worked. Besides, he deserved to hear what was going on since most of it was going on in his house and garden.

'Yeah, we could,' Darren said, 'but he'd never forgive me. And I don't think I could forgive myself.' Darren took out his phone and found camera mode. 'Right Sanj, stand there next to it. This one is for the album.'

Sanjay stood and grinned, his proud smile a thing of wonder.

# CHAPTER FIFTY

**KYLAH WAS IN THE KITCHEN.** She hugged Darren like a long-lost friend and, to Sanjay's horrified consternation, did the same to him.

'Sorry about your dad,' Kylah said, looking Sanjay in the eye and rubbing his upper arm. 'He says thanks for the funeral. Oh, and he says don't forget the extra insurance policy at the back of the left-hand drawer of his study bureau. Something to do with inheritance tax.'

Sanjay, who'd gone into paralysed-rabbit-in-the-headlights mode, nodded in dumb acceptance. There might have been a glint of gratitude behind his panicked eyes, but it could just as easily have been terror.

'Well,' Kylah continued, turning again to Darren, 'here we are then. Still, the good news is that everything, more or less, is back to where we began…' She frowned, noting Darren's wary, fed-up expression. 'You don't seem too overjoyed to see us, Darren.'

'Don't I? I wonder why?'

'Now, now, Darren…' Matt said.

But Darren wasn't having any of this. Someone had just tried to murder him and his best friend, and almost succeeded. The time for pussyfooting around had long passed. And Darren knew all about pussyfooting because he'd won prizes for it. Amanda and the Crays were feral felines he'd been pussyfooting around for far, far too long. Well all that had changed. And, somewhere inside the murky puddle of his self-awareness, Darren knew that he had changed as well. He took a step forward towards Kylah.

'Where the hell did you go to after I took Sanjay to see his dad in hospital? I wanted to speak to you, ask you stuff. But all you to did was bugger off, leaving me…floundering.'

Darren snapped his head around to where Matt seemed suddenly unsure of which foot to stand on. Kylah, too, looked ever so slightly less composed than usual in the fierce heat of Darren's glare.

'Yes, I can see how you might be a bit miffed at that,' Kylah said.

'Miffed? You get miffed when the shiny new games console you expect on Christmas morning turns out to be a pair of bloody stripy socks. I was more than miffed. I nearly lost it. Nearly sold out to that bunch of psychos that were here tonight. I've been a total arse to Sanjay. I almost didn't go to his dad's funeral and all because Amanda convinced me I was going bonkers. If it wasn't for George Hoblip—'

'Who?' Sanjay asked.

Matt smiled indulgently. 'Ah yes, good old George.'

'If it wasn't for him…' Darren hesitated, not letting up on his seething glare, but running out of words to add to it.

'…You would have never heard from us again,' Kylah said. Her words, in the deathly hush that the hour always brought, sounded ominous. 'You would have married Amanda and led a frustrated, unhappy life, working in Health and Safety at Dobson and Crank's for the next twenty-three years. You would have had no children, and your wife would leave you after six years for a supervisor in a call centre called Vim. You'd become a reclusive alcoholic by the age of forty and die alone by inhaling your own vomit at the age of fifty-two.'

Both Darren and Sanjay were staring at Kylah, though Sanjay's was more a goggle-eyed, full-on glare a few millimetres short of spontaneous dislocation.

Kylah sighed. 'Do not ask how I know all that. I've already broken a dozen rules in telling you.'

'And you were willing to let that happen?' Darren muttered after trying, and failing, to swallow twice.

Kylah wasn't smiling any more. 'There are forces at work in this world and others who would like to bury people like you, Darren.'

Darren didn't say anything, though his mouth did open and shut three times. She'd said two things that sent his brain on a snapped-cable ride down the elevator shaft. He managed to focus in on one.

'Forces?' he croaked.

Matt was still nodding. 'People like the Crays…they're just instruments. Put here for a purpose.'

'By things like Ysbaed. And they, as you know from first-hand knowledge, are a lot worse,' Kylah added.

'Hang on,' Sanjay found his cracked voice and picked out the second of the two weird things, saving Darren the trouble of asking. 'You said 'people like you' to Darren.' He threw a frown in the direction of his friend. 'This Darren?'

'Yes,' Kylah said. 'Very much this Darren.'

'What does that mean, exactly?' Sanjay asked.

Kylah's gold-flecked gaze drifted from one man to the other. Her face was difficult to read but Darren thought he could see pity mixed in with a little bit of…what was that…hope and expectation?

'Darren has talents, Sanjay. He is a Maker. He has an ability to instil his imaginings with life. Diversity gene. Emerges every fifty or so generations. But there are those out there who want everything to be the same. Bend things to their will, control nature. They hate free spirits like Darren here.'

'But why didn't you tell me all this before?' Darren, still angry, demanded.

Kylah looked unusually uncomfortable. 'Our role is…delicate. We can't be seen to be interfering too much in the cosmic order. Okay, if a demon like Ysbaed gets loose then he's fair game and we do what we need to. When it comes to matters of conscience, it's a lot more…nuanced.'

'That sounds like one of those words that can mean whatever you want it to mean,' Sanjay observed.

'Yeah, like I've just nuanced in that room. I'd give it a couple of minutes if I were you,' Darren muttered and then his eyes narrowed as cogs meshed. 'Wait a minute, are you talking about *my* conscience here?'

Kylah nodded, lips compressed into a smile. 'You had to get to this point—painful though it was—on your own.' She grimaced and then added under her breath, 'Albeit with a little help from one George Hoblip who has a very ulterior motive called Lulem and is a loose cannon at the best of times.'

'Are you telling me that you would have been happy to let me side with the Crays?' Darren's eyes hardened.

Matt squirmed. 'Our hands were tied. But I for one had every faith in you.'

It wasn't the answer Darren wanted to hear but when it came to backhanded compliments, he'd heard a lot worse. Good God, was it really as simple as that? Had it all been a test to see if he was worthy? Because if it was he didn't much like the thought of being the guinea pig in an experiment in *morals*. The bloody things were tricky enough to negotiate at the best of times and, in his experience, even when you did manage to leap over the camouflaged traps with the sharpened spears and clamber over all the slippery obstacles to gain the high ground, the view from the top was often a misty and a lonely one.

'I almost...' Darren said, thickly.

'Almost is a very overrated word,' Matt said, nodding sagely.

'And I prefer the one that begins with R as in redemption,' Kylah said. The gold flecks in her eyes seemed to sparkle.

'What now?' Darren asked when Kylah's gaze got too much to bear.

'I have something to show you,' Kylah said. She pushed herself away from the table and walked out of the door. 'Upstairs in the bedroom,' she added.

Matt grinned and whispered. 'Bet you don't get an offer like that every day.'

'And if you continue with those schoolboy innuendos it's an offer that you won't ever be getting again,' Kylah said from the stairs.

Matt made a face. 'It's the policeman in her,' he whispered, 'and I know quite a few people who'd give anything to be that pol—'

'I HEARD THAT.'

'Including me,' Matt mouthed the words theatrically.

'AND THAT. Yellow card, Agent Danmor.'

'She doesn't mean it,' Matt made a face.

From the landing above, Darren heard a muffled, 'Yes I do.'

'She doesn't,' Matt whispered.

Despite his grouchiness, Darren found it difficult not to like Matt and Kylah. Even if they had been prepared to hang him out to dry, he got the feeling that it would have been a reluctant hanging and they'd have appealed to the Krudian supreme court right up until the trapdoor snapped open under his feet. But the little, despite-himself, smile that played on Darren's lips as he walked up the stairs was nothing compared to the hundred-watt grin that broke out on seeing what awaited him in the bedroom.

'How the hell?'

'Told you,' Matt said from behind him. 'She loves tidying up.'

Gone were the scattered individual models and plastic foliage in haphazard piles on every available surface. In their place, the trellis tables were laden with hardboard sets, each one complete; the desert, the jungle, industrial, mountain, seaside, they were all there. For the first time Darren could remember they were all on display. That in itself was miraculous since the trestle tables did not have enough room. Instead, Kylah had done something to the walls. At least Darren assumed she'd done something to the walls. Either that or the sets were floating in fresh air. Tiers of metre square hardboard seemed to hang a foot apart and when he reached his finger out to touch one it glided forwards like the drawer of a very expensive kitchen, while the one stacked beneath moved up to replace it.

'I see you worked out the souperglue's mode of action for yourself?' Kylah said.

'Eventually,' Matt nodded, still gawping.

Darren felt a tug on his sleeve. He looked down to see Sanjay's hand pulling at it. 'Is she doing all this?' he asked.

Matt answered for him. 'Oh yes, she's full of tricks like this.'

Kylah, meanwhile, was looking at Darren with unflinching intensity. 'It's all complete. Every set. The rest is up to you.'

'What do you mean, up to me?' Darren frowned.

'I mean that this is your chance to start again. This is your world, Darren. You created it and you can recreate it. All the things and places that you ever made are here. What you need to do now is breathe life into them.'

Darren stared at her. A watery sun was starting to poke its head above the horizon in the darkness of his head. 'Are you saying that if I take their photographs, there'll be a new Moldarrenovia?'

Kylah smiled and nodded. 'Just as it was before.'

'I can't believe it,' Darren said, staring at the repaired sets.

'You'd better,' she said with a grin.

'Oh, and perhaps we can make it a new and improved Moldarrenovia,' Matt said. In his hand he held the still broken model of Trey Lushton that Amanda had bought in Norwich and that Darren had once photographed for her. 'I thought perhaps we could incinerate this one. Pretty low quality anyway, don't you think?'

'I think that's the most sensible thing I've heard all night,' Darren said and smiled. It was a good, broad smile that faltered only when a fresh thought struck him. 'But what about Ysbaed? What if we incinerate him too—or not photograph him at least?'

Kylah nodded, but her lips were downturned. 'Nice theory. But he'll be in hiding.'

Darren looked around.

'Don't bother, we've looked,' Kylah said. 'And secondly, he'll happily hibernate in some dark corner of the universe for as long as it takes. Of course, he's nothing without the votives. You've unmade two. The third is still anchored, through your earlier photography, in a virtual Moldarrenovia. Once it re-manifests, that is where it will be, and you can be sure that Ysbaed will follow.'

'But if that initial photograph of the pyrite I took from the spy set is here on my camera, can't we send it to hipposync@nimbus.com too?'

'Unfortunately not. You need to recapture its image from its manifestation in Moldarrenovia. And of course, he knows that, and he'll want to protect it.' Her eyes hardened. 'But this is our chance to put one of the monsters away for good. It's a lot to ask I know—'

Darren didn't even let her finish. He picked up his camera and started taking photos. It took him a quarter of an hour, most of which was also spent explaining to Sanjay what he knew about Kylah and Matt, who were both more than happy to fill in the blanks. When he finished, they all went back to the kitchen. Seven cups were laid out on the table.

'We expecting visitors?' Darren asked.

On cue, the back door opened. 'Anyone home?' called a voice that made Darren laugh out loud in delight. George Hoblip breezed in with a reluctant Malcolm and Vivette in his wake.

'Obfuscator! Paladin!' Darren said. If he was hoping for a sign of alacrity from them, he was disappointed. They both stared at him with expressions of the kind you'd give a suspiciously steaming mound left by next-door's cat.

'Do I know you?' Vivette asked.

Malcolm merely skulked.

Darren turned to Matt. 'You wiped their memories, didn't you?'

'Had to, Darren. Them's the rules.'

'But that means we have to go through the whole explanation thing again,' Darren groaned.

'Nah we don't,' George said. 'This my tea?' He picked up a mug and drained it in one gulp, much to Sanjay's astonished delight.

'That tea was boiling,' Sanjay whispered.

'He's just showing off,' Matt said with a little shake of his head.

'Wait a minute,' Darren said, 'What do you mean by "No we don't", George?'

'Did all the explaining on the way here, bro'. Told 'em the whole thing, how he's Paladin and she's the obfowossname.'

'Obfuscator,' Darren said.

'If you say so,' George said. 'Plus that blooming ghoul on the hill, Ysbaed....' He seemed to notice Sanjay for the first time and held out his hand. His face distorted grotesquely into what was a bwbach grin. 'George,' he said.

Sanjay, once he'd recovered, shook George's hand, nodding like a China dog in an earthquake.

'This is *the* most ridic thing I've ever heard. Can someone please tell me what is going on? Is this still a nightmare? Or is this…creature…real?' Vivette pleaded.

'I am going to call the cops,' Malcolm said.

Darren grinned. 'Just like old times.'

'And who the hell are you?' Malcolm rounded on him belligerently.

Darren turned to face them. 'I know you're not going to believe any of this now, but you are about to go somewhere beyond your wildest dreams. It will be one hell of a trip, and you're going to laugh and cry, get shot at, have acid thrown at you, eat wax apples that taste like nectar and make a lot of very good friends. And, more than anything, you're going to get a chance to bring some light back to a very dark place. Consider me your slightly mad but loveable magic bus driver.'

'You're off your rocker,' Malcolm said.

'Am I?' Darren said. 'I suggest you take another look at George, pinch yourself and then reconsider that statement. Oh, and if, sometime over the next hour, you get a sudden urge to stand up and shout, "It's only a game!" do not. If you do, I will personally kick you in a very private place, and I don't mean the WC, very hard, and possibly more than once. Please nod if you understand.'

Malcolm, with the expression of a man realising that he was in very much out of his depth and that if he continued to struggle he was very likely to drown, nodded.

Darren turned to Kylah. 'Where did you say Ysbaed was hiding out this time?'

Kylah pressed a finger to a small stone she wore in her ear and listened. Eventually, she turned to Darren and said, 'In the new Moldarrenovia, he's gone north. Volcanic region. Very Reykjavikesque. Oh, and he's now got zombie orcs for henchmen. Courtesy of some other stupid PC game that you snapped.'

Darren nodded. 'And don't tell me, the Tirerenans are trying to kill them with arrows.'

Kylah nodded.

'But I've just created Moldarrenovia. How is it that you have intelligence?' Darren asked.

'In creating the physical manifestation, its history and culture come ready wrapped. We have people on the ground.'

'And don't tell me, you lot can't go over there and sort it out for some weird Krudian reason?'

'Correct,' Matt said. 'Jurisdiction issue. That and the fact that we'd be robbed of our skill sets. Whereas when you lot go over, yours are embellished.'

Darren nodded and turned immediately to Malcolm. 'Okay, zombie orcs. Weapon of choice?' He was playing the professional pride game here. Malcolm hesitated and then made eyes to the ceiling.

'I'm not biting,' Malcolm said.

Darren glanced at George Hoblip, who took a step forwards.

'Okay, okay,' Malcolm said. 'Zorcs are from *Asteroid Z1*. Libanus Games' piss poor attempt at a space cowboy shoot-em-up. It's DNA disruption rifles for Zorcs. Usually secreted in potholes. You need to deactivate a floating mine to get at the weapons cache.'

Sanjay was shaking his head. 'How do you know that stuff?'

Malcolm gave him a disdainful frown in response.

'It's what he does,' Darren grinned. 'I bet, too, that the Zorcs will not be able to see the red end of the spectrum or something like that. Think you could work up some camo for us knowing that?' he asked Vivette.

'I am a designer, not a common tailor,' she bristled.

Darren grinned even more widely. 'So long as you've got some nail varnish. Of course, neither of you have to come, do they George?'

George was eating curry powder out of a tin with a spoon. 'Nah, course not. We could go walkies in their dreams every night instead. Just a little reminder of how they refused to help me out.'

'Bastards,' Malcolm said.

'Monsters,' cried Vivette.

George grinned. Darren saw Sanjay swallow back the nausea.

'Oh, yeah,' muttered George, 'thought I'd come with you this time, bro'. I got nothing to do till teatime. 'Course you'll be in charge and all that. C'mon, take my picture.' He offered up a gurning smile.

'Can he?' Darren turned to Kylah.

'He's a bwbach,' she shrugged. 'He can do almost anything he likes.'

'And of course you haven't seen Lulem in how many weeks?' Matt said.

Darren didn't think it possible for a red and orange-skinned bwbach to blush. Purple was not a good look for him, he thought as he snapped the image.

'Welcome aboard,' Darren said. And turned again to Kylah. 'So, let me guess. All the men have gone off to fight the Zorcs and the women are holding the fort?'

Kylah nodded.

'We need to do is photograph that piece of pyrite, right?'

'The quest for fool's gold,' Matt said dramatically.

'I like it,' George swaggered.

'Darren, this is your show.' Kylah said, her vice suddenly low. 'The same rules apply as before. You can walk away from this and we'll use the pentrievant on everyone here. They won't know anything has happened.'

'And what about the Moldarrenovians?'

'They'll have to fight their own battles,' Kylah said.

'Sod that. Let's do it,' Darren replied.

Kylah smiled. Darren could almost hear male pulses surge in the room. She fished out the aperio and went to the back door. She attached it and motioned to Darren to turn the knob. It swung open to reveal a hot and humid jungle beyond.

'Go ahead, George. Wait for us near that banana tree. I'm right behind you,' Darren said and watched George gesture towards the jungle and usher the hesitant Malcolm and Vivette through. Darren put out an arm to hold them back.

'Trust me. You will not regret any of this.'

They both returned looks of abject disgust. *Yeah, go on,* he thought. *Hate me if you like. But how many chances do you get in this life to do as much good as you're going to do?*

Darren stepped back and reached for a small notebook next to Sanjay's phone. 'Can I borrow this, Sanj? Thought I'd make some notes this time.'

Sanjay reverted to goggle-eyed silence, but Darren saw him nod and hold out his hand. ''Course. Thanks for fixing my Mesopotamia, Dar. I'll see you when you get back, eh?'

Darren shrugged. 'Don't know when I'll be back, Sanj. There's not much here for me anymore. I quite fancy a touch of country life for a while. Though, thanks to the Summerville paradox, I could be away for a year and be back in time for Christmas. It's you I'm worried about. How are you going to manage? I mean, who else do you know who likes playing *Mario Kart* and watching the Babylonians fight Hannibal?'

Sanjay's hand fell, and his head followed. 'There's no need to rub it in.'

'It's true though. I hate to admit it, but Amanda was right about that. I promised your dad I'd help you find a girl. Trouble is, I don't know many females interested in military strategy and the farming techniques of ancient civilizations.'

Sanjay was shaking his hangdog head. 'You're being a knob now, Darren.'

'I'm only saying,' Darren continued, 'that you're not going to find anyone like that here…'

Sanjay turned to walk away, shaking his head. 'You can be a real sod when—'

'…in York. Whereas in Moldarrenovia,' Darren continued, 'there's this girl called Bron who's into military strategy big time, and who happens to be Roxana's sister. She'll think that you, Sanjay Bobal, are the best thing since sliced wax apples.'

Sanjay froze. He turned slowly back around. Darren was holding out his hand and wearing a stupid grin. 'You didn't think I'd leave you here a second time, did you? Not after what we've been through.'

They shook hands and then Darren pulled him in for a hug. Over Sanjay's shoulder, Darren saw Matt and Kylah silently applauding. There might even have been something moist glistening in one of those gold-flecked eyes.

Sanjay, struck by a sudden anxious thought, swung around to face Kylah.

'Will this be a problem?'

Kylah shrugged. 'This is a totally new scenario. And didn't the Maker take a snap of you standing next to your model?'

Sanjay nodded.

'Then I guess there will be a whole new Mesopotamia type country in Moldarrenovia.'

Sanjay sniffed and grabbed a paper kitchen towel to wipe his runny nose.

'Right,' Darren said, turning towards the still open door. 'Stay close, Sanj, and keep your head down.'

'This girl, what was her name again?' Sanjay whispered as he crossed the kitchen to join Darren.

'Bron. Welsh for—.'

'I know what it's Welsh for.' There was a short silence before Sanjay added in an airy tone, 'At least I know the anatomical translation. Well named, is she?'

'Behave.' Darren grinned.

Sanjay returned the grin with interest.

'And,' Darren continued, 'you're not going to believe this, but everyone over there gets lessons in… certain arts.'

'Like finger painting?'

'Some of it involves finger. Probably. But not painting.'

Darren put an arm around his friend's shoulder and stepped through into the steamy heat of another world.

# ACKNOWLEDGMENTS

As with all writing endeavours, the existence of this novel depends upon me, the author, and a small army of 'others' who turn an idea into a reality. A special mention to Bryony Sutherland for editorial guidance through the labyrinth. The Hipposync Archives are a work in progress. Special mention goes to Ela the dog who drags me away from the writing cave and the computer for walks, rain or shine. Actually, she's a bit of a princess so the rain is a no-no. Good dog!

But my biggest thanks goes to you, lovely reader, for being there and actually reading this. It's great to have you along and I do appreciate you spending your time in joining and the team at Hipposync and in New Thameswick where anything is possible.

## CAN YOU HELP?

With that in mind, and if you enjoyed it, I do have a favour to ask. Could you spare a moment to **leave a review or a rating**? A few words will do, but it's really the only way to help others like you discover the books. Probably the best way to help authors you like. Just visit the book's page on Amazon and leave a few words, or a rating, if you have the time. Thank you!

# FREE BOOK FOR YOU

Visit my website and join up to the Hipposync Archives Reader's Club and get a FREE novella, *Every Little Evil*, by visiting:

https://dcfarmer.com/

When a prominent politician vanishes amidst chilling symbols etched in blood, the police are baffled. Enter Captain Kylah Porter, an enigmatic guardian against otherworldly threats. With her penchant for the paranormal and battling against cynical skeptics, she dives into a realm where reality blurs. Her toxic colleague from the Met is convinced it's just another tawdry urban crime. But Kylah suspects someone's paying a terrible price for dipping a toe, or something even less savoury, in the murky depths of the dark arts.
She knows her career and the missing man's life are on the line. Now time is running out for the both of them…

Pour yourself a cuppa and prepare for a spellbinding mystery.

By signing up, you will be amongst the first to hear about new releases via the few but fun emails I'll send you. This includes a no spam promise from me and you can unsubscribe at any time.

# AUTHOR'S NOTE

Once upon a time, in the swirling mists of the last century, my journey into the fantastical began. A devotee of the greats like Tolkien, I found myself drawn deeper into Terry Pratchett's Discworld and Tom Holt's tilt at the modern—the holy trinity of the Ts, if you will.

Two decades ago, I embarked on a series of stories of wonder and the fantastic. Satirising our turbulent modern world with snarky humour by displacing the hapless participants of these tales into situations and places where things are very different. And, come on, who wouldn't want a quick trip to New Thameswick, or have access to an aperio? And all under the umbrella of The Archives.

The Ghoul on The Hill has its origins in many places. It's said that some cultures believed that taking a photograph might also be stealing a part of their spirit or soul. So what if, in the great scheme of things, it might be possible instead to give a soul, or existence, to something inanimate by photographing it? The one in a million, or billion, given this gift unbidden might consider it a blessing, or a curse. What sort of mayhem might that trigger, I wondered.

Enter Darren Trott. The rest, as they say...

All the best, and see you all soon, DCF.

**READY FOR MORE**

### **Blame It On The Bogie (man)**

Bobby Miracle wants a job. And she's at the point where she'll take just an about … anything.

But then she strikes lucky. And even if the pay is awful, the job is just up her street. But it isn't long before her dream internship takes a dark turn. As a trans-dimensional lockdown traps her and her coworkers, Bobby must confront her deepest fears alongside Asher Lodge, an enigmatic inspector from a Fae intelligence agency. With survival at stake and secrets lurking around every corner, Bobby must harness her inner strength to save herself and the agency from an ancient enemy, and find out that there's more to her name than meets the evil eye.

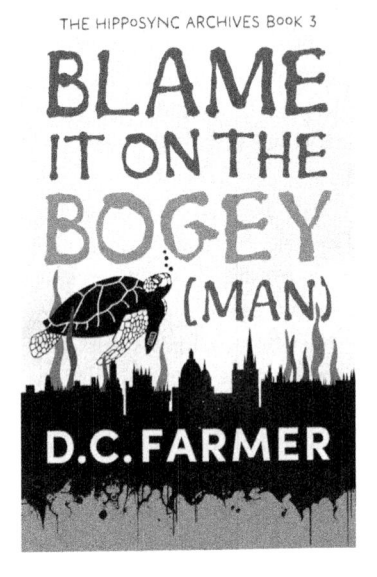

Printed in Great Britain
by Amazon